THE ROAD TO KADESH

by

A. W. Whinnett

The Road to Kadesh

by

A. W. Whinnett

Field of Reeds books

ISBN: 978-1-0685514-0-6

Cover design by Chandler Book Design

Typeset using LaTeX

CHAPTER 1

The wind shifted, bringing the tramp of marching feet and the pounding of signal drums, and on the ridge above the watching Egyptians the Amurrite infantry phalanx appeared out of the haze and settled into its battle line. From the woods beside the river to halfway along the crest it stretched, a double row of spearmen and shield bearers with a great mob of archers stationed behind. In the shimmering heat their surcoats looked invisible against the sky and the rows of dark, bearded faces appeared to hang suspended in the air. Above them danced flashes of red fire where the bronze spearpoints caught the afternoon sun.

'Gods help us, I never thought there'd be so many,' said Hetep. For almost an hour he had been waiting beside his chariot and scanning the empty ridge, his armour chafing his skin as he sweated in the heat. Now, at the first sight of the enemy army, he felt a shiver of dread – this was nothing like last year's skirmishes against the Sherden coastal raiders. Unbidden, his hand moved to touch the protective amulet he wore on a thong around his neck.

His chariot driver, Sebeku, was less impressed.

'Foreign rabble,' he said, and spat to show his contempt for their enemies. 'Remember what we were told: the infantry are dross. It's their chariots we must stop – they're the danger.'

'Of course,' said Hetep, making an effort to compose himself. After all, he was a chariot warrior now, one of the pharaoh's elite, and he had to remember to set an example to the infantry. Besides, the other men of the

1

squadron would be watching.

'Now they come,' said Sebeku. 'At last.'

On the flank of the Amurrite phalanx a row of dark, wavering shapes seemed to sprout from the bare hilltop. As Hetep watched they resolved themselves into a long line of chariots, moving slowly, the horses picking their way over the stony ground. He tried to count them and again had to gulp down his fear – there must be nearly a hundred, he thought. And then came a second wave, in a great line that almost filled the horizon. He remembered what their commanders had told them during their training, that chariot battles were won not by numbers but by speed and agility. He could only hope they were right, for otherwise they were in danger of being overwhelmed.

On either side of him waited the other chariots of his squadron, a bare fifty in all, set back from the flank of the Egyptians' own infantry phalanx; far behind, in reserve, stood the fifty chariots of the second squadron. The crews, like him and Sebeku all warrior-driver pairs, were standing by their cars, while in the intervals between waited the runners: agile, lightly armoured men carrying javelins and whicker shields. He glanced about, hoping to exchange a nervous smile or see a few worried faces, signs that others shared his unease, but all he saw was a calmness that was almost eerie. The only movement was from the horses as they tossed their heads, snorting from the dust; the only sounds the jingling of the bridle fittings and the quiet laughter from some of the runners as they shared a joke. It was as if they were standing on the parade ground back in Pr-Ramesses, instead of five hundred miles from Egypt facing the entire garrison of a defiant and hostile city.

The second wave of Amurrite chariots halted on the ridge but the first kept coming, rolling onto the plain separating the two armies. As they drew nearer Hetep could

2

make out the heavy armour on both crews and horse teams, and see how solid looking the cars were – typically Asiatic, or so he had been told. As he watched they wheeled, angling towards the Egyptian infantry and ignoring the waiting chariots, and with the horses' every hoof fall the knot of apprehension that had been forming in his gut tightened. He strained to see through the dust to where he knew Ramesses was standing in his chariot, surrounded by his personal guard. He thought he caught a glimmer of blue – sunlight reflecting from the pharaoh's war crown.

'What's Ramesses doing?' he said. 'We should attack now, before it's too late.'

'Calm yourself, you're unsettling the horses,' said Sebeku. 'There's time enough yet. You'll see.'

Now the enemy chariots were spreading out, aiming to attack the flank and front of the Egyptian phalanx simultaneously. Yet at the same time they were moving further from the support of their own battle line, and it dawned on Hetep just why his squadron had been stationed so far back. By feigning weakness they had lured the enemy forwards, and he was about to share his insight with Sebeku when Antef, the squadron's commander, came racing along the line in his chariot, yelling the order to mount up.

Hetep's pulse quickened and he threw himself into the car – clumsily, for the sudden shift of weight made the horses back. But Sebeku was there, soothing them in a quiet voice. Then he too mounted, grabbed the reins and took up his shield.

Horns sounded and the first squadron started its advance, the horses moving at a trot, the runners sweating as they strove to keep up. Then the squadron's drummers began playing, the pounding matching the tempo of the hoof falls, and as the squadron swept past the flank of the infantry the foot soldiers gave a great shout of acclamation.

Hetep gazed back at them, his heart filling with pride. At the front stood the assault troops, veterans in cloth armour with shields slung at their backs, armed with axes and khopeshes; behind were the archers, the Egyptian natives naked save for loin cloths and groin protectors, the Libyans and Nubians making a colourful contrast in their hide capes and feathered headdresses. And tall above them stood the battle standards: painted wooden fans, gilded hawks heads and great sprays of ostrich feathers. And if the infantry were an inspiring sight Hetep could only imagine how he must look to them as he went gliding past in his shining chariot. Again came a great surge of emotion and he was trying to compose a battle cry worthy of a warrior hero when he heard Sebeku's scolding voice.

'What are you doing? Ready the weapons. This is not a parade!'

'Sorry,' muttered Hetep, reddening. He reached down to take out his bow from its case; it was already strung and he tested its draw, then picked out an arrow from one of the quivers mounted on the car.

Antef's chariot was drawing ahead and Sebeku urged the horses into a canter. As they accelerated Hetep bent his knees, feeling the car flexing beneath him and smoothing out the jolts and bumps. The driver was watching his horses, alert for trouble, but they were pulling well, running sure-footed over the tufts of dry meadow grass: Phoenix, on the left and the youngest of the pair, was already half wild with excitement and straining at the bridle in his eagerness to get to the Amurrites; beside him Might-of-Set, older and steadier, was setting the team's pace, his muscles moving smoothly under the linen trapper.

4

The horns blared again, this time sounding the charge, and in a few quick strides the squadron's horses were at full gallop, leaving the runners behind. Now the car was jolting under Hetep's feet and the hooves were kicking up great clouds of grit that stung his eyes and nose. His fear was gone, replaced a keen exhilaration at the feel of the rushing air and the sight of the sunlight flashing on the wheel spokes of the racing chariots. Sebeku must have felt it too, for his habitually sour face was split into a fierce smile as he crouched, leaning into the airstream.

In moments they were bearing down on the flank of the Amurrite chariot line, and only then did the enemy commander realise his mistake in underestimating the speed of the Egyptian machines. There came a gabble of panicked orders and the Amurrite squadron came wheeling around to meet them – too fast, for a half-dozen vehicles overturned, sending their crews sprawling.

The distance was closing rapidly – five hundred paces, four hundred – and already some of the Egyptian warriors were shooting; long range, even for a composite bow, but Hetep saw one of the enemy drivers slump over in his car, an arrow in his chest. Almost too late he remembered the bow in his own hand. He drew the string and loosed the arrow – too hastily, for the shot went wide. With the next he forced himself to aim properly, and this time the shaft buried itself in a horse's neck; the animal stumbled, taking its car veering aside. Few of the other Egyptians were so fortunate and most of the Amurrite chariots came on unscathed, the arrows glancing off the horses' armour or embedding themselves harmlessly in the solid cars or drivers' shields.

The horns sounded a single long note: the order to pass through the enemy formation – a dangerous maneuver that risked fatal collisions. Sebeku readied himself, his

5

shield held high, and steered for the gap Hetep had made in the Amurrite line. As they closed Hetep reached for another arrow and fitted it to the string; his hands were shaking and he had to look down to see what he was doing. He lifted his eyes again, and there was another Amurrite chariot thundering towards them, its warrior raising his spear to strike. In panic he let fly but the arrow vanished into the dust. There was no time to get another and he stared in frozen horror at the spearpoint as it closed, its tip pointing straight at his heart...

Sebeku yanked at the reins, pulling at Phoenix's head, and with a great creaking of wood the chariot slewed sideways. The spear blade grazed Hetep's corselet as the Amurrite car went flashing past, its axle almost touching their own. Quickly he nocked another arrow, turned and shot into the cab's open back; the arrow lodged in the enemy warrior's neck and there was a scream as he pitched backwards. Then they went plunging into the Amurrites' dust trail, a thick orange fog that made Hetep's throat burn.

Well over half the Egyptian chariots had made it safely through and now the warriors were shooting as fast as they could snatch up their arrows, taking advantage of the enemy's vulnerability. Under the storm of missiles the Amurrites were trying to come around but their cars were too heavily loaded, and the wheelbases too narrow, to risk turning tightly. Not so the Egyptians machines; there was no horn blast this time, just Antef's voice screaming the order over the din, and as one the squadron began its turn. Hetep was pitched to the side as the car slewed around and the wooden frame screeched, the wheels digging curved furrows in the dirt. Right, that was their fastest turn, with Might-of-Set pulling on the inside and Phoenix racing along the outside of the arc. Sebeku was grinning again, lost in the joy of the moment; Hetep grinned back, and then the car righted itself and he grabbed for another arrow.

The Amurrites were still only halfway through their own turn. Flank on to the Egyptians they were impossible to miss and the arrows fell thickly among them, crippling the horses. Through the lingering dust beyond Hetep saw the runners coming up fast; they swarmed around the stricken Amurrite chariots, dragging the crews from their cars and butchering them.

The remaining Amurrites had finished their turn and they came slowly, the spent teams unable to drag the cars faster than a trot. This time Sebeku took them through at a walk, allowing Hetep more time to aim, and the enemy's horses kicked as they went down.

It was over. The Amurrite attack lay in ruins, the survivours fleeing, while the Egyptian runners, joined by dismounted charioteers, were searching through the wreckage, finishing off the remaining enemy wounded and cutting off hands – trophies to aid in the later counting of the dead. Others went skirmishing up towards the hill, screening the first squadron as it rolled to a stop to rest the horses.

Hetep stepped down from the car. Dust coated his front and filled his nostrils; he sneezed and wiped his hands over his sweating face, turning the dust into long smears of mud. He stretched, feeling his joints crackle; he must have shot nearly thirty arrows and his arms ached enough to make him wince. Yet for all the pain he felt like a god as he surveyed the remnants of the Amurrite squadron. In the space of a few score heartbeats he and his comrades had destroyed a force of a hundred enemy chariots. He wondered if his father would at last have been proud of him. Probably not, he decided, and sighed.

Now the second Egyptian squadron was coming, breaking ranks to flow around them. Horns blared, this time not to give commands but for the sheer joy of making a noise – or perhaps, thought Hetep, to call the attention of the gods Montu and Amun to the carnage. Then the drummers took up the paean – a wild pounding that heated the blood. His melancholia vanished and he returned the crews' salutes as they passed, then watched as they formed up again and accelerated towards the ridge in a cloud of dust and noise.

As the haze left by their passing cleared Hetep searched about him, trying to count the squadron's survivours. It looked as if they had lost about a dozen chariots, but there was a good chance many of the men who had driven them were still alive – it was, after all, the horses which were usually killed, or so he had been told.

Movement caught his eye – someone was waving. It was his friend Teppic, another of the squadron's archers; they had joined Re division together. He was shouting something and laughing, but Hetep could not hear; perhaps he was only celebrating the squadron's victory. Hetep was glad to see his friend unhurt and he waved back, grinning.

'If you're quite finished, we have work to do,' said Sebeku. He was kneeling by Might-of-Set, where he had been feeling the muscles in the horse's forelegs, and now he scowled up at Hetep. 'You may have forgotten but we are in the middle of a battle. Remember your duty. The weapons and chariot may need attention.'

Abashed, Hetep mounted the car and took out the bow to examine it for signs of wear. It was a powerful weapon, a composite of wood, horn and sinew, held together by glue that took more than a year to cure, and could send an arrow through a sheet of copper. Yet it was also surprisingly easy to damage and he was relieved to see that its bark covering was still smooth and unbroken. Next came the car, little more than a framework of bent willow, ash and elm poles bound together with leather and sinew, and so light he could lift it unaided. Such a flimsy-looking thing, yet it had cost a fortune, and the training to use it, along with its maintenance, had cost even more – a quarter of his father's land he had spent to become a charioteer. No, he told himself: *his* land. Even after three years there were moments when he forgot he was his own master now.

He forced himself to concentrate, brushing away the dust as he inspected the frame for splits in the wood. During that turn it had seemed as if the thing was going to wrench itself apart, yet for all its slightness it had held intact and he found not a single crack or loose joint. There were not even any arrow marks – which surprised him, for some at least of the Amurrite chariot warriors had carried bows. Then he noticed the arrowheads embedded in Sebeku's shield – and with a shock realised that many of them must have been aimed at him. And he had not even noticed. A little thrill of fear mingled with pride passed over him, followed by gratitude for Sebeku's skill and courage. He watched, smiling fondly now, as the driver finished tending to his beloved horses.

A wild yelling came from the hill and he looked up in time to see the second squadron smashing into the reserve Amurrite chariot line. He wondered why the enemy had not charged when they had the chance. Perhaps their commanders had been too stunned by the speed of the Egyptian attack to respond, or perhaps too blinded by the dust churned up by the wheels. Whatever the reason, they were paying for their hesitation now.

A messenger came racing towards them, jolting up and

9

down on the hindquarters of a donkey. Antef met him and after a hurried conference the commander was shouting for the squadron to mount up again. This time they were to go in against the Amurrite infantry, to prepare the way for their own foot soldiers' attack.

'Already?' said Hetep. Again he looked up at the hill where the second squadron was fighting. 'But we haven't dealt with the rest of their chariots.'

'It's getting late and we need a victory today,' said Sebeku. 'If we don't finish this rabble off now we'll have to do it all again tomorrow. We cannot fight them in the dark.'

'But it's not safe for the infantry.'

'Then go and tell Ramesses. He's the one in charge, not me.'

To say more might lead to voicing doubt about the pharaoh's godhood, so Hetep just shook his head and mounted the car in silence.

This time the squadron formed up in five columns, one for each troop, and they raced towards the Amurrite infantry phalanx, the runners toiling far behind. At the head of each column the troop commanders held their standards high so that the trailing crews could see them through the dust; the spacing between the columns had to be exact and there could be no mistakes, for they would have to turn in front of the enemy line, and even a single collision might spell disaster for the whole squadron.

As they climbed the slope Hetep saw the Amurrites growing more distinct through the haze, and again a fierce excitement welled up inside him as the god Montu filled his heart with fire. The rumbling of the wheels and the pounding of the hooves made the blood sing in his veins; to the Amurrite infantry the sight and sound of the on-rushing chariots must have been terrifying and he thought it a wonder they still stood.

The warriors in the frontmost chariots began shooting, sending their arrows high over the Amurrite shield bearers to plunge into the unarmoured men behind – two hundred paces, and already over the roar of the charge Hetep could hear the enemy's panicked screams. Then at fifty paces from the line the lead chariot in each column swept around in a tight arc, the stones flying from under the wheels, the warriors shooting now at point blank range, sending arrows through shields and corselets and killing men in swathes. The rest of the chariots followed, one after another, each matching the path of the one ahead. This was the moment when they were at their most vulnerable, with the horses flank on to the enemy line. But there was little to fear: levy infantry armed with simple wooden bows could not hope to hit targets moving at such a speed.

Hetep's car was the last in his column and as Sebeku brought them around he shot four arrows in rapid succession. Then they were away, following the rest of the troop to reform out of range of the Amurrites' bows. There he had a few precious moments to rest, to try to ease the ache in his arms, and then they went wheeling around to plunge in against another sector of the line, raking it with arrows before dashing away to safety. Six times they attacked, racing in and out, and the Amurrites were cut down like grain at the harvest.

Now they were drawing away for the final time, the horses slowing. Hetep had lost count of the number of arrows he had shot and the pain in his arms was like fire. As the vehicles rolled to a stop the runners dashed forwards to form a skirmish line in front of the Amurrite phalanx, protecting the squadron from attack by any survivours bent on vengeance.

Sebeku dismounted to inspect the horses again and when he returned he had a sour look on his face.

'Might-of-Set is becoming lame,' he said. 'Did you not feel how we were slowing after that last turn? I think already he's getting too old for battle.'

'Well, he can rest now,' said Hetep. 'We've done our job. They'll be sending in the infantry next.'

'I think we shall need a replacement by next year.' The driver spoke sadly. 'It's a shame, for he is brave and steady, as if born for war.'

'At least we don't have to pay for the horses. But you know what it's like. If we want our pick we need more seniority.'

'It'll come. I think we've lost more than a few crews this day, which means we shall move up in the hierarchy once their replacements are trained.'

Some of those crews may have been our friends, Hetep thought gloomily, but he did not say anything.

The squadron had halted to the left of the battlefield, leaving the way open for the infantry assault. On the hill the second squadron was still engaged and Hetep squinted, trying to pierce the thick layer of dust blanketing the crest. As he watched there came a tumult of noise and the dust billowed as if stirred by a giant hand. The noise grew, and out of the swirl burst a mass of Amurrite chariots in ragged line abreast, the cars bouncing over the stones, the crews whipping the horses into a galloping frenzy. In the lead was a gilded chariot drawn by a pair of magnificent, night-black horses; its warrior, a huge, bearded man armoured from head to foot in bronze scales, raised his spear and screamed a challenge as he bore down on the helpless Egyptians.

There was a moment of frozen horror, then all was yelling confusion. Hetep was shouting at the charioteers near him to mount up – as if they needed to be told. Sebeku was already back in the car; with clumsy hands Hetep handed him the reins then drew out his bow and a clutch of arrows.

A squad of runners was guarding the flank; they barely had time to hoist their shields before they were swept away like straw. Next in line was one of the chariots. Its driver, panicking, had tangled the reins and the horses were backing in confusion while the archer yammered in terror. Then the lead Amurrite chariot was on them. The armoured warrior gutted the driver with one thrust of his spear while his companion struck down the archer with an axe. Then they went thundering past.

Hetep's chariot was next in line but Sebeku already had them moving, accelerating fast and coming around in a tight curve. For an agonising moment it looked as if they would be caught; then they were pulling away, chasing after the rest of the squadron and leaving the runners to scatter behind them.

'We can't keep this up,' shouted Sebeku. 'Might-of-Set is exhausted.'

'Use the whip, you idiot. The whip!'

Hetep handed the whip to Sebeku – even now the driver was reluctant to use it – and turned back to watch the pursuit. Gradually the Amurrite machines were falling behind, all except the gilded chariot in the lead. The gods only knew what breed the horses were but despite having to haul the massive car they were closing steadily; the warrior was still brandishing his spear and yelling like a madman, and his driver, a cruel-faced man with pale green eyes, glared his hatred.

Hetep shot but the jolting of the car threw off his aim and the arrow skidded from one of the armoured horses. As if in response the warrior took out his own bow from

13

its holder. He fitted an arrow and drew, aiming straight for Hetep.

'Faster,' yelled Hetep. He loosed another arrow, only to watch as the Amurrite driver batted it away with his shield. Then the warrior shot. Hetep flinched as the arrowhead slashed a furrow along his cheek, and he felt the blood cooling in the air flowing over his skin.

'Faster!'

At last Sebeku was lashing at the horses. Another arrow lodged quivering in the frame and in panic Hetep shot again. This time the Amurrite driver was too slow; the arrow pierced his arm and the shield dropped. With shaking hands Hetep nocked another arrow and drew until his arms creaked; a heartbeat to aim, knees bent against the motion of the chariot, then he released. The arrow vanished and reappeared buried deep in the Amurrite warrior's face. Hetep gave an exultant shout as the warrior slumped over the front of his car, his hand flailing for the rail. For a moment he hung there, caught on the chariot's pole, while his driver tried to grab him with his uninjured arm. Then he vanished under the chariot. The car bounced as a wheel struck his body, and the whole thing swerved aside and tumbled over. Hetep caught a glimpse of the following chariot running the warrior over, its team trampling his body into the dirt, before they were lost in the trailing dust.

Now they were drawing ahead of the pursuit and Hetep felt weak with relief. Yet something was wrong: arrows were falling about them like rain. He looked around and saw to his horror that their flight had taken them right up to the Amurrite infantry phalanx and they were racing along parallel to its front.

'Turn,' he yelled. 'Get us away!'

Sebeku dragged on the reins and they slewed around,

14

heading back to their own lines, but also partly towards the pursuing Amurrites. Most of the rest of the Egyptian chariots had already done the same and were speeding for safety, all except one, slowed by an injured horse. Hetep stared, sickened, as both its driver and warrior went down together in a hail of arrows.

Another fifty paces, he thought, and we'll be safe – gods willing. He was about to turn again to check on the pursuit when something came hissing down from the sky and he heard a cry of pain. Then Sebeku was sagging backwards, an arrow lodged above his collar bone and blood pouring down his chest.

Hetep made a grab for the driver, slowing his fall, but he could not stop him rolling out of the back of the car. The shift of weight checked both horses and they slowed to a canter. In desperation he lashed the reins, imploring the horses to move faster, yet it was Sebeku's voice they were used to hearing and they ignored his pleas. Then a volley arrows caught Might-of-Set in his flank and the horse slowed to a limp, his head drooping. Phoenix, taking his pace from the older horse, matched his gait and the chariot came to a stop, side on to the oncoming Amurrites.

Hetep scrabbled for another arrow but the quivers were empty. Screaming curses he snatched up a javelin and twisted the cords with shaking fingers. He turned, picked out the nearest chariot, aimed at one of the horses and threw with all his strength. The cords unwound, spinning the javelin as it flew, and the blade pierced the horse's cheek, driving up into its brain. The animal collapsed, dragging its companion with it, the end of the chariot pole dug into its flank and the car leaped into the air, flinging out its crew. Round it came in a huge arc, a great lump of wood and bronze, growing until it filled his vision. Then like a hammer it came smashing down. He flung himself aside, arms raised; there was a crash of splintering wood, something struck his torso, and then he was lying on the ground with a burning agony in his ribs.

Through a haze of pain he saw Egyptian chariots racing past and heard yelling and the clashing of weapons; he was sure that he saw the pharaoh among them. With an effort he reached out for his bow, only to find it broken in two. A horse lay nearby, shuddering in pain; it kicked out, struck his head a glancing blow and he fell back, senseless.

CHAPTER 2

Consciousness returned slowly and with it came a ringing that filled his skull. He opened his eyes but all he could see was a bright haze, like sunlight through fog. He rolled over and pushed himself onto his hands and knees, and pain stabbed through his head. Gradually the pain receded and as it did so the fog thinned, revealing all around him indistinct, fast-moving shapes. He heard the noise of the battle, but muffled as if from far away, and what sounded like a pair of bellows working, accompanied by a nauseating bubbling sound.

Still on his hands and knees he groped his way towards the source of the noise and came upon the remains of his chariot. Its wheels were gone and the pole had been snapped clean off, while the rest was little more than a mass of splintered wood where it had been crushed by the impact with the Amurrite car. He remembered the sound it had made as its frame had split apart – almost like a scream.

Beside the wreck lay Might-of-Set, dead with the arrows thick in his body like spines. But Phoenix still lived; one of his forelegs was broken and a shard of blood-flecked bone was poking out through the flesh. The horse kept trying to stand; as his lungs laboured red foam bubbled around his mouth, and Hetep realised he had found the source of that awful noise.

He drew his knife and edged closer, trying to mimic the soothing sounds he had heard Sebeku make so often. Bracing himself he drove the knife blade through Phoenix's throat; the horse convulsed, air hissing out of his severed windpipe, and jets of warm blood spurted over

17

Hetep's arm. In another moment the horse lay still.

Almost at once Hetep's vision cleared. All around him lay the ruins of that last Amurrite charge: horses, broken pieces of chariot cars, and dead and dying charioteers; the Egyptian counterattack must have swept over him as he lay insensible. Beyond, on the ridge, the Amurrite infantry was still holding its position, but the ranks looked ragged, with piles of dead filling the gaps – his own work, he realised, and that of the rest of the squadron. A skirmish line of runners was moving up the slope, screening the enemy phalanx, while to the right a troop of Egyptian chariots was wheeling about, the warriors shooting at something hidden by the dust.

He crawled on and found Sebeku lying where he had fallen. The driver was on his back, his eyes closed and his breathing quick and shallow. His tunic was thick with blood and a great pool of it lay soaking into the earth by his side. The arrow's shaft was gone; softened by his body fluids the glue holding it to the head had dissolved and it had fallen away, allowing the wound to partially close. Which meant that the head was still embedded deep in his flesh. Hetep cut away a piece of Sebeku's tunic with his knife and pressed it gently onto the wound; the half-clotted blood was as thick as honey and the cloth stuck fast.

Drums rolled and horns brayed out, and Hetep looked up to see the Egyptian infantry beginning their advance. The assault troops came first, marching under the golden battle standards with their shields held high, the section leaders yelling out commands as they attempted to keep the ranks in order. Behind them came the lines of archers, followed by the musicians, and the drum rolls seemed to echo from the very sky. On the flanks came chariots, the last of the reserves, shepherding the strike force and

18

ready to pursue the Amurrites the instant they broke. And there among them was Ramesses, resplendent in his bronze scale armour, standing in his gold-plated chariot and looking like the god that he was, his bow in one hand and a brace of arrows held high in the other.

The Egyptian phalanx was drawing nearer and Hetep was kneeling right in its path. He was too hurt and tired to drag Sebeku clear; unwilling to abandon his friend he cradled his head, as if his arms could protect them both from being trampled by the soldiers' marching feet. At the last moment the troops broke ranks to flow around him. He stared at them numbly as they passed, receiving only a few strangely hostile glances in reply, and as the last of archers marched by the files closed up again, leaving him staring after them.

The infantry reached the slope and at a hundred paces from the Amurrite line the archers halted and loosed volleys of arrows, high over the ranks of the still-marching assault troops. The drumming rose to a crescendo and a thousand throats roared the name of Montu, the god who lays low foreigners and rebels alike. Then the assault troops charged.

Hetep saw the flashes of sunlight on metal as the axes and khopeshes did their work, and heard screams of pain which quickly built up to sounds of terror. In moments the Amurrite line was buckling under the Egyptian onslaught; then it crumbled, and as the men took flight the chariots swept in like diving hawks, turning the flight into a bloody rout. Clouds of dust rose over the hillside, reddened by the afternoon sun, and then the slaughter disappeared over the ridge, taking the sounds of battle and the cries of the vanquished with it.

A quiet settled over the plain and in the drifts of haze Hetep saw a few scattered groups of men moving about –

stragglers from the advance, and those among the injured who were still able to walk. From the other direction came a party of camp followers; many had come to strip the enemy dead of valuables and soon they were making piles of booty among the corpses, but others were searching out the Egyptian wounded to give what aid they could. Hetep called out, waving, and a pair of them came over.

'Please, be careful,' said Hetep. 'He was hit in the neck.'

The men lifted Sebeku and bore him away towards the camp, leaving Hetep to follow on shaking legs. Others joined them and soon Hetep found himself part of a procession of wounded men, all walking in silence, their faces looking old with pain and exhaustion.

They neared the camp: a square of bare earth bordered by a ditch, behind which had been placed a row of shields. At the centre stood the royal enclosure – a cluster of tents surrounding the pharaoh's marquee – but most of the rest was open space, dotted with piles of stores and corrals for the chariot horses and pack animals. And at the far corner, downwind from the royal enclosure, was a makeshift infirmary, staffed by the army's magicians, diviners and physicians, and separated from the rest of the camp by a line of oxhide screens.

Sebeku was groaning in pain and his wound was bleeding again. At the entrance to the infirmary he was laid on the ground and Hetep fussed over him, until a harassed-looking man with a blood-encrusted torso came hurrying over.

'Help us, please,' said Hetep. 'He's got an arrowhead lodged in his neck. You're a physician?'

'Of course.' The man squatted down beside Sebeku. 'You know him?'

'He's my driver. Do you think he'll live?'

'Charioteer is he?'

'We both are.'

'I see.' The physician teased away the corner of the makeshift bandage and prodded at the wound. The way the glistening blood moved under his fingers made Hetep's stomach clench and he looked away. Then he wished he had not.

Everywhere in the infirmary lay wounded men, many covered in blood. None could have been there for more than an hour, yet Hetep was convinced he could smell the tang of putrefying flesh. Worse than the smell was the noise: an unending chorus of moans, whimpers, babbled prayers and cries of agony. He knew from talks with the army's veterans that it was in the aftermath of a battle that most of its casualties would die: arrows, spears, and even the fearsome axes and khopeshes, tended to wound more often than kill outright, and death would usually come only after hours or days of suffering – at least to those on the winning side. If an army lost a battle its wounded were often killed where they lay, and he wondered if they were not the more fortunate for it.

For all the apparent disorder he realised there was a clear demarcation in the arrangement of the patients. On the far side of the infirmary lay the most grievously wounded: men with shattered limbs or gaping stomach wounds, or faces half ripped away by axe and sword blows. It was from there that most of the noise came; a handful of magicians and lector priests attended them, intoning spells to ease their journey to the West. It was better on the near side, where lay the men who looked as if they had a chance of living beyond the next sunrise. There the physicians were at work bandaging limbs and staunching wounds.

By now the physician had finished his examination.

'This is an injury I can heal,' he said. 'We shall take him this way.' And to Hetep's relief he indicated the near side of the enclosure.

Together they carried Sebeku over to a clear patch of ground. The physician squatted beside him and pulled away the rest of the cloth plug.

'Now hold him tightly,' he said. 'This is going to hurt.' He drew a knife and, as Hetep gripped Sebeku by the shoulders, cut into the wound, enlarging the hole. Sebeku shrieked and writhed while the sweat poured off him but Hetep held on, trying to pin him with his body weight while fighting against his own pain and nausea.

The physician dug probing fingers deep into the wound. He frowned and tilted his head. 'Almost there,' he muttered, while Sebeku's whole body shuddered. 'Got it!' he said, and drew out the arrowhead. 'Can't leave it in, of course: it'll just fester. Something in the metal attracts all the bad fluids in the body.'

Hetep swallowed and closed his eyes, and when he looked again the physician was threading a strip of linen through a stained copper needle. Humming softly to himself he stitched the wound up, while Sebeku moaned in renewed pain. As a final touch he took out a lump of fresh meat from a bag beside him and slapped it over the would.

'Horse,' he said dryly. 'There's a lot of it going spare today.' He bound the wound up, meat and all.

'Is that it?' said Hetep. 'Will he live?'

The physician shrugged. 'Only the gods know, and they're unlikely to tell me. Now let's have a look at you.' He prodded Hetep's ribs, provoking a yelp of pain. 'Nothing broken there – only a little bruising. You'll be fine.'

'What about my head? Something hit it and I still feel sick.'

'Hm.' The physician probed around Hetep's skull. 'That doesn't seem broken either. It may feel worse tomorrow, or it may feel better – I can't say. But if it starts to feel as if your brain's swelling you'd better come back and we'll open a hole in your skull. Until then there's nothing I can do.'

'A hole?' said Hetep weakly.

'Yes, a hole. It relieves the pressure. Now please go away. I'm busy. If you want any more help try praying.'

CHAPTER 3

With the battle over the last of the haze had settled over the plain, and for the first time Hetep could clearly see the rebel town that had supplied the bulk of the troops they had fought. Irqata it was called, the southernmost bastion of the kingdom of Amurru, and it stood beyond the ridge on which the Amurrite infantry had deployed. From a distance it seemed a fine-looking town, its buildings and walls glowing pink where they caught the last of the day's sunlight. He guessed it must be a dismal place now, its streets filled with people mourning their dead sons and husbands. He wondered why the town's rulers had chosen to resist.

By now the victorious Egyptian troops were returning to the camp. The infantry came first, some marching in formation, others alone or in little groups. The chariots followed, shepherding the foot soldiers as if by instinct, although with the enemy army destroyed there was no danger now. Hetep was saddened to see how depleted the squadrons were, and how many of the crews were on foot, limping along beside the cars.

As life returned to the camp the watch fires were lit, and growing activity near the bread ovens signalled that it was time for the evening food ration. Hetep joined the queue and found himself among an exhausted-looking group of charioteers; only a couple were from first squadron and they exchanged a few words, mostly about missing comrades. None spoke of the battle and the glorious annihilation of the rebel army, and none had any news of his friend Teppic.

As usual there was a single loaf for each man, accompanied by goat's cheese, onions, leeks and garlic; a scribe stood nearby, recording the issue of each ration against a list of names. There was beer too; because of the battle they were being given a double ration, and it was not the usual stuff, either, but the more potent variety drunk during the Sekhmet festival back home.

The first squadron's sleeping area was near the far end of the camp – just a patch of bare earth, its borders delineated by little piles of stones. There Hetep squatted down and placed his beer jugs in front of him. He turned the bread over and over in his hands, staring at it blankly; he had eaten nothing since dawn and knew he should have been ravenous, yet all he felt was a dull sickness in his belly, as if the fear he had known during the battle was still with him. So this is victory, he thought; Amun spare us from ever having to suffer a defeat.

In the end he forced himself to eat, biting off lumps of bread and chewing doggedly, his teeth crunching on the grit left from the mill stones. He took a swig of beer to wash the food down; the soupy liquid had a refreshingly sweet taste and he finished the rest of it in a couple of gulps. No sooner had he set the empty jug down than his mood lifted. The sky took on a rosy tint as the sun slipped behind the horizon and he murmured a prayer of thanks to Menquet, the brewing goddess. Content at last he lay back on his elbows and smiled. His smile broadened when he spotted his friend Teppic limping towards him, carrying his own ration of food and beer.

'Gods what a day,' said Teppic, and sat heavily beside him. 'I heard about your chariot. How's Sebeku?'

'Alive, for now. But what about Ipu?' This was Teppic's driver. 'Why isn't he with you?'

'Don't worry, he's fine. He's still out there somewhere, sawing off the last of the hands and piling them up.' Teppic gestured towards the darkening plain. 'He told me it was the bit he'd been looking forward to the most. I didn't have the stomach for it myself, so I left him to it.' He grimaced. 'He said the piles remind him of home – he thinks they look like pyramids.'

'He wasn't injured in the battle was he? On the head, I mean.'

'If he was I didn't see it. He's got his work cut out for him, though. I've never seen so many corpses.'

'I saw the last attack, when the infantry and the reserve chariots went in,' said Hetep. 'I can't imagine there's an Amurrite left alive. Which is good, I suppose.' His earlier feeling of contentment was fading and he stared out into darkness between the watch fires. 'You know, I say the words, but I can't make myself believe it. Do you think it's always like this? After a battle, I mean.'

'Don't forget this is my first time as well.' Teppic drank and looked down at his jug, swirling the remaining contents. 'My father never did talk much about how he used to feel after the slaughter was over. Neither did my uncles. It was as if it wasn't a fit topic for discussion.' He shrugged. 'But if you're bothered, just remember the Amurrites had a choice. They could have paid the tribute.'

'I suppose so. Although it's not as if we gave them much time to reconsider.'

It was only late that morning that the Egyptian scouts had found the leading units of Irqata's garrison moving towards the ridge to oppose them – unexpectedly, for all the other cities they had marched against had offered not even a hint of resistance, their terrified mayors and princes instead making grovelling obeisance at their first sight of Ramesses. Like many in the army Hetep had expected the pharaoh to issue an ultimatum, but instead he had ordered an attack as soon as the camp had been pitched.

It was as if he could not wait to test himself against an Asiatic army, for this, the fourth year of his reign, was the first in which he had marched into Canaan, and the people of Irqata were the only Canaanites to offer him any resistance.

Hetep wondered if there would be more fighting after this, for he was sure that Amurru had many more towns besides Irqata, and doubtless thousands more troops, too. Perhaps they were already on their way to try to recover their southernmost settlement. And more than half of Re division's strength was still many days' march away, subduing the inland towns; what if the Amurrites attacked before those scattered units could rejoin them? Hetep remembered how he had felt when he had first seen the size of the Amurrite host, and experienced again the terror of being pursued by a relentless and seemingly invincible enemy that he could not outrun...

'You should drink the rest of your beer,' said Teppic. 'You look as of you need it.'

'No, I've had enough.' Hetep pushed his jug away. 'I was speaking to some of the others just now. You know we lost Kai and his driver, Pentu. Rama too, and at least a dozen others. They say second squadron lost even more. So many dead, and so far from home; what kind of a funeral can we give them here?' He shuddered. It was a fate they all dreaded and one of the risks of serving Pharaoh in the army, for an improper burial meant the dissolution of the *akh* and the final, second death.

'Some of them might make it to the West,' said Teppic. 'We just need to remember their food and drink offerings. And we might as well start now.' He raised his jug. 'To the happy dead. May they find their path to the Field of Reeds an easy one.' He poured out a couple of drops of beer as a libation, then drained the jug and smacked his

27

lips. 'That's better. I tell you, if we had this stuff every day I'd never want to go home. Come on, cheer up. We won, after all.'

'Yes, I know. I was there too,' said Hetep, forcing a smile. 'But I keep thinking about those chariots when they were coming after us. And the warriors – all that armour, and on the horses, too. They must have been rich men. Who were they?'

'I heard it was their reserve squadron, lead by the prince of Irqata himself. Second squadron never saw them coming through the dust. The Amurrites caught them at rest – you know why we have to keep moving – and just smashed their way through. Then they came for us. But their prince was shot in the face and killed.'

Hetep's heart quickened and he sat up straight. 'The face, you say? This prince... what did he look like?'

'A big man in scale armour – like Pharaoh's only heavier. I saw the corpse. Someone got him with an arrow, just under the eye.'

'And he was the town's ruler?'

'So they say.'

'That was me,' said Hetep. 'I did that. What I mean is, I shot him in the face. We were last in the line, trying to get away. And I killed him.'

Teppic's eyes widened. '*You* killed him? Then we owe you a debt. It slowed their attack, gave Pharaoh time to deploy the reserve chariots. Only the gods know what would have happened had that man not been stopped.' He raised his second jug in a salute. 'Life, prosperity and a goodly burial,' he said, and drained it in one go.

Hetep's gloom lifted again; perhaps there was more good to the day than he had supposed. He gazed out over the camp, which was now filled with men, all eating and drinking; most were mere black outlines against the fires.

The volume of conversation had been steadily growing and now somewhere in the darkness a man started to sing a battle hymn to Montu. A hundred raucous voices joined in, and Hetep found himself humming along and smiling.

'But it shouldn't have happened,' said Teppic. His face was growing flush as the beer did its work. 'The battle, I mean.' He belched and reached for Hetep's second jug. 'You sure you don't want that?'

'No, take it. What do you mean, it shouldn't have happened?'

Teppic took a gulp of beer and wiped his mouth. 'I told you: the battle. At least not today. If Ramesses had any sense he'd have waited. But no: he was too eager to fight; reckless, even. I heard some of the commanders – Antef, a few others – told him to wait. But he wouldn't listen.'

'Hush!' said Hetep, scandalised. 'It's not safe to talk like that.' He glanced anxiously around, but all the men nearby looked to be deep in their own conversations.

Teppic leaned closer; his face shone red in the light and his voice sank to a hoarse whisper. 'A couple more days we'd have had the rest of the division with us. Five thousand men – five thousand! And we'd have annihilated these foreigners, and not suffered a scratch.'

'But Pharaoh's the son of Amun-Re.' Hetep was whispering back. 'How can a god make a mistake?'

'How long's he been on the throne, eh? Not even four years. Perhaps his godhead hasn't properly settled in yet. He's not like his father, you know.'

Ramesses' father, King Seti, had captured territory all the way to the northern border of Amurru and had even beaten the fearsome Hittites in battle, briefly wrestling from them control of the city state of Kadesh. Yet for all his campaigning he had also appreciated the benefits of

29

being at peace and had quickly made a treaty with his former enemies, so that for a decade all of Canaan had been quiet.

'Give Pharaoh time. I'm sure–' A noise from behind made Hetep break off and he twisted around to see a man coming to his feet – a man who, only moments before, must have been sitting right behind him. 'Why didn't you tell me he was there?' he said to Teppic, horrified.

His friend just stared back, eyes glassy from the beer. Hetep craned his head around again, trying to determine who the man was, but all he saw of his now retreating back was a silhouette against the firelight.

'It's only Baya,' said Teppic. 'Didn't you recognise him?'

'Gods, not him! What was he doing here?' Baya was the commander of the second squadron, a deeply unpleasant man of grasping ambition whose family had been military aristocracy since the time of the wars against the Hyksos. 'What if he heard us? Those things you said, about Ramesses...'

Teppic belched and waved a dismissive hand. 'Don't worry about that: he can't have heard much. Besides, we're charioteers. We're allowed more freedom than lesser men.' He picked up the beer jugs and shook them, one after another. They were all empty and he frowned.

'You, maybe,' said Hetep. 'Your father's rich. But what about me? What if I'm accused of impiety? They could have me beaten.'

'Not the hero of the battle they wouldn't. No, it's a reward you'll be getting. You killed the prince of Irqata, and probably saved the army. Or at least saved Ramesses from an embarrassing setback.'

'Reward?' said Hetep. He stared blankly, until finally he understood. 'Oh yes, of course. I hadn't thought of

30

that.' It was a sign of the extent to which the day's slaughter had disordered his wits that he had forgotten one of the reasons he had been so keen to become a chariot warrior. The Gold of Valour it was called: a gift from the pharaoh for distinguished conduct in battle. Sometimes it really was a gold artifact – a neck torc, an insect-shaped nugget, or some other beautifully worked artifact – but often it was more. He might have a new chariot and some metal armour, or perhaps a grant of land back in Egypt and a gang of slaves to work it. He was smiling now, his good feeling restored. 'You really think I'll get it?'

'Why not? This could be the start of great things for you. You're moving up.' Teppic grinned and clapped him on the shoulder. 'Now let's see if we can find some more of this beer.'

CHAPTER 4

That night Hetep dreamed of being chased by a glaring, pale-eyed enemy, and he woke feeling nauseous and with a pounding headache. He remembered drinking and singing late into the night with Teppic and wondered if there had been something evil in the beer – it would not be the first time a bad batch had made its drinkers sick. Then he remembered what the physician had told him about his head swelling up and wondered instead if he should go back to the infirmary to ask for a charm to dispel the sickness. But the thought of having to endure the smell of all that corrupting flesh made him retch and he sank back down again.

Gloomily he watched the work gangs as they finished preparing the graves for the army's dead. The embalmers had worked quickly to preserve what they could of the corpses of the wealthy, but the common soldiers had to make to with a simple linen wrap and the hope that the soil was sufficiently dry to preserve them from complete dissolution. All were interred together while lector priests recited spells to aid their souls' journey to the West. Incense drifted over the camp, mingling with the smoke from the braziers that had been lit to greet Khepri, the dawn sun.

Hetep found he had no stomach for the morning beer ration and he poured it out as a libation for the dead. Afterwards he slept, and on waking found that the sickness in his belly had lessened, only to be replaced by a feeling of melancholy that not even thoughts of his coming reward could dispel. For the next two days he rarely stirred from the sleeping area, while the life of the camp went on around him as if in a fog, and his nights were rest-less and filled with evil dreams. Perhaps it was a blessing he had no chariot or team that needed attending to, for he doubted if he would have been fit for even the lightest work. Then, on the third sunrise since the battle, his head cleared and his gloom lifted.

As the smoke rose from the bread ovens Hetep joined his comrades for the morning meal and listened to the lat-est camp gossip. It seemed that the royal enclosure was sealed off, the senior officers sequestered with the pharaoh and his priests, and there were rumours that one of the commanders was in trouble because of mistakes made dur-ing the battle. The talk reminded him that by indulging his sore head he had been neglecting Sebeku, and feeling guilty he made his way to the infirmary.

Halfway there he spotted Baya crossing the camp on some errand; the second squadron's commander saw him, checked, and walked quickly away, leaving Hetep feel-ing both puzzled and worried. He remembered Teppic's drunken talk on the evening of the battle; how much of it had Baya really overheard? He told himself he was wor-rying over nothing, that their talk was just the typical griping of soldiers tired after a battle; besides, neither of them had seriously doubted Ramesses' godhood. Still, he could not shake the feeling that Baya now had his eye on him.

The infirmary was far less crowded than before, and he guessed that most of the missing had died rather than recovered from their wounds. He found Sebeku awake, lying motionless and staring up at the sky. Someone had wiped the dirt from his face and he looked grey with blood loss.

Hetep squatted beside him.

'You're still alive, then,' he said, speaking lightly to

33

hide his anxiety over his friend's condition.

'So it would seem,' whispered Sebeku. He swallowed and passed his tongue over parched lips. 'How long have I been here?'

'A few days. I would have come sooner, only I haven't been well myself.' Hetep held up a water skin. 'I brought you this.'

Sebeku drank and lay his head back again. 'Thank you,' he said, his voice a little stronger.

'Do you remember what happened?'

'No. And nobody here can tell me, even the few who are fit for conversation.' The driver grimaced; Hetep took it to be a smile. 'But I heard we won the battle. Is it true?'

'You wouldn't be here if we'd lost now, would you?'

'No, I suppose not.' Again came the rictus smile. 'It's all so dim. I remember the Amurrite chariots coming for us, and then pain – lots of pain. But after that, nothing.'

'You had an arrow stuck in your neck. That's how you got the wound.'

Sebeku put a hand to his throat, where lay a thick wad of bloodstained cloth and raw meat. 'Yes... yes, of course.'

'Some god must have been watching out for you. If that arrow had hit another finger breadth further up it would have cut your vein and killed you.'

'Perhaps so.' Again Sebeku touched the wound. 'What happened after? Did we crash? It's all blackness.'

'The chariot's wrecked. One of the Amurrites collided with us. We were lucky to survive.' Hetep paused.

'Go on,' said Sebeku, looking at him intently. 'What of the horses? Phoenix and Might-of-Set – are they hurt?'

'They're dead. I'm sorry.'

34

Sebeku exhaled a ragged breath and closed his eyes. 'Then we were not lucky at all.'

'We'll get replacements,' said Hetep, speaking quickly now. 'And a new chariot, too. That armoured man I shot was the Irqatan prince. We'll be getting a reward – Teppic's sure of it. We'll have gold, land, slaves... it might be anything. And then we can buy a whole stable full of horses, the best in Egypt.'

Sebeku turned his face away. 'Please, I can't think of gold today. Just let me rest.'

'It'll all turn out well,' said Hetep. 'You'll see.'

Sebeku did not reply but lay still. After a while he drifted off into what looked to be an uneasy sleep. Hetep rested a hand on his friend's brow, feeling the heat of his skin; there's fever coming, he thought, and he reexamined the wound, noticing this time how red and swollen the flesh around it had become. He called one of the physicians over.

'The breath of an evil god has entered the wound,' said the physician. 'We have applied honey, and the patient wears the red carnelian amulet. Beyond that there's nothing we can do.'

Hetep stayed by Sebeku's side, watching as the driver twitched and mumbled through his fever dreams. As the day's heat grew the charnel smell of the infirmary built until it became an almost tangible thing. At last, unable to bear both his growing nausea and the increasingly urgent buzzing of the flies, he stood and hurried out, a hand over his nose and mouth.

Back in the clean air of the main camp he began to feel better. A crowd was gathering near the gate and he went over, curious to see the cause of the commotion. He worked his way to the front in time to see a detachment of Re division's infantry, escorted by a squadron of chariots, arriving along the inland road. The troops looked tired, but it was only from long days of marching – they lacked the dead-eyed exhaustion of men who had been in battle. They came to a halt outside the gate and stared about them at the plain, which was still littered with what the dogs and vultures had left of the Amurrite dead, and the graveyard, with its fresh mounds of earth and hastily carved monuments. Then their officers dismissed them and their ranks dissolved into a gaggle of chattering men.

The camp's troops crowded forwards to meet them, hungry for news of the campaign and gabbling questions. What had they seen? Had the other cities surrendered? When were they all to go home? Many of the new arrivals were even younger than Hetep, newly recruited for the year's campaign, and it took a while to piece together their excited accounts. It seemed that all Canaan had surrendered without so much as a hint of resistance; everywhere the troops went they had found city gates standing open and the late tribute payments – metal ingots, bolts of cloth, beams of cedar, and a hundred other things – laid out for them in piles. Some of them laughed at how easily they had cowed the foreigners. This was proper soldiering, they said: parading about, singing and showing off the battle standards, while terrified Canaanites prostrated themselves in the dirt in their thousands.

'Then you didn't get to fight,' said Hetep. 'I'm sorry.'

'Sorry? What in the name of all the gods for?' said one of the newcomers, a spearman barely out of adolescence. 'Marching is hard enough. You think we're fools, lusting for bloodshed and risking our necks?'

'But you won't be rewarded.' Hetep looked around him at the now silent crowd. 'If you don't fight you don't get anything.'

'So? I just want to go home and see my family again.

36

The same for the rest of us. Isn't that right?'

There was a chorus of agreement.

'All fighting gets you is an early grave,' said another. 'Who'd want that instead of a happy old age and a goodly burial?'

'I'm a charioteer,' said Hetep, letting his pride rule his tongue. 'We had a battle here and I killed the enemy commander, and Ramesses is going to give me some gold.'

'Well that's good for you. But what makes you think we should care?' The young spearman was frowning and his companions closed in around Hetep.

'I didn't mean any insult,' said Hetep. 'I'm sorry. It's just... I thought we'd joined for the same thing, that's all.'

'Charioteer, you say?' This was a deeper voice, coming from behind, and Hetep turned to see an infantry commander shouldering his way through the ring. He was one of the assault troops, a thickset, brutal-looking man with a scowl made worse by a long gash down the side of his face, the scab so heavily ridged it looked like a strip of crocodile skin. 'Which squadron are you?' he demanded.

'The first,' said Hetep warily. 'Why?'

'So you're one of *them*, eh? Well, I was in the battle too, and all I saw of your lot was when you were running away.'

'Then you didn't see much at all.'

'It was enough,' said the commander. 'Listen, friends,' he shouted, turning to address the newcomers. 'Don't you believe his lies about rewards and gold. If there's any justice the only payment those accursed charioteers will be getting is a good whipping. They ran away, and it was *we* who did the fighting: the infantry.'

'That's not true,' protested Hetep. He looked appealingly at the ring of now hostile faces. 'We destroyed a

37

whole squadron of Amurrites.'

Another infantryman came barging forwards. This one was a Nubian mercenary with a bloodstained bandage around his thigh.

'I was with him,' he said, jerking a thumb at the commander, 'and what he says is true. You filthy cowards ran and left us to the foreign chariots. It was Pharaoh who saved us, while you fled like sheep.'

'You all hear that?' roared the commander. 'They're supposed to protect us!'

'You lied,' said the young spearman. 'How dare you sneer at us for not wanting to fight!'

Hetep rounded on him. 'But you weren't even there! And as for you,' – this was to the infantry commander – 'I fought until I ran out of arrows; I must have killed a dozen men, including their prince. How many of you can match that?'

'If there's one thing I can't stand it's hearing one of you chariot men giving himself airs. You think the infantry are just a bunch of mud-shovelling peasants, don't you?' The commander jabbed Hetep in the chest, pushing him back. 'Well let me tell you, you stuck-up piece of vulture filth, I've been fighting Libyans and Nubians for years, and I've been given gold from the hand of Pharaoh himself. And I say you're a liar – a liar and a coward.' He shoved his face into Hetep's, his fist gripping his tunic. 'So what you going to do about it, eh?'

Hetep's frustration burst into fury. The battle had cost him almost everything he had; he remembered his fear as he had watched that huge Amurrite chariot closing, and the last desperate arrow shot that had saved him – and perhaps saved the rest of the army. And now this leering brute was telling him it was all lies.

'I'm not a coward,' he shouted, and smacked the commander in the jaw with the heel of his palm.

In an instant the crowd became a jostling, yelling mob. Blows rained down on Hetep from all sides, but there were so many assailants and such a tangle of limbs that they did little harm. He saw the face of the commander looming near and struck again, this time with his fist. A jolt of pain shot up his arm as his knuckles met bone, then someone tripped him and he went down. He curled up, shielding his head with his arms, while his assailants clustered around him, kicking and punching. A foot jabbed into his bruised ribs and he twisted, screaming in sudden agony.

'What in the name of the gods are you doing?' The voice was Teppic's, sounding faint through the roaring in Hetep's head. At once the blows stopped and Hetep felt more than saw the ring of attackers pulling away. His friend swam into his vision, a blurred outline against the sky; there were others with him, all charioteers, and they formed a cordon around him.

Slowly Hetep regained his feet, wincing with pain.

'Thank you,' he said. 'That was getting unpleasant.'

'You,' snapped Teppic, pointing at one of the infantry-men. 'Who's your file leader?'

The newcomers shuffled back, avoiding Teppic's eye, but the wounded commander stood his ground.

'Let me guess,' he sneered. 'More chariot men.'

'You guess right,' said Teppic. 'My name's Teppic – son of Khor, former Commander of the Host and now Scribe of Sacred Writings at the Re temple in Heliopolis. And when my father's finished with you, you'll be spending the rest of your life digging mud for brick making with no hands!'

The commander hesitated, his lip curling. He looked around at the others for support, but found none.

'It's nothing,' said Hetep, shocked at the anger in his

friend's voice. 'Just a misunderstanding, that's all.'

'You heard him,' said the commander. 'It's nothing to get bothered about. So just calm yourself, all right?' He turned and swaggered off, taking the Nubian with him. Deprived of a leader the young recruits dispersed, leaving the charioteers standing alone.

'What an unpleasant man,' said Teppic. 'I tell you, some of these commoners are no better than bandits. Did the rabble hurt you at all?'

Hetep probed his tender ribs. 'Just a few more bruises, that's all. It was my fault: I got a bit carried away. I can't really blame that commander for being angry – you saw he'd been wounded in the battle.'

'So had you. So had many of us. That's no excuse.'

'It's the newer recruits who bother me more,' Hetep went on, speaking with all the wisdom of his two years' seniority. 'It's as if they don't understand what we're doing here. We're restoring Ma'at and keeping Egypt safe from chaos, and all they want to do is go back to their farms.'

'What do you expect? They're only levies, after all. Still, I agree they could be trained better. Remember what we saw back home at Pr-Ramesses: they were still recruiting the day we marched.'

'You still think it's to get them ready for next year?'

'Has to be. The Hittites won't stand idle after what we've done here, and from what I've heard Ramesses will stop at nothing to eclipse Seti. We'll be back here again or I'm a goat herder. And speaking of lowly folk, there's a reason I came looking for you, and it wasn't just to save you from the brute soldiery. Your uncle's asked to see you.'

Hetep grimaced. 'What does he want?'

'You think he'd tell me? You'd better go, just to hu-

mour him – he did say the summons has the force of a
royal command.'

CHAPTER 5

Royal command, thought Hetep, as he paced back across the camp – what's the man up to now? His uncle, Nebenteru, brother of his dead father, was a low-ranking scribe attached to the commissariat and barely had the authority to issue an extra bread ration. The man had managed to get himself assigned to Re division and had been an almost constant nuisance throughout the campaign.

At the gate to the royal enclosure stood a pair of Sherden – warriors in horned helmets carrying great bronze swords. They were the very same sea raiders who had attacked the villages in the Delta last year, seeking plunder and slaves. Ramesses had met them in battle and destroyed them, and the survivours had chosen service in Egypt's army rather than slavery in the mines and temple farms; by all accounts they had become as loyal to Ramesses as men whose families had served the pharaohs for generations. They watched Hetep suspiciously as he approached, but let him pass once he had mentioned Nebenteru's name.

Ramesses' tent dominated the enclosure, and in its shadow stood a row of smaller tents housing the princes, the Royal Butler and the Chief Physician; a dozen or so priests, diviners, astrologers and royal scribes; and the army's senior officers. Smaller still were those for the lesser commanders and scribes, and at the far side of the enclosure, furthest from the Son of Re's radiance, were the smallest tents of all: those occupied by the clerks and lesser functionaries. And in the endmost of these, standing with his arms folded and a scowl on his face, was Hetep's uncle Nebenteru.

'You took your time getting here,' he said. He had thick, dark eyebrows, and they were drawn together to form a continuous line across his brow. 'But it's no more than I've learned to expect.'

'I'm sorry,' said Hetep. 'I came as fast as I could, but I was wounded in the battle.'

'So I heard. They tell me you hit your head. But your legs should still be working fine.'

'I've bruised my ribs as well – it makes walking painful.'

Nebenteru snorted. 'You're fortunate it was only a few bruises. From what I've heard half your comrades are dead or maimed, and all after being tossed from those wretched contraptions.'

'Please, not the anti-chariot lecture again. I've heard it before and I'm too tired to listen to it again.' Hetep turned to leave.

'Just you stop right there!' barked Nebenteru. 'There's a reason I summoned you, young man, and it wasn't to hear more of your insolence. For three years I've stood by and watched you squander your father's wealth on that abominable machine. Three years! And now I've had enough.'

'Why can't you just leave me alone and stop meddling in my affairs?'

'Because everything you do dishonours your blessed father's memory. How can I tell him all is well when I go to his tomb, when everything he worked for – the career he built for you, the land he cultivated to pay for the schooling – is left to go to ruin?'

'That land is mine now,' said Hetep in a low voice, 'and there's not a thing you can do about it.'

'We'll see about that. No, don't speak – listen. I said be silent! Because at last, Thoth be praised, I've been given the chance to undo the harm you've done.'

'I don't know what you're plotting but I'm a chariot warrior now, and you can't push me around like you used to.'

'A chariot warrior with no chariot. Is there anything under the whole vault of heaven that's more useless?' Nebenteru gave a short, barking laugh. 'But you will be useful again. Oh, yes. Because on this day you are to resume the career you were trained for, the one you abandoned when you took up this chariot nonsense. You are to stay in Amurru and work as a scribe. There's to be a new Egyptian commissioner here and you'll be assisting his staff.'

'No, I don't think so. I'm an archer in the first squadron of Re division. Do you know what that means? Do you know how hard I had to work to get this far? So I lost my chariot – but I'll be getting another, and if I have to sell more land to pay for it, that's my choice. You can't stop me.'

'Oh, but I already have,' said Nebenteru, smiling in triumph. 'The order has already been decreed by Ramesses himself, may he be given life, breath and health. There, I knew that would make you stare.'

Hetep's immediate though was that Nebenteru had to be lying, but he dismissed the notion as impossible: the man was far too pious and respectful of tradition to take Pharaoh's name in vain.

'Why can't you stop interfering? Are you trying to ruin me?'

'So that's my reward, is it? Insolence, when instead you should be thanking me for saving you from more folly. Still, we know who's to blame: that good-for-nothing Teppic. I always said he was a bad influence.'

'Don't you bring my friends into this. Anyway, Teppic's family is one of the most respected in Egypt.'

44

'Military aristocracy,' said Nebenteru with a sneer. 'A necessary evil, nothing more. It'll do you good to be away from his influence for a while. What you need is a few months spent earning a respectable living again. And afterwards, when your duties here are finished and you return to your lands in Egypt – lands administered by me in the interim, I should add – we shall see about finding you a job in the town granary. And then you can marry, and provide this family with the heirs it so sorely needs.'

'I see you have it all planned,' said Hetep.

'You are not a child anymore and it's time you faced up to your responsibilities.'

'You're right: I'm not a child. You may not have heard but I'm an important man now – or soon will be. I'm getting a reward. Some gold at least, and maybe even some land. So if you think you can steal my property, then think again.'

'A reward? What, for the most spectacular chariot crash of the day?' Again came the short bark of laughter. 'That blow on the head has made you delusional.'

'It's true. I killed the commander of the Amurrite army. He was a prince.'

'Foolish boy! Another man's already being rewarded for killing him. So you can save your lies for another time.'

Hetep felt a sudden chill. 'Which other man?'

'One of the scribes has just finished writing out his new commission. Pharaoh made the decree only yesterday.'

'Who's commission? Will you tell me what's happening!'

'Someone called Bui – something like that. See? I've forgotten it already. He's one of your chariot men.'

'You mean Baya, commander of second squadron?'

'Hm? Ah, yes, of course, Baya. That's the one. They say he saved the army by killing the Amurrite leader and

45

he's to be rewarded with some sort of diplomatic posting under the new commissioner.' Nebenteru gave a dismissive sniff, as if such appointments were beneath consideration. 'Anyway, you're finished with these people now. Remember what you were taught: the only life worth living is the scribal life, and it comes with real rewards, earned by hard graft and not by this squalid killing of foreigners. And scribe is one of the oldest careers there is – and that makes it respectable!'

Hetep's mind was still reeling. 'How can that man be getting my reward? It's impossible.'

Nebenteru was not listening. 'It is through wise administration that one increases Ma'at; the very words we write strengthen the world and bring order to chaos. And in doing so you improve your own standing with heaven. With the gods' blessing you could end up as chief overseer of a whole street full of granaries.'

'Gods help me,' said Hetep weakly. 'I need to find Antef, tell him there's been a mistake.'

'You're going nowhere, young man. Besides, Antef isn't permitted to talk to anyone at the moment. There are questions being asked about his fitness for command and he's been confined to his tent. The god Amun is deciding his fate.'

'Confined? What ever for?' said Hetep, puzzled. During the battle the men of first squadron had fought until they had run out of arrows, and if they had not retreated when the Amurrites had charged them they would have all died. Who could blame Antef for that?

'Good, so it's settled,' said Nebenteru, seeming to take Hetep's confusion as a sign that it was. 'Now that you're a scribe again you have many duties, and they start today. Pharaoh is receiving the formal surrender of this wretched land and what passes for its king is coming to make his

46

obeisance. He'll be here within the hour and I've arranged for you to join Pharaoh's entourage, so you can see how these things are done. There's just time for you to get changed.'

Hetep stared at his uncle. 'How can this have happened?'

'I see we're still going to have to work on your manners. Any other young man would give an eye for the chance to stand in the shadow of the Son of Re. Now come along. We need to make you presentable.'

Hetep stumbled along after his uncle, still dazed with the news of Baya's promotion. It has to be a mistake, he thought: somebody must have misreported what had happened in the battle and Baya had gained the credit by default. Then why had he not been honest and admitted that a different man had killed Irqata's prince? Whatever the truth Hetep had to let the army's commanders know, and quickly. In the meantime he would just have to humour his uncle, for disobedience would only make his situation worse.

At another tent Nebenteru summoned a slave who helped Hetep into a clean linen kilt. The fabric was soft and light, and dazzled where it caught the sunshine; after spending the past two months wearing armour Hetep felt almost naked – although he had to admit the clothing was comfortably cool.

His uncle cast an approving eye over him. 'It's good to see you dressed like a civilised man again,' he said. 'Now follow me.'

At the camp's entrance waited a little group of scribes, accompanied by a priest of Amun, a royal fanbearer and a pair of slaves, the latter holding a gilded chair. Beside them stood the Royal Butler; he cast a critical eye over Hetep and with a tilt of his head indicated that he had passed the inspection and was permitted to join the others. Then a body of Sherden warriors came to escort them from the camp and they trooped onto the plain, the slaves with the chair struggling to keep up.

'Who's this king we're meeting?' asked Hetep. 'I thought I'd killed the city's ruler.'

'His name is Benteshina and he's the king of Amurru,' said Nebenteru. 'He's come here from Sumur.'

'Where's that?'

'On the coast, a day's march from here. It's the capital of this Amun-forsaken land.'

'And he's coming all the way here?'

'Do you expect the Son of Re to go to him? The Lord of the Two Lands does not wait on barbarian kings. Now be quiet!'

They stopped at the edge of the battlefield, on which the remains of the Amurrite dead still lay unburied. Hetep wondered at the wisdom of such a callous policy, for without whole bodies and the proper funeral rites they would be unable to reach the next life, and he feared the harm they might yet do to the men who had killed them.

Nearby, dissolving in the sun and crawling with flies, lay piles of severed hands – the trophies taken from the enemy dead after the battle. Heaped up and counted by scribes, then viewed by Ramesses, they had afterwards been left to rot in the sunshine, like the bodies they had come from. Fortunately the wind was blowing the smell away.

Beyond the trophies stood a crowd of Amurrites: olive-skinned men with black hair and beards, and wearing loose-fitting robes, many of which were brightly patterned in red and blue; they made a striking contrast to the

Egyptians who, save for the Sherden, were clad in plain white linen kilts and body wraps. Many of the Amurrites sported bruises and crudely stitched wounds; soldiers, Hetep realised, who had fought in the battle and had escaped the massacre after the rout. Some looked to be charioteers, standing tall despite their defeat, and he experienced a sudden sense of fellowship, for all that they were enemies. He wondered what stories they could share of their training and their deeds in the battle. Then he remembered that he was no longer a charioteer – no longer fit company for those proud Asiatic warriors – and his *ka* was filled with a bitter misery.

One of the wounded Amurrites caught his eye. He had deep grazes down one cheek and a bandage around his forearm, and something about him filled Hetep with a vague disquiet. Then the man turned, fully revealing his face, and with a jolt Hetep realised it was the driver of the Irqatan prince's chariot, whom he had shot in the arm. Quickly he stepped back, hiding behind one of the Sherden.

From the camp sounded a peal of horns, and a blazing figure emerged and came racing towards them. It was Ramesses, approaching from the west in his chariot, with the morning sunlight reflecting from his armour and the gold plating on the car. Hetep turned his head away, blinking the great purple blotches from his vision, and when he looked again the pharaoh had stopped and a pall of dust was drifting over the Amurrites, making them cough.

Ramesses dismounted, and the instant his foot touched the ground the slaves hurried forwards with the chair, placing it in the chariot car. Then he sat, facing the Amurrites with his sandals resting on the ground, while his fanbearer took up station, drying the royal sweat with wafts from his ostrich-feather fan.

The sight of the Son of Re in the fullness of his majesty was too much for some of the Amurrites, who wept and fell on their faces, appealing for mercy. But Ramesses ignored them and just sat, a faint smile on his face and a distant look in his eye, as if he was seeing and hearing things that were beyond mortal senses.

Another chariot came rumbling towards them. This one was Canaanite, drawn by a pair of horses armoured from neck to rump in thick linen; a wagon followed, and Hetep saw that it carried a corpse. A stillness fell on the Amurrites, and they watched the chariot's progress in nervous silence.

The driver dismounted and approached Ramesses. He looked sleek and well fed, and had a dark face and hooded eyes; around his waist he wore a plain woolen kilt and his oiled beard curved outwards, ending in a point like a spear blade. Hetep noticed that the wounded charioteer was following the man with his eyes, his chest working visibly as he breathed.

'I am King Benteshina, your slave,' said the newcomer, speaking Babylonian, the common tongue used between Egypt and its Canaanite vassals. 'I am the dust under your feet. Seven times I prostrate myself on my face; seven times on my back.' He bowed low, his beard almost touching the ground.

The wounded charioteer shoved his way forwards.

'It that it?' he shouted. 'We don't even ask for terms?'

Benteshina jerked upright and wheeled to face him. For an instant he stared, appalled, as if seeing a man just risen from his tomb, and then his face lit up with a look of wonder.

'My dear Zuratta,' he exclaimed. 'How I exult to see you among the living!'

'Where are the troops you promised, you fawning dog?'

The Royal Butler stepped forwards as if to shield Ramesses from the sight of the unruly foreigners and the Sherden advanced with him, full of menace and with their swords out.

'Who is this man?' he demanded. 'You!' – this was to the charioteer, the one Benteshina had called Zuratta – 'hold your tongue, or it will be removed.'

Zuratta was still glaring at Benteshina but he held silent, allowing himself to be pulled back a couple of paces by his terrified companions.

Benteshina turned a nervous smile on Ramesses.

'Forgive my servant, Majesty,' he said. 'His wounds have doubtless clouded his wits. I promise that he will not speak in such a disrespectful way again.'

'Let us hope not,' said Ramesses with a chilling mildness. 'Now bring forth the rebel, that he may receive his punishment.'

A pair of slaves began manhandling the corpse out of the wagon. Curious, Hetep moved forwards to get a better view and saw that it was the body of an Amurrite chariot warrior, heavily built and clad in a bronze hauberk. For a moment it caught on the rail at the wagon's side and teetered, its limbs splayed grotesquely. Then it fell in a clatter of metal scales.

The slaves lifted the corpse by its armpits and dragged it up to Ramesses' chariot. One of them gripped its hair and raised its head, revealing a savage, bearded face, the mouth hanging slack, the eyes staring straight at Hetep as if livid with hate. An arrowhead was still embedded in the left cheek, the skin around the wound a bruised contrast to the yellow corpse sheen of rest of the flesh.

With a start Hetep recognised the face. It was the warrior he had killed – the Irqatan prince. Zuratta must have realised it at the same moment, for he gave a howl of anguish and struggled forwards, and it took two men to hold him back.

'This is the rebel, O Great King,' said Benteshina. 'He alone defied Your Majesty. He alone bears the responsibility for the sin.'

Ramesses stood and advanced on the corpse.

'I arrived in this land like Montu in his power, and all bowed down before me,' he said, his voice filling the vast area of the plain surrounding them. 'All except you, vile rebel.'

Ramesses reached forward and gripped the corpse by its hair. He held it up while the priest handed him a mace, its haft made of dark, polished wood, its head a ball of gleaming stone. Ramesses raised the mace above his head and as he did so the priest began an incantation praising the goddess Ma'at, the embodiment of order, justice and all virtuous conduct.

'Like Re in his glory I came, to kill and to pile up the rebel corpses,' intoned Ramesses. 'With my arm alone I slew those whom Re abominates.' As he spoke he struck the head of the dead prince with the mace, again and again. The waxy flesh yielded like clay under the blows; the dull thudding made Hetep feel sick. At each blow Zuratta convulsed with anguish and fury, straining against the men who held him back.

The pharaoh opened his hand and the corpse fell into the dust. As if prodded by a spear Benteshina lay flat on his face.

'May the gods you love bring you all you desire,' he said. 'May you celebrate a thousand jubilees. May the light of your face shine on all the lands. I have brought gifts as tokens of submission: gold, slaves and chariots – all are yours. This land is yours – its cities and its people.

Life and health for king of the world!'

Ramesses returned to his chariot and seated himself.

'Now Amurru is subdued,' he said. 'Now it is under my sandals, as it shall be under them forever.'

With a violent lunge Zuratta broke free, and he pushed his way to the front of the crowd.

'You miserable cur,' he roared at Benteshina. 'You've sold us to our enemies! Where are the troops you said would come? Where are the men of Sumur, Arwada and Tunip? Where –' Then he saw Hetep and stopped rigid, as if struck by a blow. 'I know you,' he said, and pointed at the prince's corpse. 'You did this. You killed him!'

It seemed to Hetep in that moment that the whole crowd had receded and all that was in the world was he and the enraged charioteer.

'I'm sorry,' he said. It was a foolish thing to say – why apologise for what was done during war? – but he could think of no better reply. Then the moment passed and all was roaring chaos, with the Sherden advancing again and beating back the yelling crowd.

Zuratta was still raving. 'I swear, by the storm god Teshub, there will be retribution!'

'But it was a battle,' protested Hetep. 'It wasn't murder.'

He was aware that Ramesses was looking at him. This could be my chance to claim the credit that is mine, he thought. But he dared not turn to face the pharaoh, let alone plead with him. He felt guilty, as if he was the cause of the disorder, and his cheeks burned. Yet why should he be ashamed for doing his duty?

'Blood pays for blood,' cried Zuratta, still glaring at Hetep. 'You are a dead man!'

The Sherden waded in. Hetep saw Zuratta take a blow to the head and reel back, and then the Sherden's swords were hacking up and down, while the angry shouts of the Amurrites turned to screams.

The Butler was roaring orders, calling the Sherden back, and after a while the screaming subsided. Silence fell, save for weeping and the groans of the wounded.

Benteshina hesitated, then bowed low at the waist. 'Majesty, I swear, in the name of the god Ba'al, that this will not happen again. All Amurru will see the wisdom of submission.'

'You had better make sure of it,' said the Butler. 'The Son of Re has been more than generous. You would not like him to alter his judgement on this town, let alone the whole kingdom.'

They all looked at Ramesses, but the pharaoh seemed as unmoved by the altercation between Hetep and Zuratta as he would by a squabble between ants. He shifted on his chair and his eyes strayed to the rotting piles of hands, and as they did so he gave a faint smile of satisfaction, as if all that mattered was his victory in battle over the only people in all Canaan who had dared to resist him.

CHAPTER 6

Hetep's uncle was pale with fury all the way back to the camp.

'What in Thoth's name do you think you were doing?' he cried, once he and Hetep were alone. 'And in the Royal Presence, too!'

'How can you blame me for what happened?' protested Hetep. 'That man threatened me; you must have seen it. He tried to assault me.'

'You're going to be here for months with these people. The last thing you should do is antagonise them.'

'I can't stay, not now. What if he tries to have me killed?'

Nebenteru snorted. 'He wouldn't dare. Besides, we're leaving a garrison. So there'll be troops to protect you.'

'How many?'

'Two, maybe three hundred. All foot soldiers, mind – none of your stuck-up chariot men.'

'I thought we'd need thousands for a place like this.'

'And how do you propose we feed and maintain such a force? No, a few hundred are more than sufficient. You saw that peasant who calls himself a king. He was in awe of the Son of Re – he couldn't surrender fast enough.' Nebenteru gave a derisive chuckle. 'They say he was sending peace offerings even as Irqata's garrison was lining up to fact us. So there's nothing for you to worry about.'

'Peace offerings? I don't understand. If he wanted to surrender why did he have Irqata's troops fight us?'

Nebenteru shrugged. 'Who knows the mind of an Asiatic? Ma'at-less foreigners – they make their own chaos. Which reminds me: you'll need a mentor once I'm gone.

55

I've had you assigned to Merimose, the Chief Scribe of the Commissariat. You'll be making inventories of bread and beer rations for the garrison. See that you do as he says.'

Merimose turned out to be a kindly-looking ancient with cloudy eyes and an inane, toothless smile. Hetep greeted him politely but had to hide his despair as he listened to his list of duties. He wondered how he was going to stand the tedium.

He knew that others would think him a fool for being so ungrateful. A scribe's life was indeed a good one – clean linen every week, soft hands, limbs not worn out by endless toil, and the respect afforded to that great rarity: the literate man. But such a life could offer no experience to rival that riding in a charging chariot with the horses at full gallop, and there was no honour to compare with that of serving under Ramesses as a member of Egypt's new elite, where one might gain rewards for valour from the hand of Pharaoh himself.

And now there was no doubt that he had lost it all. While he had been moping about the camp after the battle and nursing his sore head, Baya had indeed been acclaimed as the man who had killed Irqata's prince and stopped the enemy attack, and had been honoured with a lucrative posting in Amurru's new Egyptian administration. The thought made Hetep squirm with frustration. The reward was his by right; how could Ramesses and the other commanders have been so mistaken?

A visit to Sebeku did little to improve Hetep's mood. The driver was sinking deeper into fever and the flesh around his wound was hot to the touch. The physicians had laid a pile of dung near his head to draw out the evil; beyond that they could recommend nothing but prayers.

Benteshina departed as discreetly as he had arrived, reportedly to prepare his city to accommodate the Egyptian garrison's three hundred men. At the same time Ramesses announced the name of the commissioner he had appointed to ensure the king's continued loyalty: Nui, Re division's Commander of the Host, a huge, belligerent-looking man in his mid forties, with a great bald head and a body covered in battle scars. Hetep had only spoken to him once, at his recruitment, and the memory of their meeting still made him tremble.

Within an hour of receiving his commission Nui summoned his staff to his tent. Hetep, at Nebenteru's insistence, joined them and with a sinking heart he examined the men with whom he would be working, likely for the next year or more. Most were career bureaucrats, with stooped shoulders and ink stained fingers, their flesh soft and pale from a life spent almost wholly indoors. The remainder were ex-charioteers: straight backed, lean and tanned; among the latter was Baya, lurking at the back and avoiding Hetep's eye.

Nui addressed them in a voice more suited to roaring orders across a battlefield than the confines of a tent. He told them that he was to be Pharaoh's representative in Amurru and had been granted the authority to do everything short of declaring war on the Hittites if it suited him, and that he would brook no insolence from mere foreigners and he expected them to do the same. He asked for neither questions nor suggestions and nobody dared to offer any, and he dismissed them as if they were troops on the parade ground. Hetep was the last to go and just as he reached the tent's entrance Nui stopped him with a hand on his shoulder.

'Wait. I want a word with you.'

Hetep swallowed nervously as he stared at Nui's huge,

scowling face. He told himself he had nothing to fear: having been on the man's staff for less than a day it was impossible for him to have yet done anything wrong.

'You were in first squadron, weren't you?' said Nui.

Hetep nodded but did not speak.

'And now, for my sins, you've been assigned to me. The other men I know, by reputation if nothing else. You I do not. So tell me: are you going to be of any use?'

'I don't know. I've never been much good at scribal work, and until yesterday I was a chariot archer. I think there's been a mistake. If I could just talk to Antef I'm sure he'd–'

'Antef's in no position to rectify whatever mistake it is you think's been made. No, you're stuck here, just as I'm stuck with you. So we return to the question of your usefulness. Did you finish your scribal training, at least?'

'Mostly. I know the common script, but not the hieroglyphics.'

'We don't need any fancy work – you're not decorating tombs. You'll just be keeping records and maybe writing down what people say. That's if I let you attend any meetings. Other than that, I suppose we could do with some help carting things around and taking inventories. I assume you can count.'

'My uncle said I was to count bread rations. But please, not that. I can do other things, help in other ways.'

'Such as?'

'I can speak the local language – or at least one of the southern dialects, which is close to what I've heard the Amurrites speaking. And some Babylonian, too; it's what everybody uses as a common tongue, you know.'

'So I've heard,' said Nui dryly. 'Where did you learn all this?'

'My mother was from Sidon. She was taken as a slave when she was young and she ended up marrying my father after he freed her. He let her teach me her language. He thought it might be useful. That was when I was still training to be a scribe. She also told me some of their gods' stories, and a bit of the history.'

'I don't need to know about their gods, so you can keep all that yourself. But the language might be some help.' Nui considered a moment, while rubbing a hand over his jaw; it sounded like a piece of pumice scraping on sandstone. 'We need more baggage animals for the garrison's move to Sumur. We can't have the army's: they're being used to carry the rest of the tribute home. So we have to make do with what we can get from the locals – donkeys, oxen, whatever they have. We were promised some yesterday, but you know what these people are like for organisation. More likely they're just being awkward. Normally I'd send some troops over to hang a few of the malcontents from the walls and take what we need, but Ramesses told me not to kill too many of these people – not unless I have to. So we'll try persuasion. I want you to go to the town and organise it.'

'Me, go to Irqata?' said Hetep, remembering the pale-eyed charioteer, Zuratta, and his threats of vengeance. 'It might be dangerous. Some of the people might be angry they lost the battle.'

'Not scared, are you?' said Nui with a snort. 'And you say you're a chariot warrior!'

Hetep reddened. 'It's not that. I just wondered if they might be a bit difficult if it's just me on my own.'

Nui laughed. 'All right, you can stop shaking: you'll have some company. A few scribes, of course, and I'll send some soldiers – a dozen of the new spearmen should do. I'll have Yuya lead them. He's a good man – tough and

59

experienced. He'll be garrison commander once the rest of the army's gone, so mind you don't upset him. There's a palace of sorts at the town's centre; go there. I'll send a message ahead so they'll be expecting you. And don't take any nonsense. These people are Pharaoh's subjects. He owns them, as much as he owns the land they stand on.'

CHAPTER 7

The day's heat was building and the air over the plain shimmered. From the camp the town of Irqata looked distorted in the haze; partly hidden by the ridge, it seemed to Hetep like some vast, malevolent creature, waiting to pounce and crush him. And somewhere within its walls was Zuratta, doubtless nursing a new collection of injuries after the Sherden's massacre and set more determinedly than before on the path of vengeance. The thought made his stomach turn over.

He knew that in battle he would be able to face Zuratta without a qualm: the recent fight had given him confidence in his skills as a chariot warrior, especially when Montu was with him. But he was going to have to enter Irqata unarmed and unarmoured, while Zuratta would enjoy the full support of the town's remaining garrison. For the first time he missed his linen corselet, even though it chafed his skin and made him sweat; more so he missed Sebeku and his ready shield and keen vigilance. Yet taking either a shield or armour was out of the question – scribes simply did not use such things. They also rarely went armed, but that was one custom Hetep was determined to break. Knowing that it would take a while for Nui to assemble the scribes and their escort he searched out Teppic.

'I heard about Baya,' said his friend when they met. 'I'm sorry.'

'So am I,' said Hetep. 'Listen, I need a dagger. They've taken all my weapons away.'

'Already? You're a keen one for revenge,' said Teppic. He eyed Hetep, his expression concerned. 'Just be careful.

Baya might prove harder to kill than you think. And don't forget murder's a sin.'

'Murder? What do you mean? I need it because Nui's sending me to Irqata. I guess you heard about that insane Amurrite charioteer. I might run into him and I want to be armed if I do.'

Teppic's face cleared. 'Ah, I see. Then you'd better take this.' He unbuckled a sheathed dagger from his waist and handed it to Hetep. 'It's Cypriot bronze and it'll cut through anything. But you're going to have to hide it, and that scribe's kilt wouldn't cover a fruit knife.'

Hetep looked down at himself. 'I hadn't thought of that.'

'Give me a moment. You still have time, don't you?'

Teppic vanished into the camp. A while later he was back, grinning and holding up a tunic. 'It's proper scribe's wear, so they won't object. Just don't ask me how I got it.'

Hetep strapped the dagger to his torso then pulled the tunic on to cover it.

'I'll tell them I'm feeling the cold,' he said.

Teppic raised an eyebrow. 'At this time of the year?' He tugged a fold straight in Hetep's tunic. 'There, you'll do. Just be careful, will you? And we can talk about Baya when you're back.'

The scribes were already waiting at the assembly point. Among them was Merimose, who squinted at Hetep and smiled amiably. Soon their escort appeared in the shape of a dozen conscripts, none of whom looked as if they had any battle experience. Not so their commander, who turned out to be the same scab-faced veteran Hetep had brawled with the day before.

'Well if it isn't our mouthy chariot hero,' he said. He took in Hetep's attire and smirked. 'My, you've come down in the world. Demotion for cowardice, was it?'

'There's been a mistake, that's all. And I told you: I'm not a coward.'

The commander – Yuya, Nui had called him – sneered. 'Well, I say you are. And watch your mouth: your fancy-talking friend isn't here to save you this time.'

Yuya formed his troops into a column and lead them off at a quick march. The scribes wheezed as they strove to keep up but, as was expected of men in their profession, without a word of complaint. Hetep laboured along beside them, and every footfall sent stabs of pain through his ribs.

'Can you please slow down a bit,' he said after a while. 'I'm injured, and some of these men aren't used to this.'

'Tough,' said Yuya, and increased the pace.

'What's wrong with you? Slow down!'

Yuya halted and wheeled to face him. 'Who in the name of all the gods do you think you're talking to?'

'Nui said you're here to assist me, which makes me senior to you. Go back and ask him if you don't believe me.'

'I don't take orders from a grain counter.'

'Can you read?' said Hetep.

'What's that got to do with anything?'

'There might be documents to check, or an inventory to make out. We're not here to plunder the town, you know. We're just here for a few animals, and we should probably get a receipt.'

Yuya frowned. 'A what?'

'A receipt. A sealed list of what we've taken.' Hetep smiled at Yuya's confusion. 'Everything in that town be-longs to Pharaoh. What if someone accuses us of taking

63

some of it for ourselves? Without a proper inventory it might be hard to prove our innocence. Do you know what the penalty is for stealing Pharaoh's property? You could be burned to death or impaled.'

'Well, now you put it like that...' Yuya gave a mocking bow and held out his arm. 'Since you're in charge you'd better take the lead. And when we're there you can do all the talking you want, and take all the blame if anything goes wrong.'

They moved now at an easier pace, past fields of yellowing grain and meadows bright with summer flowers. A few farm labourers were about, some leading donkeys and oxen, but for the most part the land was empty. As they drew nearer to Irqata it rose steadily against the sky and for the first time Hetep could clearly see its walls. Built primarily for keeping out raiding nomads, they would have offered little hindrance to a determined assault by Egyptian troops. It was no wonder the garrison had decided to meet them on the open plain, he thought, where they could at least use their chariots – and to good effect too. He felt again the fear that had come to him during the battle, which only became more acute when he remembered Zuratta. He told himself that he had nothing to worry about, not with a whole squad of soldiers to protect him, although a glance at Yuya's scowling face made him wonder how much use they would be to him if there was any trouble.

They marched through the town's gate, ignoring the two Amurrite soldiers who stood on guard, and headed straight for the palace, a walled building of faced stone standing on a raised mound of earth. At the entrance a little knot of men was waiting. All were slaves except one, a corpulent man in a patterned wool robe, sporting a curled beard and a greasy smile. He bid the Egyptians welcome in the name of Amurru's many gods and introduced himself as Ayub, cupbearer to the late prince and now the town's mayor.

'I have received the requisition order from the peerless Nui and have read his words,' he said, holding up a clay tablet. 'Of course, it would bring me joy beyond measure to supply what he needs. But alas, there is not a single animal to spare in all Irqata. Our tears fall like silver shekels. Please convey to him our regret.'

Yuya was glowering suspiciously. 'What did he say?'

'Nothing worth translating,' said Hetep. 'Just leave this to me.' He turned back to Ayub. 'No animals, you say, in the whole kingdom? I think you're just trying to waste our time.'

'Not at all,' Ayub assured him. 'I said there are none in the town. But I have sent scribes and counting men out to the villages and farms. Give them a few days – a half-month, no more – and then we shall know what we can spare.'

'I saw oxen and donkeys in the fields. Why can't we take those?'

'But they're private property,' said Ayub, scandalised. 'We cannot take the farmers' animals. There would be a riot!'

Hetep considered Ayub, his eyes narrowed. He had only a hazy idea of the laws of ownership in these northern lands, but he could not believe that even here the will of the palace could be defied by mere farmers. No, the man had to be lying. He turned to the scribes for advice but they were all looking studiously at the sky, or the buildings, or the road leading back to the town's gate – anywhere else but at him.

'I don't suppose anybody has any suggestions,' he said.

Merimose held up his hands as if to push away responsibility. 'We are here simply to record. It is not fitting that we recommend a course of action. But I am willing to pen a dispatch to Nui, asking for instructions.'

'And in the meantime I suppose we just stand here?'

'We shall send the youngest of us as courier. I am confident that he will be back before sundown, and then we shall know what we are to do.'

Yuya was watching with a smirk. Hetep felt his face grow hot and he rounded on Ayub.

'Listen to me. These animals now are property of Ramesses, beloved of Amun, as are you, your people, and everything else in this kingdom, and you know it. I expect donkeys and oxen to be delivered here within an hour. If they're not, I'll instruct the troops to take what we need, and kill any "private citizens" who defend their property rights. Do you understand me?'

Ayub's hands fluttered in agitation. 'There's no need for threats. We are doing all we can. We–'

'Be quiet!' snapped Hetep. Then, in Egyptian, 'Commander, have your men draw their weapons.'

Yuya shrugged, but gave the order. At the sight of the gleaming dagger and khopesh blades Ayub blanched and took a step back.

'Let us not be too hasty,' he said. 'Perhaps there is a way we can accommodate you.' He turned and spoke rapidly to one of the slaves, who ran off. 'If you'll kindly wait I shall have refreshments brought. The animals will be delivered within the hour.'

The Egyptians were lead to a walled garden adjoining the palace and immediately made for a grove of trees, whose shade gave some respite from the day's growing heat. A slave brought them wine; it had been mixed with cold water and Hetep gulped down a whole jugful. Afterwards the soldiers lay down under the trees and slept, while the scribes stood patiently in a little group.

The wine, as much as his victory over Ayub, had done much to abate Hetep's fears, and feeling restless and curious he wandered off through the garden. He came to a gate in the wall and heard voices on the far side. One of them sounded familiar and he stopped to listen. He could not catch any of the words but he was sure that the speaker was Baya. Now what's he doing here? he wondered.

He went up to the gate. There he hesitated, looking back. The Egyptian soldiers were still asleep in the shade, but if there was trouble they could be roused with a word. Reassured, he went on, slipping silently through the gate.

He found himself in a courtyard bordered by more trees, and so quiet was it that he could hear his sandals crunching on grit as he walked along the tiled path. He saw a figure moving beyond the trees and stopped, crouching in the shadows by the wall. The figure came into the light. It was Baya for certain.

There was nobody else about; whoever he had been talking to must have just left. Baya glanced furtively around and hurried off – to Hetep's relief towards an archway at the far end of the courtyard – and in another moment was gone.

Now what was that all about? thought Hetep. Faintly came the sound of the Egyptian soldiers' snoring, a sign that they were still within calling distance. His curiosity outweighing caution, he left his hiding spot and crept along beside the wall.

A doorway in the palace wall opened on his right, and he ducked through and into the passage beyond. After waiting for his eyes to adapt to the semi-darkness he advanced, slowly and with his ears straining. Voices came from ahead and he stopped, listening. They were Amurrites for sure and something about the tone set the hairs prickling on his neck. It was time to go back.

He turned, and found Zuratta blocking his way. The Amurrite still had the bandage around his arm and now he had another around his head, and his face was bruised and swollen. He wore a short sword at his waist, and one hand was resting on the hilt.

'I have prayed to Teshub for this moment,' he said. 'I did not expect the god to answer so soon.'

'There are Egyptian troops in the garden outside,' said Hetep, trying to keep his voice steady. 'One word from me—'

'Will be your last.' Zuratta drew his sword and advanced on Hetep. 'You're doing well not to appear afraid. But you are afraid, aren't you?'

Hetep backed away, keeping his distance, and wondered how quickly he could get to his dagger. Not quickly enough, he decided.

'If you kill me, Nui won't rest until this city's been razed to the ground.'

'Not if he thinks you died in an accident,' said Zuratta. He called out, softly; answering voices came from behind Hetep and a pair of Amurrite soldiers appeared from the gloom.

'Now you will come with me,' said Zuratta. He added something in a language Hetep did not understand and pushed past, heading down the passage. One of the soldiers followed him, while the second drew a sword and prodded Hetep along in front of him.

They passed a guard room, from which a group of spearmen watched them curiously, then a smaller side corridor. With every step they were moving further from the garden and the Egyptian soldiers; better do something now, thought Hetep, before it's too late. Deliberately he caught a foot on the edge of a flagstone and stumbled sideways against the wall. For an instant his arm was hidden, and he drew the dagger out from under his tunic. As his guard made to grab him Hetep twisted and thrust the dagger upwards with all his strength, driving it through the man's armour and deep into his guts. He felt the soft yielding of viscera and heard the guard's dying exhalation – a grunt of shock as much as pain. Then he was off, sprinting back the way he had come.

It took a long moment for Zuratta and the other soldier to realise what had happened, and then they came racing after him. Remembering the guard room ahead Hetep took the side corridor, hoping it would lead him out of the palace. The way was dark and he tripped on a stone and went sprawling, the dagger spinning off into the shadows. No time to look for it now, he thought, and he was up and running again in a few heartbeats. He shot around a corner, scattering a startled gang of slaves, and saw an archway ahead, through which came the glare of daylight.

His legs were aching and pain was stabbing through his bruised ribs, but the sight gave him renewed vigour and in a few strides he had emerged into a courtyard. A moment to scan all around, eyes shaded – four walls, a gate, a pair of astonished-looking spearmen... and a flight of steps, leading up to the palace roof.

He raced up the steps, two at a time. At the top he turned and saw Zuratta, halfway up, red faced with rage and exertion as he laboured against his own injuries. Hetep lashed out with his foot, caught Zuratta on the jaw and sent him tumbling back down, then raced off across the roof.

At the edge he looked down at the road below. Too high to jump, he thought; I'll break a leg for certain. A squad of soldiers – archers as well as spearmen – appeared from a stairwell ahead, while from behind came the sound of Zuratta in raging pursuit. Trapped, he thought, and he stared wildly about him. There: a low wall abutting the palace where the road turned aside. He sprinted towards it, leaped and landed on the wall's top. For a moment he teetered, before dropping to his hands and knees. Then he lowered himself over the wall's far side and dropped to the ground, just as the first arrows rattled against the stonework all around him.

He found himself in an alley scarcely an arm span wide and blocked at one end; the other end opened into what looked to be a main street. He heard Zuratta screaming orders, but fortunately the wall blocked the solders' line of sight and for now he was safe. He rested a moment, leaning against a buttress to catch his breath, before stumbling forwards on shaking legs.

There were a dozen or so people in the street beyond, all Amurrites, and all staring at him open mouthed. Now where? he thought. As he stood looking about him there was a shout and Zuratta came into view, far down the street. He was staggering as he ran, roaring curses and clutching his forehead as if pained by the loudness of his own voice. Then a band of Amurrite spearmen appeared and came charging towards Hetep, overtaking Zuratta.

Hetep turned and stumbled away as fast as he was able, knowing that he was too injured and used up to get away, but unwilling to just surrender. His back was bent and his eyes were on the road, and he collided with Yuya, who was coming around a corner with his detachment of soldiers.

'Where in Montu's name have you been?' demanded Yuya, grabbing him and jerking him upright. 'The animals are here.' Then he saw Zuratta and his men. 'Local trouble, eh?'

Hetep nodded, too breathless to speak.

Yuya gave a quick order and his soldiers formed up in a line, their spears at the ready. It was enough to check the Amurrites' advance and two sides faced each other in the now empty street, like battle lines in miniature.

For a while nobody moved or spoke. Then Zuratta caught up with his troops. Blood was running from his nose and he had a bruise developing on his jaw where Hetep had kicked him, and he was wheezing so much that his curses caught in his throat.

'That man tried to kill me,' said Hetep, pointing at Zuratta. 'You should arrest him.'

'I can't,' said Yuya. The road they stood on ran beside the palace wall and he pointed up at the battlements, where a line of Amurrite archers stood silhouetted against the sky. 'In case you haven't noticed, we're outnumbered and outmatched. And Nui told me there was to be no fighting. Which means we're just going to walk quietly away from here. So tell your new friend if he doesn't make any trouble, neither will we.'

'Didn't you hear? He tried to have me murdered.'

'Really? And what about you?' Yuya looked pointedly at Hetep's blooded hand. 'Who have you just killed?'

By now Zuratta had recovered from his exertions. The sight of Yuya's men seemed to have blunted his rage but not his hatred, and he glared at Hetep.

'It seems vengeance must wait,' he said. 'But I'm a patient man. Tell your men to stand down, or there'll be more blood spilled here than either of us wants.'

Yuya frowned at Hetep. 'Well?'

'He's says we're to back off. I think he's letting us go.'

'Sensible man,' said Yuya. 'Tell him we'll do it, but only if he makes the first move.'

'But he'll be getting away with attempted murder,' protested Hetep. 'You can't let him.'

'I can, and I will. Now do as I say or we'll all regret it.'

Hetep looked up at the archers, who were standing ready to draw and shoot, arrows nocked to their bow-strings. He realised Yuya was right and they would never survive a battle in the open street.

'We'll leave,' he said to Zuratta, 'but not until you've dismissed your men.'

'Don't trust me, is that it?' said Zuratta. 'Very well.' He barked a series of orders and the bowmen vanished, while the spearmen backed away to the far end of the street.

'Feeling safer now?' He advanced to within a dagger thrust of Hetep, who stood his ground, willing himself not to flinch away. 'Because you're not, you know. It's very dangerous for Egyptians here – as others of your kind have already found out. And I'm told you're going to be with us for a very long time.'

'There'll be a garrison,' said Hetep.

'Of a mere three hundred men, while I command the loyalty of twice that many kinsmen in the hills and up-lands. And once I've been confirmed as ruler of this city I'll have just as many soldiers, all devoted to me.' A smile twisted his bruised, swollen features. 'I look forward to introducing you to some of them.' Still smiling he nodded to Yuya, turned and limped back down the road.

Hetep exhaled. He found he was shaking all over.

'You seem to have a talent for making enemies,' said Yuya, looking amused. 'And now, if you're quite finished stirring up the locals, you've got work to do. These peas-ants have rounded up a few donkeys for us. You'd better come and count them – it's what you're here for, isn't it?'

The scribes had already done most of the inventory work and one of them was holding a sheet of papyrus, both sides of which were covered in writing – although what there was to say about a few score of pack animals Hetep could not imagine. He made sure the donkeys were adequately roped together, assigned the fittest of the scribes the task of guiding them, and lead the way down the street, leaving the others to follow. So upset was he by his encounter with Zuratta that it was only once they had all passed through the town's gates that he realised he had forgotten to get a receipt after all.

It was a slow journey back to the camp, for the scribes proved to be inept donkey drivers and Yuya would not allow his soldiers to help.

'What if your friend causes trouble?' he said. 'My men need to be ready.'

'I don't think he'll bother us again today,' said Hetep.

'Just what did he say to you in the street back there?'

'If you must know he threatened me. He told me it's dangerous here for outlanders. But he was probably lying.'

'Oh no he wasn't. Years ago the Egyptian commissioner here was murdered, along with his whole staff. Throats cut, head bludgeoned into pulp, that sort of thing. They left a terrible mess – blood everywhere. Of course the crime was avenged, but it was too late for the dead commissioner and his scribes.'

'How do you know this?'

'My father told me. He served hereabouts, under Seti.'

Hetep closed his eyes briefly. 'Gods,' he said, 'I need to get out of here.'

'Still,' went on Yuya cheerfully, 'I'm sure the prospect of being massacred by angry natives wouldn't daunt one of the pharaoh's brave elite.'

CHAPTER 8

At the camp Yuya and his men sloped off, leaving Hetep to see to the corralling of the animals. It took some time, and only when he was satisfied did he make his way to Nui's tent to give his report.

Nui was pleased about the pack animals, but less so when Hetep described his encounter with Zuratta.

'Yuya's already told me about that,' he said. 'According to him you went off on your own and caused trouble with the locals.'

'It wasn't like that, not really.'

'So he lied, did he?'

'Well... not as such,' said Hetep. 'But he didn't see everything. Zuratta tried to kill me, and afterwards he threatened me. Didn't Yuya tell you that?'

'He said you'd made this foreigner angry, probably by killing one of his friends. Well? Did you kill somebody?'

'No! I mean, yes... but it wasn't murder.' Hetep noticed that Nui was staring at his blood-encrusted hand. He slipped it behind his back, as if to hide the evidence.

'I see.' Nui glowered at him for a moment. 'Do you realise what could happen if you provoke these people? At the first act of defiance I'm going to have to start hanging some of them from scaffolds. And Ramesses won't like it, and it'll be your fault. So there's to be no more fighting with the locals. Do you understand me?'

Hetep realised that any protest he could make would be futile. 'Yes, I understand,' he sighed.

'Good. Then that's the end of it.'

'But what if Zuratta tries to kill me again? I haven't got any weapons – they won't give me any. And my driver's still too wounded to protect me.'

Nui gave a dismissive grunt. 'Whoever this Zuratta is he wouldn't dare kill an Egyptian – not with the entire Re division only a few miles from his town's gates.'

'And afterwards, when they're all marching back to Egypt... what then?'

'You're trying my patience,' growled Nui. 'You've made a decent start, all things considered, but you've a long way to go before you earn my trust, and even further if you want my respect. Now get out of my sight. I'm busy.'

That afternoon the last detachments of Re division came marching into the camp. The campaign was over; the subject kingdoms of Canaan, which had tested the new pharaoh's resolve by their insolence, had been cowed and were once again loyal vassals of Egypt. Only Irqata had chosen to resist, and Ramesses had met the rebellious foreigners in battle and annihilated them. Now the whole division – four thousand infantry and five hundred chariots, save those lost in the battle and the few who were to remain behind as a garrison – was to return home, on the way linking up with the five thousand troops of Amun division, which had been tasked with subduing the settlements along the inland road, from Meggido to the border of Kadesh.

Ramesses appeared among them, hurrying the preparations for departure. Some claimed that the god Amun had spoken to him in a dream, demanding to see for himself in his temple at Karnak the booty from the campaign; others repeated rumours of Libyan incursions on Egypt's western border, where another show of strength was needed to pacify the tribes. Whatever the reason the last of the newly arrived troops had scarcely broken ranks before they were ordered to form up again, ready to begin the journey home.

Hetep made a last effort to talk to Antef, who was still confined in the royal enclosure, but the Sherden barred his way; it seemed that the disgraced commander's sins were so grave they could be transmitted like a disease, and nobody was permitted to go near him. His hopes for early reinstatement fading he went searching for Teppic and found him at the chariot corrals, arguing with his driver, Ipu, about some new harnesses they had been given for their horse team.

'Does it matter if one's red and the other's blue?' Teppic was saying. 'The horses don't care, I don't care, nobody cares except you!' He saw Hetep and his look of exasperation dissolved into a grin. 'Back from the crocodile's jaws, I see. I heard you were safe, but you know one can never rely on hearsay.'

'It's busy here,' said Hetep, looking around.

'We're leaving today. Provided we can get the horses hitched in time,' he added, with a dark look at Ipu. 'Come over here where it's quiet and tell me how you did. Was there any trouble from your local friend?'

'A little.' Hetep held up his hand to show the dried blood under his fingernails. 'It's not his, unfortunately. I lost your dagger, too. I'm sorry.'

'Don't worry, I can get another. I'm just glad it was useful.' Teppic's easy expression turned to one of concern. 'And I'm sorry we're leaving you behind. What are you going to do once we're gone?'

Hetep shrugged. 'Try to get my credit back, of course. Somebody has to be told that there was a mistake and it was I who killed the Irqatan prince, not Baya.'

'That was no mistake,' said Teppic quietly. 'I thought

76

you realised that. What I said, when I gave you the dagger...'

'You really thought I was going to kill Baya?'

'No, of course not. You're far too sensible.' Teppic patted him on the arm. 'But the truth is Baya lied. He swore he killed the prince in the fighting up on the hill.'

'Swore? You mean in front of a god?'

Teppic nodded. 'I heard him say it, as well. He claimed that second squadron held back the enemy chariots and only a few broke through to attack us, and that if we'd stood our ground the infantry would never have been in any danger.'

'But that's not true. There was a whole squadron of Amurrites coming after us. We both saw it. Gods, the whole army must have seen it! And any chariot warrior knows we had to get out of the way or we'd have been overrun. It's what we're supposed to do: skirmish. If anyone's to blame it's Baya. Second squadron should never have let the Amurrites get near us.'

'Remember there was a lot of dust. Only the gods – and Pharaoh – know the full truth.' Teppic glanced around him. 'Come with me,' he said, and lead Hetep through the bustle of the camp to the lee of a pile of grain sacks, where they could talk without being overheard. Hetep looked questioningly at him but said nothing.

Now listen,' said Teppic in a low voice. 'When my father and uncles used to talk about their campaigns I'd overhear certain things that probably weren't meant for my ears. Such as how King Seti won his victories, and how the accounts on the monuments and my father's memories would often differ. Do you understand me?' He held Hetep's eye for a moment. 'What's important is that Ramesses remains blameless. To deny Baya's claims

77

would be to suggest that the pharaoh sent first squadron to attack the enemy's infantry too soon, before their chariots had been neutralised.'

'But that's what happened,' said Hetep. 'We both know it. How can we just forget?'

'At the same time we both know that it can't have happened. Ramesses is a god, remember? And a god can't make a mistake. At least this one can't, anyway. So Baya's account has to be true. Which means that first squadron, and Antef in particular, are guilty of failing to stop a mere handful of chariots.'

Hetep remembered that Antef was one of the commanders who had argued against Pharaoh's plan of immediate attack. Perhaps that was the true reason he was being punished.

'Poor Antef,' he said. 'Baya's really seized his chance there.'

'Our second squadron commander is nothing if not opportunistic,' said Teppic dryly. 'He must have been waiting years for this moment.' It was common knowledge that Baya and Antef had long been rivals for honours and postings.

'I still can't believe the whole army would have taken Baya's word about what happened,' said Hetep. 'They must have found the prince's body well away from the hill. Didn't anyone question it?'

'Who remembers now where the body was found? And Baya produced witnesses. His driver was one, but he was badly wounded and died that night, and there was a man named Mehy – one of Baya's troop commanders. They both corroborated his story, that he killed Irqata's prince on that hill.'

'What about *my* witnesses?' said Hetep. 'Zuratta for instance. He knows I did it. He accused me of it, openly, in front of the Royal Butler. In front of Ramesses, too.'

'So I heard. But who'd believe the word of a foreigner against the decree of the living god?'

'So that's it, then. I'm stuck here.'

'I'm sorry.' Teppic laid a consoling hand on Hetep's shoulder. 'But don't worry. You'll see home again soon – a year, maybe two at the most. They don't keep scribes out here forever, you know. And you'll have Sebeku to look after you once he's well enough.'

'He might still die, you know. His fever's getting worse.'

'Oh, come on, he'll be fine. Could you imagine him in the Field of Reeds, with nothing to complain about? I always did wonder how you put up with him.'

Hetep shrugged. 'We just get on. And he knows horses; I wouldn't have had a clue on my own. I'd never have got this far without him. Or without you, either.'

They heard orders being shouted and the volume of noise from the camp increased.

'The squadron's forming up,' said Teppic quickly. 'I must go. But as soon as I get home I'll see if there's anything I can do about Baya.'

'Be careful,' said Hetep. 'His family's powerful, you know.'

'So is mine. And they never did like any of his lot; they'd be glad to do him an ill turn. Oh, and I'll look in at your farm when I can and see if I can stop your uncle from stealing it. And don't worry about Zuratta. Nui will keep the local rabble in line, and you'll have soldiers to protect you. They're only infantry, but they do soak up the arrows.'

'I don't know how I can repay you for all you've done for me.'

'Just come back safe to Egypt.' Teppic turned to go,

then stopped as a thought struck him. 'Here, you might find this useful,' he said and pulled an amulet from over his head. It was a gold *wadjet* – a depiction of the eye of Horus – inlaid with lapis lazuli. 'I got it made before we set out, to see me safely through the campaign. Looks like it worked. So now we can see how well it does for you.'

He dropped it in Hetep's palm. The metal had the soft heaviness of pure gold; Hetep turned it over and saw that the back was inscribed with a powerful protective formula.

'No,' he said after a moment, and tried to hand it back. 'I can't take it. The gold alone must be worth–'

'A lot. Yes, I know. Go on, keep it. It'll make me feel better.'

There was no fanfare to mark the division's departure, no drums or hymns, just the tramp of thousands of feet on the dusty road. Like many of those left behind Hetep watched them go and he was still sitting, staring morosely down the road, long after the last of their trailing dust had settled over the southern hills. Only when night began to fall did he stir, joining the remaining troops for the evening meal. Nobody sang and there was very little talk. Instead the men huddled close around the watch fires, staring gloomily at the flames or out into the darkness – perhaps, thought Hetep, already yearning for the day when they too would return to the Nile valley and decent living.

The following dawn they were given the order to form up for the march to Sumur. It was a relief for Hetep, but also the cause of a new anxiety: Sebeku, along with the rest of the wounded deemed too sick to move, were to be left at Irqata in the care of the handful of Egyptian administrators who were to oversee the town, and Hetep had little doubt that as soon as the Egyptian troops were gone Zuratta would kill him. Stretching his limited scribal authority he bribed one of the animal drivers with an extra beer ration to secure Sebeku a place on a transport wagon, and half an hour's careful forgery with a sheet of papyrus and a borrowed writing kit put his friend on the garrison's ration strength.

They set out in the morning sunshine, with Nui and the senior staff leading in their chariots, the infantry under Yuya following in a column, and in the rear the scribes, slaves and auxiliaries, and the baggage train of donkeys and ox-drawn wagons. It was a hot, uncomfortable march, and Hetep kept close to Sebeku, whose fever seemed to be building to its crisis point. He wondered if, in his attempt to save him from Zuratta's wrath, he was only speeding him along to the West. But it was too late now to send him back to Irqata.

After a couple of hours the Irqatan uplands gave way to rolling hills covered in dense forests of cedar, oak and pine. Hetep wondered how far King Benteshina could be trusted and half expected to see an avenging horde of Amurrite soldiers come bursting out from ambush, but the land remained quiet.

By midday they had reached the coastal plain. Much of the land here had been cleared of trees and they passed villages surrounded by olive groves and fields of barley. They trudged on, wearily now, following the road until at last, an hour before sunset, they crested yet another rise and had their first sight of Sumur, capital of the kingdom of Amurru.

On a hillside by the shore of the Great Green it stood, a city of shining white masonry, protected by a wall of dressed limestone blocks. A harbour, thick with shipping, lay at the western end; beside it, nestled against the battlements, stood a large walled enclosure two storeys high that Hetep guessed was the royal palace. Beyond that lay the rest of the city: a tightly packed jumble of houses, shrines, granaries and halls, rising in concentric rings all the way to the walled acropolis at the peak, where stood the temples, their towers gleaming like polished bone.

At the main gate the Egyptians were met by Amurrite officials with fluttering hands and acclamations of loyalty and welcome. The rest of the city was quiet and as the garrison made its way between the looming buildings anxious-looking residents peered out from their doorways, as if afraid that the Egyptians would yet sack the city.

As the troops marched into the plaza beside the palace Nui ordered the musicians to play, but the drums sounded flat and the horns thin and brassy in that great open space. When the last notes had died away the Amurrites, many not bothering to hide their disdain, indicated the complex of houses that had been reserved for Nui and his staff, and the barracks that was to house the garrison. Nui dismissed the troops and as they dispersed Hetep turned to follow them, but Merimose stopped him.

'You are one of us now,' he said, and pointed out the dormitory that was to house the scribes, a narrow little building nested between a storehouse and a potter's workshop.

After depositing his bed roll Hetep went to tend to Sebeku. The driver's fever was breaking at last and he seemed dimly aware of the people around him; Hetep found an unused annexe nearby and laid him inside on a blanket, with a promise to return later with food.

At sundown, after the evening ration had been issued and he had fed Sebeku, he joined Merimose and the others in the dormitory. Already they had set up a little shrine to Thoth, patron of scribes, with a statue of the god in his baboon aspect forming the centerpiece. One of them lit the incense lamp and they recited a few prayers, and afterwards Merimose assigned them their sleeping places. It seemed that the deciding factor in who got the best spots was seniority and Hetep, as the most junior, ended up near the door. It was draughty and, once the sun had set, cold, and he shivered as he lay on his mat waiting to fall asleep.

Chapter 9

In the morning the scribes held a little worship ceremony in front of the Thoth statue before trooping out, blinking, into the sunshine. Nui was waiting for them, and while Merimose was giving the others their instructions he called Hetep over.

'We're meeting our new subjects today,' he said. 'You did well with the pack animals so I'm giving you a chance to show your worth again. Behave yourself today and you may find this the first day in a rewarding new career.'

'Will it have anything to do with bread rations?' said Hetep.

'Bread? What are you blathering about?' said Nui, frowning. 'You told me you speak these people's language. So I want you to listen to what they say – especially Benteshina, and especially anything in his native tongue.'

'What do you think he'll say now that he didn't to Pharaoh?'

'Probably quite a lot. I don't think he's going to like what I'm going to tell him, so watch him closely and see how he reacts. But don't speak. You're a scribe, a man with no opinion, which means you keep silent. Do you understand me?'

They were joined by a squad of Egyptian spearmen headed by Yuya, and two of the scribes. There was no sign of Baya.

Hetep eyed the escort, which seemed to him rather small. 'What do we do if the locals cause trouble?' he said.

'They wouldn't dare,' said Nui.

The city's limestone buildings shone in the sunshine

and its streets were alive with people. The previous day's fears appeared to have left them and now they watched with open interest as Nui lead his party down to the palace gatehouse. A little group of Amurrite officials was there to welcome them; the almost ritualised words of greeting were spoken and Nui replied in kind, and then they were lead into the palace.

They crossed a wide courtyard. Beyond was a porch, the roof supported by great columns of wood, and then came an entrance hall, its walls painted with scenes showing bearded men hunting or wrestling, or taking their ease in lush, water-filled gardens. Back in Egypt it was usually only the walls of tombs which showed scenes of everyday life – images that ensured the deceased would experience all the pleasures he had enjoyed during his life and none of the miseries. Here it gave Hetep the odd impression that he was about to meet a man already dead.

At the far side of the hall a pair of huge bronze-sheeted doors opened soundlessly at their approach and Nui lead them through into the throne room. It was pillared, with a roof spanned by huge beams of carved cedar. A row of high-set windows admitted shafts of light thick with dust motes, while lower down the walls were painted with scenes of battle and slaughter in which a king towered over the ranks of his soldiers.

Waiting to greet the Egyptians was a line of courtiers with curled hair and pointed beards, wearing dyed woolen tunics. Then the line parted to reveal Benteshina himself, sitting enthroned at the far end of the room and flanked by guards. He wore a robe as brightly patterned as a bird's plumage and was decked with enough gold to fill an Egyptian vizier's tomb. Beside him sat a woman in a fine linen dress, with dark, almost black eyes which gleamed with reflected torch light – Benteshina's queen for sure, thought Hetep.

The king was lounging, seeming confident and at ease. Gone was the grovelling penitent who had promised the pharaoh a lifetime of servitude; here, secure in his own domain, surrounded by his soldiers and courtiers, he was indisputably king, and his hooded eyes held an ill-concealed loathing for his new overlords. Hetep remembered his uncle's words about how much in awe the men of Amurru were of Egypt's might, but there was precious little sign of that here. The memory of the cheerful, sunlit city and its peaceful-looking people vanished; now, suddenly, he was aware than he was in the heart of what until recently had been an enemy kingdom, ruled by a Ma'at-less barbarian, and Pharaoh's army already seemed very far away.

Nui was speaking; it sounded like more formulaic words and Hetep stopped listening, his attention drawn instead to the woman. She was searching the faces of the Egyptians as if looking for someone. As her eyes rested on Hetep he felt the sudden urge to hide and without knowing why he became certain that she was an associate of Zuratta.

She waved one of the courtiers over, and Hetep recognised him as one of the Amurrite charioteers who had been standing near Zuratta on that day outside Irqata. Now what's he doing here? he wondered. The courtier peered at Hetep then bent to whisper in the woman's ear, and as he did so her eyes widened.

Hetep's puzzlement turned to fear. He had no doubt now that this woman was one of Zuratta's agents. He had barely escaped from the man at Irqata; what chance did he have here, under the baleful eye of Amurru's king and his scheming wife, when all he had protecting him was a bare three hundred troops, under the command of a man who hated him?

By now he had lost the thread of Nui's words, and it was only when he heard a gasp from the Amurrite courtiers that his mind came back to the room. He looked about him and realised the mood had changed. Nui was standing squarely with his arms folded and his jaw set, while the courtiers were muttering angrily.

'This is not a negotiation,' said Nui, his voice raised. 'Thirty tons of copper from the Cyprus trade, three tons of tin from the east, a hundred tons of cedar, and ash, elm and willow for chariot making. I want it all ready by the turn of the season. And that's just the beginning.'

Hetep winced. It was an exorbitant amount of tribute; no wonder the Amurrites were looking angry. But Benteshina simply gazed placidly at Nui, as unmoved as if he had just been read the contents of the garrison's laundry list.

'You are as gracious as your pharaoh is just,' he said. 'All will be settled in time.'

'There's more,' said Nui. 'From now on this kingdom is going to be governed as a province of Egypt. Which means all royal commands will have to be approved by me.'

For the first time the woman spoke. 'Why are you treating us this way? Before now we were always left to order our own affairs.'

'Because by the decree of King Seti you should have been paying tribute to us. But since Ramesses' accession it's all been going to the Hittites.' Nui did not look at the woman, instead keeping his eyes fixed on Benteshina. 'There's to be no more scheming with the Hittite empire. You're subjects of Egypt again and you'll behave as such. This is the will of Ramesses, the Son of Re, and don't you forget it.'

Benteshina's eyes half closed. 'Ramesses' servants have

come to us like Yam's envoys to the court of the god El, demanding much in their master's name. The hero Ba'al gave Yam his payment, and it was more that Yam asked for. And in a like manner we shall pay our Egyptian guests.'

Hetep looked from Benteshina to Nui and the scribes. The king's comment was a threat, yet none of the other Egyptians seemed to realise.

The woman was still livid. 'What kind of a peace settlement is this? These are not the terms we agreed to. Show me where it is written.'

This time Nui addressed the woman directly. 'The terms of Amurru's surrender are being carved onto a stone monument at the mouth of the Dog River. I invite you inspect it once the masons have finished.'

The woman sat back, speechless. Benteshina gave her a sidelong glance and smiled. 'Be at peace,' he murmured to her in Amurrite. 'As Yatpan rewarded the hero Aqhat, so I shall reward our foreign guests.'

Nui must have understood a few of the words, for he frowned at the king. 'What's that about serving?' he said. 'Speak up, in Babylonian, so we can all understand.'

'I was agreeing to your terms,' said Benteshina with a sly smile.

'No he wasn't,' said Hetep, stepping forwards. First the comment about the gods Yam and Ba'al and now this, he thought; the king's threatening Nui and mocking his ignorance, and nobody else realises. 'He said he's going to betray you.'

There was a stunned silence, as if Amurrites and Egyptians alike could not believe that a mere scribe would dare to speak in the king's audience hall. Only the woman showed no outrage, instead watching Hetep with interest.

'Not now,' growled Nui.

'But I know the story,' said Hetep. 'Yatpan was a–'

'You will be silent!' barked Nui, his face livid. He signed to one of the soldiers, who pulled Hetep back out of sight, then addressed Benteshina again. 'I am... sorry... for the breach of protocol,' he said, as if uttering even a word of apology pained him.

Benteshina waved a hand airily. 'Consider the incident forgotten. And in the meantime, please allow me to reaffirm my loyalty, as strong as Yassub's was to his father Kirta.' His eyes met Hetep's and he smirked, as if they were sharing a secret. 'As for the matter of the tribute, all will be as you say. And now, since our business appears to be concluded, it only remains for me to say that I wish your pharaoh all speed on his long, long journey back to his very distant home.'

Again Hetep was in trouble, but had to admit that this time it was partly his own fault.

'Who do you think you are?' roared Nui. 'I ordered you to keep silent!'

They were in the dormitory. Merimose was fussing in the background and a couple of the other scribes were looking on, nostrils flared, while from the shadows the Thoth statue watched with stony-eyed disapproval.

'You said you wanted my help,' said Hetep. 'Benteshina was lying to you.'

'Of course he was! He's an Asiatic; they lie as easily as they breathe. But we don't tell him that to his face!'

'What he said about Yatpan... None of you know who he is, do you?' Hetep looked around at the scribes, who shook their heads, blank faced.

'Well, what of it?' said Nui.

'It's in one of their stories. Aqhat offended the goddess Anat, so she sent Yatpan to kill him by treachery. Benteshina was saying he'll serve you in the same way.'

'Very well. I didn't know that.' Nui exhaled and passed a massive hand over his head. 'But you have to understand there are gods-given rules of diplomacy that must be obeyed – for our sake as much as for the foreigners'. I know Benteshina hates me. He hates all of us: he's under Pharaoh's sandal and he doesn't like it. But he knows that if he doesn't do what I tell him our army will return, his city will be razed to the ground and every single one of its inhabitants sold into slavery.'

'Perhaps he'd hate us less if we weren't taking so much tribute,' said Hetep.

It was the wrong thing to say, for it roused Nui's anger again. 'Criticising Pharaoh's policy now, are you? Is there no end to your conceit?'

'But the amount... its not just a few pack animals this time. You're stripping the kingdom bare. They'll rebel.'

'Listen and learn something. We're going to be at war again next year, and we'll be taking the whole army: all four divisions. And we need to pay for it. These coastal cities – Sumur, Tyre, Sidon – they're all rich, and they're the ones who are going to feed and equip us. Not to mention all the stuff they'll be sending to Egypt for the building projects. Do you understand? We need these people's wealth.' He took a breath to calm himself. 'There's another thing you don't know. Benteshina's still conspiring with the Hittites. There's even some in this city, although they're keeping well hidden. Which means we have to show him that it's *we*, and not the king of Hatti, who's in charge here. If we show leniency he'll take it as a sign of weakness.'

'Hittites? But I thought we were at peace with them.'

'For the time being, yes.' As Nui eyed him Hetep remembered what Teppic had said about the Hittites not standing idle after Amurru's defection. 'But that's none of your business. What *is* your business is scribal work. But it seems even that is beyond your capabilities.'

'I'm sorry. I told you I was never much use as a clerk. It was my uncle who had me assigned here.'

'You mean Nebenteru? It's true he started pestering to see Ramesses almost as soon as he heard you'd lost your chariot. But it was Baya who got Pharaoh to listen. His grandfather's a priest of Amun at Karnak, so he tends to get what he wants.'

'Why would Baya want to keep me here?' said Hetep, surprised.

Nui shrugged. 'You'll have to ask him about that yourself. Just don't bother me with it. In fact, I don't want you anywhere near me. And if you even think of stirring up more trouble I'll have you skinned. Understand?' And with that he turned and stalked out.

As soon as he was gone Merimose came over.

'You give the calling a bad name by offering opinions like that,' he said. 'In my day a transgression like yours would have merited a dozen blows from a stick at the very least. But not in these decadent times.' He shook his head sadly. 'There's no respect for the traditions any more. Ma'at can just fade into nothing for all anyone cares.'

In his reedy voice he gave Hetep his new list of duties, including mixing ink and paint, keeping the dormitory's shelves stocked with papyrus, sweeping the floor, and the most important task of all: keeping the incense lamp by the Thoth statue burning. Then he gathered up his pens and ink palettes and lead the rest of the scribes out, leaving Hetep standing alone in the dusty gloom.

CHAPTER 10

With nothing better to do Hetep swept and re-swept the floor until the flagstones gleamed. As he worked the eyes of the Thoth statue never left him; it may have been just the play of shadows across the god's face but Hetep was sure he was laughing at him. Then the incense lamp went out. He knew that to leave it unlit would only bring more trouble, so he propped his broom up against the wall and went out to find some more fuel.

The streets were busy and it took him a while to reach the storehouse. He found the lamp fuel and was standing outside again, about to head back, when a change in the breeze brought the fresh smell of the sea. Unwilling now to return to the stuffy confines of the dormitory he turned and headed across the main plaza and down towards the harbour district. At a gatehouse a flight of steps took him to the top of the harbour wall and there he sat, gazing about and breathing the salt-tanged air.

Below him a quay stretched away in a long curve, its berths crowded with ships; a few were Egyptian, larger versions of the Nile boats that were as much a background to his life as the great river's palm trees and reed beds, but most were strange-looking things whose origins he could only guess at. Beyond the quay lay the open sea – the Great Green the sailors called it – and for the first time in weeks he could see the far horizon.

Gradually the sun reddened as it dipped towards the encircling ocean, transforming from Re, the god of the midday sun, into Atum, the god of the evening disc. Then it disappeared to begin its journey through the Netherworld and as the light faded the great sky bridge, the body of the goddess Nut, came into view above him. It was comforting to see her holding back the waters of chaos here just as she did over Egypt, and for a long time he gazed up at her, oblivious to the passing of time.

The breeze from the sea became colder, making his skin prickle. It was getting late and he thought guiltily of the still-unlit incense lamp in the dormitory. He stood, then hurried down the steps and on through the now empty streets. Reaching the dormitory he found it silent, its windows dark; no doubt Nui has the others out working late, he thought. He was about to cross to the door when he noticed a pair of figures standing among the trees lining the road. Something about the way they held themselves made him uneasy and he ducked into hiding while keeping them in view. Staring, he saw that they were Amurrite soldiers, armed with axes and daggers. They were talking, and he strained to hear the words.

'Then where is he?' one of them was saying. 'We know he's not with the other Egyptians. He should have been here.'

'If we don't find him tonight she'll have our heads,' said the other.

'He must be away on some errand. Let us stay hidden and keep watch, and we shall have him when he returns.'

Hetep backed away, his heart beating fast. He had no doubt these men had been sent to murder him by the woman he had seen earlier. What could he do? He considered going to Nui but immediately dismissed the notion; the man barely tolerated his existence as it was, and would be unlikely to believe wild tales of murder plots and lurking assassins. And there was nobody else he could turn to for help, not even the Egyptian troops, commanded as they were by the brutish and hostile Yuya.

He put a hand to his amulet and muttered a quick

93

prayer; never had he needed a god's protection more. Then his fingers touched the *wadjet* that Teppic had given him. He weighed it in his hand, feeling again the solid heaviness of pure gold, and as he did so a plan began to form in his mind. It was reckless – dangerous, even – but what choice did he have?

As silently as he could he crept through the shadows to the annexe by the dormitory. Sebeku was still there, muttering in his sleep, a sheen of sweat on his face. Hetep woke him with a gentle shake of his shoulder.

'Don't speak,' he said softly. 'We're in danger. We have to get away.'

'What?' The driver blinked, his eyes unfocussed.

'We're leaving, now. Here, I'll help you up.' Hetep moved to put an arm under Sebeku's back.

'Leave? What's happening?'

'Come on. Try to stand.'

'Will you let me alone,' cried Sebeku.

'Be quiet,' whispered Hetep fiercely. 'Some men have come kill us; they're nearby. You have to stand up.'

The urgency in Hetep's voice, if not the words, seemed to penetrate Sebeku's fevered confusion and he half stood.

'That's better. Now can you walk?'

Even with Hetep's help Sebeku could do little more than stagger, but they managed to get across the road unseen. Hetep glanced back towards the dormitory and was sure he could see the outline of one of the assassins standing motionless near the trees.

'This way,' he said, and half carrying Sebeku he headed for a nearby alley, hoping it would lead them past the main plaza.

'Where are you taking me?' said Sebeku.

'Somewhere safe. Just try to support your weight a bit more, will you? My ribs are still sore.'

'No.' Abruptly Sebeku's knees buckled and he slid to the ground. 'Not another step. Not until you tell me where we're going.'

'For the gods' sake keep your voice down!'

From near the dormitory they heard a man calling in Amurrite. 'Who's there? Show yourself!'

Hetep looked meaningfully at Sebeku. 'See?' he said, noiselessly. He tilted his head, listening for the sound of approaching footsteps, but none came. Touching his pendant he thanked the god for his protection, then hauled Sebeku to his feet again.

'Now this time try to walk,' he said.

It took a while but at last they reached the harbour entrance, and without meeting a soul.

'Where are we going?' asked Sebeku, looking at the gate.

'Back to Egypt.'

'Have you lost your senses? Nui will have us impaled for desertion!'

'Only if he catches us. Besides, he doesn't want me here – he's said as much already.'

'Then you go – risk your own neck if you want to. Just leave me be, can't you?'

'I told you, there are people trying to kill us. We haven't got a choice.'

He helped Sebeku through the gate and up the steps to the quay. To one side stood bales of wool and cloth, and ranks of jars holding oil and wine. Hetep caught the silhouette of a soldier standing at the quay's far end; as he watched the soldier turned and started pacing towards them, and quickly he lowered Sebeku to the floor and crouched beside him.

'Ouch!' said Sebeku. 'Can't you be more careful?'

'Shut up, will you? There's someone watching the

cargo.' Hetep dragged the driver into hiding behind the jars. 'We'll stay here until dawn. If the gods are kind nobody will find us.'

'And if they're not?'

'Don't worry. We'll be fine.'

Hetep propped Sebeku up and examined his neck. The scab over the wound had thickened and although the nearby flesh was still swollen it was much cooler than before.

'You're healing well,' he whispered.

'No thanks to you. Don't think I was too ill to remember that journey here in the wagon. And now you drag me down here to the docks. It's a wonder I'm still alive.'

'You'd be dead if I'd left you behind.' Speaking quietly, Hetep told Sebeku how Baya had stolen his credit, and then about Zuratta and his threats, and the woman at the audience. 'So now you see why we have to go home.'

'Gods help us,' said Sebeku weakly, and he lay back with his eyes closed.

'It'll turn out for the best – you'll see. And once we're home I'll be able to stop my uncle seizing my land and get something done about Baya. I'm sure I'll find someone who'll listen to me.'

Sebeku remained silent and after a while he fell asleep. The night became cooler and he started to shiver, and the best Hetep could do was use his body to shield his friend from the wind.

CHAPTER 11

Hetep woke with a start. For an instant he could not understand why he was lying with his face against cold stone; then he remembered where he was and why, and he groaned quietly. Sebeku was still alive, asleep but with a touch of returning fever showing on his skin. Hetep shook him awake.

'Wait here,' he said. 'I'm going to find us a ship.'

He crept out from hiding and stood, looking about him while working some life back into his chilled and cramped limbs. It was only just after dawn yet already the harbour was filling with sailors, merchants and toiling slave gangs, all jabbering away in languages that meant no more to Hetep that the cries of the gulls wheeling overhead. He walked along the quay, asking anyone who looked like a sailor in both Egyptian and Babylonian for passage to Egypt. Most of the men he spoke to ignored him; a few others simply stared at him. None offered him a berth, and he was growing increasingly anxious when, near the end of the quay, one of them indicated with a nod of his head a man standing by one of the gangplanks. He was dark and thickset, with gold earrings and great whirls of black hair over his chest and arms.

'Sir, are you the captain of this fine ship?' said Hetep, going up to him.

'I might be. Who wants him?' The captain's eyes darted over the length of the quay.

'I do. I need to get to Egypt, and I must leave today.'

'In trouble are you?' The captain looked Hetep over as if appraising a piece of livestock. 'You look like a scribe. Don't tell me: you've been caught embezzling the stores.'

'I just have to get home, that's all. And I've a friend who needs to come with me.'

'Two of you, eh?' said the captain. 'And all the way to Egypt. It'll cost you.'

'I have this.' Hetep took Teppic's golden *wadjet* from around his neck and, not without a qualm, handed it over.

The captain examined the charm through narrowed eyes and tried to scratch its surface with his thumb. Then he looked Hetep over again.

'Yes, I think this will fetch a decent price,' he said, half to himself. He smiled, his teeth glinting like metal. 'We sail in an hour, as soon as the cargo's loaded.'

'How long's the trip?' asked Hetep.

'Hm? To Egypt, you mean? Oh, about a week or so, with decent weather. But you'll see. Now go and get your friend.'

Back at the hiding place Sebeku was still barely awake.

'I've bought us passage home on a ship,' said Hetep. He put an arm under Sebeku's shoulder and heaved him up. 'Come on. One last effort.'

He staggered out, supporting the weakly protesting driver. They were partway to the ship when Hetep saw the captain stiffen, his eyes fixed on something near the harbour gate, then turn and hurry up the gangplank. He looked back, almost tripping over Sebeku's legs. A trio of Amurrite soldiers was coming towards him, and he was sure that among them was one of the men who had been searching for him last night.

His first instinct was to run, but that would mean leaving Sebeku behind. And even if he did, there was nowhere to go except the sea. He lowered Sebeku to the floor and stood over him, like a man defending a comrade's corpse on a battlefield, and searched around vainly for something he could use as a weapon.

'You've lead us quite a chase,' said one of the soldiers as they drew near. 'But it's over now and you're coming with us.'

'Who are you?' demanded Hetep.

'My name is Hiziru, captain of the temple guard,' said the soldier. He gave a polite little bow. 'I have been asked to find you. There's no reason to be afraid. Somebody wishes to talk to you, that's all.'

'You were sent by Zuratta. Admit it.'

Hiziru looked surprised. 'You know that name?'

'We waste time here,' said one of his companions. 'Listen, Egyptian. If we wanted you dead we would kill you now, and not one of the people here would stop us. Have the sense to see reason.'

That at least was the truth, as Hetep saw, for although the harbour had grown busy, nobody was paying them any attention; indeed, the crowd was avoiding them, so that they stood in the centre of a little bubble of calm. He looked back at the ship but there was no sign of the captain, and he realised he had probably lost Teppic's amulet for good.

He sighed, resigned now to his fate. 'Very well, I'll come. But what about my friend?' He indicated Sebeku.

'We were told to bring only you,' said Hiziru.

'But he's sick. He needs help.'

'One of us will stay and tend to him, and I swear in El's name that he'll not be harmed. Now come, you've wasted enough time as it is.'

From the harbour gate they crossed the plaza and climbed the road leading to the acropolis. Neither Hiziru nor his remaining companion would answer any of Hetep's questions about whom he was being taken to see. Perhaps it was Nui, thought Hetep, and he wondered nervously how he was going to explain away his attempt to abscond. But they passed the Egyptian quarter and kept climbing, and as they reached the acropolis gates he only grew more puzzled.

Beyond the gates lay more open space than Hetep had yet seen in Sumur, and around it stood the temples: huge limestone structures with towers and pillared entrance porches. From the offering fires on the roofs thin columns of smoke rose in the still air, taking the morning's sacrifices up to the abode of the gods.

His escort lead him to one of the largest of the temples. Figures were moving on top of its tower and he heard voices calling to a Canaanite goddess in a strange mixture of Amurrite and an unknown language. He balked, remembering his mother's tales of the dark practices in Canaan's past, of child sacrifices and the annual killing of kings, but Hiziru assured him that all was well and lead him through a side door in the temple's wall and into the corridor beyond.

It was dark after the bright outdoors and a faint trace of incense hung in the air. Ahead a few lamps shone, casting blood-coloured patches of light onto the pink plaster walls, and he heard echoes of a woman chanting. They passed a series of painted images, and in the lamp light one stood out plain: a goddess wearing a necklace of human heads and a belt adorned with severed limbs. Again he checked his pace, and looked nervously at his escort.

'There's no cause for alarm,' said Hiziru. 'It was only our lady you heard, talking to the goddess.'

The words explained nothing; instead they only added to Hetep's disquiet. There was foreign sorcery here – he could feel it, thick in the air like fog. As he walked he gripped his amulet, praying silently and wishing that he was not so far from home, where the daily temple rituals performed by the pharaoh and his proxies the priests cast their blanket of protection over the land.

The passage ended in an archway.

'You are expected,' said Hiziru. 'Please go in. We shall wait for you here.'

In the room beyond the arch a pair of braziers burned with a smoky crimson fire. Between them stood a high-backed chair, on which sat the woman from Benteshina's throne room. She wore a long pleated dress fringed with purple and her face was a brightly painted mask, with kohl-blackened eyes and scarlet lips – the very image of the bloodthirsty goddess he had seen on the corridor wall. But her necklace held only a row of bright red crystals and from her girdle hung nothing more sinister than triangular pieces of lapis lazuli.

So striking was the woman that it was a moment before Hetep noticed the others in the room. Two were spearmen, standing guard either side of the throne, but it was the third who made him stare. He was a burly, pale-skinned man in a fur-trimmed robe, and had long black hair hanging down over his shoulders. It made Hetep think of the rich women back home with their luxuriant wigs, but he knew this was no wig. The man had to be one of the Hittites Nui had mentioned – former enemies who were now at peace with Egypt thanks to the treaty signed by Ramesses' father, King Seti.

'That ship you were about to board was bound for Cyprus,' said the woman. 'Its captain is little better than a pirate. He would have sold you and your friend at a Cypriot slave market. You're fortunate I had my brother's men search for you.'

'Brother?' said Hetep. 'I don't understand.'

'I am Elissa, the sister of King Benteshina. Did you

101

think I was his wife?' She regarded him with amusement – or was it contempt? What with the shadows flickering over her face and the bright cosmetics Hetep found it hard to tell. 'I am also the widow of the prince of Irqata, a man my Hittite companion here tells me you killed. Is it true? Did you really kill my husband?'

Gods help me, thought Hetep, the woman's after revenge. He fought down the beginnings of panic while she studied him, her eyes shining with what he was sure now was a cruel pleasure. He glanced at the Hittite but there was no help there – the man just stood impassive, as silent and still as a carved image in a temple. He wondered if he should call for help, but realised it would be futile.

He moistened his lips and swallowed. 'Yes, I killed him,' he said at last. 'I admit it. Although another man has taken the credit.'

'So I've heard. But I've also heard that this other man lies and it is you who did this thing. And the goddess Anat has spoken to me, confirming the truth – and she sees and knows all that has happened, and some things that have yet to happen.'

'It was done in battle, fairly,' said Hetep. 'So if it's vengeance you want–'

Her sudden laughter made him stop. 'Vengeance?' she said. 'Is that what you fear? No, I wish only to thank you. You have done me a service, ridding me of that Habiru filth.'

'I don't understand,' said Hetep again. He forced himself to concentrate; the smoke from the braziers had an odd smell and he wondered if it was drugged.

'For two years I had to share that filthy animal's bed; in twice that time I'll not be able to wash his stink from my body. I can only thank Anat that I was here for the Festival of the Gracious Gods when the news came, else I

102

would still be in that squalid little town, wearing mourning clothes and rubbing my eyes with ashes to bring forth the tears.'

For the first time the Hittite spoke, in precise but faintly accented Amurrite. 'My lady Elissa, perhaps you say too much. The Egyptian should not be allowed to know such things.'

'No, he is to be trusted. The goddess has seen inside his heart.' She held Hetep's gaze as if she too could divine his thoughts. 'And now let me tell you why I had you brought here, for it's not only to thank you for my deliverance. I wish to discuss the tribute payments. Your pharaoh's mouthpiece, Nui, asks too much of us. In the days when we owed fealty to the Hittite king the burden was much less – for which I am told many in this city are still grateful.' She glanced at the Hittite, who inclined his head as if acknowledging a compliment. 'We want you to talk to Nui and persuade him to lessen the amount.'

'I can't do that,' said Hetep. 'He barely tolerates me as it is, and even if he did listen he can't change Pharaoh's decrees. Nobody can.'

'Oh, but you will help us,' she said. 'And in return I offer you my protection. My husband's brother, Zuratta, is a vengeful man and he'll not rest until he has your head.'

So Zuratta was the prince of Irqata's brother, thought Hetep. He might have guessed, given the violence of the man's reaction to his death.

'I see from your expression that you've already met him,' said Elissa.

'He tried to kill me in Irqata. But he wouldn't dare harm me here in the capital.'

'What's to stop him? Your commissioner commands a scant three hundred soldiers. Zuratta has at least that number of supporters in this city alone. And in the hills there are many hundreds more – kinsmen, and others of the Habiru who owe debts to his family. Which makes your position, and that of Nui, more precarious than you think. And yours is the most precarious of all. You cannot guard yourself all the time and Zuratta needs only moments to take his revenge.'

One of the braziers flared up and a shift in the air currents sent out a tendril of smoke. It made Hetep's heart race, and he had to fight the urge to cough.

'Are you threatening me?' he said hoarsely.

'Not at all. I wish only to help you and your people. Zuratta will use the heaviness of the tribute as an excuse for rebellion; as I said, he has many supporters in the city.'

'Then tell Nui yourself, or get your brother to do something. He's the king, isn't he?'

'You know full well that Nui would never listen to me,' she said. 'And as for my brother...' A troubled look crossed her face. 'He acts as if he does not care.'

'I'm sorry about the tribute,' said Hetep. 'But as I told you, there's nothing I can do to change it.'

'You mean there's nothing you *want* to do. But I know differently. The goddess has revealed that you are destined to save this city from rebellion. What better way is there than by persuading Nui of his folly? And remember: I can protect you from Zuratta. Do you really think your household gods can keep you from harm, this far from home?' The words echoed Hetep's earlier fears and he wondered how much she guessed about him. 'And as payment for my protection, there is another thing you can do for us. We wish to know what Nui is planning.'

' "We?" Do you mean you and your brother, or you and him?' He pointed at the Hittite.

'Both of us,' said the Hittite, breaking his silence again. 'Why the heavy-handed approach? What does Ramesses plan? Is war coming next year?'

'I wish I knew, really,' said Hetep. 'But again you're asking the wrong man. Nui has me sweeping the floor and mixing paint for the scribes.'

'For now,' said Elissa. 'But change is coming – I have seen it. And regardless of whether you want to or not, you *will* help us.'

Hiziru escorted him out and at the acropolis gate they met the third man who had intercepted Hetep at the harbour.

'What have you done with Sebeku, the man I was with?' said Hetep.

'He is unharmed,' said the man. 'He insisted we take him to a room near your scribes' sleeping place. He said he feels safe there.'

'Very well – and thank you,' said Hetep. Then, to Hiziru, 'Tell me, does Benteshina know I've been here?'

'The lady Elissa's loyalty to her brother is unshakeable, yet for his own good she does not inform him of all that she does. And neither do we, although we serve both faithfully.'

Hetep nodded. 'I understand. May I go now?'

He descended the twisting main street, barely seeing the crowds as he passed among them, thinking about his strange interview with Elissa. There had been an earnestness about her that left him oddly moved, and in other circumstances he might have been willing to try to help her. But what she asked of him was impossible: he could no more influence Ramesses' policy than he could hold back the Nile's annual flood. Besides, Nui would have him skinned if he found out he was conspiring with the locals. Still, he would have to go carefully and avoid giving a flat refusal to do as she wished, and not only because she was the sister of Amurru's king. She had a power from the gods' world itself, which made her far more dangerous than the usual palace schemer.

Her goddess, Anat, was well known in Egypt, where she was worshipped as a daughter of Re and had many temples; indeed, Ramesses himself revered her as one of his many protective deities, and called her the Lady of Heaven. Ruthless and warlike, she was a goddess to be feared; what would she be like here in her native land, untamed by the influence of Egypt's gods? He remembered the image of the goddess he had seen in the corridor and felt a chill at the thought of being caught up in her machinations, and his hand strayed to his amulet. He could only hope that Egypt's tutelary gods would prove the stronger here, as had its armies against their more temporal enemies.

Someone touched his shoulder and he spun around, his heart jolting. But it was only the Hittite, and he was smiling.

'Do you not find the air from the sea refreshing?' he said. 'And after a meeting with the lady Elissa, it is doubly welcome. I don't know what she puts in those braziers, but it makes my head swim.'

'Why are you following me?' demanded Hetep.

'Because I wish to talk to you.'

'Not more plotting. I've had enough for one day. And if Nui sees me with you he'll have me impaled.'

'Then we'd best go somewhere more private. Come with me.'

The Hittite crossed the road and after a nervous glance to see if any of his fellow Egyptians were in sight Hetep followed. They ended up in a walled courtyard nestled between a shrine and a three-storey housing block. A stone water trough stood at one end and they sat on its rim, in the shade.

'There, that's better,' said the Hittite. 'Now allow me introduce myself. My name is Mursili and I am something of a merchant.'

'I guess you know who I am.'

'Oh, yes. You are – or rather were – one of your pharaoh's chariot archers, but you have since fallen from grace. Tell me, was there some scandal, perhaps?'

Hetep wondered if the Hittite was mocking him but the expression that met his own showed nothing but a good-natured curiosity. Still, he had to be cautious – the man was a foreigner, after all.

'Perhaps first you should tell me what a Hittite is doing conspiring with a Canaanite princess,' he said.

'Conspiring?' said Mursili, with a laugh. 'Such a strong word. But perhaps not entirely inaccurate. Let us make a bargain. You tell me your secrets, and I shall tell you mine.'

'It's no secret my chariot was destroyed in the battle at Irqata, and that thanks to my interfering uncle's malice I've been demoted to scribe.'

'It seems we have something in common. I too have a most insufferable uncle, and he has been a constant nuisance ever since my manhood rights. He never lets me forget that I am the son of a junior wife. But I have interrupted – you must think me rude. Please, continue.'

'There's not much more to say. You already know that in the battle at Irqata I killed the city's prince. But another man – Baya, one of our squadron commanders – has taken the credit, and without it I've no chance of getting reinstated.'

'There are, of course, charioteers among my own people and I understand that theirs is a proud profession. I

107

am truly sorry for your loss. And having the credit for your achievements stolen must make it doubly hard to bear.' He shook his head sadly. 'The gods are just – of that there can be no doubt. It is we men who bring evil and inequity into the world.'

Hetep found himself warming to Mursili, despite the man's foreignness.

'That's very kind of you,' he said. 'But I wonder if even the gods are as just as you say. Ramesses is half divine and he must have known what really happened in the battle, but he didn't do anything about it.'

'What do you mean?' asked Mursili.

'Baya and the other commanders must have told him what he wanted to hear. Either that or he just ignored any uncomfortable truths. I wonder if he only really listens to the voice of the god Amun, and anything anyone says that doesn't fit with what the god tells him he just ignores. I think–' He stopped talking, suddenly aware that he had just openly criticised Egypt's living god in front of a foreigner.

Mursili was watching him. 'Go on,' he prompted.

'Oh, there's nothing more to say,' he said, feeling uncomfortable. Then, more quickly, 'And now you've heard all there is to know about me, what about you and the princess?'

'You mean the lady Elissa? Remarkable woman, isn't she? I made her acquaintance at Irqata when I arrived there a few months ago. It was obvious that she hated her husband and we became... friends, shall we say. She trusts me.'

'You were at Irqata?' said Hetep. 'When?'

'Oh, until a little while ago,' said Mursili vaguely. He half stood and spent a moment fussing with his robe. 'There,' he said, 'that's far more comfortable. These things do tend to bunch up. Now where were we? Oh yes, the rebellion. Elissa has foreseen it, you know, and her premonitions are to be taken very seriously.'

'Is she really Benteshina's sister? When I saw her I thought she was his queen. She certainly acts like one.'

'The king had a wife but she died in childbirth some months ago, and his diviners have yet to find an auspicious day on which he can take another. The poor man has only daughters and is quite heirless, you know – a situation which, as you can imagine, causes him some distress. Not to mention the fact that it is a source of instability in the kingdom. I'm told that the charioteer you killed had some claim to the throne.'

'Then Benteshina must be as happy with the outcome as his sister.'

'I suppose, now that you mention it, he must be,' said Mursili. 'Now listen. You have to do as the princess asks, or the city will suffer. The tribute was already too much to bear, and only this morning I heard that Nui is to have half the kingdom's grain harvest set aside. I can only assume it is to feed Egypt's armies during some new campaign.'

Hetep avoided Mursili's gaze. 'I wouldn't know anything about that.'

'Of course not. Still, whatever the reason it'll mean hardship for these people and it might push them too far. Nui must be made to see the danger, and that a rebellion here is in nobody's interest. But he is a hard man and clearly has his instructions, and he will no more discuss them with me than he will with Elissa. Which is why he must be made to listen to you.'

'I think you both overestimate my influence.'

'I am well aware of your status. Now let me tell you something that may enhance it. I know that this Baya you

109

mentioned has twice met with Zuratta in Irqata, but to what end I can only guess. I also know that he is taking an interest in the trade that flows east from here, not to mention the storehouses that are to hold the tribute before it is shipped. I wouldn't be surprised if a portion of the goods that enter Sumur go astray sometime in the near future; doubtless Zuratta will receive a share for his assistance. Tell me, is it the custom among your people for an underling to steal wealth that belongs to his master?'

'No, it's not.' Hetep thought back to what he had seen and heard at the palace in Irqata, when Baya had been talking with Zuratta. He knew that one of the trade routes from Sumur passed through Irqata and he remembered Zuratta's claim that he would soon be the town's ruler – the ideal position from which to assist Baya with his schemes.

'I see that I have told you something useful,' said Mursili.

'Perhaps you have.' Hetep looked searchingly at the Hittite. 'After all this, will you still claim you're a merchant? Because you sound more like a spy to me. Tell me the truth. What are you really doing here?'

Mursili laughed lightly. 'Oh, I see I cannot fool you. Yes, I admit it: I am more than just a simple trader. You see before you the man charged by my king to set up a colony here – a colony of merchants, you understand. Which is why I have such an interest in what goes on at the harbour. But don't tell anybody, least of all our new Egyptian overlord. I don't think he's quite ready for such a revelation.' Mursili stood and again straightened his robe. 'And now I must leave you, for I have much to do. We shall meet again.' He gave a curt little bow and strode off into the street, leaving Hetep staring thoughtfully after him.

Once Hetep would have dismissed Mursili's suspicions about Baya as lies intended to weaken Egypt's position in Sumur. But not now, after all he had recently seen and heard. Teppic had already convinced him of Baya's greed and dishonesty; now it seemed that the man was corrupt, and to a degree that few others would dare to approach. The theft of tribute, wealth that belonged to Ramesses and to the gods of Egypt's temples, was an unforgivable sin, and if caught Baya would at the very least be sent back to Egypt in disgrace. He might even be impaled. Hetep smiled as he pictured his rival's ruin and the restoration of his own fortunes that would surely follow. Recognition for his deeds at Irqata, reinstatement as a chariot warrior... it was all that he dreamed of. Then his smile faltered as he realised that it would remain just that: a dream, unless he could find proof of Baya's crimes.

Chapter 12

A ship arrived from Egypt bringing craftsmen and architects for a new construction project. To strengthen Egypt's grip on Amurru a fortified manor was to be built for the commissioner and his staff, designed by Egyptian expertise but erected using local forced labour. Another cause for resentment, thought Hetep when he heard the news. Still, it did bring an unexpected opportunity. Nui was to hold a meeting to discuss the plans with his senior officials – including Baya, who had been appointed Overseer of Local Labour – which would leave the scribes' offices, and in particular the annexe Baya used as his private tablet house, empty. Hetep was hopeful that a search of the latter would turn up something damning.

On the morning of the meeting, after Merimose and the scribes had left the dormitory, Hetep abandoned his broom and snuck out into the street. From hiding he watched Baya emerge from his quarters and join the others, before they all trooped across a nearby plaza and into the building where Nui had his office.

Now all Hetep had to do was get into Baya's annexe, a simple matter were it not for the Egyptian soldier posted by the door. He had the look of a man who had been staring at the same patch of wall since dawn and was contemplating hours more of the same, and was leaning on his spear for support. Still, bored or not, there was no getting past him, and all Hetep could do was remain hidden, watching and waiting for his chance.

The sun climbed, shining fully onto the soldier's face, and sweat began to pour off him. He licked his lips and wiped his hand over his brow. Finally, after a guilty glance up and down the road, he marched away from his post, straight towards a nearby drinking trough.

Instantly Hetep was up and running. He reached the door, slid through and pushed it closed behind him. For a moment he stood, waiting for the shout of alarm that meant he had been spotted, but there was not a sound.

The lamps inside were unlit but a pair of slit windows let in just enough light to allow him to see. An alcove in one wall held shelves of scrolls and clay tablets, while across the room there stood a low table on which rested a stack of fresh papyrus sheets and a scribe's writing kit, with a cushion tucked beside it. A curtain at the far end indicated the presence of either another alcove or a private writing room.

The shelves looked the most promising. He took a step towards them, then recoiled when he saw the accusing eyes of baboon-faced Thoth staring at him from the shadows. He wondered if the god would punish him for what he was doing – after all, snooping on a fellow Egyptian was hardly acceptable scribal behaviour. He whispered a quick prayer and a promise to light an extra incense lamp in the dormitory, then set to work.

He examined a few tablets at random, but as he feared they were written in Babylonian symbols – an incomprehensible jumble of wedge-shaped marks pressed into clay. The scrolls were better; some were covered in the local script, as unreadable to him as that of the Babylonians, but most were written in the signs used by Egyptian scribes. But there was so much of it. What to read?

As quickly as he could he scanned through the newest. They were administrative documents, one of which was a list of workers' names set against tallies of food rations, and held little of interest. Only the last, and most recently filed, was different, and held accounts relating to an estate back in Egypt that seemed to indicate a deficit somewhere and was bundled with a request from a steward asking for permission to sell off more land. Which was interesting, but far from the proof he was searching for.

He replaced the scrolls and looked around again, feeling a growing sense of desperation. There had to be something compromising. He spotted a written sheet on top of the stack on the table and picked it up. His eyes, already aching from the unaccustomed strain of reading in the dimly lit room, moved slowly over the page as he tried to make out the words. It was a letter, and included a list of metal ingots with weights and shipping dates; it was marked as a translation of a message sent by a certain Zuratta – assuming he was correctly reading the signs rendering the name.

Footsteps sounded on the road outside and he heard voices from just beyond the door. One of the speakers was Baya.

He dropped the papyrus and darted through the curtain at the back of the room, and found himself in a dark little alcove containing an empty scroll rack and no window. A gap showed between the curtain and the wall and he put his eye to it in time to see Baya striding in through the door, a scribe at his side.

'Now remember,' said Baya, 'just take a hundredth part of the tribute, no more. And don't forget the trade levy – tell the merchants they'll lose their licenses if they object. Send it all to the storehouse on Fish Street; it's to be loaded onto the *Ivory Wind* as soon as it docks. Write it down so you'll remember. Oh, and don't forget to give the Habiru his share – although only the gods know if he's worth it. And be sure to tell no one about this. It's Pharaoh's private business, you understand?'

The scribe nodded and left. In the quiet that followed

Baya looked about him, and as his gaze fell on the table he frowned. He stepped over and realigned the sheets of papyrus while Hetep watched, his breath held and his pulse hammering in his ears. Slowly Baya straightened, then he turned to face the curtain.

'I know someone's there,' he said. 'So you might as well come out.'

Hetep backed away half a step and stood rigid. He's only guessing, he thought. He cocked his head, listening; with his eye no longer at the gap he could see nothing inside the room. He heard Baya take a pace towards him and what sounded like a blade being unsheathed.

'I'm armed,' said Baya. 'Don't make this worse for yourself.'

Hetep, feeling suddenly foolish, stepped out through the curtain.

'Now what are *you* doing there?' said Baya. He had a dagger in one hand, the blade pointing at Hetep's midriff.

'Hiding,' said Hetep. He could think of nothing better to say, and certainly no lie that would make him appear innocent.

'So I can see. And before that?'

'I came to find you. To ask you something.'

'Really? And then you hid because... well, perhaps you can tell me.' Baya's knife hand moved as he talked and Hetep stared at the patch of reflected light as it ran up and down the blade. He cleared his throat.

'If you want to know I came to ask you why you kept me here in Sumur,' he said. 'You arranged it, didn't you?'

Baya frowned. 'Now who told you that?'

'Nui.'

'I see.' The dagger point dipped a fraction. 'If you must know, it was to keep you from mischief. Better to have you here under my eye than allow you to go back

115

to Egypt, where you might embarrass yourself by making wild, unsubstantiated claims.'

'You mean about the Irqatan prince, don't you? But you must know that I killed him!'

'Must I?' said Baya, with a faint look of surprise. 'You weren't the only chariot warrior to kill Amurrites that day. And then there was all that dust. Are you absolutely certain the man you killed was the one presented to Pharaoh? Certain enough to swear to it on your life?'

'I know what I did. The credit's mine, as should be the reward.'

'There were witnesses who saw what *I* did. My driver, for one – may he find eternal joy in the West. And the second man of my squadron, Mehy. We all swore before the gods that what I said is true. So it has to be.'

'But it's a lie,' said Hetep. 'And the gods will punish you for it.'

Baya shrugged. 'It's this world that concerns me, not the next. After all, it's not as if anyone's ever returned to tell us what it's like over there. Besides, even if what you say was true, it's too late for anything to be changed now. The monuments have already been carved, the decrees made and the honours given out.'

'And now you're taking advantage of your new position by stealing from the tribute.'

Baya's eyes widened. 'Ah, so *now* we get to the truth. You're spying... on a fellow Egyptian, as well. Did Nui put you up to this?'

'Hardly. He barely tolerates me; he'd never ask me to work for him.'

'Really?' Baya glanced around the room. 'I don't know what you were instructed to find here, or what you did find, but it doesn't matter. There's nothing you can do to stop me. But there's much that you can do to help.'

'What do you need me for? You seem to have everything organised.'

'You'd think so, wouldn't you? You know, these foreigners are useful enough in their way, but I need a man I can trust, a man who knows our ways and can talk directly to the Egyptian ship captains, so I can run things properly. And you may find the work more rewarding than counting bread rations or whatever it is Nui's got you doing.'

'I take it that Zuratta's not much help. Don't act all innocent. I know who the "Habiru" is – I saw you talking to him in that garden in Irqata. What have you promised him in exchange for his cooperation?'

'You needn't concern yourself with that.'

'You can't trust him,' said Hetep. 'He hates us, and he'd kill you if he had the chance. He's just using you.'

'You forget: these people have been pacified. Zuratta assists me because he's too afraid not to. But you are right in a way: I could use more, shall we say, civilised assistance. So I repeat my offer. Help me with my work here and I'll help you in return.'

'A bribe, eh? How much do you think I'm worth?'

'Don't worry, I'm not going to insult your sense of honour by offering you wealth. Instead I offer reinstatement. That's what you really want, isn't it? My family has a great deal of influence, as you well know. I'm sure any one of them could talk Ramesses into having you back as a charioteer – after all, the military does tend to get what it wants. What do you say?'

Hetep searched Baya's face. 'How do I know you'll keep your promise?'

'You doubt the word of a man from one of Egypt's leading families? If you like we'll go to the Amun shrine and I'll swear it before the god.'

117

Hetep knew that such an oath would be binding to most men, even to the point of death, and acceptance hovered on his tongue. Yet he also knew what kind of a man Baya was – impious, driven by greed and ambition – and he realised that the moment he ceased to be useful Baya would destroy him.

Baya was still waiting for his answer. 'Well? You'll find that I can be a loyal friend, but a dangerous enemy. What do you say?'

'No,' said Hetep, with an effort. 'No,' he said again, this time more loudly, as if to affirm to himself as much as to Baya what he had decided. 'What you're doing here is wrong. And I cannot be bought.'

Baya's face flushed with anger. 'You think it matters what happens here? Who cares about a bunch of Asiatics? We own these people, and if I want to profit from them that's my right!'

'Don't you think they resent us enough as it is? Extorting wealth from their merchants could tip them into rebellion. And what about the tribute? It belongs to Pharaoh and stealing it is the same as stealing from him. It's a sin, and it offends Ma'at. You may as well be robbing his ancestors' tombs!'

Baya suddenly went very still. 'And just what would you know about that?' he said quietly. The dagger was pointing straight at Hetep's sternum.

'What do you mean?' said Hetep, alarmed by the sudden change in Baya's demeanour. 'You can't frighten me. Get out of my way. I'm going to Nui. We'll see what he has to say about this.'

'I'm sorry, I can't let you do that.'

Baya's grip tightened on the dagger and Hetep tensed, ready to fling himself aside – as if it would do him any good. The next moment they heard voices and a pair of scribes came bustling into the room. Instantly the dagger vanished under Baya's tunic. He and Hetep stared at each other while the scribes, sensing that something was wrong, fell quiet.

'I think we're finished here now,' said Hetep. 'If you don't mind I have a meeting to arrange with Nui.' He pushed past the glaring Baya and walked quickly to the door, while the scribes looked on, puzzled.

It was only once he was outside that he felt his body reacting to what had happened and he wiped his sweating palms on his clothes. Gods, he thought: was Baya really going to kill me? He searched his memory, recalling the cold, deadly look on Baya's face as he came towards him, the dagger held ready to thrust into his midriff.

No, it was impossible. The light was poor and he must have misread Baya's expression. It was unthinkable that the man would try to murder a fellow Egyptian – at least not in a place like Sumur, where he could not hope to keep the crime hidden. Still, Hetep was in no doubt that he now had another enemy in Amurru alongside Zuratta.

CHAPTER 13

Nui refused to see him; indeed, Hetep could not even get past his secretary, who sent him away with scolding words about wasting the commissioner's time. Then Merimose appeared, wanting to know why he was disturbing the other scribes at their work and if he had finished his day's chores, and ordered one of the guards to escort him into the street again.

Unable to face the suffocating gloom of the dormitory he kept walking, choosing streets at random, his mind repeatedly going over his catalogue of misfortunes. He had always tried to live a virtuous life and had never deliberately done anything to diminish Ma'at. So why was he being made to suffer? What god had he angered? Even as the question formed in his mind he knew the answer. It was no god who had singled him out for punishment but his father, cursing him from beyond the grave.

Hetep never had been a dutiful son, and in the three years since his father's death his failure to uphold his filial duties was little short of criminal. Only rarely had he made the long journey to the village cemetery to make the proper offerings to his father's *ka*; much easier was it to put off the task for one more day, one more week, and spend his time at Pr-Ramesses enjoying the easy camaraderie of his fellow charioteers. Perhaps if their relationship had been more amicable he might have made the journey more frequently, but his father had been a hard man to respect, and an even harder one to love – harsh, dull humoured, always finding fault with Hetep's conduct, and miserly almost to the point of madness. Hetep remembered how, during his childhood, his father used to issue him, his sister and his mother with a daily grain ration, as if they were a gang of corvée workers instead of a family.

When the news had come of his father's drowning in a ferry accident on the Nile Hetep had secretly rejoiced, and with Teppic's encouragement and the patronage of Teppic's family had lost no time in bartering away sufficient land to pay for the chariot and the training, and to enter the life he had come to yearn for – and that his father had disapproved of so strongly. In the week before the army had set out for Amurru he had tried to make amends by hiring a *ka* priest to make offerings to his father in his absence, but at the same time the chariot had needed some gilding for a parade and the best he could afford to hire was a local scribe's assistant whose assurances even Hetep did not fully believe. He suspected the man of neglecting his duties, leaving his father's shade hungry and thirsty – and growing in malice.

Of course his mother would be on hand to keep an eye on the *ka* priest, but he had little confidence in her effectiveness. Throughout his life she had been a gentle, reassuring presence, but never a forceful one, and as both an ex-slave and a foreigner of low standing she had no authority over native-born Egyptians. From there his thoughts turned to his uncle and he groaned as he pictured the man plotting to seize control of his land while his mother stood by, powerless to intervene. It was maddening: here he was, stuck hundreds of miles from home, with no chariot and no prospect of ever getting one again, cursed by his father's spite while his uncle plotted to steal his remaining wealth.

He closed his eyes and took a breath. Stay calm, he told himself, and settle your own *ka*; it's not all hopeless. Teppic would have reached Egypt by now, and he knew that his friend would not stand idly by while his uncle schemed. And there was always the hope that he would yet find a way to bring down Baya.

A change in the quality of the street noise made him stop and look around, and he realised that his walk had taken him to the foot of one of the towers by the city gate. On a whim he ducked inside and climbed the steps to the roof. The stairs were steep, and the stone walls felt cold against his sweating arm. At the top an Amurrite spearman saw him but let him pass and he walked across the tower roof to the battlements. The effort of the climb had burned off the worst of his resentment and he leaned his elbows on the parapet and gazed out at the countryside.

Olive groves and fields of ripening grain stretched away before him, bordered by patches of forest, and through it all ran the coastal road, a ribbon of pale earth winding towards the horizon. He followed it with his eyes until it disappeared into the haze. What if he climbed down and just started walking? he wondered. In a month he could be home in Egypt... provided Nui did not send out troops to arrest him, and he survived the marauding gangs of Habiru. He sighed and shook his head.

He heard the city gates creak open below him and saw a squadron of chariots rolling onto the meadow in front of the city. They were Amurrite, with wheels mounted under the cab to support the weight of the armoured crew – the same type he and the rest of Re division had fought outside Irqata. And the horses were big to match them: powerful-looking things imported from a place called Mannea, somewhere to the east. Nui had been asked to ship as many as he could find back to Egypt as part of Sumur's tribute.

Hetep watched as the chariots wheeled and charged, the crews shooting at targets with javelin and bow, and his longing to join them was almost painful. But he was also aware of a new feeling, mingling unpleasantly with the yearning: an echo of the sick horror that had gripped his belly when he had seen Sebeku falling from the cab, the arrow stuck in his neck, as the Amurrite chariots thundered towards them. He shook his head as if to clear it, and told himself that if he was ever back with the squadron again his fears would vanish.

'Quite a view, isn't it?'

Hetep jerked upright and turned to see Mursili emerging from the tower stairwell. The Hittite was smiling and he came over to join him at the battlements.

'You're following me again,' said Hetep, but not without a smile in return. 'Admit it.'

'Not at all. I've just heard a disturbing rumour and I've come to see if it's true.'

'Is it?' said Hetep, glancing around. 'True, I mean.'

'It is too soon to tell. But the moment I find out you shall be the first to know.' Mursili shaded his eyes and scanned the southern horizon. Evidently what he was looking for had yet to appear, for he dropped his hand and, just as Hetep had done, leaned out to watch the maneuvering chariots.

'I heard a rumour that Nui is to have weapons and chariots made here, and that already he's storing up raw materials,' he said after a while, his eyes still on the Amurrites. 'One might almost imagine he's expecting to fight another battle hereabouts. You wouldn't know anything about that, would you?'

'Is this the news you were talking about?'

'No, that is a different matter. I'm just curious – from a merchant's point of view, of course. Because if he is building a new chariot force he's going to need wood and metal, and plenty of other things besides. I wonder if I

123

might be able to arrange to supply him with some.'

'I'll mention it at our next meeting,' said Hetep bitterly.

'Ah, yes... of course. Please, forgive me. I forgot that you're a little out of favour at the moment.' He frowned down at the Amurrite chariots. 'Their troop commander's a bit of a firebrand. Listen to him: charge, wheel right, shoot, charge again... no wonder the horses look tired.'

'They're pulling too much weight. It's all that armour they're wearing, and on the crews, too. It makes them clumsy.'

'Still, they gave you a fair bit of trouble, eh?'

'What do you mean?'

'Remember, I was at Irqata, too. I saw the battle from the top of the walls, and I may have been mistaken – there was, after all, an awful lot of dust – but some of your chariot men were almost overwhelmed by these supposedly clumsy Amurrite machines.'

'They caught us by surprise,' said Hetep stiffly. 'Perhaps you didn't see the start of the battle when we cut them down in droves. Our chariots are better – faster and more maneuverable. We just have to keep moving.'

'Of course,' said Mursili, in a tone that only increase Hetep's irritation. 'A resounding victory for Egyptian arms, if I may judge from the conduct of the town's elders. They were absolutely pulling out their beards at what they could glimpse through the dust. Your pharaoh must be pleased.'

'You could say that.' Hetep remembered the look on Ramesses' face as he had gazed at the piles of hands on the day of Benteshina's surrender.

'Then again, outnumbering the enemy as you did, you could hardly lose, could you?' said Mursili in the same infuriating tone.

'If you really did see us, you'd know that it was *we* who were outnumbered. Less than half the division was there!'

'Only half, eh? And your pharaoh still attacked. He must be very brave.'

'Reckless, more like. Antef told him not to fight, so did the others. A few more days and we'd have the whole division with us. But no. He had to attack, there and then.'

'These kings – they're all the same,' sighed Mursili. 'They just don't listen, do they?'

'He didn't that day. I know he's a god but still...' Hetep shut his mouth, aware that what he was about to say was blasphemous. 'What I mean is, he's only been on the throne four years. It's still early days, you know. But what do you care?'

Mursili shrugged. 'Just idle questions, that's all.' Suddenly he tensed, looking keenly down at the meadow. 'Oh, good shot,' he cried. 'Well done!'

One of the Amurrite chariots was wheeling away from a target in which two arrows were stuck quivering.

'Not bad,' said Hetep. 'But any man from Re division could do the same, and at twice the range, too.'

'That's the third time you've used that word. "Re" I understand: it is the name of one of your gods. But "division"? I'm unfamiliar with the term.'

'Four thousand infantry and five hundred chariots with crews. That's Re division. Plentiful of Valour – that's what they call us.' Hetep remembered how proud he had been of the title, and tasted again the bitterness caused by his loss.

'A fine epithet. I don't think we use such things in Hatti, which is a pity. I remember once hearing about Egyptian troops called Strong of Bows. I wondered then

125

what it meant.'

'That's Set division's title – the fourth one.'

'You mean there are *four* of these fine units? I had no idea! They must be an awesome sight when they're all marching at once. No wonder so many people are afraid of you Egyptians.'

'Oh, we don't march them together,' said Hetep. He knew he was boasting, but Mursili's earlier criticism of Egypt's chariotry still rankled and he was anxious to persuade the Hittite of the superiority of the Egyptian military. 'The divisions go separately, half a day apart, so that each doesn't camp in land stripped by the other.'

'Do they now?' Mursili's eyes shone. 'How very clever.'

'We're Egyptian,' said Hetep. 'We've been organising things for thousands of years. Perhaps you should try it yourselves.'

'Hittites, behaving like Egyptians? Now *that* I would like to see.' Mursili chuckled. Then his smile vanished as he straightened and peered out at the far horizon. 'Ah, now,' he said quietly. 'I do believe my informant was right. Look there.'

Hetep followed his gaze and saw, beneath a column of wind-blown dust, a dozen chariots moving fast. Soon they were close enough for Hetep to see the crews. None were armoured, although the cars were hung with bowcases and full quivers.

'Who are they?' said Hetep.

'Trouble, I think,' said Mursili. 'Let us go and look at them as they come through the gate.'

They hurried down the steps to street level. By now a crowd had gathered to see the newcomers and they wormed their way forwards to get a better view. The first of the chariots passed under the arch; it was drawn by a pair of black horses, and again Hetep thought uncom-

126

fortably of the battle at Irqata. Then he saw the warrior riding in the cab, and his unease turned to horror. It was Zuratta. He still had a bandage around his head and his face still bore traces of bruises from where Hetep had kicked him.

'Well this is an interesting development,' said Mursili.

'You knew he was coming, didn't you?' said Hetep.

'Just a rumour, nothing more. I was hoping it was untrue.'

As the chariots drew near Hetep backed into the crowd but Mursili stayed where he was. Zuratta was scanning the people as he rode past, as if looking for someone. He spotted a squad of Egyptian infantry, who had been posted with the locals to keep order, and sneered. So the hatred is still there, thought Hetep; he was glad he was hidden. Then Zuratta's eye fell on Mursili and he went rigid, glaring at the Hittite. Mursili met his gaze without apparent emotion, but once Zuratta had passed a troubled look came to his face and he shook his head.

Chapter 14

Hetep was back in the shelter of the dormitory, sitting propped against the wall and for once oblivious to the Thoth statue's hostile gaze. Over the past few weeks he had become increasingly preoccupied with his more recent troubles and his worries over the distant Zuratta had faded. But seeing him in the city, armed and full of menace, brought back all his old fears. What chance do I have if he comes for me now? he thought; I've no armour, no weapons, just a broom made of rushes and a handful of scribes' pens.

He was wondering if he should make another attempt to board a ship for home when he heard footsteps at the doorway. He tensed, searching around for anything that would serve as a weapon, and slumped back again when he saw that it was Hiziru.

'What is it?' he said.

Hiziru bowed. 'My lady Elissa wishes to see you at the palace. She said to tell you that the time the goddess foretold draws near.'

As if I don't have enough troubles, thought Hetep. But how can one defy the will of heaven? He pushed himself to his feet. 'I'll come,' he said.

He followed Hiziru to the city's main plaza, but instead of heading for the palace gate they took a side road that lead to a small postern door hidden behind a projection in the wall. They had to crawl to get through, and once inside they paced in silence down a series of corridors until they reached a guard room. A woman was there, evidently waiting for him, and it took him a moment to recognise her as Elissa, for she was plainly dressed and her face was

128

unpainted.

'Zuratta's in the city,' she said. She looked tense.

'Yes, I know,' said Hetep. 'I saw him arrive.'

'He's speaking to my brother now. Come with me.'

Hetep followed her and Hiziru through a dark little passage. It ended in a dim, musty-smelling chamber with a door at one end. Hiziru posted himself at the door while Elissa went to the far wall, which was pierced by several small triangular holes. She waved Hetep over; from the other side came voices.

'We must be quiet or my brother may hear us,' she whispered. 'Now look.'

Hetep put an eye to one of the holes. It looked into the throne room; Benteshina was there, seated, and standing before him was Zuratta.

'The city should have gone to me,' Zuratta was saying. 'I was next in line.'

Benteshina's reply was a barely audible purr. 'Lordship of my cities is not always hereditary. Besides, the decision was not mine to make. Times have changed and we must do as our Egyptian masters require – at least for now.'

'Is that true?' whispered Elissa.

'If it is I haven't heard,' said Hetep. 'I don't think Nui cares who rules Irqata.'

Zuratta was shouting now. 'And who governs there instead? Ayub, a man who licks the dust from the Egyptians' feet and dishonours our gods!'

This time Benteshina raised his own voice. 'I told you, Nui gave me no choice.'

'And what about the troops you failed to send on the day of the battle? Did you have a choice about that?'

'Not this again,' said Benteshina wearily. 'You have been told why. We had to repeat the closing rites during the Feast of the Gracious Gods – the diviners insisted upon it. I could hardly march the army out and leave them undone, could I? It would have brought misfortune on us all.'

'You mean you bribed the diviners to delay the end of the festival. Don't lie to me, you cur. You'd spit at the gods if it would serve your scheming purposes.'

Benteshina's face darkened and he held out a clenched fist. 'With every word you talk yourself closer to the gibbet,' he shouted. 'If I say the gods delayed the festival then that is what happened. Now that's enough!'

Bootsteps sounded from outside the room and Hiziru hissed a warning.

'My brother's men are near,' said Elissa. 'We must go.'

She grabbed Hetep's arm and pulled him away from the eye holes. They hurried through the far door and down a short passage, and came to the waiting chamber that lead to the throne room. It was deserted. They heard Zuratta shouting again, his voice growing louder; in panic Hetep looked about for a place to hide. Then the doors crashed open and Zuratta came striding out, his face livid. He saw Hetep and stopped, his mouth open.

'You!' he said, his voice tight.

Hetep stared back, only partly hidden by a pillar and feeling foolish, like a child caught trespassing by an adult.

'You're the architect of all this,' roared Zuratta. 'And now it's time you paid.' He advanced on Hetep, his hands clawing and his features twisted with hate.

'Stop!'

Elissa darted out from hiding and placed herself in front of Hetep. The effect on Zuratta was startling. He gave a strangled cry and flinched back, one hand raised in a gesture of warding.

130

'You forget yourself,' she said. 'This is my brother's city – he rules here. The Egyptians are under his protection. And this one is under mine.'

Zuratta grimaced as if in pain. 'Witch! Is it not enough that you shamed yourself with a Hittite spy and sent my brother to his death? Will you curse me too with your sorcery?' He was backing away as he spoke, his eyes wild. 'Protect him if you can. But you are not as powerful as you think. The time of reckoning will come, and when it does I swear this city will run with Egyptian blood!' He turned, and in another moment was gone.

Elissa let out a long breath and looked at Hetep. 'I'm sorry. It wasn't my intention that you meet him.'

'Really?' said Hetep. 'Then what was your intention?'

'I wanted you to see my brother's reaction to Zuratta. And to convince you of the danger Zuratta poses to the city.'

The doors to the audience chamber were still open and she stepped over the threshold. Hetep followed her inside. By now Benteshina had gone, leaving the room silent and empty.

'Do you think the king heard Zuratta threatening me?'

Elissa shrugged. 'I'm not sure if it would have made much a difference if he had. I think he's up to something.'

'You mean because he lied about Nui?'

Elissa nodded.

'Why doesn't your brother just have Zuratta arrested?'

'Because Zuratta has too many followers in the city, as I think you already know. There would be riots, which is precisely what we're trying to avoid.' She took a last look around the audience chamber. 'We shouldn't be here – especially you. It's time to go.'

They returned to the postern door without being seen by any of the palace guards. Once outside they separated,

Hiziru and Elissa heading for the acropolis and leaving Hetep standing alone in the street.

To one side of him rose the palace wall, while to the other stood tall rows of tenements; the air, trapped in the narrow street, was hot and stifling. Yet it was not the buildings that made him feel as if the city was closing in around him but the intrigues of its inhabitants.

His mind had already been troubled by Elissa's attempt to recruit him as her and Mursili's spy in the Egyptian bureaucracy; more troubling still had been the knowledge that her goddess was working alongside her to trap him in a web of prophecy. And now it seemed that Benteshina was hatching his own scheme, and although Hetep could not guess its purpose it clearly depended on provoking Zuratta's resentment of the Egyptian occupation. And even without Benteshina's influence Zuratta would still be waiting for his chance to kill him, his hatred raging unabated like a wildfire. Never had Hetep so missed the simplicity of his old life as a chariot warrior, when his enemies always stood in plain sight and all he needed to fear were their arrows and javelins.

A visit to Sebeku went some way towards settling his mood. The fever had gone and the wound in his neck was sealed with a thick ridge of healthy-looking scar tissue. He was on his feet, too, although his steps were a little unsteady.

'Don't strain yourself,' said Hetep anxiously, his arms held out ready to catch his friend if he stumbled.

'I have to get out of this room or I'll go mad,' said Sebeku.

'I'll see about getting you some extra food, so you can build up your strength. But don't overdo it. And try to stay hidden, will you?'

'Why?'

132

'There's trouble coming. Zuratta's arrived, for a start.'

Sebeku frowned at him. 'We have a garrison don't we? Surely they'll protect us.'

'I wouldn't count on it. I'm not exactly on friendly terms with its commander. And Nui, our commissioner, doesn't like me either.'

'Have you made enemies out of everyone here?'

'Not everyone, no. There's Benteshina's sister, Elissa – she's friendly enough, but seems to think the goddess Anat has set me up to save the city from a rebellion. And there's a Hittite who I think I can trust. His name's Mursili and he's a merchant, and he seems to know a lot about what's going on here.'

'Don't tell me you've been conspiring with these people while I was lying here ill. And with a Hittite, too! Don't you know they're our enemies?'

'We have a treaty with them; King Seti made it. And the Amurrites are subdued.'

'Only trust a foreigner when you have your foot on his neck. And even then be cautious.'

'I think I liked you better when you couldn't talk.'

'You'll see,' said Sebeku. 'One day your Hittite friend will betray you, as will that Amurrite woman.'

'Just let me deal with them. In the meantime, don't let Baya or Zuratta see you. They don't know you're here.'

CHAPTER 15

It was late afternoon, three days after Zuratta's arrival, and Hetep was once again sweeping the dormitory, battling against the never-ending stream of dust that the wind kept blowing through the gap at the bottom of the door. He had just worked a particularly stubborn patch of grime from between a pair of flagstones when the door opened, admitting a swirl of grit. He looked up sharply and saw Paneb, one of the more independent minded of the Egyptian scribes, standing breathless at the threshold.

'You're needed at the storehouses,' said Paneb. 'We've some wood that needs to be inventoried.'

Hetep stared, the unexpectedness of the request making him stupid. 'What, me?'

'You're the only one here – except the god, of course,' said Paneb, with a nod to the baboon statue. 'He said be quick. So get your kit.'

'Who said? Nui?'

'Ships have come from Egypt to collect some of the tribute. Most of it's wood, and Nui wants it all counted and recorded by sundown. But some of the scribes are off sick with hangovers and we need help.'

Hetep dropped the broom. At last, he thought: a chance to do something other than sweeping.

'Give me a moment,' he said, and searched around for his writing palette – a wooden box holding ink cakes and a pair of reed pens. He found it buried under a pile of unwashed clothes.

He followed Paneb through the crowded city streets and down towards the harbour. Through its gate he could see the Egyptian ships moored beside the quay and the sight of the crews in their native garb brought on a pang of homesickness.

'The wood's in a storehouse at the end of Fish Street,' said Paneb. 'I've been told to send you there.'

'What?' Hetep blinked at him. 'Sorry, I wasn't listening.'

'It's that way,' said Paneb, pointing. 'Take the second opening on the left; the wood should already be there. And now I must go. We've a mountain of copper ingots to send as well, and we haven't even began sorting them.' Then he was off, heading for the busy chaos of the harbour and shouting for a gang of slaves.

Hetep hesitated at the entrance to Fish Street. There was something about the name that filled him with disquiet, but he could not say why. Yet he could see nothing to be afraid of, just the usual crowds of city folk going about their business, and there was even a pair of soldiers posted at the far end, keeping an eye out for trouble. There was no danger there, and he felt suddenly foolish standing afraid in the bright sunshine.

He headed down the street, the writing palette gripped in one hand, and soon came to the entrance Paneb had indicated. Beyond lay a small courtyard, floored with gravel and stones; beyond that was a doorway, leading to what must be the storehouse.

The moment he stepped through the entrance the high walls cut off the sound of city life and he paused to look back at the street. People were still passing by, but now in apparent silence, and he had the odd feeling that he was viewing a procession of the dead. Idiot, he thought: some chariot warrior you are. Trying to ignore the pricking of his skin he advanced a few more steps towards the far doorway.

'Hello?' he called. 'I'm here.'

Behind him a foot crunched on gravel and he turned to see a figure blocking the way back to the road. Robes, heavy boots – definitely not an Egyptian, he thought, and with unease turning to panic he fled.

Beyond the door there was indeed a storehouse, dark and empty save for the wind-blown dust. He heard the man's bootsteps behind him and he kept going, heading for an opening he could just make out in the far wall. He was halfway there when someone stepped out to block his way. It was Zuratta, and he was smiling in triumph.

Hetep stopped and whirled about, but the booted man was filling the other doorway, and he saw a third figure coming up behind. He turned again, and now Zuratta was striding towards him. Without pausing Hetep stepped forwards, raised his arm and flung his writing palette at Zuratta's head with all his strength. A corner caught Zuratta in the eye and he howled, bending over with one hand pressed to his face. Hetep sprinted straight for him, hoping to shove him aside and escape, but Zuratta's free arm came flailing out, checking him, and in another moment the booted man had his arm locked around his throat. He struggled, then a foot struck the back of his knee and he went down. Now the third Amurrite was on him, forcing him onto his front; a rope was tied around his arms, pinning his elbows together behind his back, and another around his legs, and then all three of his assailants stood back.

Zuratta's eye was half closed and already swelling, with a trickle of blood running from the corner. He wiped it with his hand, making a red smear along his cheek.

'You'll pay for that, tenfold,' he snarled. Then, to his companions, 'Begin!'

The second Amurrite was holding a sack, from which he pulled a block of incense and a fire starter. In moments he had the incense burning and was kneeling and praying in a language strange to Hetep. Meanwhile the third Amurrite went to the shadows in the far corner and came back dragging a block of stone. It looked to Hetep very much like an altar on which one would sacrifice an animal.

'What are you doing?' he said, his voice breaking with fear. 'Let me go!'

'You are going to die,' said Zuratta. 'Not as slowly as I would like – we lack the time for such amusement. But the manner of you death will please my brother's shade.' He glared down at Hetep, a bruise spreading over his face like an opening flower and blood clouding his eyeball. 'And know this, you Egyptian filth. Your flesh will be eaten by wild dogs and your bones scattered in the wilderness. An eternity of torment is waiting for you.'

'But you can't do that,' protested Hetep. 'It's a sin. The gods won't allow it!'

Zuratta drew out an engraved dagger and ran a thumb across the blade. 'The more you fear, the more the god Teshub will relish the sacrifice.'

'You're making a mistake,' said Hetep, trying to keep his voice even. 'You think Nui won't notice I'm gone?'

'What if he does? He'll never find your corpse. Are you done yet?' This was to the man with the incense.

'Patience. It must be done correctly lest the witch see what we do and tell her filthy goddess.' He chanted more words in the same strange language as before, brought his hands together and snuffed out the incense burner. 'There,' he said. 'It is finished. We may begin.'

Hetep struggled vainly against his bonds as Zuratta dragged him over to the stone. The second man produced a blood-encrusted copper bowl from the sack; at the sight of it Hetep started gabbling a mixture of prayers and entreaties, interspersed with calls for help. Zuratta hit him across the head, twice, and he went limp. As the other two Amurrites pulled his head over the altar he heard his protective amulet clattering against the stone. Gods help me, he thought, they're going to cut my throat, like an animal's. He felt bile rising in his gullet and he swallowed it down, desperate not to choke. Again he called for help, his voice shrieking. He twisted his head, and out of the corner of his eye he saw the blade poised, a fingerbreadth from his neck.

'What in the name of Thoth are you doing?'

The blade withdrew. Hetep swiveled his eyes around until they ached and through a watery blur made out a figure standing in the doorway.

'You there – untie that man.' The figure came striding into the storehouse, and Hetep could scarcely believe what he saw. It was Merimose, and he was shaking with anger.

'I said untie him, this instant!'

The men gripping Hetep relaxed their hold, but Zuratta raised his knife.

'One scribe or two,' he said, 'what does it matter how many we kill?'

Still Merimose came on, undaunted; it was one of the bravest acts Hetep had ever seen.

'You scoundrels! Do you think you can frighten me? Put that knife down or there'll be consequences!'

Hetep felt as if his tongue had swollen to fill his mouth and he had to swallowed repeatedly before he could speak.

'One Egyptian death might be explainable as an accident but not two,' he croaked. 'Especially when one of them is Chief Scribe. Nui will tear this city to the ground looking for our bodies and our killers. And you know it.'

Zuratta's bruised face darkened further and he took a step towards Merimose. 'I'll not be denied my revenge.'

'Wait,' said one of his companions. 'The Egyptian is right. We cannot kill them both.' He looked down at Hetep. 'But Teshub will have his sacrifice yet. The day of reckoning has merely been postponed.'

Still fuming, Zuratta looked first at his companions, then at Hetep. Finally he slid the dagger into its sheath.

'We go. Now.' He indicated the incense lamp and the bowl. 'Bring those.' Then he turned, kicked Hetep in the face and stalked out, his companions with him.

'That's them told,' said Merimose, with satisfaction. 'Wicked brutes... how dare they!'

'If you could give me some help...' Hetep's head was ringing from the kick and he could feel blood running from his nose.

'Of course.' Merimose untied the ropes and helped Hetep to stand.

'Thank you,' said Hetep. 'You just saved my life.' For the first time he felt respect – he might even say admiration – as he looked at Merimose.

'Oh, I wouldn't go that far. Still, I think it's high time we did something about the city's brigands. It's scandalous that an Egyptian could be waylaid like this.'

'They weren't brigands. Didn't you see?'

'They must have been. If I'd have had soldiers with me I'd have ordered their arrest. But where's the garrison when you need it, eh? You tell me that. Still, I don't think we'll see them again in a hurry – not after the scolding I gave them.'

Hetep opened his mouth to explain, then closed it again. What's the point? he thought. He doubted if Merimose's weak eyes had seen more than a few blurs. He rubbed his arms and legs where the rope had bitten into his flesh, then probed his face. No teeth missing, at least, and his nose seemed unbroken. But he knew it was going to start hurting soon.

'How did you know I was here?' he asked.

'Nui wants to see you. Paneb told me you'd been called away to help with the inventory so I went to look for you, but you weren't in the storehouse with the others. Then I heard you calling out, so I came here.'

'Are there really stacks of wood that need counting?'

'Oh yes. Baya's been supervising.'

At the sound of that name Hetep's insides went cold.

'Did Baya order Paneb to send me here?' he said.

'Of course! As I said, it was Baya who was put in charge of making the inventory.'

Hetep wondered if the attempt to kill him was at Baya's instigation. More likely Baya was just helping Zuratta take his revenge, in payment for the latter's continued cooperation in his embezzlement scheme.

'And now,' said Merimose, 'if you've quite recovered, you must come with me. Nui has asked to see you. And as you know he's not a patient man.'

CHAPTER 16

It was Hetep's first visit to the building that Nui had adopted as his formal residency. Considering its importance its interior was surprisingly drab, the pillars and walls lacking the cheerful, decorative paintwork one saw in official buildings in Egypt. It was as if Nui cared nothing for aesthetics, an impression only reinforced by the state of the rooms he had chosen for his offices. The furniture was sparse – little more than a few folding stools – and aside from a pair of daggers and a khopesh the wall niches were filled with nothing but protective devices and scribal paraphernalia, including piles of blank papyrus sheets, wet clay for tablet making and a stack of writing kits. There was, of course, a statue of Thoth, sitting at the back on one of the shelves; unusually, it was of the god in his ibis form. Hetep ducked his head in a nervous greeting to the god and brushed his hands down his tunic, aware of how shabby he must look after his encounter with Zuratta.

A scribe appeared and lead him to a side room. There Nui was standing, holding a clay tablet and wearing a troubled frown on his face. When he saw Hetep his frown deepened.

'Took your time, didn't you?' he growled. 'I summoned you nearly an hour ago.'

'I would have come sooner only someone was trying to kill me,' said Hetep. 'It's how I got the bruises.' He pointed to his face.

'I thought I told you there's to be no brawling with the locals. We've enough trouble as it is.'

'It was Zuratta, the man I told you about back at Irqata. He's here in the city.'

'Then I'll get Yuya to send out some extra patrols. Now to business.'

'It won't be enough. I think Baya's protecting Zuratta.'

Nui looked at him sharply. 'What did you say?'

'I don't mean to criticise Yuya or anything. It's just... well, I've been wanting to tell you this since we came here. Baya's working with Zuratta, the brother of the Irqatan prince I killed. They're stealing tribute and levying their own private tax on the merchants.'

'Have you lost your senses? First this nonsense criticising Ramesses' policy here and now this. Well I won't have it, do you hear me?'

'I'm sorry but I can't let you ignore this,' said Hetep. A part of him wondered where he was finding the courage to talk back – a month ago he would not have dared. 'Baya's corrupt, and I can prove it. And just now he tried to have Zuratta kill me. Why do you think I'm covered in so much blood?'

'I said that's enough!'

'Remember when I went to get those pack animals at Irqata? I saw Baya in the palace gardens, talking to Zuratta. Did you send him to Irqata on that day? Well?'

Nui exhaled noisily. 'No, I don't recall that I did. But there could be a number of explanations for what you saw.'

'There's more. I was in his annexe and I heard him telling one of his scribes to load the stolen goods onto the *Ivory Wind*. You should check the ship, see what it's carrying. And you should go and see the Hittite merchant, Mursili. He knows what Baya's doing and he might have more proof.'

'You've been talking to *him*? A man who would like nothing better than to sow discord among us for his own filthy purposes?'

'Won't you at least have the ship searched before it sails? If Baya's really stealing from the merchants it'll only make the Amurrites hate us more. And what about the tribute? He's giving a share of it to Zuratta. What if someone at home finds out that a foreigner is taking what belongs to Pharaoh? You might get blamed for that.'

Nui's jaw clenched and he gripped the tablet so hard that bits of it broke off and fell to the floor. 'Gods curse the man,' he muttered. He fixed a warning eye on Hetep. 'You keep away from Baya, understand? I'll deal with him in my own time. And not a word to anyone else.'

'But the tribute; the ship–'

'Enough! This is not your affair. I said I'll deal with it.'

There was something odd about Nui's expression – a hint of evasiveness, perhaps, mingled with embarrassment – and Hetep realised, to his astonishment, that he was afraid of Baya. Gods help us, he thought, if even our mighty commissioner daren't bring the man to heel.

'Now if you're quite finished,' said Nui, 'perhaps we can get back to business. Which is this.' He held out the tablet so that Hetep could see it.

'I can't read the Babylonian signs.'

'Well I can. It's from a priest in one of the temples on the hill. He says the god El wants to see us at a festival they're having next month and predicts all sorts of trouble if we don't go.'

'A what?' said Hetep, blinking. It was the last thing he expected to hear.

'Are you going deaf? I said a festival. Their god wants to get a look at us, and at me especially.'

'I don't understand. What festival?'

'Apparently El's having some sort of drinking party. You said once you knew about these people. So you can

143

tell me what to expect, and why it's so important that we go. Well?'

'I don't... I mean... Please, give me a moment.' Hetep took the tablet from Nui's hand and examined the tangle of symbols covering its surface. How did anyone ever learn to read this mess? he thought. He noticed Nui glaring at him. 'Sorry, I was thinking. Yes, I know a little – if it's the one I suspect. It's a feast where the leading men of the city gather to honour the god and discuss the city's business. They offer El food and drink – especially drink. That's the most important part.'

'So only the god drinks,' said Nui with relief. 'That's good.'

'No, they all do. They emulate the god. In the story El drank so much wine he couldn't stand and ended up soiling himself. I think the idea is that Benteshina and the others have to do the same. Well, maybe not the last bit, but they'll get pretty drunk.'

'I see.' Nui looked displeased. 'Why do you think we're invited?'

'El is the king of their gods, so obviously he's important. If he's to see you it has to be on a festival day when he's out of the temple and on public display. You can hardly go and visit him in his inner sanctum.'

'I suppose not. But if they expect us to get drunk like the locals they're going to be disappointed. I'll have to issue orders – we're to remain sober.'

'You mean you're going?'

'Of course. And it's not just me this god wants to see. Pretty much everyone bar the garrison troops are going. Which means scribes are included – even you.'

'All of us?' Hetep had a sudden premonition if danger. 'Don't go,' he said. 'Something's not right.'

'What harm can it do, as long as we keep our heads?

144

And it might help placate this rabble I've been given to govern. It's their chief god who wants to see us, after all, and if the god's happy with us...'

'Then so are the people. Yes, I know.'

'Don't forget we're a long way from Egypt,' said Nui. 'And one thing I've learned in all my years is that although you can grind the people into the dirt it's not a good idea to upset their gods, not when you're in their own lands.'

'I suppose not,' said Hetep, his hand straying towards his amulet.

In the corridor outside Hetep exhaled and ran a hand over his brow. That could have gone better, he thought. He had hoped for at least a few words of commendation for exposing Baya but instead he had only roused Nui's anger. Worse, Nui's rasping voice and stern disapproval had reminded him unpleasantly of his father – a man always ready to administer a beating when Hetep did not learn his letters properly, or to tell him that he was too lazy to ever amount to anything.

No, he was being unfair. For for all his bluntness of manner there was a decency to Nui that Hetep's father had never possessed, and he was nowhere near as judgemental. Still, it was obvious that Nui had no intention of curbing Baya's excesses; commissioner of Amurru he might be, but he was clearly reluctant to cross Baya and his dangerously powerful family.

As if summoned by the thought Baya appeared, striding in through the entrance gate. He was smiling and had the air of a man satisfied with a job well done, but when he saw Hetep he stopped as if he had walked into a wall and his smile vanished.

'Surprised to see me?' said Hetep.

'I don't know what you mean,' said Baya stiffly.

'You know exactly what I mean. You sent me to that storehouse, knowing Zuratta was there.'

Baya frowned. 'Storehouse?'

'Don't play the innocent with me. Merimose already told me it was you who ordered Paneb to send me there.'

Baya stood for a moment, his mouth working, then his eyes widened. 'Of course! I remember now. You were supposed to go to the north storehouse. Paneb must have sent you the wrong way. We waited for you, but in the end I had to do your part of the audit myself. Now if there's nothing more, I wish you good health and a joyful day.'

He nodded curtly and walked on down the corridor, then disappeared into Nui's office.

CHAPTER 17

Back at the annexe by the dormitory Hetep told Sebeku about his encounter with Zuratta.

'We've been too soft on these people,' said Sebeku. His voice was sharp, as if his wound was paining him. 'If Ramesses had burned Irqata to the ground as an example we wouldn't be having this trouble with them now.'

'He wanted these people as willing allies, not corpses. Dead people don't pay tribute.'

'Perhaps not. But at least when they *are* dead they can't stop you taking what was theirs.'

'It's not the Amurrites that worry me, anyway,' said Hetep. 'It's Baya who's the real menace. But Nui's too afraid to reign him in.' Hetep took a pace up and down the annexe. 'If only I can find some proof, something that Nui can't ignore, we can bring Baya down. And then there'll be nothing protecting Zuratta.'

'But Nui's our Commander of the Host, and now he's the commissioner,' said Sebeku. 'Only Ramesses and the gods have more authority here. Are you sure of this?'

'I saw the look on his face. Don't forget he's the son of a commoner, like me. Baya's got the influence to do him a lot of harm, so it's no wonder he's reluctant to upset him. Which means we'll have to deal with things ourselves. I want you to keep an eye on Baya; you could do with getting some exercise anyway. He doesn't know you're here so he'll have no reason to look out for you, but I'll get you some local clothing and something to cover your head, just in case.'

'You want me to go skulking around dressed like a foreigner?' said Sebeku with disgust. 'Are you mad?'

147

'Please, just do it. For me. I want to know where and when Baya meets Zuratta. You do know what he looks like, don't you?'

Sebeku nodded. 'Green eyes, red beard, angry sneer, and bruises from where you keep whacking him on the head. I'm not surprised he doesn't like you.'

'The feeling's mutual.'

'What did Nui want, anyway?'

'To tell me about a festival.' Hetep related what Nui had said, and when he had finished the driver looked worried.

'If they wanted to kill us all at once we couldn't make it easier for them.'

'I don't think even Benteshina would murder guests in the middle of a festival to Amurru's greatest god. It would destroy him, and curse his kingdom for generations. Still, we'll be careful. Nui's no fool, you know.'

'And we'll all get drunk, just like that?'

'Not quite all. Yuya, our garrison commander, isn't going. You're not invited, either.'

'That's the best news I've heard yet. I don't think I could stand an evening of wine drinking. Beer is the only drink fit for a civilised man.'

'Well, you'll get plenty of that from now on, and I'll see about some extra meat rations. Anything to get you strong again.'

'So I can go skulking after Baya. Thanks. And in the meantime, what will you be doing?'

'I think it's time I paid my respects to the king.'

Despite being a member of the conquering power it was not easy for Hetep to arrange to see Benteshina. The king spent much of his time in a state of ritual purity,

148

presiding over the sacrifices and ceremonies that fed Amurru's gods and kept his kingdom safe from divine wrath, and was only approachable for one or two hours each day. And even then he was shielded from contact by an army of courtiers, which Hetep knew he had no hope of penetrating.

But there were ways of bypassing the king's bodyguards and officials. After a morning's nervous skulking about the city's streets, watching out for Zuratta and his men, Hetep managed to track down Hiziru who, after some persuasion, agreed to escort him to the temple where Elissa was paying her respects to her goddess.

She was dressed in her finery, her face and arms covered in intricate henna-drawn patterns, and her robe was so saturated with incense smoke that Hetep could smell it from a dozen paces. Traces of blood stained her hands and forearms; evidently she had been sacrificing, and her depurification ritual had been too rushed to have removed it all.

'The goddess has sent me a dream,' she said. 'I saw a scorpion burned by its own shadow and a man who was once a beggar become a prince. Then the shadow passed across the face of the Shapash, the sun goddess, and from the sky came rain, the droplets bright and red. The meaning is clear.'

'It is?' said Hetep. The dream symbols meant nothing to him, and he wondered if Elissa had been sleeping too close to her incense lamps.

'To those who possess sufficient knowledge in these matters, yes. Now tell me what news you have for my brother. That is why you've come to me, is it not?'

Hetep nodded. 'Zuratta's helping Baya, who's protecting him. I don't think your brother realises how closely they're working together.'

'The shadow draws near the sun – Zuratta's strength grows until it threatens to eclipse the men of Egypt. Do your people not worship the sun? And you say your man Nui, for all his power, cannot stop him. Why is that?'

'There are a few... complications. That's why I need to tell your brother. He's the only one who can help.'

'I see,' said Elissa. 'Wait a while and I shall see what can be done.'

The king received Hetep in his throne room. As before he was sitting at ease, his feet resting on a stool and one elbow propped on an arm rest, but this time he was attended by only a single courtier and a pair of guardsmen.

Hetep thought about bowing, but remembering Nui's words about how they owned Amurru he settled instead for a brief nod of his head.

'Thank you for agreeing to see me,' he said.

'You gave us such an entertaining performance at out last meeting that I felt unable to refuse my sister's request,' said Benteshina.

'I'm not here to entertain you this time, O King,' said Hetep.

The courtier cleared his throat. 'My lord, the outlander is still on his feet. A more prostrate attitude would–'

Benteshina silenced him with a gesture. 'Hush, please, my loyal chamberlain. Remember what I told you: the Egyptians are an insolent people. They come to us like Yam's messengers to El: unbowed and with tongues as sharp as swords. But remember how Ba'al rewarded Yam for his conceit and be patient.'

The same threat as before, thought Hetep, as the king studied him with an amused contempt. And he knows that I know. What's he playing at?

'But you are Ba'al's chosen!' said the courtier, scandalised. 'It is not–'

'I said be quiet,' snapped the king. 'And leave me. You men, too. I wish to speak to the Egyptian alone.'

The courtier glared suspiciously at Hetep but did as he was told and after gathering the two guards swept out of the room.

'A tiresome but useful man,' said Benteshina. 'Now don't tell me. You've come about Zuratta, haven't you?'

'Yes, O King. He tried to murder me, as if there are no laws in the city. And he's helping one of my compatriots, a man named Baya, steal from the tribute that's meant for Pharaoh.'

'Is he now? And you've come to me about it. I must say it's not very honourable to betray one of your own to a foreigner. Or is that how you Egyptians always conduct your business?'

'Baya is a lying, thieving scorpion and a threat to Ma'at. He has to be stopped, and Zuratta with him.'

'And you ask that I do it instead of Nui. Interesting. It suggests to me that Nui's position here is weaker than I supposed – information which I am sure will be most useful.'

'Weak? Hardly, O King. He still controls the city, doesn't he?'

'For the time being,' said Benteshina with a chilling mildness. 'Now tell me: why should I care about this Baya? Whether he steals from the tribute or not, the wealth is still lost to my city and my people are still impoverished.'

'Baya's also extorting goods from the merchants, and that's wealth that shouldn't be lost. He's giving a share of it to Zuratta. And the richer Zuratta becomes, the more

151

of a nuisance he'll be. There could be disorder – rioting, even – and neither of us wants that.'

'Indeed not. But I assure you that Zuratta is no threat to me. It is you Egyptians he hates.'

'Because we conquered his town.'

'Indeed. But more so because you killed his brother. And that is a wrong he will never forgive. A bare three generations ago his family were living among the Habiru, and although since then they have ruled Irqata they have not lost their taste for blood vengeance. Zuratta in particular is a man to keep his old traditions alive. You do know about the Habiru, don't you?'

Hetep nodded. 'My mother often told me about them. She was from Sidon.'

As far back as he could remember his mother's reminiscences about her life in her native city would invariably end with a bitter tirade against the Habiru and their depredations. In a voice filled with a rare hatred she would talk of their violence and treachery, and how they infested the Canaanite uplands and delighted in terrorising the region's city folk. Never settling yet never fully nomadic, it seemed many had been civilised themselves until driven into the wilds by debt or social upheaval, while others were from families who had been Habiru for generations. And all were thieves and murderers, respecting no law of gods or men.

'Tell me, O King,' said Hetep, 'why did you let one of these people govern Irqata?'

'It was my great grandfather Aziru's doing, not mine. While liberating Amurru from the Egyptian yoke he found the Habiru to be useful mercenaries, and afterwards rewarded one of Zuratta's forebears with the title of Prince of Irqata. An act of generosity that has since proved unwise, for recently Zuratta and his brother had become

152

somewhat troublesome vassals.'

A chill of suspicion began to form in Hetep's mind.

'I suppose you couldn't just order Irqata's prince to relinquish his power,' he said.

'Sadly not. He was a popular man – one might say dangerously so. Of course his people mourned his death, but they can take comfort in knowing that he died a warrior hero and has joined the ranks of the Rephaim.'

'And he was killed by us Egyptians. By me, to be more exact. Which leaves you entirely blameless.'

'Naturally. I was many miles away when the deed was done. How could I possibly have been involved?'

The king smiled thinly and a sly glint came to his hooded eyes, and Hetep's suspicion hardened into certainty.

'O King, does Zuratta suspect you had a part in this?'

'What he thinks is of little interest to me. And let me remind you: he's not my enemy, but yours. To me he is again just another Habiru, a man without a city.'

'Like the god Attar he has neither palace nor court; he is no king,' quoted Hetep.

'Impressive. And I take it you know what happens next in the god's tale.'

'He discovered he was too small to occupy Ba'al's throne.'

'He most certainly was,' said Benteshina. 'I like you, despite your impertinence. You've shown yourself to be a man who understands our ways – unlike Nui and the others, who are mere brutes, like Litan, the great beast from the sea. I can do nothing about Baya of course; Nui will have to deal with. But let me offer you an assurance. I have come to an understanding with Zuratta and I swear, in the name of the god Ba'al who raised me to kingship, that from this day he'll not pursue his vendetta against

153

your person. There: that's what you really wanted from me, wasn't it?'

As he stepped out into the clear sunshine of the plaza Hetep felt as if he was emerging from the suffocating atmosphere of a charnel house. He always knew that Canaanite kings, Ma'at-less foreigners to a man, could be treacherous and self-serving. But Benteshina was a schemer without peer, and hearing him slyly hinting at his monstrous act had made Hetep feel unclean, as if he had been witnessing a man deface the statue of a god.

A king's primary duty, after seeing to the needs of his deities, was to protect his people, and yet Benteshina had sacrificed the bulk of Irqata's garrison just so he could eliminate some bothersome subordinates. And instead of hiding his sin he seemed proud to have committed it. The depth of the man's impiety was breathtaking. As was his stupidity: he had all but admitted openly that he was planning a revolt; he must know that Hetep would report what he had heard to Nui.

And then all at once Hetep understood the true extent of Benteshina's scheming, and he stopped in mid stride and turned to face the palace, his mouth open. He knew, from what he had overheard that day with Elissa, that the king was inciting Zuratta's hatred of the Egyptians. Now he realised that at the same time he was making sure that Nui and the garrison would be prepared for the inevitable revolt so that they would crush it and kill Zuratta. And all without a drop of blood staining Benteshina's hands, or any risk of him reneging on the oath of loyalty he had sworn to Ramesses.

Despite his dislike for the man Hetep found himself impressed by the ease with which he had once again maneuvered Egypt's military into acting as his agent of execution. Yet there was a flaw in the king's scheme: even with the few hundred supporters in the city that Elissa claimed Zuratta had, Hetep could not see how he could be persuaded to attack the heavily armed Egyptian garrison. No, for that he would need an army of his own.

CHAPTER 18

It was the middle of summer and the god Ba'al had been killed and dragged to the Underworld by Mot, its dark and sinister overlord. With the Rider on the Clouds dead there would be no more rain, and for two days the people of Sumur mourned his passing. In the temples the lector priests offered prayers to Anat, Ba'al's warrior sister, asking that she kill Mot and free her brother, so that he could restore life to the land. Each year the cycle repeated itself, and although Ba'al was always freed in the end there were times when Anat's struggle with Mot dragged on, delaying Ba'al's return and the beginning of the autumn rains. Then the following year's harvest would be poor, leaving the people reliant on the reserves held in the royal granaries. But with the grain surplus due now to be taken by the Egyptians the people feared that, were this year's rains to fail, Mot would walk the land unbound and they would starve in their thousands.

There were reports of malformed sheep births in the upland farms and rumours that diviners were finding the animals they examined empty of entrails. A riot almost broke out when Saturn appeared hanging low on the horizon, looking oddly coloured and shrouded by mist. The city's people studied the patterns made by everything from flocks of birds to the wind-blown dust that swept the streets, and found little that was good in what they foreboded. At the busy street markets and in the meeting houses they talked openly of how much easier the Hittite yoke had been to bear compared to the Egyptian, and looked forward to the day when their new masters would be overthrown.

Nui, concerned about the growing tensions in the city, began to take Hetep more into his confidence, although there was little Hetep could recommend beyond easing the burden of the tribute, arresting Baya and promising to take a smaller share of the harvest – none of which Nui was prepared to even consider. He had, however, listened to Hetep's suspicions about Benteshina and Zuratta, and now spent his spare moments with Yuya, deep in plans to bolster the defences of both the barracks and the residency.

It was a few days after his audience with Benteshina and Hetep was out in the city, returning from conducting yet another audit of the scribal stores. He was ducking his way through the passively hostile street crowds, head down and pretending not to notice their muttered curses and threats, when he heard a babble of raised voices from around the next bend in the road. He turned the corner and found himself at the back of a crowd of city folk, all facing a granary at the road's far end. After setting his writing kit down he clambered onto a nearby wall to see what was happening.

The granary's doors were open and in front of it stood Paneb and a party of Egyptian scribes carrying measuring sticks; one held a piece of papyrus on which he must have been recording the granary's capacity. Among them was an Amurrite priest holding the purification implements he had used to make it ready to receive the grain and keep it free of vermin. They were looking frightened, and from the crowd Hetep heard cries of 'Blasphemy' and appeals for the gods Dagan and Ba'al to curse the grain so that it would choke the Egyptians.

Paneb stepped onto one of the roadside stones protecting the doorposts and in a loud voice appealed for calm. There would be enough food for all, he said; Nui had given

157

his oath that nobody would starve, even if next year's harvest did fail. But the baying of the crowd drowned out his words. Loudest of all was an Amurrite merchant Hetep recognised from the dockside storehouses. Emboldened perhaps by the absence of guards, the man rushed forwards and yanked the papyrus sheet from the scribe's grip. Then he tore it into pieces and stamped the pieces into the dirt, as if by destroying the Egyptians' records he could stop the grain being taken.

Why aren't there any soldiers here? wondered Hetep. He craned his neck, trying to search the nearby streets, but there was no sign of any troops, Egyptian or Amurrite. But he did spot Baya emerging from a side alley, seemingly deep in thought and oblivious to his surroundings. When Baya did at last notice the Amurrite mob he stopped and stared, appalled. Then he began to slink away, looking to see if anyone was watching.

Hetep jumped down and pushed his way along the edge of the crowd, shouting to draw Baya's attention.

'Go and get help. Call out the garrison and get some troops here.'

Baya gaped at him, shaking his head in disbelief. 'This shouldn't be happening,' he said. 'These people are subjugated.'

'Don't just stand there, you fool. Go to the barracks. Run!'

'Don't you speak to me like–'

'There's no time. Yuya won't listen to me – it has to be you. Get a squad of spearmen here, quickly!'

Baya took one last panicked look at the mob then fled up the street. With a snort of disgust Hetep turned and plunged into the crowd, trying to reach Paneb and give what help he could. One or two of the Amurrites struck out angrily at him, but most were still directing their ire at the Egyptian scribes and the priest.

He reached the front of the mob, where the merchant was working his followers into a frenzy. Paneb was still trying to reason with them, but his voice was beginning to crack and Hetep could see the fear in his eyes, and the scribes were looking terrified.

'Get in,' shouted Hetep, pushing one of them through the granary door. 'The rest of you, too. There's steps at the back. Get up to the roof.'

The noise was building, a hundred voices now screaming their hatred. Then a stone came flying out of the crowd and struck Paneb on his temple. He fell, and with a howl the mob surged forwards.

Hetep found himself pinned against the granary wall, blows raining down on him from all sides. He fought back, blindly; then something struck him in the ribs and the pain made him double over, breathing hard. More blows fell on him and he curled up, trying to protect his head and ribs with his arms.

He heard orders shouted in Egyptian and screams. The crowd fell away and he stood shakily, leaning against the granary for support. As space opened up around him he saw the priest, pale with shock, his face bruised and his ritual implements broken; he was trying to speak, but Hetep ignored him. He went over to Paneb and found him lying curled up, his tunic filthy from where he had been trampled. He was dead, with his skull split open and a great, sticky pool of blood congealing around his head.

Hetep turned and saw Egyptian troops dispersing the last of the crowd. Leading them was Yuya. Hetep marched over, his grief quickly turning to anger.

'Where were you?' he demanded. He grabbed the front of Yuya's tunic and shook him. 'Where were you? You're suppose to protect us!'

'Get your hands off me!'

Yuya wrenched himself free and stepped clear. Hetep lunged towards him again, his arm raised, but a pair of Egyptian solders pulled him back.

'What in the name of all the gods do you think you're doing?' shouted Yuya.

'You were meant to be here, protecting us.' Hetep pointed at Paneb's body. 'I'm holding you responsible.'

'Now just you wait,' said Yuya. 'I–'

'I've hardly seen an Egyptian soldier anywhere in this city, not for weeks. We're in the middle of an enemy kingdom, surrounded by people who hate us, and you, and all your men – where are they? In the barracks drinking beer and playing senet. You think I haven't seen it?'

Yuya started to protest but Hetep cut him off. 'Did you know a man tried to murder me last week? Zuratta – remember him? And now they've killed one of our own, in the very street!'

'You think I can have troops everywhere at once? You're not the only Egyptian in the city, and this wasn't the only work gang we had out today. We've just stopped a riot near the harbour. But you didn't see that, did you?'

Hetep took a deep breath and let it out in a long sigh. 'No, I didn't,' he said. 'I'm sorry. I should have known. But this...' He gestured around him at the granary, the priest, the terrified scribes who were only now reemerging onto the street, and lastly at Paneb's body. 'Someone has to pay.'

'Did you see who did it?'

'No, but I think I know someone who did. His name's Dashru. He's one of the merchants, a grain exporter; I've seen him before at the harbour. He was there, stirring up the crowd. He'd have seen who killed Paneb.'

Nui looked grim as he listened to Hetep's report.

'I've told you before, Yuya's a good man,' he said,
once Hetep had finished. 'He's doing his best, but he's
stretched thin. I'm sorry about Paneb, but that's one
of the risks of serving Pharaoh in a foreign land. These
people have no concept of Ma'at and it gets a bit rough.
Still, justice must be done.'

Less than an hour later Nui had the grain merchant,
Dashru, in custody. So brave when backed by a mob, the
man absolutely wept when threatened with a beating and
could not give the murderer's name quickly enough – that
of a local charcoal burner.

Yuya found him and dragged him into Nui's presence
with his arms bound behind his back. It took two men
working in tandem to beat the confession out of him and
by sunset his corpse was hanging on a scaffold above the
granary gate.

'It'll quieten them,' said Nui, when he and Hetep went
to inspect the executioner's work. 'You'll see.'

'I wonder if we got the right man,' said Hetep. The
whole incident was starting to make him feel a bit queasy.

'Does it matter as long as someone's punished for it?
Anyway, we did a divination. Our gods won't lie about
something like this.'

'No, I suppose not,' said Hetep. 'So Ma'at's been restored, eh?'

'You can spare me the sarcasm. It'll work, I tell you:
there'll be no more trouble now.'

'I think there will. Those riots today were Zuratta's
doing – I'm sure of it. Remember what I told you: Benteshina's been working up his hatred of us. I think Zu-

ratta's testing us, gauging our response. I can almost feel him watching us.'

'If that's the case Yuya would have seen him.'

'You said so yourself: he hasn't enough men. And there's still the matter of Baya. I saw him at the start of the riot. He was just standing there, watching. He's incompetent – you must have realised that by now.'

'Of course I have. But you have to understand there are certain... limits to what I can do when it comes to Baya.'

'Then let me try. Send me home and I'll get someone to listen, and then we can get him relieved. I know people who can help – Teppic, for one. And if you get rid of Baya then Ramesses might send out a replacement who can really help you here.'

'I already have someone who does that.' Nui gave him a brief smile, then turned and stalked off towards the residency.

Hetep stared after him, and it was a moment before he realised what the commissioner meant. He felt brief glow of pleasure at the compliment, quickly replaced by the gloomy realisation that he had made himself far too useful to be allowed to return to Egypt now.

CHAPTER 19

The harvest took place under the gaze of the city's gods, who sat protected from the harsh summer sun in wooden booths built atop the temple towers. The grain dance, which should have been a joyous occasion thanking Dagan and Ba'al for the gift of food, became a city-wide dirge, the people covering themselves in ashes and asking Mot to spare them, as if for years they had been in the grip of famine. Nui had the garrison out in force while the Egyptian portion was measured out and stored. Then the granaries were sealed shut and guards posted at the doors.

The city became quiet, the people tense and watchful. Benteshina kept himself hidden away, worshipping Amurru's gods and communing with his ancestors, and avoiding contact with both the Egyptians and his own people, as if content to let events run their course. Rumours of an imminent Hittite invasion swept the population and Nui sent out patrols to gather news. Hetep, at Nui's request, went to interrogate Mursili but he found the Hittite compound empty save for a pair of Amurrite guards, who told him that the Mursili and his entourage were away negotiating trade deals. He thought of asking Benteshina what he knew but realised that, even if he was granted a second audience, Amurru's scheming king would be unlikely to tell him anything useful.

It was near sunset, a week after the harvest, and he was returning from another fruitless visit to the Hittite compound when he came upon Zuratta in the street. It had been so long since their last encounter that he had grown complacent, walking openly in the city without even an occasional glance over his shoulder; now the memory of his ordeal in the storehouse surfaced and with it came fear, which quickly faded – after all, he told himself, what could the man do to him here, surrounded by all these people? He became easier still when he saw Sebeku watching from the concealment of a doorway.

'How's the eye?' he said. 'It looks painful.' The whole of Zuratta's left eye was still clouded with blood while the socket around it was heavily bruised, giving it a deep, shadowed look.

Zuratta snarled, his hands clawing as he lunged at Hetep.

'Now now,' said Hetep, darting out of the way. 'Remember, Benteshina told you to keep away from me.'

'Gloat while you can,' said Zuratta. 'Vengeance is coming, sooner than you think.'

'You haven't enough followers for that. Even your king doesn't like you.'

'And what would you know about that?' Zuratta's good eye narrowed, glinting with suspicion. 'They said you were with him, alone. What did he say about me?'

'Nothing.' Hetep remembered Benteshina's sly boast about how he had left Zuratta and his brother to die outside Irqata. How much of it did Zuratta guess? 'It was nothing about you.'

Zuratta advanced a step, his face dark with suspicion. 'What did he say?'

Sebeku stepped out of hiding and crossed the street. 'No you don't,' he said, putting a restraining hand on Zuratta's arm. 'Remember, you've been told to behave.'

Zuratta turned his glare on him. 'I remember you – from the battle. You were with him. I was told you were dead.'

'So I was,' said Sebeku with a twisted smile. 'But like Osiris I live and walk again.'

164

'Not for much longer.' Zuratta shook his arm free. 'The time of blood draws near. Teshub is coming and he will not have to wait long for his sacrifice.'

Such was the menace in Zuratta's voice that Hetep looked up at the sky, half expecting to see the vengeful god come raging down from the heavens that very instant. Instead, there was a cry of alarm from the sentries on the walls.

'What's that?' he said, staring around him.

Zuratta gave a gloating smile. 'Your days are coming to an end.'

Hetep pushed past him and ran for one of the towers in the city wall, Sebeku close behind. People were standing in the street, looking up at the battlements or talking in anxious voices; others appeared on the roofs of their houses, staring over the city.

They climbed the steps to the top of the wall. At the parapet one of the Egyptian soldiers made space for them and pointed east where, beyond the fields and meadows, the land rose in a series of wooded hills. And winding its way over the far crest and down through one of the valleys was a long column of figures. There looked to be hundreds of them, although in the fading light it was hard to make them out.

'It's an invasion,' said Hetep. 'The Hittites have come.'

'If so then their plan is to overwhelm us with waves of sheep and goats before sending their children to storm our walls,' said Sebeku. 'Will you look properly?'

Sebeku's sharp eyes had picked out what it took Hetep and the garrison troops a while longer to realise, that they were seeing a whole tribe of men, women and children, accompanied by flocks of goats and sheep, and trains of laden donkeys.

By now a few Amurrite troops had joined them and

165

they called the Egyptians fools for panicking the city folk.

'Who are they?' said Hetep.

'Habiru,' said one of the Amurrites. He spoke the name like a curse. 'It's no invasion, but they'll steal the eyes out of your head if you're not careful. We'll have to shut the gates against them and patrol the hills to guard the flocks in the uplands.'

As the sun set the newcomers set up their camp a mile from the city. One by one their dark leather tents went up, covering the fields like a pestilence, and their harsh, alien voices drifted over the city as they gave worship to gods known to the Amurrites only by rumour.

The people of Sumur spent the night in watchful fear, while on the acropolis lector priests sang prayers to Ba'al, promising the god a sacrifice of a score of bullocks if he would drive the Habiru from the city's walls. Then came the sunrise, and the fear vanished as the clearing mist revealed a camp of peaceful animal herders, with the women out collecting water from the nearby river, the children thick about them, and the men already laying out trade goods in front of the main gate. Many in the city now recognised kinfolk among the Habiru and were eager to share news about lands they might only hear about once in a decade. Mindful that he needed to make some concessions to keep the people he governed happy, Nui had Sumur's gates opened and he allowed small groups of tribesmen to enter under escort.

Hetep spent the day walking the streets and talking to the newcomers, and was unsettled to learn how many were Zuratta's kin. If Elissa was right Zuratta already had supporters in the city; now it seemed that at a stroke he could call on many hundreds more. Meanwhile Sebeku had news that was as unwelcome as it was half expected.

'Baya's been to the camp, with Zuratta,' he said. 'He

had his face covered, but I know his gait – haven't I been following him for long enough? He stayed for over an hour, talking with some of the elders.'

'Is he still there?'

'He came back this afternoon. I think he spent some time afterwards at the new arms storehouse, but I lost sight of him.'

Hetep went straight to see Nui at the residency. A pair of scribes tried to keep him out, insisting that the commissioner was busy, but he ignored them and strode past; it was a sign of the extent to which his status had increased that they did not call the troops to have him thrown out. As he neared Nui's office he heard Baya talking, his voice sharp with irritation.

'Is that so?' he was saying. 'Well I wouldn't trust Benteshina to tell me that the sky's still in place. And he's plotting with that Hittite merchant. I've told you before: you must depose him and replace him with someone we can trust.'

'Must I?' said Nui. 'And who do you recommend we appoint instead?' It sounded as if he was having trouble containing his anger.

'Zuratta. He's loyal to Egypt and would make a fitting king.'

Hetep came into the room in time to see the look of incredulity on Nui's face.

'Loyal, after we crushed his army at Irqata? Have you been at the wine store?'

'He's seen reason,' said Baya. 'He knows we're here to stay and he's decided to cooperate.'

'Cooperate, with the man who *claims* to have killed his brother? Sorry, but you've come to the wrong place if you want regime change. Now if that's all, please leave. I'm busy.'

167

Baya turned to go, and only then noticed Hetep. A look of sly understanding spread across his face and he glanced between Hetep and Nui, his head nodding.

'Now I see why you've turned against me,' he said. 'I warn you, Nui, not to let this peasant upstart dictate your policy. It is breeding that makes a man fit for command. And I advise you, for your own good, to do as I say.'

Nui seemed to tower up like a thundercloud and his hands twitched. 'Get out. Out, is say! Before I forget myself.'

Baya shrugged. 'You'll see.' He turned and sauntered out.

Nui exhaled. 'One day he'll push me too far,' he muttered. 'And I suspect I'll regret it more than he. Now what do you want?'

'I was going to tell you I've uncovered more evidence of Baya's disloyalty, although after what he's just said I don't think I need it. He all but admitted to conspiring with Zuratta.'

'I can't condemn him on the strength of his preferences about who should be king.'

'Then what about this? My chariot driver, Sebeku, saw him with Zuratta. They went to the camp outside the city. Some of those tribesmen there are Zuratta's kin; they may owe him favours. So now Zuratta has the army he needs for a rebellion.'

'I see.' Nui passed a hand over his head and exhaled. 'Gods, what a mess.'

'You should have the Habiru searched at the city gates in case they try to bring in weapons.'

'Should I now? First Baya and now you. I'm certainly getting my orders today. It's just as well I've already told the gate guards to do just that. You think I don't know my job?'

'I'm sorry,' said Hetep. 'I didn't mean...'

'Forget it. It's nice have someone agree with me for once. As I said, not one of this Habiru rabble with get in here armed. And if they still want to kick up a fuss, let them try pitting bare hands against spears and khopeshes.'

'Zuratta could still get support from the city's soldiers. *They're* armed, at least, and a lot of them hate us for taking all that grain.'

'I can't disarm them all. No, we'll be alright. I'm turning the barracks and the residency into fortresses – Yuya's helping with that. There is something else I want done, though. They tell me Mursili's back from his trading expedition, or wherever it was he went. Talk to him, see if he'll tell you anything about Hittite troop movements. He'll lie to you, of course, but he might let something out.'

Hetep hesitated. 'So I'm an envoy now, am I, and not just a scribe?'

'You'll keep your station for now, for appearance's sake. Understand?'

Hetep nodded, trying to stop himself from smiling at this new change of fortune.

A short walk from the residency took him to the Hittite compound: a pair of tall stone buildings flanking a courtyard, and all enclosed by a mudbrick wall. The gate was open, and blocking it was a Hittite with brutish features and scars left by weapon cuts on his forearms.

'Good day to you,' said Hetep. 'I'd like to see Mursili. He knows me.'

'He's out, on business,' said the Hittite in thickly accented Canaanite. 'Go now. Go away!'

'I know he's here. He was seen earlier.' Hetep moved to peer past the Hittite and into the courtyard.

'And I tell you no! Now go away, or I break your head.'

Hetep eyed the Hittite, who was shorter but much stockier than he.

'Look, there's no need to be difficult,' he said and tried to push past. 'If you just–'

'No. Leave now!' Moving with the speed of a striking cobra the Hittite grabbed him, twisted and threw him to the floor.

Hetep stood, rubbing a graze on his elbow.

'It's like that, is it?' he said, and charged the Hittite, his head down. They locked together, feet skidding in the dirt as they pushed each other back and forth. Hetep managed to hook a leg around the Hittite's calf and was about to trip him when someone grabbed him by the arm.

'What in the Storm God's name do you think you're doing?'

The newcomer pulled Hetep and the Hittite apart. It was Mursili, glaring and angry.

'Is this how a representative of the great Ramesses conducts himself?'

'Sorry,' muttered Hetep, reddening. 'I just got a bit carried away.'

'And Tagi,' said Mursili to the Hittite sentry. 'Where are your manners? This man is a friend!'

The Hittite, Tagi, turned his glower on Mursili. 'The Egyptian was rude. He needed manners taught.'

'But not like that. Apologise, and we shall say no more about it.' There was a hardness in Mursili's voice that Hetep had not heard before.

Tagi mumbled something that may just have been an expression of regret.

'That's better,' said Mursili. 'Remember, these people are not our enemies – despite what others might tell you.' He smoothed his hair and tugged his robe straight. 'And now, my dear Hetep, to what do we owe the pleasure of your visit?'

'I've come to ask if there's a Hittite army on its way here,' said Hetep. 'Half the city seems to think so.'

'I have absolutely no idea what you're talking about,' said Mursili. He glanced up and down the road. 'But let's not stand out here gossiping. Come, we shall go inside and talk like civilised men.'

They ended up in a room furnished with couches and decorated with brightly patterned wall hangings; Hetep wondered what Nui would have thought of such luxury. A servant brought him a cup of iced wine. It was sweet and well watered, and he drank it thirstily.

'Benteshina has the ice brought down from the mountains,' said Mursili. 'I hope you find it sufficient recompense for my colleague's roughness.'

'It's good,' said Hetep. He rarely got to drink wine at home because of its expense and he gladly accepted a refill.

'Now what's this you say about an army?' said Mursili.

'I thought you might be able to tell me.'

Mursili raised his eyebrows a fraction. 'I doubt very much that my king is leading one here. From what I hear the royal army is rather hard pressed. The Assyrians are causing trouble again, not to mention the Gaskans and the Arzawites. Besides, Hatti and Egypt are still at peace.'

'But for how long? Amurru was a Hittite vassal until we arrived with Ramesses. Don't you want it back?'

'Perhaps you do not know, but we are a people who do not lightly wage war. We prefer order and good governance. It encourages trade, which benefits us all.'

'I had no idea you revered Ma'at,' said Hetep, surprised.

171

'Another new word. What does that one mean?'

'Ma'at is a goddess. Her name also means order, justice and stability – all that's good in the world. It's what we desire the most in Egypt, and what we have when the pharaoh's strong. But you're foreign – you're supposed to be a threat to Ma'at.'

'Am I really?' said Mursili, and laughed. 'Yet as you see, it's not just you Egyptians who desire a peaceful life.'

They drank and Mursili refilled the cups, splashing wine over the table. Hetep watched his flushed, cheerful face and realised that he was already half drunk. Let's see what he really knows, he thought. 'So about this Hittite army that's on its way...'

Mursili shook his head. 'I tell you, there is no such thing.'

'But what if it's a surprise attack? You wouldn't tell me, would you?' Hetep watched Mursili's face over the top of his wine cup.

'If my king wished to wage war he would declare it, not come in secret, like an assassin. Our peoples have a treaty, sworn before all the gods of Hatti, and to renege on such an agreement without just cause is a sin that would be punished severely. Long ago King Suppiluliuma, before he became a god, violated the terms of a similar treaty with you Egyptians, and the plague our gods sent as punishment killed both him and his son, and left Hatti empty for a generation.'

'So no attack?'

'No attack.' Mursili finished his wine, waited for Hetep to do the same, and again refilled the cups. 'Besides, we can regain Amurru by other means,' he said, his voice slurring. 'Your pharaoh will find it far too costly to maintain a garrison so far from his home. But not so Hatti. Soon the natural order will restore itself – you'll see.'

172

'Not once we've captured Kadesh it won't,' said Hetep. 'I don't know who controls it now, but they're in for a bit of a shock when Ramesses leads the army there. And after that we'll control the entire east-west trade route, and there'll be wealth for a whole division of new troops.'

Mursili belched and looked at his cup, frowning. 'I don't think this wine quite agrees with me. It feels as if there's a fire rising from my belly. Perhaps you'd better finish it.'

Hetep filled his cup with the last of the wine.

'Better get some practice in for the festival, I suppose,' he said. 'Mind you, we won't be drinking much.'

'The El festival, you mean? I understand there's to be a lot of wine.'

'Nui'll see us right. He says he can outdrink any man living. Besides, we'll be careful: one cup each, that's all. Are you going?'

'Oh, no. The Hittites are a familiar presence in Amurru and are well known to El. After all, we were here long before you.'

For a moment Hetep wondered if Mursili was making a threat but one look at his open, wine-reddened face allayed his fears. Such a decent fellow, he thought – for a foreigner. Not like that duplicitous reptile Benteshina.

'Yes, a very long while indeed,' went on Mursili with a sigh. 'It grieves me when I think of all the festivals I've missed back home. Especially the Crocus Festival – the one we hold in the spring.' His eyes grew distant as his thoughts turned inwards.

'Tell me about it,' said Hetep.

'There are hymns and processions of gods, drinking and laughter, and women in flowers and woolen tunics dancing the rite of sowing. The king himself presides over the sacrifices, you know. On such rituals hinge the fate

173

of our empire, for if they were to fail, so would we as a people.'

'Can that happen?'

Mursili talked on, as if he had not heard. 'For the second year now my duties have kept me away from home and I have missed it. They say that this year some of the animals used for the auguries were sick – black spots on the livers, malformed lungs and spleens, that sort of thing. Next year the festival will have to be lengthened and the rites repeated to undo the harm. And the king has to attend until they're all done, even if enemies are crossing the border.'

'Are your gods really so harsh?'

'Harsh?' Mursili looked at him and frowned. 'My dear Hetep, of course not! They give us so much, and have made us the strongest people in the world. A thousand gods we worship, and do you know why? Because we have absorbed such a great many people into our empire, and with them their gods. Can you Egyptians boast of worshipping so many?'

Hetep shook his head, smiling at Mursili's earnest pride in his people's achievements, none of which could possibly match Egypt's.

'Without the Storm God's favour a king, no matter how large his army or how skilled he is at war, can only be defeated. But with it he is invincible. Although I do admit the price of piety can be high. Next year will not be the first time a king sets out on campaign late because of a festival. And would you believe that one year a king had to break off a campaign early to complete a ritual back home?'

'I don't think Ramesses would ever do that.'

'No? Then perhaps your king does not care much for his gods.'

There was a long silence.

'You were saying about next year...' prompted Hetep.

'Hm? Oh, only that I fear that when my king sets out late the Assyrians, or one of our other enemies, might take advantage of us.' Mursili frowned at his cup and wiped a hand over his face. 'Perhaps, on reflection, I shouldn't have told you that. Still, that's the way of it.'

'No, it's all right,' said Hetep. 'It's just the wine.' He put his empty cup down. 'Well, I guess I should go.'

'I'll have Tagi see you back. It's getting dark, and there's Habiru about in the streets. And this wine is rather strong.'

Hetep protested but Mursili was very insistent and in the end he could not refuse. As he walked back, a little unsteady on his feet and with the brooding Tagi a couple of steps behind him, he smiled when he remembered how quickly Mursili had become drunk. Perhaps they only had beer back in Hatti and he was not used to anything stronger, he thought. The poor man would never have said so much about his king and the spring festival if he had been sober. Hetep resolved not to embarrass him by mentioning it on their next meeting.

'An interesting evening,' he said to Tagi outside the dormitory.

Nui's scouts returned without finding a trace of a Hittite army anywhere within the borders of Amurru. When the news spread the nature of the rumours flying about the city changed. Now the Habiru were Hittite mercenaries, sent to infiltrate Sumur; worse, the other Canaanite cities to the south had thrown off the Egyptian yoke and declared loyalty to the long-dead kingdom of Mitanni. Then it was the Assyrians who were the threat; known

175

mostly by hearsay as a cruel and warlike people, they were said to have overrun the Hittites' eastern provinces and were poised to invade Amurru. But as the El festival approached the rumours died away, and the city's mood became one of watchful expectancy.

'I keep seeing Zuratta in the streets,' said Hetep. He was in Nui's office helping with the accounts. 'He struts around like he owns the place and more of his supporters have slipped into the city. And Yuya can't watch them all.'

'Let them swagger,' said Nui. 'Without weapons, what can they do?'

'I suppose it's too late to write home and get some reinforcements.'

'I've already done it,' said Nui. He eyed Hetep as if defying him to make a comment. 'But they won't be here until after the festival.'

Hetep realised how much the admission had cost Nui in injured pride. 'It was the right thing to do,' he said. 'Ask for help, I mean.'

Immediately Nui bridled. 'I didn't ask for your approval, or for your sympathy either.'

'I'm sorry. I meant no slight.'

'No, I suppose not.' Nui exhaled and rubbed his face. 'We'll make do with what we've got. Thanks to Yuya they'll need a siege train to get into the residency, and the whole garrison is going to be mustered and under arms, all night. I'm even posting troops outside the hall where the drinking's happening, so if there's any trouble there we'll crush it at its source. I've told Benteshina it's an honour guard to welcome the god as he comes down from the temple.'

'He didn't object?'

'He had no choice,' growled Nui. 'This is still our city,

after all.'

'Do you trust him?'

'No. But he's a frightened man. He needs Egypt's armies to protect him – from the Hittites for one thing, now we've made him turn his back on them. And he's sworn loyalty to Ramesses, and in front of his own gods, too – the kind of oath that'll kill a man if he even thinks of breaking it.'

'Just be careful at the festival,' said Hetep. 'The wine's going to be strong and you're going to have to drink something.'

'Don't worry about me. There isn't an Asiatic alive who can match me cup for cup with wine.'

'But can you keep up with a god?'

'I shall relish the challenge,' said Nui with a grim smile. 'Then once this is over and we've shown these people that their god has to accept us, we'll kick this Habiru rabble out and start clamping down a bit more.'

Chapter 20

It was the day of the El festival and Hetep was standing on the barracks roof and searching the crowds as they assembled along the processional way.

Since midday the city's people had been gathering in the streets and alleys, the richest clad in embroidered robes, others in tunics of red- and blue-dyed wool, and all wearing wreaths of summer flowers; many were passing wineskins from hand to hand and the air was filled with laughter and snatches of song. And for much of that time Hetep had been scanning the rows of happy, shining faces, looking in vain for a sign of Zuratta or his Habiru kinsmen.

An hour before sunset a horn sounded from the acropolis and all eyes turned to the temple of El; in the expectant hush the priests' songs could be heard drifting down from the temple towers. All at once the bronze bands on the acropolis gates caught the sunlight and blazed like strips of fire. Then the gates swung open and the city's people in their thousands gave a great shout of joy as El, the Father of Humanity, appeared. He was a huge figure made of wood, ivory and gold, wearing a robe and garlanded with flowers; seated on a throne, he swayed ponderously as his bearers carried him down the roadway.

Hetep ran down the steps to street level and went out into the crowds. He worked his way up the hill to halfway along the processional route, then back down along the roads near the barracks, but still he could find no trace of Zuratta's men. By the time he had made his way to the residency it was late and Nui was waiting with the Egyptian scribes and officials. A squad of assault troops stood by.

'Now we're all here,' said Nui, with a pointed look at Hetep, 'perhaps we can start.'

'Sorry. I got stuck in the crowd. I've been out in the streets, searching. There's no Habiru – not one. They were everywhere this morning.'

'So?' said Nui. 'They've no weapons. What harm can they do?'

'Why are they missing? It bothers me.'

From the shadows Baya appeared and stood at Nui's side.

'One cannot expect to find a handful of vagabonds in a city of ten thousand people,' he said, his voice scathing. He turned to Nui. 'We should go now. El will soon be in the drinking hall and should not be kept waiting. Remember, this rite is important.'

'So I've been told,' said Nui. He cast a considering eye down the street, where Egyptian troops were manning a barricade, and up at the file of archers standing on the barracks roof. Finally his gaze settled on the soldiers of their escort and he nodded, satisfied.

'Right, let's go,' he said. 'Scribes at the back, troops at the front. And keep your heads up. Remember, our gods are stronger than theirs, and we own this city.'

They marched through the back streets to avoid the revellers and reached a plaza to the north of the royal palace, where stood the hall that was to hold the opening banquet: a squat, multi-columned building abutting the palace wall. Its main door was open, but inside there was little to see except a fog of smoke shot through with flickering orange firelight. Beside it stood a file of Amurrite spearmen.

At an order from Nui the Egyptian infantry deployed into two lines, flanking the doorway. Only once they were

179

properly in position did he turn to greet the Amurrite contingent sent to welcome them.

'At last!' said one of the Amurrites, in a tone that had Nui grinding his teeth. 'El will be here in moments.'

The noise from the crowd grew and the god came into sight, far across the plaza. He had lost his flowers and was spattered with wine, flung at him by his adoring worshippers. The Amurrite soldiers hurried forwards, clearing the way for him to be taken in through the hall's doorway, and after a short wait the Egyptians were permitted to do the same.

The hall was dominated by a vast wooden table laden with jugs, goblets and plates. Down one side a row of deer and aurochs carcasses were roasting over a fire pit, the flames sending out great clouds of greasy smoke. Benteshina and his courtiers were already present, seated at the far end; the king's face and arms were spotted with blood from where he had lead the sacrifices of the animals. There was no sign of the god.

The Egyptians were shown to their seats. Nui was placed beside the king, with the senior scribes nearby; Hetep, officially still the most junior, ended up by the entrance where, mercifully, he could feel a draught of cool air from outside. He pitied his compatriots, most of whom were closer to the fires. He looked from one anxious, sweating face to the next, and it was a moment before he realised that Baya was missing. Now how did he slip away? he wondered.

A noise like the crashing of a sheet of metal distracted him and at the far end of the hall a pair of huge bronze doors opened to reveal El, enthroned and gazing down at them from the head of his own table. Someone had wiped the wine stains from his face and had dressed him in a fresh robe, and before him had been placed a great silver goblet, a cubit across at the rim; a priest was already filling it with wine. The light from the fires cast moving shadows over the god's face, animating his features, and his eyes shone as if in anticipation of the revelry to come.

Slaves carved off great hunks of venison and piled them onto the plates. Then the wine goblets were filled – the Amurrites' by ladle from a stone basin near the god's table, the Egyptians' from tall, thin pottery jars painted with images of squid and fish.

'We drink both to honour the god and to emulate him,' said Benteshina to Nui. 'But this is also a chance for us to meet and discuss the ordering of the city. Wine loosens the tongue and brings out the truth.'

He raised a brimming goblet, drained it in a few gulps and banged it down on the table. Silence followed, in which the Amurrites looked on expectantly. Nui cleared his throat, shot warning glances at the other Egyptians, and sipped from his own goblet.

'Excellent,' said Benteshina.

A group of musicians filed into the hall and began to play, and soon a steady hum of conversation was coming from the Amurrite end of the table. The Egyptians, following Nui's lead, drank sparingly, and remained silent and watchful. Hetep, feeling thirsty in the heat, took a swig. He found the wine refreshing but unusually tart, with an odd aftertaste he could not place. Frowning, he pushed his goblet away.

The music grew louder and the Amurrites drank as if racing each other to intoxication. By now Benteshina was deep in a rambling, largely one-sided conversation with Nui, whose only contribution was to grunt a few monosyllabic replies. More wood was heaped onto the fires and the air grew so thick that Hetep could only dimly see El and his attendant priests. Where in all this was the test? he wondered. What was the god looking for in us?

A slave came to fill the Egyptians' goblets but Nui shook his head and covered his with a hand. Benteshina frowned, the music stopped, the talk died away and a shadow passed across El's face.

'Is the wine not to your liking?' said the king, his voice slurred.

In the silence the flames in the fire pit sounded like distant thunder.

'It's fine,' said Nui. 'Just a bit sharp. But perhaps I'll have a little more.'

'The god insists that you do. All of you.'

Nui raised his cup and took a sip, yet still El and his worshippers looked on in disapproving silence. Nui hesitated, then drained his goblet; following his lead, the other Egyptians, including Hetep, did the same. There was a collective sigh from the king's courtiers and the tension vanished. The music resumed, and now El seemed to be smiling at both Amurrites and Egyptians alike.

The banquet went on, with the Amurrites eating sparingly and drinking copiously. Benteshina had resumed his talk with Nui, but with the other conversations growing increasingly loud Hetep could not hear a word. Then, prompted by some sign that Hetep could not detect, all fell silent once more while Benteshina and his god waited for the Egyptians to drink, and only once they had done so did the hubbub resume.

Time passed, although it was becoming impossible to tell how quickly. Every now and then a lull fell, during which Nui and the others drank with increasing abandon; whatever impulse drove the timing of the rite Hetep could not fathom. The wine was making him feel sick and a strange fuzziness was gathering at the corners of his vision; furthest from the god that he was, nobody saw him as each time he now tipped his portion out under the table.

By now the Amurrites were bellowing tuneless hymns to El or laughing in high-pitched giggles. Nui was sweating and frowning at his goblet; beside him Merimose sat unmoving with his face on the table, while another of the scribes slid to the floor, to be rescued and propped against the wall by the slaves. This is no ordinary wine, thought Hetep, as his stomach churned and his head span. Something was very wrong and he had to warn Nui, but his whole body was numb and he found he could not speak. Then movement under the table distracted him; it sounded like a dog, snuffling around for scraps, but when he looked there was nothing there.

At last the rite was over. Benteshina stood, swaying like a tree in the wind, with dribbles of wine running down his face.

'El is pleased,' he said thickly. 'Now go. It's time... time for...' He belched. 'Secret rites. Not for you, just us. No outsiders.'

The Egyptians stood up – all except one who pitched over backwards, to be caught by the ever-attendant slaves. Nui lead them out, his knees sagging; Hetep felt the floor shifting underneath him as he walked.

'Do you need help?' asked one of the slaves.

'No,' said Hetep. His tongue seemed to fill his mouth. 'Manage... I can manage.'

Outside, the cool air hit Hetep like a blow from a club. They must have been drinking for hours, he realised, for the night covered the city like fog. The Egyptian soldiers were still at their posts and he heard their officer reporting to Nui. The latter swayed as he stared back, uncomprehending, then staggered, retching, and were it not for the officer's quick reactions he would have fallen.

'Need sleep,' mumbled Nui and he staggered off to-

183

wards the residency. Most of his staff followed, but a few sank to the floor, and the soldiers rushed to help them.

Hetep looked back at the hall. Benteshina was gone and the slaves were clearing the table, but El was still there, smiling at him. Then the bronze doors closed.

A wave of nausea swept over him, and with it came a nameless feeling of dread. All at once he knew that he had to escape from the plaza. He stumbled away, heedless of the shouts of the soldiers and the pleas of the stricken scribes behind him.

Chapter 21

The night air was heavy with the reek of incense and spilled wine, and beyond the plaza the streets were packed with men and women, all laughing wildly or roaring out hymns to El. He tried to push his way through but a half-naked man wearing a wreath of jasmine flowers shoved him and he nearly went down under the feet of a ring of dancing women. Staggering, he fetched up against a wall and stood, clutching a buttress for support, while the starlit sky wheeled above him and sweat ran down his face. He forced himself to think. Where was he going? To the barracks, of course; something was very wrong and he needed to summon the troops. He pushed himself away from the wall and reeled off down the street.

Faces swam in and out of his vision, some shouting ecstatically, others singing, and many with wine running from their mouths. His sandals crunched on bits of pottery – empty jugs and food bowls, thrown aside and trampled into fragments by hundreds of feet. Again someone shoved him and this time he fell, and felt only dully the pottery shards digging into his palms and knees. Then he looked up and saw looming over him a robed, bearded man, his mouth set in a sneer.

'I have waited a long time for this day,' said the man. It was Zuratta, his face bruised and his left eye a single, crimson orb, glowing like charcoal in a fire.

Hetep stumbled to his feet and fled, back past the ring of dancing women. He looked back but saw no sign of Zuratta following. He kept going, sliding along a wall for support, until a figure ahead blocked his way – tall, robed and bearded, laughing a cruel laugh; Zuratta again, for sure. But how? Hetep wiped his hand over his eyes and looked again, and realised the man was just another reveller, still laughing as he offered wine to a companion.

Hetep's head began to clear. Had the first man also been one of the revellers and not Zuratta? He tried to remember what he saw. What was in that wine? He thanked whichever god was watching over him that he had drunk so little. But Nui, and most of the others, had been closer to El and had been unable to tip the stuff away. It was no wonder most of them could barely stand by the end of the ceremony.

He moved now through the less-crowded back streets, still heading for the barracks. The way was narrow, the closely packed houses blocking out the sky; he rounded a corner, and almost collided with a band of Habiru jogging along the street towards him. They were armed with Egyptian khopeshes and axes, and the torch light reflected like red sparks in their eyes. There was nowhere to escape to and he stood, numbed by wine and shock, as they came straight for him... and kept on going, jostling him as they passed.

'Not so quick, brothers,' shouted one of the men at the back. 'Remember, until they have the gates open we're to wait, and block Barley Street.'

Hetep turned, astonished to still be alive, and watched the Habiru as they turned and vanished down a side road, heading away from the Egyptian barracks. Barley Street; why was the name so familiar? Then he remembered it was one of the main approaches to the royal palace, and all at once he understood. The revolt had started, there was no doubt of that, and Zuratta was about to take his revenge – but not on the men of Egypt, as Benteshina had planned, but on Benteshina himself, the man who had betrayed him. And with both Nui and the king either drugged or drunk on wine there was nobody to lead the defence of the palace.

He ran, the sweat now feeling cold on his skin. He heard screaming in the distance – or was it just the cries of drunken revellers? And was that the tang of wood smoke, or just the smell of the torches and braziers that had lit the processional way for El? A wave of nausea came over him and he stopped, leaning against a wall and breathing hard. Then he vomited, copiously and with barely any effort, and when he finished his head was clearer than it had been all evening.

At a plaza he met a squad of Amurrite troops marching up the road to the temple district and recognised Hiziru among them.

'Wait,' shouted Hetep. 'You're going the wrong way. Get to the palace – Zuratta's men are going there.'

Hiziru looked puzzled. 'But I am to be at the acropolis gates to welcome El at the end of the festival.'

'Where's the rest of the city's solders?'

'They were dismissed an hour ago and are at home, celebrating with their wives,' he said. 'It is, after all, festival time.'

'Listen to me,' said Hetep. 'El's safe. In fact, all the gods are safe tonight. Even me and the other Egyptians are safe. But Benteshina's in danger. Zuratta's going to kill him.'

'But El–'

'The god can look after himself. And I'm sure he'll be happy to reward the man who helped to save his king. But you'll have to hurry. There's armed Habiru storming the palace.'

'Me, save the king?' Hiziru spoke slowly, as if his mind could not grasp the concept.

Hetep wanted to shake the man but instead forced

himself to speak calmly. 'You heard what Elissa said. I'm the one destined to help the city, remember? Her goddess Anat told her. And I swear that what I say is true. If Zuratta's revolt succeeds he'll kill Benteshina and Elissa, and anyone who's loyal to them. Do you doubt that?'

'No... no, I do not,' said Hiziru, the uncertainty clearing from his voice. 'What is it you want me to do?'

'Round up as many soldiers as you can find and meet me here. I'll be back soon.'

'Where are you going?'

'To try to get our garrison moving. And to find some weapons.'

Egyptian troops were blocking the street but their commander recognised Hetep and let him pass. More spearmen were stationed outside the barracks, while on the roof the archers were still posted, watching over the city.

Hetep strode up to the soldiers at the gate.

'Where's Yuya?' he demanded.

'Inside. Why, what do you want?'

But Hetep was already marching down the entrance passage, roaring Yuya's name. He burst into the eating hall to be met by a row of astonished faces.

'Where's Yuya?' he said again.

A moment later the commander emerged from the adjoining room. His mouth was full and he had a beer jug in his hand.

'What are you doing here?' he said, spitting bits of food.

'Your men are in the wrong place,' said Hetep. 'The Habiru are heading for the palace. We're needed there.'

Yuya chewed for a long time, staring at Hetep. Then he swallowed.

'Get back to your ink pots, scribe,' he said. 'Nui told me to guard the barracks and the residency, and that's what I'm doing. I don't take orders from you.'

'Nui's too drunk to help. So are the others – someone drugged the wine. There's only us now.'

'If anyone's drunk it's you.' Yuya set his jug down. 'But I can see I'll get no peace until I have a look. Come with me.'

He pushed Hetep out ahead of him and once in the street called up to one of the archers on the roof. 'What do you see?'

'There's some firelight down near the harbour and there's more noise than before,' said the archer. 'It might be something.'

'Another torch procession,' sneered Yuya. 'These Asiatics do like to see stuff burn. And we've been hearing their racket all night. Now if it's all the same to you I'd like to get back to my food.'

'Just listen, will you?' shouted Hetep, growing desperate. 'It's Zuratta – he's trying to kill Benteshina.'

'Why in the name of Montu would he do that? They're both Amurrites!'

'Gods, what's the use?' said Hetep. 'At least give me some weapons. Even a dagger would help.'

'Scribes aren't allowed to go armed, you know that. Now get out of my sight, or I'll have you dragged away by your nose.'

There was only one other person Hetep could turn to for help and he ran to the scribes' dormitory. The whole place, including the annexe, was in darkness and it looked deserted, and he was beginning to despair when he saw Sebeku appear at the doorway.

'My, you're a noisy one when you're angry,' said the driver. 'I could hear you shouting at Yuya even from here.'

189

'Zuratta's men are heading for the palace and Yuya won't believe me. We have to do something ourselves.'

'Then it's good I found you these.' Sebeku ducked behind the doorframe and came back with a bow, a khopesh and quiver full of arrows.

'Don't tell me you've been stealing,' said Hetep with a smile.

'Not at all. I'm on the garrison's ration strength, remember? So I have a right to them. Even the scribe at the armoury agreed, after a little persuasion.'

Hetep took the bow and strung it, then buckled on the quiver and grabbed the khopesh. As he armed himself all his fears and anxieties fell away. He smiled as he ran a thumb across the khopesh's blade, feeling its sharpness.

'Thank you,' he said. 'Now I must go: Hiziru's waiting. If I'm not back–'

'You think you're leaving me behind?' Again Sebeku vanished behind the doorway and returned with a shield and another armful of weapons.

'But you've been ill. You should stay here and rest.'

'Yes, I know. But it's my job to protect you – from folly as much as arrows. Even when we're on foot.' He hefted his shield. 'Shall we go?'

They moved fast, almost invisible in the shadowy alleys and streets. As they ran Hetep felt the quiver bumping against his back. He thought how much easier it is to be in a chariot, with everything carried by the car.

'Where's the rest of the troops?' said Sebeku. 'Are we storming the palace on our own?'

'Yuya's too stubborn to help. But we've got some of the locals on our side. See?'

Hiziru was waiting for them at the end of the street. He had a bare dozen soldiers with him – a couple of spearmen with armour and shields, the rest unarmoured

190

archers.

'Is this it?' said Hetep.

'It was all I could find,' said Hiziru. 'Even the men assigned duty this night are nowhere to be seen.'

'Then we must make do with what we have,' said Sebeku. 'Now what's that?'

They all heard it at the same time: the rattle and tramp of marching troops, coming from the direction of the acropolis. They barely had time to form a battle line when a group of Amurrite soldiers came into view, lead by Elissa. Her face stood out pale in the darkness and in one hand she held an axe.

'What are you doing here?' said Hetep. 'And what's that for?' He pointed at the axe.

'These men are from the temple guard,' she said. 'The goddess told me my brother's in danger.' She held up the axe. 'And did not Anat take up arms when Mot killed her brother Ba'al?' Her words were brave but she looked afraid – with good reason, thought Hetep: if Zuratta managed to seize control of the city her life would be quickly, and painfully, over.

'Had we not better get to the palace?' said Sebeku.

They ran, Hiziru, Hetep and Sebeku leading. By now many of the city's people had drunk themselves unconscious; others were leaning against the walls and vomiting up the wine as freely as they had drunk it down. With the noise of revelry lessened Hetep was sure now he could hear the sound of fighting.

They met a courtier running up the street. He looked sober, but his eyes were wild with panic and he careered blindly into Hetep.

Hiziru grabbed him by the sleeve. 'Wait! What news from the palace?'

'All dead,' said the man. 'The king, everyone – dead.'

'Dead? How so?'

Hiziru shook the courtier but the man broke free and went reeling up the street, shouting, 'Long life to Zuratta, king of Amurru!'

'It's a lie,' said Elissa, with a certainty that she could not possibly have felt. 'Even so, such a claim might unsettle the less loyal in the city. We had best get my brother out in the open so his subjects can see him.'

At the main plaza people lay among the discarded jugs and scraps of food, insensible with wine and heedless of the rats crawling over them. Near the palace gate stood a cordon of armed Habiru tribesmen; behind them more were clustered at the gate itself and Hetep could hear the periodic crash of a ram as they tried to batter the doors open.

'We cannot fight our way through all that,' said Hiziru.

'We don't need to,' said Elissa. 'There's another way in. But to use it we shall have to get past these men unseen.'

They hid, watching the tribesmen at the gates and waiting for a chance to move. A drunken cheer sounded from one of the side roads and as they looked the god El wobbled into view. His drinking over, he was being carried back along the processional way to his home in the acropolis, escorted by a band of priests beating on drums. Around him clustered a mob of worshippers, a hundred strong, perhaps all that remained in the city able to stand. They were singing hymns as they stumbled and danced, and as they jostled the bearers El lurched drunkenly from side to side on his throne.

'The goddess watches over us this night,' said Elissa with a smile. 'Follow me.'

They waited until El and his entourage were well out into the middle of the plaza before leaving cover, bent over to avoid the tribesmen's gaze. The chief priest looked at the Amurrite soldiers goggle-eyed and when he saw Elissa his mouth hung open. She spoke to him, while Hetep and the others wormed their way in among the worshippers, and the god swung around as the bearers turned towards Barley Street.

Someone shoved a jug of wine under Hetep's nose. Another made a grab for his quiver and he felt hands snatching at his khopesh, but now Sebeku was beside him, pushing them back with his shield. He drank the wine – a few quick sips – then passed it on, and as the Amurrites started a new hymn he joined in as best he could.

Perhaps it was El himself who clouded their enemies' eyes, or perhaps it was just the thickness of the crowd, but they escaped the tribesmen's vigilance and left the procession halfway along the street.

'Here we are,' said Elissa, after leading them to the concealed postern door she and Hetep had used before. She banged on the wood with her fist and shouted, and from inside came a muffled reply. Evidently the speaker recognised Elissa's voice, for there came the sound of bolts being drawn back and the door creaked open.

One by one they squeezed through the tiny doorway. Waiting for them on the other side was a trio of frightened-looking palace guardsmen. At the sight of Elissa and Hiziru their faces cleared.

'Come with us,' commanded Elissa. 'The king is in need.'

They ran, Elissa guiding them, the clatter of their armour and weapons loud in the narrow corridors. Faintly they could hear the pounding of the ram against the main gate. Then came a splintering of wood and a roar of triumph; 'The gate!' said Hiziru, and they quickened their pace. The cries of the Habiru grew louder and Hetep recognised Zuratta's voice exhorting his men to kill anyone they found. Then came an answering challenge and the clashing of weapons, this time from somewhere ahead.

More corridors, and then they were in a courtyard with a pillared colonnade down one side, the rest open to the starlit sky. A dozen bodies, both Amurrite soldiers and Habiru, lay scattered on the flagstones where they had been cut down in a running fight, and all was still and silent. They passed through an archway, Hetep and Hiziru taking the lead, turned a corner, and the silence was abruptly broken as they ran into a pitched battle.

A mob of Habiru was fighting to gain entry to the royal apartments, yelling curses and calling Benteshina's name in voices like carrion birds'; opposing them, and blocking the doorway, was a squad of palace guardsmen. There was no time for Hetep to use his bow; raising his khopesh he charged, Hiziru and the Amurrites close behind, and with cries of alarm and sudden fear the tribesmen turned to meet them.

Hetep hacked down the nearest with his khopesh. A spear came stabbing towards him; Sebeku darted forwards, his shield up, and batted it aside before driving his dagger into its owner's midriff. They pressed forwards, the Amurrites close around them, and Hetep felt the god Montu guiding his arm and banishing his fatigue as he cut and stabbed at his enemies. Then, in moments, there were no more Habiru standing, and the only sound was the groans of the wounded.

Hetep wiped the sweat from his face and looked around him, his pulse slowing as the god's fire drained from his body. Twenty tribesmen lay dead or dying, and six of the Amurrites were down. A pair of the palace guardsmen was tending to the latter while another came over to Hiziru. He saw Elissa and stopped, amazed.

'What in Ba'al's name is this? The princess, here. And an Egyptian...'

'There's no time to explain,' said Elissa. 'Where's my brother?' She looked wild and the blade of her axe was dripping blood.

'Safe in the inner chamber. Not one of these pigs' sons got past us.'

Hetep made a quick search of the Habiru corpses.

'Zuratta's not here,' he said. 'It's a diversion. There must be another way to the royal apartments.'

The guardsman hesitated. 'There's a hidden passage. But no outsider would know of it.'

'Zuratta does,' said Hetep. 'Or else where is he?'

They pressed on deeper into the palace, until again they heard the noise of battle ahead, and came upon Zuratta and a group of his followers assaulting a line of guardsmen. Among the defenders were Tagi and Mursili; both were shieldless and unarmored, but they held swords and were hacking desperately at the tribesmen. No time to wonder about that, thought Hetep, as he charged forwards.

He saw Zuratta stabbing at the defenders and Tagi fell, blood pouring from a wound in his thigh. Then one of the Habiru turned to meet him, his shield up and spear poised to strike. Hetep ducked, hooked the end of his khopesh over the lip of the shield and pulled. As the tribesman staggered, off balance, Hetep thrust his arm forwards and sent the tip of the khopesh into his face. Then he started laying about him, slicing at arms, heads – any exposed flesh he could see – while Sebeku stood beside him, protecting them both with his shield.

Mursili was shouting from somewhere in the melee and Hetep fought his way towards him. Another tribesman fell and he drove forwards, his sandals sliding on blood,

195

and there in front of him was Zuratta, jerking his spear from a guardsman's writhing body, and with only Mursili now opposing him. Beyond, at the back of the room, stood Benteshina, swaying drunkenly, his eyes wide with a mixture of horror and disbelief.

Zuratta stabbed with his spear, slicing through Mursili's sword arm. As he drew the spear back for the killing thrust Hetep flung his khopesh, point first. It caught Zuratta on the side of his head, slicing into his ear, and the spear went wide. Tagi was still down but he had managed to crawl over to Zuratta and now he grabbed his legs. Zuratta staggered, off balance; then a pair of Amurrite guardsmen were on him and he went down under a flurry of blows.

It was over. The surviving guardsmen were seeing to their wounded, while Hiziru and his men were binding the arms and legs of the few tribesmen unfortunate enough to still be alive.

Mursili was staring at Hetep. Blood welled over one hand where it gripped his injured arm.

'You do turn up in some odd places,' said Hetep.

Before Mursili could reply Benteshina came lurching forwards, pushing him aside. He seemed to have mastered his fear and was glaring around him.

'What is this?' he said, his voice thick. 'You!' – this was to Hetep – 'Who allowed you in here?' Then his eye fell on one of the Habiru corpses. 'Traitors!' he shouted, his face twisted with a sudden rage. 'Offal! Vagabond Habiru filth! What of you promise?' He kicked the corpse in the head. 'Attack me, will you? Renege on your sworn oath?' His voice rose to a scream. 'I am your king! I rule in Ba'al's name; the gods themselves have placed me on Amurru's throne!'

'Brother, please, calm yourself,' said Elissa, grabbing

196

the king's arm. Her earlier wildness had gone and now her face looked grey and tired. 'We must let the people see you.'

The king's bout of fury drained away as the wine once more reasserted its grip on his mind. His face went slack and he stared about him, swaying and with sweat dripping from his forehead.

'Help me take him,' said Elissa to Hiziru. 'There's a stairway to the roof just down the passage.'

'If Your Majesty would permit me...' Hiziru grabbed Benteshina by one arm and invited Hetep to take the other, and together they propelled the bewildered king down the passage, followed by a band of Amurrite archers. Sebeku kept close by; he was limping and had a long cut down one arm, but he still had his shield.

They half carried Benteshina up the steps and onto the roof. The moon had risen and a cold wind blew across the rooftops, bringing with it panicked cries and the sound of fighting. By the harbour two of the storehouses were burning; silhouetted against the flames were Amurrite soldiers, trying to stop the fire from spreading.

'A diversion to draw away the men still under arms,' said Hiziru. 'That explains why I could find so few.'

From the plaza came screams and the din of battle, and they heard a man shouting, 'Long life to king Zuratta!' Hetep crossed the roof and from the lip looked down onto a scene of chaos. A band of loyal Amurrite spearmen was fighting to clear the area in front of the palace gates and trying to stop them was an assorted mob of tribesmen, turncoat Amurrite soldiers and confused revellers, many of the latter still garlanded with flowers and brandishing wine jugs. As Hetep watched the loyalists fell back, leaving their dead and wounded to be trampled by their enemies. At the head of the tribesmen a rebel Amurrite officer raised his spear.

'Zuratta for king!' he cried.

The loyalists, uncertain and leaderless, were wavering. Quickly Hetep unslung his bow and fitted an arrow to the string. He drew and aimed, gritting his teeth against the pain in his ribs, then shot, and one of the tribesmen next to the officer went down, an arrow in his side. Then the palace archers were beside Hetep, loosing a volley that felled two more of the rebels.

The officer roared out a barrage of orders and a band of rebel archers formed themselves into a line. Two of them shot, aiming for Hetep, but Sebeku was there in time, his shield up; one of the arrows struck it with a thud and the second went skidding off over the rim. Hetep shot back, hitting one of the archers in the arm. The man cried out and dropped his bow, and the others fell back under a hail of missiles.

By now Hiziru and another guardsman had Benteshina propped up between them at the lip of roof. The king was staring down at the plaza, disbelief gradually turning to rage.

'Say something,' said Hetep. 'Talk to them.'

Benteshina harangued the crowd, accusing them of treachery and threatening death and torture for the whole city. Fortunately few of the listeners could understand his drunken ravings, but they could see him and they recognised his voice.

The rebel Amurrite commander looked up at his king. He held a javelin and weighed it in his hand, his eyes narrowed – judging the range, thought Hetep, or perhaps considering where his loyalties lay. Hetep drew his bow, aiming for the commander's heart; sweat started on his back and face as his arms quivered with strain. The commander saw him, and nodded. The he turned to his followers.

'Long life to King Benteshina!' he shouted and flung his javelin at the nearest tribesman. There was a cheer and the loyalist spearmen surged forwards.

CHAPTER 22

The rebels fought on with desperate courage, for they all knew the fate they would suffer if captured alive. Had it not been for Yuya, who at last listened to Hetep's pleading and lead the Egyptian garrison into the streets to restore order, the rebellion might yet have succeeded, but by dawn the city was secure, with the gates closed and guarded, sentries posted on the walls and El safely back in his temple home.

In the clear morning sunshine Hetep trudged across the main plaza towards the residency, his sandals sticking to pools of congealed blood and spilled wine. Corpses lay everywhere, and the air was so heavy with wood smoke and the reek of human gore that he had to cover his nose with his hand to avoid retching. Beside him walked Yuya and Elissa, both silent with fatigue, their ashen faces speckled with blood.

Nui appeared at the doorway, his eyes screwed up against the sunlight and one hand clutching his brow.

'Gods, it feels like someone's been stamping on my head,' he said. Then he saw the bodies. 'And by the looks of it on a lot of other people's, too. I think one of you had better tell me what's been going on.'

'Zuratta tried to murder Benteshina but we stopped him,' said Hetep. 'It's all quiet now.'

'Quiet?' Nui reeled and grabbed the doorframe, his face breaking out in a greasy-looking sweat. 'What in Montu's name did they do to that wine?'

'It was drugged by Zuratta, so you wouldn't be able to interfere when he stormed the palace,' said Elissa. 'He did something similar once to one of my husband's enemies.

I only realised last night – and I was almost too late.'

'The palace, eh?' Nui grimaced and rubbed his eyes. 'You'd better tell me everything. But come inside. It's too bright out here.'

In the room at the back of the office they found Baya searching though a bundle of papyrus documents. When he saw them he set the sheets down in a pile and squared their edges with an exaggerated air of innocence.

'I wondered when you'd show yourself,' said Nui. 'I'll want a word with you later. But not before I've heard what this lady has to say. Well?'

'My brother thought he could use Zuratta to free the city. He's afraid that if the Hittites take over again they'll punish him for handing it over to you without a struggle. He couldn't lead a revolt himself because of the loyalty oaths he'd sworn but he knew that Zuratta had made no such promises. He even helped him by arming the Habiru.'

'No, that wasn't Benteshina,' said Hetep. 'The ones I saw in the street were carrying Egyptian weapons from the new armoury.'

'Were they now?' Nui looked hard at Baya, who was pretending not to have heard, then at Yuya, who nodded.

'I think Elissa's only half right,' said Hetep. 'Benteshina wanted Zuratta out of the way and he knew that if he provoked a rebellion we'd kill the man for him, which he couldn't do himself. But if the rebels *had* won and got rid of us he'd have gone over to the Hittites again, after mopping up what was left of Zuratta's followers. So whatever happened he couldn't lose. But it all went wrong and the Habiru attacked the palace instead of us. I think our scheming king underestimated the strength of Zuratta's hatred for him.'

'Either that or he was outbid,' said Elissa. 'Perhaps someone offered Zuratta the whole of Amurru if only he removed my brother.'

'And I can guess who that someone might be,' growled Nui. 'Where were the Hittites when all this was happening?'

'At the royal palace,' said Hetep. 'I saw Mursili there and his aide, Tagi. But they couldn't have been plotting with Zuratta. They'd hardly have taken refuge with Benteshina if they knew he was going to be attacked, would they? They were fighting against the Habiru, as well.'

Nui gave a derisive grunt. 'Typical foreigners: can't even betray us properly. No offence intended,' he added, with a nod to Elissa.

'None taken,' she said with a wry smile. 'But if you wish to find Hittite conspirators, look no further than Carchemish. It's the seat of their viceroy, who could easily have been corresponding with Zuratta. The Habiru make good messengers.'

'Then we'd best get rid of them. Now what about the garrison? How many did we lose?'

'We've about thirty dead, twice that many wounded,' said Yuya. 'I've put men on the main streets and all the gates. The city's quiet now.'

'Good. I want you to go and find Mursili and bring him here. Use force if you have to, but don't kill him. Understand?'

As Yuya hurried off Nui turned at last to Baya. 'Which leaves us with you,' he said. 'Tell me, is there anything you'd care to add to what we've heard just now?'

Baya gave a small shrug. 'Only that if you had any sense you'd have realised what Zuratta was planning long ago. Also, this was an internal squabble, between the king and one of his subjects. We had no right to interfere.'

Nui stared at him. 'Are you trying to say you *knew* this was going to happen?'

202

'We should have given Zuratta more support. He'd have made a far more loyal king than Benteshina, as I'm sure even you can see. I never was happy with your policy of trusting him.'

'Am I still drunk?' said Nui, looking around at the others.

'Baya's the one who let the Habiru into the armoury,' said Hetep. 'It had to be him. I don't know if you noticed, but he slipped away last night before the drinking ceremony.'

Baya sighed. 'It was obvious that Benteshina was selling us to the Hittites,' he said with a bored patience. 'Even you admitted they were with him last night. Which meant Zuratta's men needed help. And with Zuratta as king instead of Benteshina, Amurru would have been governed by a useful ally.'

'I don't believe it,' cried Nui. 'You were assigned to help me govern these people, not plot to usurp their king's throne! Do you realise what you've done?'

'It is *you* who has made the error here. And now, thanks to this low-born peasant's meddling,' – he threw a poisonous look at Hetep – 'the whole scheme's been ruined.'

'Scheme?' roared Nui, his temper exploding at last. 'You conceited worm! This is *my* city – *I* rule here, not you.' He was shaking with rage, his huge hands clawing. 'Get out! Out, I say, before I forget myself! Go to the barracks and stay there – you're under arrest.'

Baya drew himself up. 'I shall write to my grandfather about this. He's a priest of Amun, you know, at Karnak. There will be consequences.'

'You're right about that.' Nui advanced, full of menace, but Baya just turned his back and sauntered out. Nui watched him go, his teeth grinding.

'You knew what kind of man he is the day I spoke to you at Irqata,' said Hetep.

Nui exhaled loudly. 'All right, I should have listened. Happy, now?'

'He has to be prosecuted – you must see that now. He admitted to conspiring with rebels, and arming them, too. And don't forget he was stealing from the tribute. His family can't protect him now, not after this. Send me back to Egypt with a written statement and I'll go to the vizier, or even to Ramesses himself if I have to. Then you'll be rid of him for good.'

'Sorry, I can't do that. I need you here.'

'You're wrong,' said Elissa. 'Hetep's work here is done. You must let him go to Egypt.'

Nui turned his glower on her. 'I'll thank you to remain silent. This is not your affair.'

She matched his gaze calmly. 'It is the will of the goddess,' she said. 'You'll see.'

The words seemed to unsettle Nui and Hetep remembered what the commissioner had said about not upsetting the local gods.

'She's right, you know.' Hetep spoke quickly; this could be my chance, he thought. 'Do you know what Baya will say when he writes to Egypt? He'll tell them about the rebellion, and about how it was put down by foreign soldiers while you were lying prostrate with a sore head. How's that going to look?'

Nui's hands started twitching again. 'I'll strangle him if he tries,' he growled. 'Very well. I'll send a report to Ramesses with an account of Baya's actions. That should be enough.'

'It won't work.' Hetep tried to keep the note of desperation from his voice. 'Ramesses, the vizier... they'll have questions you haven't anticipated. But if you send me I can vouch for you, tell them what really happened.'

'I need you here to help order the city. Now that's enough!'

Bootsteps sounded from the corridor outside and Mursili appeared, escorted by a pair of infantrymen. He looked filthy, his tunic stained by patches of blood from the fighting, and one forearm was swathed in a thick grey bandage.

'You were in Benteshina's private chambers yesterday evening,' said Nui. 'Why?'

'For the first time since you arrived at Sumur you grant me an audience and you don't even offer me the courtesy of a greeting,' said Mursili.

'We were drugged and I have a headache. Which means I don't want to have to ask you again. What were you doing?'

'I took a wrong turning on the way back from the festival.'

'You're lying. You were conspiring with Benteshina, against us.'

'Conspiring with a man too drunk to stand? Credit me with some wisdom, please. I only deal with sober men. I find it better if all parties remember what was agreed to when they wake up the next day.'

Elissa was eyeing him coldly. 'I think you knew about my brother's scheme to have Zuratta attack the Egyptians. And you went somewhere you thought would be safe, leaving the rest of us to take our chances in the city.'

'My dear lady, it grieves me to hear such a thing and know that you, too, suspect me of dishonesty. Whatever you all believe of me – and I see that your minds are made up and it would be futile to try to explain myself – please know that I am as surprised as you by the unexpected turn of events last night. I would never have wanted any of you hurt.' He turned to Hetep. 'Especially you, my friend.'

Nui made a disgusted sound. 'More lies. Your days of plotting with the Amurrites are over. You have a week. After that, any Hittite I catch inside the border of Amurru will be killed.'

'My lady, is this just?' said Mursili, appealing to Elissa. 'After all I have done for you, will you not vouch for me?'

She shook her head, tight lipped. 'You lied to me. But that is a personal matter and is not to be discussed here. As for the rest, I have nothing more to say.'

Crestfallen, Mursili looked from her to Hetep, and finally to Nui.

'One of my men was wounded in the fighting,' he said. 'Against the rebels, I should add. If he is forced to move–'

'One week,' repeated Nui. 'Now get out.'

'Your reputation does you no justice at all,' said Mursili. He inclined his head courteously to Hetep, cast a last, remorseful look at Elissa and left, his shoulders bowed.

'I thought you told me we don't accuse these people of lying to their faces,' said Hetep once Mursili had gone.

Nui shrugged. 'Circumstances change.'

Elissa was watching the empty doorway. Her expression had softened and now she gave a sad little shake of her head.

'I think he was telling the truth when he said he didn't want you harmed. He's a decent man at heart, and if he's guilty of anything it's of being naive. I think just wanted Zuratta out of the way and he trusted in Benteshina's scheme.'

'Well he backed the wrong man there, didn't he?' said Nui, grinning. He clapped his hands together. 'Right, then. Let's get this mess of a city cleaned up.'

CHAPTER 23

Over a hundred Amurrites and Habiru had been killed during the revolt and the funeral dirges lasted all day. Meanwhile the Egyptian dead were buried with as much ceremony as Nui's meagre allotment of lector priests could provide, although with their graves so far from Egypt Hetep doubted if many would reach the West. He pictured himself one day lying in a shallow pit in a foreign land, with his *ba* unable to recognise his decaying body and his *akh* fading into nothing, and he ached to return home, where if the worst happened he would at least be given a decent burial. But what chance did he have of ever leaving Sumur? Nui said he needed him, and that was that.

With the funerals over Benteshina renewed his loyalty oaths to Ramesses and together he and Nui sacrificed a donkey at the Ba'al temple as a sign of reconciliation. Hetep, now Nui's adjutant in all but name, was present, and watched with disgust as the king fawned over his Egyptian master like a beaten dog. He might have got what he wanted – the removal of another troublesome subject – but it was at the price of angering his Egyptian overlords and his expression now was tinged with fear.

Benteshina had the captured rebels executed in public on the meadow outside the city. And that would have been the end of the affair had he not saved the choicest victim until the last: Zuratta, who had survived the fight in the palace and, unknown even to Nui and Elissa, had been held captive ever since. Traitor, oathbreaker and leader of the revolt against the Ba'al-given authority of his king, there was no law or custom now that could save him, and no protest his surviving kinsmen could make that would not call down the wrath of the gods.

Hetep supposed he should have rejoiced at the prospect of Zuratta enduring what was certain to be a painful and ignominious death. After all, the man had tried not only to kill him but also to leave his *akh* in torment afterwards, and he would doubtless have slaughtered every Egyptian in the city had his revolt succeeded. Yet Hetep's reaction was one of sadness, accompanied by an uncomfortable feeling that an injustice was being committed. As a foreigner Zuratta could not help being what he was: it was in his nature to destroy and kill, and to be a threat Ma'at. If anyone deserved execution it was Baya, a man who, despite his gods-given advantages, corrupted the very foundations of the world by his actions.

Zuratta's execution took place in the plaza outside the palace. Benteshina declared a daylong festival, and there was food and wine for the people. Hetep did not go to see Zuratta die but he heard him – a shrill screaming that drowned out the cries of the gulls from the harbour.

Benteshina, after a long day of prayer in the El temple, let it be know that the god and his household were pleased with Amurru's Egyptian masters, a pronouncement that made Nui smile as much with cynicism as with satisfaction. With the gods appeased, the last traces of the revolt removed from the streets and the Habiru driven at spear point from Amurru, the city settled down, the people seemingly resigned at last to Egyptian suzerainty. Meanwhile tribute poured in from the outlying towns to be weighed and shipped to Egypt, and work on the commissioner's new manor resumed.

Nui was now openly seeking Hetep's advice on the administration of the city; in consequence, and to Sebeku's wry amusement, Hetep found himself being treated with a respect that he had rarely been awarded even as a serving charioteer – and not only by the Egyptian scribes and those Amurrite soldiers he had fought alongside during the rebellion, but also by Yuya and the other commanders of the Egyptian garrison.

But all the accolades under heaven would not make him a chariot warrior again; indeed, it seemed now that nothing ever would. Nui still could not bring himself to make Baya answer for his sins, instead confining him to his quarters, and without official acknowledgement of Baya's treachery Hetep knew that there was little chance of his deeds in the battle at Irqata being acknowledged and none of reinstatement. As the days dragged on and his new duties became routine his despair grew, and in his dreams he often saw his father looking on from the West with a malicious satisfaction.

It was another blisteringly hot day, a week after the rebellion, and Hetep, weary even of Sebeku's companionship, had climbed to his usual spot on the battlements above the city's main gate, where he could trace with his eye the road that lead south to Egypt. Although sunk in his own thoughts he still heard the quiet footsteps as they came up behind him and he straightened.

'I wondered when you were going to show yourself again,' he said. He turned to see Mursili standing beside him, a look of pained dignity on his face.

'If you must know I've come to thank you for saving my life. And to bid you farewell. Nui won't let us stay any longer.'

'Then I wish you a safe journey. Now if that's all...'

'I never lied to you. And I never wanted any of you harmed.'

'Really?' said Hetep. 'Are we done here?'

Instead of replying Mursili stepped over to the parapet and looked south towards the distant hills. 'How far is it to Egypt?' he said. 'A month's march? Yet scarcely a week's journey will take you to our viceroy at Carchemish.'

'Did you come here to threaten me?'

'You misunderstand. What I'm trying to say is your people don't belong here. You can barely maintain a garrison of three hundred men as it is, while we'd be able to feed a thousand troops here – more if necessary.'

'We've enough food stored to feed a whole division.'

'At the risk of starving half the kingdom's people. They'll not endure this for long, you know. Zuratta's rebellion is only a foretaste of what is to come. One way or another – violently or by persuasion – your Ramesses will be made to realise that he cannot hold Amurru and that it is ours by right.'

'I wouldn't be so sure about that,' said Hetep. 'We took the place easily enough, and we'll hold it too. Our army's strongest, and so are our gods – we've proven that.' He thought about the relief troops who Nui had been told were on their way and wondered what Mursili would say if he knew, but kept quiet. Let it be a shock to him, he thought: he deserves it.

Mursili was still gazing over the southern hills.

'You Egyptians still have no idea what you've done here, have you? My king rules over a region that stretches from the lands of sunrise to the lands of sunset and can raise an army so numerous that it will darken the hills for miles around. And one day – soon, I fear – he will lead it here to retake what is his. And when that happens there will be nothing you or any other Egyptian will be able to do to stop him.' He turned and looked intently at Hetep. 'Please, my friend, listen to me. It is not safe here. You

211

must do all you can to get away before it's too late.'

Mursili's warning sounded like a prophecy of doom and in the face of it Hetep's confidence in Egypt's might faltered. He searched his mind for a reply that would both strengthen his *ka* again and rebut Mursili's claims, but before he could speak there came a shout of alarm from the Amurrite sentries on the nearby tower.

'Not now,' said Mursili, suddenly ashen faced. 'Not so soon.'

Hetep backed away, frightened as much by the change in Mursili's demeanour as the sentry's cry, then turned and ran for the nearest tower. A flight of steps lead up to the tower's battlements and he raced up them two at a time; he was aware of Mursili behind him, but paid him no heed.

'What is it?' he said, breathless, as he fetched up at the parapet. For answer one of the sentries pointed to where a long column of marching figures was descending the road from the inland hills, much as the Habiru had done a few weeks ago. Only this time there was no mistaking that this was an army. The Hittites had come at last.

Mursili came to stand beside him.

'I'm sorry,' he said, with a quiet regret. 'Please believe me when I say I knew nothing about this.'

CHAPTER 24

It was not a large army – only about three thousand infantry and six squadrons of chariots – but it outnumbered the Egyptian and Amurru forces combined. Still, there was no question of surrendering and from the barracks the drums beat, mustering the garrison. Archers poured up the tower stairwells and lined the parapets; Nui appeared with them, and when he saw Hetep and Mursili he came stomping over.

'You!' he snarled at Mursili. 'When this is over I'll have your skin hanging from the wall.'

'Spare me the threats, please,' said Mursili. 'We have a treaty, remember?'

'Treaty?' said Nui, almost spitting the word. He turned to survey the advancing Hittites. 'Gods, there must be thousands of them.'

'At least it's not enough for a full invasion,' said Hetep.

'No, but it's enough to have secured the city once it had been handed over by the rebels.' Nui shot Mursili another glare.

'If the rebellion had gone otherwise you might have welcomed the assistance these troops would have provided.'

'Somehow I doubt that.'

At a thousand paces from the walls horns sounded and without breaking step the Hittite infantry deployed into its battle formation: a triple line of armoured spearmen supported behind by ranks of archers. Meanwhile the chariot column split into two and swept outwards like a gigantic pair of vulture's wings, to take up station on the flanks.

213

'Impressive,' said Nui, grudgingly.

The army came on, men and horses trampling the stubble in the fields, while the defenders watched in nervous silence. Closer still, and Hetep saw Nui draw a breath – perhaps, he thought, to give the order to the archers to draw their bows. Then from the Hittite army the horns sounded again, and as one man the entire host stopped.

Nui exhaled; it sounded like a sigh of relief.

A knot of charioteers gathered in front of the ranks of infantry – clearly the Hittite general and his staff. They took in the city's closed main gate and the garrison manning the walls, and after a quick conference a single chariot detached itself and came rolling over. Its driver wore nothing but a plain-looking linen hauberk, but the warrior was dressed in a full suit of bronze scale. He dismounted and pulled off his helmet, releasing a long mane of black hair, then strode up to the gatehouse and stood, glaring up at Nui and Hetep.

'Where is the man Zuratta?' he demanded in thickly accented Babylonian.

'He's dead,' shouted Nui. 'If you've got anything to say you can say it to me. Or if you prefer we can go straight to the battle, in which you, of course, will be the first to die.'

'I do not fear you, Egyptian. The goddess Ishtar stands with me – she is my shield and my guide. And it is her desire that we talk.'

'Then you'd better come inside. And no tricks, or my men will shoot you down where you stand.'

'If it's any help to you, these are not royal troops,' said Mursili. 'They're part of the garrison commanded by the viceroy at Carchemish. What they're doing here I cannot guess. But let me assure you that until the gods will it

214

otherwise, the peace treaty stands and this man will not attack the city.'

They waited in one of the guard rooms by the main gate: Nui, Hetep, and a pair of Egyptian infantrymen. The Hittite came to meet them alone. He was a gaunt-looking man with yellowish skin stretched tight over lean, knotted flesh, as if he was suffering from a long illness, and he walked with a slight limp. But his body scars showed him to be a veteran of countless victorious combats, and he met and held Nui's gaze with eyes as unmoving as stones.

'My name is Hattusili,' he said. Just that, thought Hetep: no titles, no introduction and no mention of the Hittite king, as if the presence of his army alone gave him all the authority he needed.

'Nui. Commander of the Host, Re division, and now Commissioner of Amurru in the name of Ramesses, the son of the god Re.'

'You rule here? Then I greet you and wish you a long life and many children.'

'Thank you. I hope the same for you, if that's the right reply. If not, let's just pretend I said the right thing. Now tell me: why have you come here with an army? As I keep getting reminded, our peoples are at peace.'

'We heard there was disorder in Sumur and we came to end it.'

'By storming the city?'

'I was informed that the gates would be standing open and a different man would be here to greet me.'

'I told you: that man's dead,' said Nui. 'His rebellion failed.'

'What of Benteshina, dog of Amurru? Does he live? My king would have words with him.'

'He's alive. But he's not taking visitors at the moment. You have to deal with me.'

'I see.' Hattusili's face registered no emotion. 'In that case I must ask, in the name of my king Muwatalli, favourite of the Storm God, and in the name of the shade of your King Seti, with whom he made peace, and of all the gods who witnessed the signing of the treaty that made Amurru a vassal of Hatti, that you return Amurru to the rule of Hatti's king and the protection of its gods.'

'You know I can't do that,' said Nui quietly. His face was stern but there was a lively glint in his eye; he's enjoying this, realised Hetep.

'The gods of Sumur are now also gods of Hatti, and the unrest is a sign that they do not want you here,' said Hattusili.

'Yet here we remain. And there's not a thing you can do about it.'

'The army of Amurru is no match for the army of the king of Hatti and your garrison here is small; I know its number to the last man.' A threat, given with the same lack of expression as Hattusili's other pronouncements. Then his face softened the barest fraction. 'I also know that I have seen my share of war, and I think you have, too. I would prefer that Sumur's surrender be peaceful. So again I ask that you and your people leave Amurru.'

'Again, I say no. And please, no more threats. You haven't enough men to take this city.'

'What you see is only the smallest part of my king's army. Surrender and you may march away, to your homes and gods, and the peace between our peoples will be maintained.'

'If your royal army really was on its way here we'd

216

not be having this conversation,' said Nui. 'My answer stands.'

Hattusili sighed. 'Then I shall return to my troops and await my king's response.'

They saw Hattusili out of the city and as they watched him go Nui smiled thinly.

'Expecting someone else to be in charge, was he?' he said. 'At least he was honest about it. Makes a change, eh?'

'I was with Mursili on the wall when the Hittites were first seen,' said Hetep. 'He looked just as shocked as everyone else.'

'Did he, now? So you're saying I've been too hard on him, is that it? Very well, he can stay: he might still be able to tell us something useful. But I'll have Yuya watch him; after all, we don't want him doing anything foolish like trying to open the gates at night. Meanwhile we still control the city. And that's what counts.'

The Hittite army spread out, forming not so much a siege line as an extended encampment. Only their chariot force remaining battle ready and the following day Nui and Hetep climbed to the battlements to watch them at their practice, driven as much by curiosity as by the professional need to gather intelligence on an army they might soon have to fight.

The chariots proved to be heavier and slower than even the Canaanites', with solid, boxlike cars walled by sheets of wood and holding three armoured crewmen, while the horses were decked in thick linen trappers. Yet they were well handled, and with bow and javelin the warriors were as expert as any Hetep had seen Egypt's squadrons. And carrying that third crewman, along with their abundant supply of close combat weapons and javelins, they would be deadly in a melee against stationary enemy chariots. The familiar feelings of longing came to Hetep, but also dread as he remembered the battle outside Irqata. Gods help us if we do have to fight them, he thought. Beside him Nui watched in thoughtful silence, keeping whatever misgivings he had to himself.

A week passed without incident and the mood of the city became more relaxed – so much so that an informal market sprang up outside the main gate, where some of the bolder Amurrites traded with the Hittite soldiers. Then, at last, the Hittite king's emissaries arrived, in the shape of three dour, veteran chariot warriors, who insisted, politely but without any softening words, that the message they carried was for Ramesses alone and they required nothing from Nui but a guarantee of safe passage to the Egyptian capital. A few veiled threats on Nui's part – it seemed that for once he dared try nothing more overt – failed to learn anything more and in the end he decided to grant their request. After all, as he confided to Hetep, any delay was welcome while he waited for the Egyptian reinforcements to arrive.

On the afternoon of the emissaries' arrival Mursili once more came to find Hetep on the city's battlements.

'Still here?' said Hetep.

'The situation has changed, as you well know. And I have news. The envoys will not be travelling alone. A delegation of Amurrites is to accompany them with gifts for your pharaoh.'

'They'll be lucky to get back alive considering they tried to rebel,' said Hetep.

'If your king would kill such men then you are indeed a barbarous people.'

'I was joking,' said Hetep.

'Is that so?' Mursili eyed him doubtfully. 'Whatever the case, I have persuaded my king's envoys that they would be more favourably received if they were accompanied by a party of Egyptians, and I have arranged for you to be one of that party.'

'Me?' said Hetep, surprised. 'Why?'

'One of the envoys owes my family a favour. He spoke to Nui and insisted that you accompany him. He said he will trust nobody else.'

'That's telling me how. I asked you why.'

'Because I owe you my life and I wish to return the favour. Events are likely to turn out badly for you Egyptians here in northern Canaan, as I am sure you now realise, and I'd rather you were safely at home.'

'Now this time you *are* making a threat.'

Mursili gestured in exasperation. 'When will you understand that Amurru is Hittite territory? My king is going to take it back, one way or another, and if it is to be by violence then I want you out of harm's way. Besides, you have often hinted at how much you wish to return to Egypt and deal with your affairs there.'

'True. But what about you? Are you staying?'

'There's nothing more for me to do here. And now that Hattusili has come I am somewhat superfluous. So I shall return to Hatti. And perhaps,' he added wistfully, 'next year, I shall see the Crocus Festival.'

Hetep remembered what Mursili had told him about the near disaster during this year's ceremony and the delays expected next year because of it. How can they think of taking Amurru, he thought, when they're so clearly out of favour with their gods? Especially after we have another division's worth of troops here. Hetep felt sorry for him and the last of his coldness vanished.

'Then I suppose we'll both be enjoying the pleasures

of home,' he said, smiling now.

'Indeed we shall. And I hope, my friend, that you will enjoy yours for many years to come. And if in more settled times you should ever visit Hatti, you'll find a welcome there.' He gripped Hetep's shoulder. 'Have a safe trip. And remember: stay away from northern Canaan. For my peace of mind as much as for your own good.'

CHAPTER 25

The next morning Hetep was standing at the quay and blinking in the sunshine as he waited to board the ship that was to take him home. It was a day he had long anticipated, yet also one tinged by an unexpected feeling of melancholy. At dawn he had taken a last walk around Sumur, saying his farewells to Merimose and the other scribes, and to Hiziru and the men of the palace guard, and as he had done so he had realised that he was going to miss both them and the city – a sentiment bordering on the blasphemous for a man from Egypt, the envy of the world.

He had seen Elissa too. She had received him in her full regalia, incense swirling about her like fog, and had given him a charm to keep him safe.

'The goddess is grateful for your aid,' she had said. 'It is as much a gift from her as from me.'

At the centre of the charm was a gold figurine of the goddess Anat. It was Egyptian made and clearly extremely powerful, intended more for protecting a pharaoh than a scribe, or even a charioteer; how it had ended up in Sumur he could not guess. Some local craftsman had mounted it in a pectoral decorated with pieces of lapis lazuli and the mismatch of styles – Egyptian and Amurrite – was oddly attractive.

He had tried to refuse the gift but Elissa had been insistent. 'One day, when you are in a foreign land, you will need Anat's protection,' she had said.

He smiled as he recalled the earnest look on her face. Her concern for his welfare was touching, but misplaced: he was returning to Egypt now, whose native gods needed no help in shielding him from harm.

The quay grew warm as the sun climbed. It was now full summer and with Ba'al still held captive in the Underworld the only moisture to wet the parched fields and orchards was from the night-time dew, which vanished with the dawn. In the oven-hot air the slaves and freemen worked listlessly and even the merchants at the docks seemed to have been drained of their appetite for profit.

Nui had accompanied him to the harbour, ostensibly to oversee the auditing of yet another shipment of tribute, but he was behaving oddly and Hetep suspected he had an ulterior motive. After taking a cursory look at some piles of wood he came stomping over, sweating in the heat and scowling with displeasure.

'Montu curse these idle foreigners,' he said. 'At the rate they're working we'll be lucky to get even half the tribute sorted by the end of the month.'

'You could have a few of the slower ones impaled,' suggested Hetep.

'Don't think I haven't considered it,' said Nui, before settling into a long, brooding in silence.

'Well, that's it then,' said Hetep after a while. 'I'll be going soon.'

'Yes.' There was another long pause. Twice Nui cleared his throat and appeared to be on the verge of speaking but he said nothing, instead turning his glower towards the open sea.

'Is there something on your mind?'

'No.' Again Nui cleared his throat. 'I mean yes. What I want to say is, you'll be seeing Egypt again. Soon.'

'I'm surprised you let me go,' said Hetep, feeling both intrigued and amused by Nui's uncharacteristic reticence. 'It must be for an important reason.'

'Yes, it is. Things have changed. The truth is...' Nui

took a breath. 'The truth is that woman, Elissa, was right: I do need you in Egypt more than here. One of those accursed envoys let slip that he was going to have to tell Ramesses what's been happening recently. If I could stop them going I would, but as things stand...' He shook his head.

Hetep waited in polite silence, although it was obvious what Nui was going to ask him. It must have been Mursili who was behind the envoy's veiled threat to Nui. The scheming dog, he thought, and he wondered if Elissa had encouraged him; if so it would mean the two were on speaking terms again, which was a pleasant thought.

'The thing is,' said Nui, breaking his thoughts, 'I'm worried people back home might get the wrong impression of things. And of me. Do you understand?'

'I think so, yes.' Hetep remembered saying the very same thing to Nui a few days ago, but he did not think a reminder would be tactful.

'I need a man there I can trust, who'll tell Ramesses the truth. You know what I mean by that, don't you?'

'Don't worry. You can rely on me.'

'Good,' said Nui, sounding relieved. He seemed about to pat Hetep on the shoulder but his hand withdrew and instead went to a satchel he was carrying. 'Here, you'd better have this.' He drew out a folded sheet of papyrus and handed it to Hetep. 'It's a sworn statement of everything I know about Baya's schemes. It's addressed to the mayor of Pr-Ramesses. He's a decent man and has no love for Baya, and he knows the vizier. So you should be able to get some help from him.'

Hetep took the papyrus and looked it over. 'Do you mean his plotting with Zuratta or him stealing my reward at Irqata?'

'Both. But it's only what I know for sure. There's too

few witnesses to say what really happened in that battle.'

'Baya's driver is dead, but I know there was another man – Mehy is his name. He should be back in Egypt by now.'

Nui nodded. 'One of second squadron's troop leaders. Yes, he was wounded and got sent home. If you find him perhaps you can get something useful out of him. Oh, and be wary of the Royal Butler. His brother married one of Baya's aunts.'

'I'll remember. You know Teppic? He's one of my friends; he'll help me.'

'Good. I think you're on firmer ground with the embezzlement charge. I've been looking over the accounts and Baya certainty stole from at least one of the tribute shipments. And there's no doubt he armed Zuratta's men. But I warn you: he's a dangerous man to cross. If it goes wrong I can't protect you.'

'Thank you,' said Hetep. 'It's more than I could have hoped for.'

'Right. That's it, then. Have a good journey.' Nui hesitated; again he seemed about to pat Hetep on the shoulder. But instead he withdrew his hand, wheeled about and strode back along the quay towards the gate.

Sebeku, even now leery of Nui's presence, had been loitering at a safe distance. Only once the commissioner was out of sight did he come over.

'Emotional farewell?' he said.

'You might call it that. Are we ready?'

'Since we own nothing but the clothes we stand in I suppose we are. The foreigners are waiting for us.'

And so they were. The Hittite envoys and their staff were standing under a sun shade at the far end of the quay, and among them, to Hetep's surprise, was Tagi; their eyes met and the Hittite nodded gravely in greeting. Beside

224

them waited the party of Amurrite courtiers who were to convey their king's renewed loyalty oaths to Ramesses. None of them looked happy to have been chosen for the assignment, and given Sumur's recent history Hetep could understand why. Nearby were the gifts that Benteshina had been persuaded to send with them, among which was a pair of chariots complete with horse teams, all in the care of a party of Egyptian scribes. None were ex-army officers, which was a relief to Hetep: he had been appointed as the delegation's commander and would have felt awkward giving orders to men who had been charioteers.

Sebeku looked their companions over with a disparaging eye. 'Gods, what a rabble,' he said. 'Shall we get started?'

Their ship lay moored nearby, a gang of slaves standing ready to take the gifts aboard. And striding down the gangplank, grinning and with his eyes gleaming in his wind-battered face, was the very same captain Hetep had bribed all those weeks ago – and who in return had intended to sell him into slavery.

'It's you,' said Hetep. 'The pirate.'

'Wounding words,' said the captain. 'There was a mis-understanding, nothing more.'

'So this time we're really going to Egypt?'

'We are indeed – upon my oath. And while I remember...' He fished around inside the recesses of his tunic and produced Teppic's gold *wadjet*. 'Here, you can have this back.'

'Why?' said Hetep, with a twinge of suspicion.

'You're the hero of the city, the man who put down the revolt. So think of it as a token of gratitude – you've no idea how much armed rebellion can upset trade. Also the princess Elissa told me she'd be wearing my entrails for a belt if I didn't.'

Hetep hung the amulet around his neck. He took its return as a good omen for the future.

'Right, then,' said the captain. 'As soon as we've stowed all that cargo we'll be off. We've got a wind to catch.'

They climbed the gangplank, and at the top Sebeku paused and looked around at the deck.

'Where are we supposed to sleep?'

'On shore, of course,' said the captain. 'You don't think we're stupid enough to sail at night, do you?'

The last of the tribute had just been loaded and the crew were about to cast off when there they heard a disturbance on the quay and saw a pair of Egyptians marching through the crowds, shoving the slaves out of the way. One was Baya; the other was one of the scribes on his staff.

Hetep met him at the gangplank.

'What are you doing here?' he said. 'You're supposed to be under arrest.'

Baya ignored him and held out a written papyrus sheet in front of the captain.

'Orders,' he said. 'From Nui. Look, there's the seal. I'm being sent back to Egypt.'

'He's lying,' said Hetep. 'It's forged.'

The captain looked back and forth between Hetep and Baya, then shook his head. 'I don't know...'

'Do you want to take this up with Nui in person?' said Baya. 'He's not a patient man and he can revoke a trading license with a word. And with your reputation you need to be careful.'

'Send someone to find Nui,' said Hetep. 'Ask him.'

'There's no time,' said the captain. 'The wind's veering. If we don't get away now we could be harbour locked for days.'

'But the ship's got oars.'

The captain bristled. 'Are you trying to teach me my trade? No, we have to leave now. Besides, the princess was very insistent.'

'But Baya shouldn't be here.'

'I said we sail now. You can argue about it on the voyage.'

The captain gave the order to cast off. Meanwhile Baya was looking around and smiling brightly.

'It seems I was just in time,' he said, as he watched the gangplank being pulled in.

'As soon as Nui realises you're missing he'll send someone to get you back,' said Hetep.

'How, once we're at sea? Besides, he's got a whole army of Hittites to deal with at the moment, and I'm relieved of duty – it'll be days before he knows I'm gone. And who are you to say my reason for leaving is not legitimate?' Baya tapped his papyrus and smiled again. 'You know, I'm very much looking forward to this trip. It should prove to be most interesting. But even more so, I can't wait to be home.'

By the afternoon the wind had strengthened and the ship was wallowing in the increasing swell. Hetep, who was uncomfortable sailing even the placid waters of the Nile, felt his stomach clench.

The captain came stumping over, his long hair streaming out sideways like a banner.

'Better than chariot driving, eh?' he said, grinning. 'Just feel that wind!'

'Does it get any worse than this?' said Hetep. Saliva was beginning to fill his mouth and he swallowed.

'This is nothing. You should see what it's like when it really starts to blow.'

In less than an hour the swell had picked up, the waves rearing up like mountains – or so they seemed to Hetep, who was terrified that the ship was going to roll itself over. His nausea built and he fought it doggedly, repeatedly swallowing bitter-tasting saliva as he tried to maintain the dignity of his rank. But his stoicism could not last, and as the ship caught a cross sea and began to pitch in earnest he staggered to the rail and vomited until his belly muscles ached.

The next few hours passed in torment. The rest of the crew sat clustered in the shade behind the mast, but Hetep stayed by the rail near the bow, cold sweat and sickness sweeping over him in waves. Even when his stomach was empty he kept retching, and it was agony to do so.

Another paroxysm had just passed and in the brief period of lucidity which followed he was suddenly aware of someone approaching. He turned his head and saw Tagi, standing by the rail, his face set in an expression of – what? Murderous hostility? Hetep's stomach quivered again, but this time in fear.

Then he saw the Hittite's eyes move to focus on a spot just behind him. He twisted around and there was Baya, poised not two paces away, with his arms out and his legs braced against the motion of the ship. For an instant all three stood, frozen. Then Baya straightened and gave Hetep a curt nod.

'I hope to see you recovered soon,' he said and sauntered off, as casually as the pitching deck would allow, to join the others by the mast.

Tagi watched him go then faced Hetep again, one eyebrow raised.

'Thank you,' said Hetep. He looked back over the

ship. With the sail and cargo blocking the view none of the others would have seen him pushed overboard.

That night, at their first stop, Sebeku was outraged when Hetep told him what happened and it was all Hetep could do to stop him from killing Baya there and then.

'It has to be done properly,' said Hetep. 'Ma'at depends on it.'

For the remainder of the journey both Tagi and Sebeku kept close to Hetep, even when the ship put into the shore at night. Baya never spoke to him after that, but now and then Hetep would catch him watching him, a calculating look on his face.

CHAPTER 26

On the eighth morning of the voyage they reached the barren shore of the Way of Horus, the fort-studded eastern approach to Egypt, and saw their first glimpse of the Delta – little more than a smudge of green on the horizon. The Egyptians grew excited, telling the foreigners on board of the many wonders they were to witness in Egypt, that most blessed of lands, and they rushed to the bow, staring eagerly ahead.

By the afternoon the ship had reached the Delta and they sailed past clusters of date palms and great beds of reeds, while in the distance flocks of wading birds rose like smoke in the vast clear sky. Then it turned into the widest of the eastern tributaries and with the cutting off of the coastal breeze there came the smell of fresh water, mud and lush greenery, spiced by the tang of rotting vegetation from the marshes. Hetep breathed it all in, feeling the air's moisture reaching deep into his lungs. This was perfection, he thought – as indeed it was, for the Field of Reeds where the blessed dead went was just like the Delta, a world of inexhaustible fertility, moisture and growth. Already the memories of his time in Amurru were fading. Here was the only place that mattered: Egypt, the land at the centre of the world, order standing against chaos. Here he was safe from the influence of corrupt foreign rulers and the machinations of their strange deities. Surrounded by the richly scented air and thick vegetation he felt the protective power of Egypt's gods envelop him like a cloak. Beside him Sebeku was smiling, his eyes alive with a rare delight, and Hetep grinned back, even as he slapped away the first of the mosquitoes that descended on them in a cloud.

At Hetep's insistence they put in at a village near the mouth of the tributary, where he had messengers dispatched to warn Ramesses of their arrival. The crew took on water and bartered for dates, beer, bread and fish; as the Egyptians stood at the jetty eating, they all agreed that the food tasted much better than anything they had eaten in Canaan. Afterwards, as they waited for some cargo to be restowed, Hetep walked about near the shore and it was a pleasure to feel the soft black mud oozing over the sides of his sandals. Then it was time to reembark for the journey to Pr-Ramesses, Egypt's newest and greatest capital.

On the eastern flank of the Delta it stood: the House of Ramesses, Great in Victory, the centre of Egypt's military might. Founded only three years ago, and closer to the potential trouble spots of Canaan than the old capitals of Memphis and Thebes, already it was a mighty city, a sprawl of loosely connected districts built on the humps of silt and earth that rose above the level of the Nile flood. To the east lay a jumble of peasant houses and workshops; to the west stood the great mounds holding the royal city, with its palace, mansions, armouries, storehouses, barracks and temples; to the north and south lay cemeteries and more residential blocks; and all threaded by a network of canals and surrounded by reed beds, clumps of palm trees and fields of wheat and barley.

They docked at the main harbour. The Royal Butler was there to greet them, accompanied by an escort of palace troops; cold and aloof, he set about ordering the disposition of the Hittite and Amurrite delegations. Baya sidled off to talk to him and Hetep, remembering what Nui had said about the Butler's closeness to Baya's family, experienced a pang of unease as he watched them together. He thought he heard Nui's name mentioned and once they both turned to stare at him. Finally, their business concluded, Baya strolled off, smirking.

'He's getting away,' protested Sebeku.

'Where to?' said Hetep. 'It's not as if he's going to abscond from Egypt.'

Tagi was looking on and shaking his head.

'You are a strange people,' he said. 'That man is a liar and has conspired with evil men. In Hatti he would be put on a spike.'

'I don't suppose you'd like to stay and help me explain that to the authorities here, would you?' said Hetep.

'My task here is done and I must return to Sumur. I have only one more duty, which is to say to you, as Mursili said: do not go back to Amurru or any of the lands near it. Stay in this land. Live; do not die.'

'Now what was that all about?' asked Sebeku as he watched Tagi stride off.

'A warning, I suppose,' said Hetep. 'Or perhaps a threat. It doesn't matter, though: we're home.'

By now a gang of slaves had been assembled to convey the Amurrites' gifts to the pharaoh. The chariots were to be ridden, and to Hetep's delight he and Sebeku had been chosen to drive the lead vehicle.

'Perhaps it'll make Ramesses look more favourably on us when he sees us driving his gift from the Amurrites,' said Hetep, for he was beginning to feel a degree of trepidation about being the bearer of what he was certain would turn out to be bad news.

'Gift?' said Sebeku. 'It's a wreck! We'll be lucky if Ramesses doesn't use it as an excuse for another war against the Amurrites.'

'The old wound getting a bit painful is it?'

'I'm serious. And look at the horses! I've never seen

such a sorry-looking pair of nags. What do foreigners know about keeping chariot teams?'

'They wrote the manual. No, really. Mursili told me the instructions they use for training the horse teams is Mitanni. He said their empire had chariots long before either we or the Hittites.'

'More foreigners,' said Sebeku, as if that settled his argument.

On the road to the palace they passed monuments celebrating Ramesses' greatness, all bearing his many names in interlocking patterns of hieroglyphics carved deeply into the stone. Most impressive of all was a pair of giant statues of the pharaoh himself, brightly painted in shades of red, blue and yellow, staring over the city with eyes as white as a gull's plumage. One was still partly caged in scaffolding and a gang of masons was working on the inscription on its base, and it was only as he drew near that Hetep realised the statues were not as new as they at first appeared, but were in fact images of Ramesses' father, Seti. The last traces of the former king's name were being erased, to be replaced by that of his less accomplished son. But what did it matter? he thought. Father and son were one and the same god, after all. Still, he wondered if speed of carving was not the only reason Ramesses had chosen sunken relief instead of the more usual and time-consuming raised relief for the wording on his monuments, for it meant that his descendants would have trouble erasing *his* name in turn.

Courtiers were there to greet them at the royal palace, a rather plain-looking building fashioned from the same mudbrick as the peasant hovels on the city's outskirts. The chariots were lead away – to Sebeku's obvious relief but Hetep's disappointment – and they trooped in, escorted by a squad of Sherden guardsmen.

From the entrance gate a long, pillared hallway took them to the heart of the palace. It was cool and deeply shadowed, the air pierced by shafts of sunlight which lit the murals on the walls in brilliant patches of green, red and gold. The decorations and the shapes of the pillars evoked the First Moment when Montu made the world, raising the land from the waters of chaos, and the proximity of so much divine power made the hairs prickle on Hetep's skin. He reached for his amulet, and as he did so his hand brushed the whicker case hanging under his arm, in which he had placed Nui's papyrus. He had almost forgotten! Not only was he to face Ramesses but he intended afterwards to accuse one of Egypt's noblemen of treason. It was a daunting prospect, on which he was thankfully given no time to dwell, for the next moment they were trooping into the audience chamber and the presence of Egypt's living god.

He was seated on a gilded throne, its arms shaped like the protective wings of the vulture goddess Nekhbet, its backrest topped by the ever-vigilant serpent goddess Wadjet. He wore the crown of the two kingdoms and across his chest he held a grain flail and a crook, for he was both the source of Egypt's abundance and the shepherd of its people; in the handles of each were carved the likenesses of Nubians, Libyans and Asiatics, so that even here in the palace he was crushing them in his hands, and thus keeping subdued the foreign menace. On his feet he wore sandals whose soles were embossed with images of the same, so that wherever he walked he was trampling Egypt's enemies underfoot – as he would do forever. At his waist he wore a sword, its hilt studded with gems.

He was flanked by courtiers and officials, and Hetep

gulped to be in such august company. Most he had seen before at the parades and festivals, or at the public displays of the pharaoh's largesse when they stood beneath one or another of the Windows of Appearances to receive gifts for good service. There was General Huti, the Field Marshall of Chariotry, a wiry man with a fiery temper and limb muscles like twisted ropes, and beside him was the Royal Butler, his sharp eye ranging over the Hittites and Amurrites, alert for the first sign of impropriety. Behind the throne stood the two eldest royal princes, both barely out of childhood and yet one already with the rank of First Charioteer of His Majesty, and the other a Standard Bearer of Chariotry, and at Ramesses' side stood the vizier, a lean, wizened ancient with the wisdom of Thoth and eyes as bright at a bird's. There were others too, of lesser rank: guardsmen, both Egyptian and Sherden, the royal fanbearer, scribes and body servants, the mayor of Pr-Ramesses, and last of all a lector priest, who was praying quietly to Amun, asking that he grant the Son of Re perpetual life, health and prosperity.

The priest finished his prayer and the Butler signalled for the Hittite envoys to approach the throne. The most senior among them must have been schooled in proper etiquette for he bent low at the waist, his upper body as horizontal as his straining muscles could manage; not so his attendants, who simply bowed their heads, until a pair of Egyptian guardsmen stepped over and forcibly bent them into the correct position.

With the foreigners now properly subservient the Butler gave them permission to deliver their message. Still bent over the lead envoy opened the satchel slung about his neck and drew out a thick sheet of papyrus. It was covered in writing and had clay bullae hanging from its end, and he proffered it to Ramesses, his arms outstretched.

235

The Butler took the papyrus and handed it to a waiting scribe.

'What words has the king of Hatti placed in his letter?' said Ramesses. 'Recite, so that all might know them.'

The envoy was quivering with the effort of holding his body at such an awkward angle, yet his voice was steady.

'Say to Ramesses, king of the Egyptians, thus spoke Muwatalli, Great King: "The people of Amurru are Hittite subjects and long ago I, My Sun, made a treaty with them and took them under my protection. But then you, Ramesses, king of Egypt, marched your army against them and they broke off their friendship with My Sun. But then the people of Amurru realised their error. They tried to cast off the Egyptian yoke – proof that the Storm God, and all the other Thousand Gods, desire that they again enjoy the protection of Hatti."'

The envoy paused and swallowed to moisten his mouth. Hetep guessed he was aching to look up and see the effect his words were having but he had obviously been told that it was forbidden to face the pharaoh directly without permission. Hetep, under no such restriction given his distance from the Royal Presence, saw a flush of anger appear behind the pharaoh's carefully rigid mask, and he dreaded the eventual explosion of royal rage that would mean death to the envoys and all those who accompanied them.

The envoy went on with his recitation. ' "So I, My Sun, say to you, my Egyptian brother: return my Amurrite subjects to me, so that the peace agreed by Seti and My Sun is not broken. Or if it is your desire to contest the ownership of Amurru, I say: up with you, and let us fight! At the plain of Kadesh, where My Sun fought King Seti... at that place let our armies meet in the spring, and let the Storm God, my lord, decide the matter."'

So it was a declaration of war, thought Hetep; he might have known. Some of the courtiers were thin lipped with anger at the Hittite king's insolence, while others looked on in disgust. Ramesses shifted on his throne and fixed the envoy with a cold eye.

'Stand straight and look at me,' he commanded. 'Now listen. Not one field of Amurru will I surrender to the wretch who sits on Hatti's throne, and not one of its subjects will I give up.' He stood, let fall his crook and flail, and swept out his sword. Then he advanced on the envoy, who stood as straight as a spear, hands rigidly at his sides, his only movement the twitching of one cheek.

'With my arm alone I conquered Amurru,' said Ramesses. 'And those who resisted I laid in swathes, with *this.*' He sliced left and right through the air with his sword, its tip passing a bare finger's breadth from the envoy's face. 'My father Amun gave me dominion over all Canaan and it is mine, now and forever. And to any man who tries to take it from me, I say: "you will be a man without an heir; the world will forget you existed."' Again Ramesses cut the air with his sword and this time the envoy flinched. Then came the metal ring of it being rammed back into its scabbard. 'There. You have your answer.'

Ramesses returned to his throne and sat. For a moment his eyes fixed themselves on the far wall and his head tilted, as if his mind was in another place. Then he turned to the Butler.

'The men of Hatti are doubtless tired after their journey,' he said. 'See that they are fed and given every comfort, and at dawn let them depart. Give them an escort so that they may reach the border of their land in safety.'

And that's it, thought Hetep: no outburst of rage over the foreigners' apparent ill manners, and no death sentences for the envoys and their escorts. He exhaled with

237

relief and glanced at Sebeku, who smiled weakly in return.

As the Sherden lead the shaken-looking envoys away the Amurrites were ushered forwards. Terrified, they did not bow but fell onto their faces, gabbling protestations of friendship and loyalty. Ramses barely glanced at them; after the message from the Hittites whatever they had to say was of little import.

'See that these men also return safely to their lands,' he said.

The Amurrites stood and backed towards the door, bent low and wishing Ramesses a thousand jubilees, over and over, until at a decent distance they turned and fled, pursued by their Sherden escort.

In the silence that followed all eyes turned to Ramesses. What to make of the Hittite message? Perhaps, thought Hetep, many of the courtiers had opinions or advice to offer, but only the Lord of the Two Lands could give the proper response and they waited to hear his words.

'Now this is troubling to My Majesty,' said Ramesses, with a frown. 'When my servant Nui last wrote to me from Sumur he declared that all was well with my possessions there. And yet I have heard talk of a rebellion, and now the wretched Hittites have come with poison in their mouths, insulting My Majesty by demanding from me what is mine. Where is Nui that he may explain all this?'

He looked around as if expecting the commissioner to be present – although he must have known, thought Hetep, that the man was still in Sumur. Then, as the pharaoh's eye rested on him, Hetep realised that, as Nui's representative, it was at last his turn to speak.

He felt the sweat prickle his skin. He had only just recovered from the shock of hearing the Hittite king's message. Now he had to give an account of the recent events in Sumur – events which, if reported on clumsily, might reflect badly on Nui. And as the only member of Nui's staff present he knew that it would be he who would be the first to receive the full effects of the pharaoh's displeasure.

'Oh, gods,' he whispered, and swallowed.

'What was that?' said the Royal Butler, his voice sharp. 'Speak up, and address the Son of Re in the correct way.' He leaned close to Ramesses and said, in a whisper audible across the room, 'May I caution Your Majesty that this is the troublemaker who disrupted the Amurrite surrender at Irqata.'

'Yet he is the only man here who can speak for Nui,' said Ramesses. 'So we had best let him do so.'

Hetep advanced, his body tilted forwards. 'Majesty,' he said, 'may you be given life, prosperity and health. It is no lie that all is well in Sumur, as it is in the whole of Amurru. The people are content; in fact, Nui has proven to them Your Majesty's right to rule.'

There was an intake of breath from the men flanking Ramesses.

'Was there ever any doubt?' said the Butler, scandalised. 'Remember who you are talking to!'

Blood was filling Hetep's head and he straightened a little to relieve the pressure. 'Forgive my clumsy words, Majesty. What I meant was, there were some malcontents in Sumur who caused trouble, and their gods tested us at their drinking festival. But which god can defy the will of Amun-Re? Which king can oppose the will of Your Majesty? So Nui passed the test, the malcontents were executed and now all Amurru is at peace, as it will be always.'

He risked a glance at the throne and was relieved to see a glimmer of satisfaction on the pharaoh's face. The

239

Royal Butler, however, looked far from pleased.

'A few malcontents you call them,' he said. 'Yet from what I've heard the whole city was in uproar.'

Hetep unbent a little more and twisted his head to look at him.

'My lord,' he said, 'the man who told you this, Baya, is a criminal and a liar. In truth, it was *he* who was the source of the disorder. He colluded with rebels and stole from the tribute.' Hetep tapped the scroll case he was carrying. 'I have brought proof of this, here, and intend to see him prosecuted.'

'Proof?' The Butler paled and darted a worried glance at Ramesses.

'Yes, proof. And consider this, Majesty,' went on Hetep. 'If the men of Amurru had indeed broken faith they would not have sent such fine gifts, nor such submissive envoys.'

'Perhaps not.' Ramesses turned briefly to the Butler, inviting a comment, but the latter just shook his head. 'Very well, we accept your explanation and commend Nui for his loyalty. Now what of the men of Hatti, who abused My Majesty with foul words?'

'The envoys meant no insult,' said Hetep. 'The Hittites believe that going to war without the proper declaration is a sin, and doing so would invite disaster on their king and all his lands.'

'How is it you know so much about these foreigners and their ways?' asked Ramesses, a hint of suspicion in his voice. His courtiers, taking their cue from him, glared at Hetep.

Hetep swallowed; he was sure he could smell his own sweat. 'At Sumur, Majesty, I gained the confidence of one of their merchants, a man named Mursili. He liked to talk, and he revealed to me many things about his king

240

and their ways. He told me that if they fail to follow the rules their gods set down they risk plague or worse. Their gods are often angry with their king and his troops.'

'They'll be angrier still when we have annihilated their army and brought back their king in chains,' said one of the princes, and there was a chorus of agreement from some of the others, followed by hushed, yet respectful, admonitions from the vizier. Still, Ramesses must have approved of the sentiment, for to Hetep's relief he sat back and smiled.

'Your words are pleasing to me,' he said. 'You may retire.'

'Thank you, Majesty,' said Hetep.

He backed away, keeping his body low, until he was beside Sebeku again. As he straightened he wiped the sweat from his face and exhaled noisily.

'Well done,' whispered Sebeku. 'I thought you were in trouble there for a moment.'

The Royal Butler had recovered his poise and was glowering at them both.

'Hush!' said Hetep. 'You'll get us thrown out. I want to hear the rest.'

'So the men of Hatti do not let us take Amurru without protest,' Ramesses was saying to the vizier. 'You were right to assume so.'

The vizier inclined his head. 'If I was, it was only because I reflect Your Majesty's wisdom back at him.'

'Naturally,' said Ramesses, as if stating the obvious. 'And now all that I have planned has come to pass. No one else could have done this – only I, alone, had the foresight. Now all Hatti will march to Kadesh, and I shall meet them there and destroy them at a stroke.'

'It is as if Amun himself has decided to deliver them to you for destruction,' said the prince.

There was a moment of silence – worshipful for the most part, although one or two of the older faces showed traces of doubt.

'Are we not assuming too much?' said General Huti. 'This might be a ruse. Perhaps the Hittites intend to attack some other place while we're at Kadesh.'

'That is unlikely,' said the vizier. 'The city is at a joining of lands and all trade flows past it. Whoever controls Kadesh controls all of northern Canaan. His Majesty had already chosen it for his next conquest.'

'Then if we're expected we have all the more reason to be cautious,' said Huti. 'Kadesh is a Hittite vassal and our enemies can use the city as a base.'

'There is no need to fear, my loyal general, for now our cause is just,' said Ramesses. 'We fight not as aggressors but to suppress rebels and oath breakers, men who have violated the peace made by my predecessor, King Seti, and would do violence against Ma'at. Amun himself has handed me the khopesh and the gods Montu and Re will stand at my side – as was my intention, on the very day I conquered Amurru.'

Again the prince spoke, his eyes shining. 'You are like Re himself. You only have to say "let is be so" and it is. The foreigners will lay down in their thousands and smell the earth in front of you!'

The words seemed only to deepen Huti's concern.

'Majesty, what you say cannot be contradicted. But what if the Hittites get to Kadesh before us? Though Re might still give us the victory it will be a hard-fought one, for the enemy army will be rested and deployed to meet us. We cannot march until after the spring harvest.'

There was a murmur of agreement. A frown of displeasure touched Ramesses' brow but before he could speak Hetep stepped forwards again.

242

'That might not be too late,' he said. Then, remembering himself, he bowed and said, 'Forgive the interruption, Majesty, but there is something else I heard from the Hittite in Sumur. He was drunk and his talk was unguarded, and he said his king is going to have to set out late on next year's campaign because of the spring festival. So if Your Majesty marches as soon as he can he might get to Kadesh first, with time to spare to capture the city.'

Huti snorted in derision. 'The word of a scribe, reporting hearsay from a foreigner he says was drunk... we cannot put any faith in this report.'

'Then put your faith in My Majesty and my father Re, who guides my hand,' said Ramesses in a tone that brooked no argument. 'I alone am the one who proclaims effective deeds. Remember how I conquered the men of Amurru, and before them the Sherden, the Libyans and the Nubians. In doing so, no one could compare to me. In cowing the foreigners I received no instruction, yet I mastered it, as I shall again. We shall reach Kadesh before the vile men of Hatti,' – as he spoke his eyes rested briefly on Hetep – 'and then I shall surpass the achievements of all my predecessors.'

Ramesses had spoken and the audience was at an end. Hetep and Sebeku were herded out into the corridor with the others but instead of leaving the palace they loitered in the concealing shadow of a pillar by the main gate. There Hetep took out the papyrus sheet Nui had given him. Clutching it nervously he looked back towards the audience hall, then gulped when he saw the mayor appear and come walking towards them.

'You must do it now,' whispered Sebeku. 'You won't get another chance.'

But Hetep's courage, strained by his audience with

Ramesses, failed him and he turned away. The mayor drew near, oblivious to their presence, and as he passed Sebeku shoved Hetep, sending him staggering into his path.

The mayor goggled. 'What is the meaning of this assault?' he demanded, brushing himself off. 'Explain yourself.'

'My lord, I'm sorry. I tripped,' said Hetep, with a glare at Sebeku. 'Please, I wish to talk. But in private.'

The mayor's expression cleared.

'It's you – the young man from the audience chamber. I must say, I think you conducted yourself rather well in there. Now what it is you want?'

'I've brought something to show you. It's from Nui.' Hetep held out the sheet of papyrus. 'He says you should read it, and that you're to be trusted.'

At the word 'trusted' the mayor blanched and looked nervously around. 'If this is some conspiracy–'

'Please, my lord, it's nothing base, I swear. It's about the man I mentioned in the audience, Baya. He was appointed as Nui's assistant in Sumur but he abused his position and stole from the tribute. He also stole my reward for killing the prince of Irqata.'

'I see. But what does this matter have to do with me?'

'Nui says you know him, and that you can help.'

'Of course I know Nui. A most excellent soldier and a credit to all Egypt. But this is highly irregular. Perhaps one of my scribes–'

'It has to be you, my lord, or someone else important. I want to have Baya prosecuted and I need you to help arrange the hearing. The proof's all here. Nui wrote it all down.'

Hetep proffered the papyrus to the mayor, who took it with an ill-concealed reluctance.

'Proof, you say?' He scanned the opening lines and his eyes widened. Then they narrowed as he read more, and by the time he reached the end he was looking worried. 'Oh, my dear gods,' he said softly.

'Do you see? I can't let this matter rest. Baya stole Pharaoh's property and diminished Ma'at. Who knows what he'll do next.'

The mayor considered Hetep. 'How many other people know about this?'

'In Sumur, everybody. Here, a few. Why?'

Sebeku had been closely watching the mayor's face.

'Everyone in Re division knows, including our comrade Teppic,' he said quietly. 'He'd have told his father, too, and *he's* Scribe of Sacred Writings at the Re temple in Heliopolis.'

'Is he, now?' The mayor eyed Sebeku.

'Do you think we have a case?' asked Hetep anxiously.

'What? Oh, I shall have to say yes. Provided there are witnesses, of course. You do have some, don't you?'

'For the charge of embezzling Pharaoh's goods I'd have thought Nui's word should be enough. But there'll be a record of how much tribute was received here – you can check it with the list of what was supposed to have been sent. As for the battle at Irqata, one of Baya's witnesses is alive. We know he lied and I'm certain we can persuade him to tell the truth this time.'

'I see.' The mayor handed the papyrus back. 'I hope you realise what you are asking me to do. Baya's family is one of the most well respected in all Egypt and I have no desire to expose them to scandal.' He sighed. 'Still, I cannot refuse you, not with this evidence, and certainly not now so many people know about it.' He shot a dark look at Sebeku. 'Very well. The hearing will be held in two weeks. Don't forget to bring your witness.'

245

'Of course,' said Hetep. His heart was beating fast with excitement – this was more than he had dreamed of. 'Where should I bring him?'

'The gatehouse of the Amun temple. That's where we usually deal with this sort of business. I'll try to be there myself, of course, but...' The mayor's gaze slid away. 'Well... I might have to send one of my scribes to act in my place. Now remember, you have two weeks – that's twenty days. And don't forget to bring that witness.'

CHAPTER 27

'That was easier than I was expecting,' said Hetep once they were outside in the sunshine.

'Too easy,' muttered Sebeku. 'I don't trust him.'

'Why ever not? Nui said he was honest. And the man *did* say we have a case.'

'Honest maybe, but scared. Did you see his eyes?'

'He's the mayor of Pr-Ramesses. What's he got to be scared of? Sometimes I think you're pessimistic just for the sake of it. Come on, let's go and find Teppic. I want to see how he's been doing.'

From the palace it was only a short walk to the compound housing Re division's chariot squadrons. It was no mere barracks but a well-appointed cluster of houses, like a village without the peasants, and a gift from Ramesses to his charioteers who, as Egypt's military elite, were deemed to be more deserving of luxuries than the foot soldiers. It looked deserted, with swirls of dust drifting over the practice field and the houses all silent. Disappointed, they were about to turn away when they spotted Teppic emerging from the Montu shrine. He saw them and waved a greeting, then came over, smiling.

'Welcome back!' he said.

'Where is everybody?' asked Hetep.

'At home. There's nothing to do until next year's campaign; even the horses are out in the pastures. A few of us take turns to look after the place – keep out the robbers, tend to the shrine, go mad with boredom, that sort of thing.' Teppic's smile tightened. 'The glory of the charioteer's life, eh? Meanwhile here's you, fresh from slaying the hordes of Canaan and crushing rebellions, and to top it all an audience with the great Ramesses himself. How was it?'

'Terrifying. But if that's the price for being home I'm glad to have paid it.'

'And you're well I see.' This was to Sebeku.

'Only the gods know how after I was dragged halfway across that wretched kingdom, when I should have been convalescing in comfort.'

'And miss all the excitement at Sumur? You don't know how lucky you are.' Teppic sighed. 'Come on, there's still some of this day's batch of beer left in the storehouse. You can tell me all that's happened while we drink it.'

They sat in the shade and sipped from the beer jugs while Hetep recounted the events in Sumur, with the occasional sardonic observation from Sebeku.

'So there it is,' he said, concluding. 'More fear than excitement, and lots of dead Egyptians in that revolt.'

'Still, it could have been worse,' said Teppic.

Sebeku looked up. 'Yes, we could have all been killed,' he said. 'Or executed for conspiring with the locals.'

'Hardly,' said Teppic. 'There always was going to be a war you know; the armourers and chariot makers here at Pr-Ramesses haven't stopped working since we got back. The only question was how to provoke the Hittites into making the first move, so we'd have the gods' blessings.'

'Ramesses certainly got what he wanted,' said Hetep. 'You should have seen him with the Hittite envoys. It made my hairs prickle. The man's only half here.'

'Of course. The rest of him's a god, remember?' Teppic spoke with an irreverence that made Hetep uncomfortable.

'I wish you wouldn't talk like that,' he said. 'Anyway, what about my land? What's my uncle been up to?'

'Ah, him,' said Teppic, and drank deeply from his jug. 'He works fast, I'll give him that. We'd scarcely been back a week when he managed to seize half your father's estate – your estate, I should say. Sorry.' He took another gulp of beer.

'How?'

'The overseer you appointed turned out to be incompetent and wrecked someone's irrigation ditches. Something like that, anyway – Montu knows I'm no farmer. Anyway, he was beaten, of course, but after that he turned surly and let the place go to ruin. And that *ka* priest you hired for your father swapped the grain you paid him for gold and ran off. So all in all it gave the town's mayor the excuse he needed to start getting the land deeds changed in your uncle's favour.'

'That was no priest,' said Hetep. 'I thought I'd save a bit of wealth by hiring someone cheap.'

Sebeku stared at him, appalled. 'Did you not consider the effect this would have on your father's *akh*? It's no wonder we suffered so much ill fortune when we were away. The man must be livid!'

'You survived, didn't you?' Hetep set his beer down and put his head in his hands. 'Gods, what a mess. I have to get back, see if I can make amends to my father. And my land...'

'Don't worry, your uncle's not getting the rest,' said Teppic. 'I asked my father to get one of his best legal scribes to look into things. The man's got a Thoth-given talent for prevarication and he managed to find a clause in your father's will that seems to give a chunk of the farm to your mother. Your village mayor might have ruled you unfit to own the land but he said nothing about her, so she keeps it. Of course, your uncle disputes this – after all, your mother's only a foreigner, I'm sorry to say – but

249

it's going to take a generation to sort it all out.'

'Thank you,' said Hetep, brightening. 'See?' He looked pointedly at Sebeku, who scowled.

'I've been asking around about Baya, too,' said Teppic. 'There's a rumour flying about of some scandal that's been suppressed by his family. Not only that but the man's wealth is draining away like flood water, paying for a lifestyle well above his means. He's already had to sell off half his land.'

'Which gives him a motive for stealing,' said Hetep. 'I've already asked the mayor to call a hearing into Baya's conduct. With the statement I've got from Nui I think we'll be able to get him prosecuted. Then I can get my post back as charioteer.'

'Don't be so sure. His family might not be too keen on their wayward son, but they won't relish seeing his name dragged through the slime. And win or lose, you'll have made some dangerous enemies.'

'I'll take that chance.'

'You mean *we* shall take the chance,' said Sebeku. 'You may not have noticed, but when the arrows are flying around it's always me who gets hit, not you. The same might be true in a more legal sense.'

'Will you stop moaning? We just have to find Baya's witness, that's all. His name's Mehy.'

'Already done,' announced Teppic. 'After all, I had to do something to relieve the boredom. I tracked him down almost as soon as I came back.'

'I don't know how I'll ever repay you for all this,' said Hetep.

'Just stop Baya. The man's a menace, and if he manages to get himself a command when we go to Kadesh people are going to get killed.'

'You said you found Mehy,' said Sebeku. 'Where is

he?'

'Someone found him a job as a doorkeeper in one of the shrines hereabouts. You know he was wounded in the leg at Irqata? After he got back the wound began to fester and the physicians had to saw the leg off. He survived but he's a broken man. He drinks too much, weeps almost constantly and when he's sober he's forever making offerings at the Amun temple. He thinks the wound's a punishment for some sin he committed.'

'Probably lying under oath,' said Hetep. 'We'll pay him a visit and give him a chance to repent. But first I'm going home to see if I can do something about my father.'

'And what about me?' asked Sebeku. 'I'm on the ration list at Sumur, not Pr-Ramesses. What am I going to eat?'

'Don't worry – we'll make sure you won't starve,' said Teppic cheerfully. 'Re division never forgets its veterans.'

Hetep found passage on a barge taking grain south to the construction sites near Thebes. The Nile, its flood beginning to abate, was thick with traffic and the barge maneuvered ponderously around it, propelled upstream by the unvarying north wind. In less than a day they had reached the base of the Delta where stood Hetep's home village and it was with a feeling of relief that he disembarked.

The village was built on raised ground, well above the level of the flood. Near the river, closest to the crocodiles and mosquitoes, clustered the low, mud-brick huts of the labourers and farmers; behind, and upslope from the river, stood the granary in which his father had worked as an accountant, a half-dozen white-plastered manor houses and the village's single stone building: a shrine to the region's

251

tutelary goddess.

He took the main path from the jetty. So infrequent had his visits to the village been these past few years that the inhabitants seemed like strangers and he exchanged only a few words with them. His house was just as he remembered it: a two-storey building with a courtyard and animal corral, all enclosed by a retaining wall. Before going in he paused to look up at the lintel above the gate. It bore an inscription containing his father's name and achievements, carved by his own hand and declaring to the whole village that here lived a literate man, of higher status than those too ignorant to read it. Hetep had intended to replace the name with his own, but had yet to get around to it.

Cooking smoke drifted out through the gate and he guessed that his mother was preparing her midday meal. She would have no idea that he had returned and he smiled, thinking of how she would react when she saw him. He stepped through the gate and was unpleasantly surprised to see his uncle Nebenteru, who was standing over a rack of grilling fish.

'What are you doing here?' said Hetep.

His uncle looked up and scowled with displeasure.

'You're back a bit soon, aren't you?' he said. 'Don't tell me you've been dismissed.'

'You'd like that, wouldn't you? Another chance to tell me how worthless I am. Well, you're wrong. I distinguished myself in Sumur and Nui sent me back with a message for the pharaoh himself.'

'Pharaoh, eh? I don't suppose there was any reward. Still, it's a beginning. Your father might approve – assuming you're telling the truth, of course. Although it's a pity you had to wait until after his death before making something of yourself.'

'He'll know it when I tell him: I'm going to the grave this afternoon. Why are you here, anyway? This is still my house.'

'Someone has to keep things on order.'

'I think mother's quite capable of–'

'She's dead. Why else do you think the house is so empty?'

'Dead?' The news was so unexpected that at first Hetep felt nothing more than a dull puzzlement. 'I don't... I mean, how?'

'It happened a week ago. A snake bit her, and before the Serqet priest could come she died, raving, with the poison eating her like an angry god.'

The grief came suddenly and without warning; it made Hetep feel as if the ground was pitching beneath him and he covered his eyes with one hand, as if to shut out the world and its harsh truths. Unexpected deaths and funeral processions were as much a part of the rhythms the gods had established for humanity as the annual Nile flood and the rising and setting of the sun, yet he had always thought his mother would endure. And now she was gone. He knew he would feel her loss far more keenly than he ever had his father's, and the guilt he felt on account of *that* only magnified his grief.

He was aware that his uncle was glowering at him accusingly.

'What is it? What have I done?' he said.

'It's what you have not done that's more to the point. Had you attended to your filial duties more diligently the poor woman might still be alive.'

Hetep began to protest but under Nebenteru's stare the words caught in his throat and he bowed his head, knowing that his uncle was right. Of course, there was no suggestion that his father's *akh* was directly responsible

253

for his mother's death: although harsh he was not an especially cruel man and their relationship had known the odd moment of affection. But neglect of one's duties to the dead was an offence against Ma'at and could be punished by indirect means.

'I'm sorry,' he said. 'I don't know what else to say.' He suddenly felt empty and very much alone.

'Yes, well... It's done now, and there's no changing things. It's not as if you did it out of malice.' There was a rare note of sympathy in Nebenteru's voice. 'But now you're back you can make amends by helping me put things in order again.'

'I'm only here for a couple of days. I've got business in the Delta, and after that I'll be returning to Re division.'

Nebenteru's eyebrows came together. 'You'll do no such thing, young man. I've been making a few changes while you were away.'

'Yes, I know. You stole half my land – Teppic told me. But you're not having the rest.'

'Your father was right: the boy's a menace. And that scribe of his should be thrown to the crocodiles. But I've got a few tricks left. Your mother's passing to the West is an opportunity not to be missed. You'll see.'

'She's only just gone and already you're scheming. Have you no decency?'

'You'll watch your manners or you'll find yourself without any land at all.'

'Fine. Just you keep on plotting. In the meantime I'm going in to *my* house to take some food. And then I'm going to visit my father.'

Houses, mansions, and even palaces might be allowed to fall into ruin or be swept away by the Nile's flood but the cemeteries had to endure forever and their locations were chosen with care, always high above the water table. The site that served Hetep's village was on a raised plateau at the edge of the desert and the path leading to it was long, hot and very dusty. It was also well travelled: the dead were as much a part of any community as the living and most of the latter – as Hetep guiltily acknowledged to himself – made weekly treks to commune with their deceased loved ones.

The bulk of the cemetery's dead were buried in shallow holes scraped into the stony soil, with perhaps a beaded necklace to protect them from malign influences and a few cups and bowls for them to use in their post-mortem feasts. Hetep's father, being wealthy by village standards – although not in comparison with the scribes of the temples and palaces – had made sufficient provision for a decent sending off and Hetep had spent a good part of it on the tomb. The burial was at the bottom of a brick-lined shaft, and he had paid an artist to paint images of the food and drink his father would need to keep him fed in the West. But at the same time he had needed to pay for his first foray into chariotry and he had been forced to economise, buying only a simple reed coffin to house his father for his journey and hiring the cheapest craftsman he could find to make his father's labour gang – a set of wooden figurines who would perform a share of his corvée work for him in the Field of Reeds but whose numbers were barely sufficient to give him a day off each week.

The grave was marked by a stone block carved with his father's name and achievements. Beside the marker lay the offering tray, made of fired clay and shaped like a house with an over-large courtyard. Hetep knelt in front of the tray, swept out the accumulated sand and placed on it a bowl with a petition written inside in black paint. In the bowl he put a loaf of bread – a bit stale but the largest he could find in the house – and a great pile of dates, then poured out a whole jugful of beer into the offering hole. Still kneeling he recited all the prayers that were proper, and more besides. Finally he recited the words written in the bowl, to be sure that his father's *ba* would notice them when it next returned to the corpse.

'Hetep to Ramose, my father and lord. Greetings! I constantly pray that you are well and I make obeisance. In your life I was a dutiful son and I did all that was required. In your death I have offered to you on the proper days and I have not neglected your tomb. As you were excellent upon the earth so may you be in good standing in the West.

'All that you left me I have used to serve Pharaoh and to increase Ma'at. But now an evil man has taken what is mine and I go to seek redress. I ask that you confound my enemies and petition the gods to decide my case favourably.'

He knew that his preamble was mostly lies but he was genuinely sorry to have neglected his father's tomb – if only because of the consequences – and hoped that the sheer quantity of offerings would convince his father of his sincerity. For a long time he knelt by the tomb repeating his prayers, while the sun burned his back and the wind-blown sand stung his cheeks.

CHAPTER 28

Two days later he was back at the Re division compound, sitting with Teppic and a morose-looking Sebeku.

'How are things at home?' asked Teppic.

'My mother's dead.'

'Oh.' Teppic looked at him as if unsure how to react. 'I'm sorry. As I remember you rather liked her.'

Hetep nodded. 'When I was a child, whenever I was beaten by the schoolmaster in the scribal house she'd tell me stories to help take the pain away. She was killed by a snake. Perhaps if I hadn't neglected my father so much she might still be alive.'

'You don't know that.'

'I do,' said Sebeku. 'That man's malevolence followed us all the way to Canaan. And now it's followed us all the way back.'

Hetep gave a weary sigh. 'What do you mean "us"? What's happened to you now?'

'He's back with Re division,' said Teppic.

Sebeku gave him a sour look. 'As a stable hand.'

'*Royal* stable hand. Five *hinu* of barley a day and as many pomegranates as you can eat. Would you rather be a field labourer?'

For reply Sebeku just shook his head and lapsed back into silence.

'At least you'll get fed,' said Hetep. 'What about me? Now my mother's dead I'm ruined. All that land she inherited reverts to me, and since I'm considered unfit to own it, it goes straight to my uncle.' His hands clenched. 'Gods help me, I could strangle the man.'

'Now, now,' said Teppic. 'Murder's a sin, you know.

Don't worry, though: something'll turn up. Meantime we've still got Baya to deal with. And to that end I've discovered something about Mehy that'll help us. He used to be the fence for a gang of tomb robbers and Baya threatened to expose him if he didn't do as he was told.'

'If this comes out he'll be impaled, and Baya along with him,' said Hetep, his heart leaping.

'No chance of that I'm afraid: Baya's only peripherally involved. But Mehy's a real sinner, and he's desperate to repent and clear his conscience. So all we need do is get him to testify that he lied about Baya's deeds during the battle. In return I'll offer to have him pardoned – having an uncle who's Chief of the Medjay is sometimes useful, you know.'

'Nepotism to beat nepotism,' said Hetep, suddenly deflated. 'Is there no other way?'

'Stopping Baya can only strengthen Ma'at. How can the goddess not approve? And then you get declared the hero of the battle of Irqata, earn your rightful reward and you both end up back in Re division where you belong. And then we can deal with your uncle.'

'When do you want to go and see Mehy?'

'No time like the present. It's only a short walk.'

Mehy's house turned out to be a sprawling mansion with plaster-coated walls which glared white in the sunshine. From inside came the sound of mourning and Hetep could feel his stomach sinking as they stood in the street outside, listening.

'Now we're here we might as well go in,' said Sebeku. 'Although it's obvious the man's dead.'

It was one of the house slaves who told them what had happened to Mehy. Strong in body and with the stump of his leg seemingly healing well, at the same time his mind was sick and his nights were filled with evil dreams. A new physician was assigned to care for him and at first he appeared to rally. But soon afterwards he relapsed, his *ba* fading like a lamp running out of oil. The physician did all he could and a lector priest sat up night after night reciting the proper incantations, but Mehy left to begin his journey to the West just after sunrise this morning.

'Who was the new physician?' said Hetep. His words were so much wasted breath – he had already guessed what the answer would be.

'I do not know his name,' said the slave. 'My master's former commander, Baya, hired him using his own wealth. He said the physician was the best in all of Pr-Ramesses and it was the least he could do to help an old comrade.'

The cries of the hired mourners filled the house, and in the echoes Hetep was sure he could hear his father's mocking laughter. Wordlessly he turned and lead his friends out into the street. They found a low wall and sat in a line, staring out over the silt-laden fields under the full glare of the unforgiving sun.

'I told you we're cursed,' said Sebeku, breaking their long silence. He looked accusingly at Hetep. 'And it's your fault. Your father's *akh* follows us around like a cloud.'

The words irritated Hetep enough to rouse him from his thoughts.

'Can't you be positive for once?' he said. 'You give up if that's what you want to do, but I'm going to that hearing. We've still got Nui's statement. False accounting, treason, forgery – all the proof we need. It'll be enough; you'll see.'

Teppic regarded him with pity. 'Do you still have that *wadjet* I gave you?' he said. 'Because I think you're going

259

to need it.'

The hearing took place in the courtyard behind the
gatehouse of the Amun temple. Presiding was the local
chief priest of Thoth, a gaunt, humourless-looking man
with a thin lips and purple shadows under his eyes; he
was seated on a folding stool and from his neck hung a
pendant depicting the goddess Ma'at – the sign of his authority to administer justice. Beside him stood a junior
priest and at his feet sat a pair of scribes, one equipped
with a writing kit and a sheet of papyrus, the other surrounded by heaps of leather scrolls containing years' worth
of statutes. Baya was there, looking pleased with himself,
and at the back loomed a pair of Medjay, mercenary soldiers responsible for enforcing Ma'at within the borders of
Egypt and bearing staves with which to administer sum-
mary beatings to liars and perjurers.

A man came bustling in, red faced and sweating. He
ducked his head to the priest, apologised for his lateness
and introduced himself as Qatna, the mayor's chief scribe.
From his breathless gabble it appeared that the mayor had
been taken ill and he, Qatna, was to act as his representative. Hetep, remembering the mayor's earlier evasiveness,
felt a twinge of worry.

'I told you so,' muttered Sebeku.

The junior priest made a sacrifice and the smell of
burned meat filled the courtyard while Hetep, Sebeku and
Baya swore their oath to tell the truth, ending with the
words: 'If I lie, may I be mutilated and sent into exile.'
Then Qatna, reading from a statement Hetep had earlier
written out, listed the charges: that Baya had plotted
with, and armed, rebels in a subject city and had stolen
wealth destined for the royal storehouses; and that, to

further his own advancement, had robbed Hetep of his reputation and his reward for killing the prince of a rebel city.

'We shall judge the second matter first,' said the chief priest after Qatna had fallen silent. 'Let Hetep speak and tell us on what evidence he brings the accusations.'

Second? thought Hetep. He had assumed that they would be hearing the charges of embezzlement and treason first, but his objection was stilled by a warning look from the priest. He turned to Qatna to appeal for help but the man was avoiding his gaze, and again came the premonition that something was very wrong.

He forced himself to speak clearly and calmly, describing the events of the battle outside Irqata and how, once he had recovered from his injuries, he had learned that Baya had been rewarded for his act of valour.

'He lied about what happened. Not only to get the reward, which was an important posting in Sumur, but to cover up his own failures during the battle.' Hetep looked straight at Baya. 'As commander of second squadron it was his responsibility to hold the Amurrite chariots on that hill. Instead he let them through and they nearly destroyed first squadron. And my commander, Antef, was blamed.'

'Can you produce a witness to support this extraordinary claim?' asked the priest.

'Yes. My driver – he was there. He'll tell you.'

Sebeku came forward, ran a jaundiced eye over the assembly and began his account, describing how the Amurrite chariots broke free and pursued them. 'We managed to pull away at first, but only just.'

'And what of this prince Hetep says he slew?'

'He was there, chasing us. And he was gaining on us, too.'

261

'Gaining, you say?' The priest's eyebrows shot up. 'He must have had horses made by a god to keep up with an Egyptian chariot!'

'We'd already taken part in two attacks,' said Sebeku. 'Phoenix and Might-of-Set were exhausted. If not, even the best of them would not have caught us.' Hetep heard the pride for his horses in Sebeku's voice, and the grief over their deaths. 'And then Hetep shouted, and when I looked around the prince and his chariot were gone.'

'And what of the second squadron?'

'They weren't there,' said Sebeku. 'It was just us.'

'Doubtless you did not see them because they were hidden by the dust,' said the priest. 'Now tell me: did you see the prince of the city fall? I remind you that you are under oath.' The priest's eyes were fixed on Sebeku's face. At his feet the scribe was scratching away on the papyrus with his pen.

'No.' Sebeku shook his head. Briefly he closed his eyes. 'I'm sorry,' he said to Hetep, while the priest sat back, smiling with satisfaction.

'It's not your fault,' said Hetep. He faced the priest again. 'I know what I did and I know what I saw, as plainly as I see you sitting here today. In battle Montu sharpens the eyes and quickens the heart, and everything stands out bright, just as we are told it is in the Field of Reeds. And things happen that afterwards you can't forget. It's not like making out inventories, or stacking mud bricks, or even reciting prayers. Battle is different.'

'Yes, I know,' said the priest dryly. 'I was once a chariot archer myself, and after that a Standard Bearer of Chariotry in Amun division. I was with King Seti when we fought the Hittites.'

'I'm sorry,' said Hetep. 'I didn't know. I meant no disrespect.'

'Let us hope not.' The priest eyed him. 'Do you have any other witnesses?'

'There was Mehy, one of Baya's troop leaders. He would have told us much more.'

'Is he here?' The priest made a show of looking around the courtyard.

'He's dead,' said Hetep flatly. He glanced at Baya, who could not stop a faint smirk of triumph from showing on his face.

'How unfortunate for you,' said the priest. 'And now I think it is time we heard from the accused. Well?'

'My lord,' said Baya, with a quick bow to the priest. 'Mehy, the troop leader Hetep mentioned, was wounded in the battle and the physicians had to remove one of his legs. Then his *ba* weakened and he saw his death coming in a dream, and as a final service to me he dictated again his account of events, the very night before he passed to the West.' Baya handed a document to the priest. 'You will find it matches mine exactly. A bare handful of Amurrite chariots broke away, we chased them and destroyed them, and it was my arm that slew the prince of Irqata.'

All this time Qatna had been standing in awkward silence. Now, prompted perhaps by Ma'at herself to intervene, he stepped forwards and cleared his throat.

'Forgive me, and I don't want to upset things,' he said, with a diffidence that sent Hetep's *ka* sinking further, 'but are we sure this testimony is reliable? I find it an odd coincidence that the only man who can corroborate Baya's statement died on the very eve of this hearing. What's more, I am sure that what Hetep has to tell us of the second matter will cast sufficient doubt on Baya's character to make us question his veracity. And don't forget what Nui tells us.'

Hetep felt a flicker of hope, only to have it crushed an

263

instant later by the priest's next words.

'Nui admits in his account that he did not see all that happened. And as for Baya's reliability as a witness, that has yet to be called into question.'

'But if you'd examined the treason charge first–' began Hetep.

'It is *I* who decides what we investigate here, young man, not you,' said the priest. He was avoiding Baya's eye and in that moment Hetep knew that he had been bribed. 'Now it seems plain to me that we can ponder the truth of this matter all day and get nowhere. Yet at the same time there is a higher authority to whom we can appeal: that of Ramesses himself – may he have life, prosperity and health. And he has already rewarded Baya for the deed of killing the enemy prince that day. So tell me: how can the Son of Re be in error?'

A long silence followed. Of course, there was nothing Hetep or anybody else could say to contradict the priest's words.

'Then it is settled,' said the priest. 'Now let us consider the charge of the misappropriation of royal goods. I have here Baya's statement,' – he held up another piece of papyrus – 'in which he assures me that he was consulting this Zuratta only in accordance with his duty, which was to determine the most productive and highest quality sources of wood and metal from which to take the tribute. In doing so he proved himself to be a most diligent servant of the pharaoh and a true credit to his profession.'

'What about the theft?' said Hetep. 'Nui made it plain. A ton of metal, as much again of wood, all missing from the shipments. How does Baya explain that?'

'Very easily,' said Baya smoothly. 'The missing goods were stolen by the Amurrites. By nature they are thieves, yet Nui did nothing to curb them. Is it any wonder they

264

plundered the storehouses? But for my vigilance even more might have been lost. As for what was shipped, not one shekel went missing.' He held up a bundle of closely-written papyrus sheets. 'I have here, brought from Sumur, a full inventory of the tribute that was sent, and if you compare it with the records of what was received at Pr-Ramesses, you will find the two agree exactly.'

'Just look at the colour of those sheets,' cried Hetep. 'The papyrus is freshly made. They're forgeries!'

'I remind you that you are in the presence of the god,' admonished the priest. 'You will keep your voice at a reasonable level. Baya has answered the charges to my satisfaction. Now concerning this last matter: that of treason and the arming of rebels. If he committed such a sin, why did Nui release him to come here?'

'He didn't,' said Hetep. 'Baya was put under arrest in Sumur but he absconded; he should still be there. And don't forget Zuratta, Baya's helper, was executed for rebellion.'

'Allow me to point out,' said Baya, 'that Zuratta rebelled against the king of Sumur and not against Ramesses, may he have life, breath and health.'

The priest gave a small sigh. 'If only Nui were here to clarify matters. But he is not, and so all we can do is accept the truth as it stands before us today.'

'But Baya colluded with our enemies,' said Hetep, almost choking with despair. 'He's a traitor! He armed the Habiru – the ones who helped the rebels.'

'Pharaoh himself is arming the Habiru of the nearer regions even as we speak. They are to join next year's campaign as mercenaries; all know that they are useful fighters. Would you say the Son of Re's policies are wrong?'

It was like being trapped in a nightmare. Hetep looked appealingly at Qatna but the man was refusing to look

265

him in the eye. He knew now that whatever he said would make no difference, that Baya's acquittal was as certain as the next sunrise, yet for the sake of his own pride he could not give up.

'That's different,' he said. 'The ones in Sumur were rebels.'

'Rebels against the authority of a foreign king, not Egypt,' said the priest. 'Now that is enough!' He banged a fist on his knee. 'The evidence has been presented and the charges answered. And now it is time to render judgement. The accusations brought are for serious offences – men have been impaled for less. And for this reason alone we must be absolutely certain they are not baseless. We must take into account the facts that Amurru is far away and these events occurred many weeks ago – a sufficient distance to cloud the issue. We must also take into account the possibility that Nui is using you to bring these accusations against Baya to divert scrutiny from his own mismanagement of the city. There was, after all, a rebellion. For these reasons I find that there are no grounds for a prosecution.'

'But it was Baya who was responsible for the rebellion,' shouted Hetep. 'And I was the one who put it down.'

'One more outburst and I shall have the Medjay flog the skin off your back. You are in the god's presence. Be silent!' The priest glared at Hetep, killing his protest. 'Your earlier testimony was shown to be nothing but lies, so why should we give credence to what you tell us now about Baya's conduct? However, we do still have Nui's letter to take into account. Baya stands convicted of over-familiar contact with foreigners and for that he is admonished. The other charges are dismissed.'

'How can this be just?' cried Hetep. 'Is everything Baya touches corrupt?'

'I do not like the implication of what you are saying,' said the priest. 'I could have you charged with making false statements. Indeed, I could have your ears and nose taken off and have you sent to the royal mines for the rest of your life. In fact, I'm minded to do it now.' He turned to the Medjay.

'Wait, I beg you,' said Qatna. 'Let us not commit an injustice. We have all sworn by the Ruler's name to find the truth, yet I must say its full form has eluded us. Under such circumstances it would be an affront to Ma'at if you were to condemn Hetep for any misdeed.'

Clearly the priest did not like being reminded that his primary duty as a judge was to uphold Ma'at and he glared back, even while he shifted uncomfortably on his stool.

'Very well,' he snapped. 'This hearing is closed.' He wagged a finger at Hetep. 'And don't let me find you here before me again.'

CHAPTER 29

Hetep lingered in Pr-Ramesses, unwilling to return home and endure his uncle's gloating pleasure over the crushing of his hopes. At night he slept in a palm grove; by day he hung about the docks, drinking beer to drive away his despair. Teppic and Sebeku were as sympathetic as they could be but it was not long before his black moods drove them away, leaving him to share his sorrows with those few unlucky sailors and labourers close enough to hear him.

For long hours he would sit brooding over his beer jug, reliving in his mind the events of the hearing, each time devising new arguments to try to escape the web of lies that had trapped him. And each time the priest in his imagination would find new ways to twist his words against him, or counter his protests with arguments as absurd as they were irrefutable. It was as if his own *ka* was fighting against him.

Often in his drunken fantasies he would take his revenge, stamping out the priest's contemptuous sneer with the heel of his foot, and then he would grin savagely and the dock workers would edge away from him. At other times, as he dwelled on the injustice of what he had seen and suffered, a sullen anger would flare up inside him, fuelled rather than dulled by the beer. He and his comrades had risked their lives in Amurru to increase Ma'at only for Baya, a coward who had stolen his good name, to weaken it again with lies and bribery. The ease with which the priest had been corrupted was frightening; was all society so rotten? If so he feared for Egypt's future, for without Ma'at the temple offerings would cease, Egyptian would kill Egyptian and foreigners would be able to enter the land at will. Then Egypt would become like Amurru – disordered, weak, and ruled by a treacherous, self-serving creature like Benteshina.

As the beer tightened its grip and the day's empty jugs piled up his thoughts would veer from Egypt's peril back to his own misfortunes. The destruction of his chariot and his loss of status, the theft of his land, and even the death of his mother – the last an ever-present ache in his *ka* that flared up whenever he probed it with his mind – were clear signs of a malevolence acting against him from outside the mortal world. Sometimes he would remember all the men he had killed in Amurru and picture their *akhs* following him to Egypt to work their evil against him, and he would clutch the amulet Elissa had given him and mutter prayers to Anat in both Amurrite and Egyptian. Only later, when his mind was working with that strange, altered clarity of deep drunkenness, would he admit to himself what his *ka* knew to be the truth: that all his misfortunes, his evil dreams, even his fear and self-doubt, were caused by his father's *akh*. And as the brewing goddess' gifts turned sour in his belly he would curse the old man's malice, which had reached out from beyond the tomb to wreck his ambitions far more effectively than the beatings he had administered when he was alive and trying to destroy Hetep's growing friendship with Teppic.

It was the fourth day after the hearing and again he was at the docks drinking. Nearby a raucous group of sailors was clustered around a senet game. He welcomed their racket, for it helped to drive out the endless, futile cycle of thoughts from his mind. One of the players must have just won, for there was a roar of laughter and he saw a forest of beer cups held high in a toast. He raised his own cup, drank, and banged it down again. He rubbed

269

his eyes, and when he looked up again Baya was standing in front of him.

'I've been looking for you,' said Baya. 'I didn't expect to find you among the city's dregs.'

Hetep stared. It took a moment for the anger to burn through the fog of drunkenness, and then he lunged for Baya's throat.

Baya darted out of the way. 'I'm not here to fight you.'

The sudden movement made Hetep's head reel and he collapsed back onto his seat.

'Then go away,' he said thickly, and poured himself some more beer. The jug was almost empty; he would have to find another.

'Don't you want to know why I'm here?'

'No.'

Baya snatched the cup from Hetep's hand. 'How much of this have you had?'

'Not enough,' said Hetep, and made a grab for his beer.

'Stop that! I've come to help you. I can make you a chariot warrior again.'

'I said go away.' Hetep gave up trying to retrieve his cup and drank from the jug.

'I'm serious,' said Baya. 'I'm leading a squadron to Libya to reinforce one of the western garrisons.'

'Another reward, eh?' said Hetep bitterly. He belched and wondered if he was going to be sick.

'You really are drunk. It's exile, you fool. My family want me out of the way.'

'Don't bother to say goodbye when you leave.' Hetep closed his eyes, hoping that if he could not see Baya he would go away. But when he opened his eyes Baya was still very much there.

'Will you listen? We're a crew short in the squadron. I'm offering the place to you.'

'Thanks to you I'm a scribe now. I've got no chariot, no horses and no equipment.'

'Everything you need will be provided. I know people who can help.'

'The benefits of wealth, eh?' Hetep belched again. 'Well, I don't want your charity. And I don't want to see you again. You've done me enough harm already.'

'But it's what you want, isn't it? A return to the life you struggled so much for. Don't look so surprised: everyone knows your history.'

'What I want is to have my name restored,' said Hetep, his voice rising. 'What I *want*, you corrupt, murdering sack of vulture dung, is to fight beside the pharaoh and have my achievements acknowledged instead of stolen.'

'You think you've got grievances against me?' said Baya, sounding angry for the first time. 'What about that ridiculous accusation you made against me in Amurru, and here in Pr-Ramesses? I had a guaranteed income of twenty *debens* of silver a week from that trade at Sumur. In time I could have been Royal Envoy! Who cares about a little redirected tribute? But then you had to stir things up against me. And now I'm being sent to Libya. So you've had your revenge.'

Hetep glared at Baya, trying to hold on to a hatred that was being steadily dissolved in floods of alcohol.

'Come to Libya, with me. You know what these savages are like; there's bound to be some fighting, and we can gain recognition and status. Together.'

'Why me?' said Hetep.

'Because I need experienced charioteers like you and Sebeku. You should see what I've been given to command: sons of rich families, who think it's their Amun-given right

271

to ride a chariot, when they barely know one end from the other.'

'So much for the advantages of breeding, eh?'

Baya ignored the jibe. 'We have a chariot for you. It's a little old, but it's the proper type, and you can pick your horses. We've even got new-forged weapons. And you'll be promoted. Troop commander – how does that sound?'

Hetep's earlier sickness passed and he found he was thirsty again.

'Get me some more beer and I'll think about it.'

CHAPTER 30

He woke with his head splitting and the morning sun shining fully into his face, and he groaned as the memories of yesterday evening's drinking bout came back to him: the drunken game of senet, in which he had lost his tunic in a reckless wager after insulting the dockworkers; vomiting into an irrigation canal until his stomach was empty; and lurching about, decrying the Ma'at-destroying evils of nepotism to anyone within earshot. From there he remembered what had prompted his debauch and he sat up, blinking, with Baya's name on his lips.

He pulled himself to the water's edge, bathed his head and took a long drink. Then he lay, his head sideways, staring across the farmland. Near the border of some wheat fields a gang of workers was repairing a leak in one of the water storage basins; exhausted, they were slipping and falling about in ankle-deep mud. He felt sorry for them and thanked all the gods that, as a scribe, he had little chance of ever being forced to join them.

But there were other kinds of drudgery, and he shuddered as he contemplated a lifetime of filling out ledgers and counting bushels of grain. For all its dangers there was nothing to compare with life as a charioteer, with its excitement, easy camaraderie and the feeling of doing right by keeping back the ever-encroaching chaos. And now Baya was offering him the chance to experience it again. He had not forgotten that the man had tried to bribe him before, and in doing so stain him with the taint of corruption, and he had been right to refuse. But now all he was being asked to do was join Baya's squadron and potentially fight on the Libyan border, and there all he needed to fear was injury and death. What could go wrong?

It did occur to him that Baya might only be feigning friendship in order to have a better opportunity to kill him. But with the hearing concluded in Baya's favour Hetep could see no further motive for murder. Besides, the man had sounded both sincere and desperate – at least so he remembered. There was, of course, no question that Baya had the power to do as he promised: even the mighty Ramesses had to be careful not to antagonise the old military families, and in exchange for their support had already made a number of concessions, not the least of which was providing his charioteers with housing separate from the infantry barracks.

No, this had to be the first sign of a change in his fortunes. Perhaps, he thought, his petition to his father had made an impression after all and the old man's *akh* was finally working for his benefit. It must have helped that his mother would have reached him in the West by now, and doubtless her softening influence was at work, too.

He pushed himself to his feet and stared walking, and before long was standing at the gate of the southern military compound where he knew Sebeku worked. There he waited, enviously watching a troop of charioteers as they exercised their teams. He spotted Sebeku emerging from the barracks and called out, waving.

Sebeku scowled as he came over.

'What is it?' he said. 'Make it quick – I don't want to be late again.'

Hetep was guiltily aware of how disagreeable his behaviour had been over the past few days. 'I'm sorry if I said anything I shouldn't. But I'm sober now.'

'Drunkenness is no excuse for boorishness. Now what

do you want?'

Quickly Hetep told Sebeku about Baya's offer. 'I'm thinking of taking it up,' he said. 'But if I do I need you to go with me.'

'Whenever we fight it's always me who gets hurt. The Irqatans, those rebels at Sumur – I'm turning into scar tissue. And now you want me to risk my neck again, and this time under the command of a man who twice tried to kill you and who murdered a witness before a hearing. And you say you're sober!'

'We don't really know that Baya sent Zuratta after me. It could have been a coincidence.'

'Does your desire for glory blind you that much? He's going to get you alone in the desert one night and stick a knife in your back.'

'Not if I've got you to protect me.'

Sebeku made a disgusted sound and turned to go.

'Wait,' said Hetep. 'I'm going, alone if I must. Stay here if you want, but it means I'll be facing the Libyans with a stranger in the chariot.'

'Then you're a fool. As I would have to be to go with you.'

'It's a chance to get back what we had. It'll be like old times again, like it was in Amurru. I promise.'

'What makes you think I even *want* any of that?' said Sebeku, and when Hetep just stared at him in puzzled silence he went on, 'I've spent a long time in those stables shovelling dung with nothing else to do but think, and I've come to realise a few things I've been hiding from myself. I never told you, but when I was in Sumur recovering from that wound I wondered if I'd ever have the courage to board a chariot again. Maybe it was the evil god who'd brought the fever, but I was afraid. Afraid of more pain and of being killed – or worse, crippled.'

'We all get that sometimes. I've felt it, and that's without the fever.' Hetep did not say that in some of his nightmares he was lying shrieking under the physician's knife after being hacked and slashed in battle. 'But once you're there, charging with the rest of the squadron, with the noise, the drums, the cheering... it's different then. I've never been so alive. And neither have you.'

'I know,' sighed Sebeku. He looked down and scuffed at the dirt with his toe. 'Yet still the fear is there. And it shames me.' He looked up again. 'Perhaps if it was any man but Baya I'd go. But it's too dangerous. I'm sorry.'

'What's the alternative? Sweeping stables until you die?'

'I'm no menial, you know. Sometimes I get to exercise the horses. And there's always a chance of promotion.'

Hetep saw the look of injured pride in his friend's eye. 'I'm sorry,' he said gently. 'But you can't read or write. Stablemasters, chief grooms, anyone like that, they're all literate. If you stay here all you'll ever do is sweep stables. Perhaps you don't mind that, but I do.'

They heard shouts from the barracks and a figure appeared at the doorway, angry and breathless. It was the division's Chief Scribe of the Stables. He caught sight of Sebeku and came marching over.

'Where in Sekhmet's name have you been?' he cried. 'I swear you're as lazy as the slaves – lazier, even. Get inside, this instant! If the east stable block isn't done by the midday rest I'll have you beaten.'

Without waiting for an answer he turned on his heel and stormed off. Sebeku spat where his shadow had been and watched him go, his eyes black with hate.

'You were a man of status once,' said Hetep. 'There's

no future for you here. You know that.'

'Just tell me when we start.'

Baya had called his new command a squadron, although with only thirty machines in total it barely deserved the name. The crews, all freshly recruited sons of the nobility, were boastful and full of swagger, and Hetep did not care for them much. In Baya's company they were more reserved, eyeing him with something close to awe, as befitting a man who they believed had met the foreign menace in its native land and bested it.

As their training began in earnest Hetep was ashamed to discover how weak he had become after his months of idleness and he took to practicing his archery away from the others' sight. Meanwhile Sebeku spent his time at the horse corrals until, one day, he summoned Hetep to show him the team he had chosen: a pair of bay stallions, huge and powerful, their withers higher than Hetep's chest, and among the first of the tribute from Sumur. Sebeku's face shone with pride as he introduced them.

'This one I have named Ibis, for he is as wise and graceful as Thoth himself,' he said, indicating the horse on his left. 'And here, dark and brooding, is Vengeance-of-Amun. Are they not magnificent? Only a god will be able to catch us on the battlefield.'

To Hetep the horses looked identical. Still, he was glad for his friend, who seemed happier than he had been for months. But Sebeku was less happy when they yoked the team to their chariot and took a drive around the practice field.

'It pulls too much to the right,' he said. 'See, the pole is bent.'

'They're all like that. Or the axle's a bit misaligned,

or the car's a little different. That's because they're all made by different people.'

'I liked our first one more.'

'Well its broken, so we can't have it. Anyway, you used to keep moaning that it pulled too much to the left. Why not try swapping the horses over?'

'Given your lack of expertise I think it best you leave the handling of the team to me.'

The next morning Hetep found Sebeku on the practice field again. The sun had barely risen yet already the driver was covered in dust, his sweat making long streaks down his face and torso.

'Better now?' asked Hetep.

'I have adjusted the reins so that the car maneuvers more easily,' replied Sebeku, with a stiffness that made Hetep sure that the horses had been swapped after all.

'Let's hope you're right. We're due to leave in a couple of days.'

The afternoon finished with a massed exercise, the whole squadron maneuvering together and shooting at targets. Hetep could only charitably describe the other crews as competent: although they could keep formation well enough they were slow in the turn and the warriors often shot wildly – much as he had done in the opening salvoes at Irqata, he remembered. He could only hope that, if it did come to a fight, they would learn their trade quickly enough that they would not all be killed. Still, it was a reassuring confirmation that Baya had spoken the truth about the poor quality of his command.

He shared his thoughts with Sebeku, who shook his head.

'We're off to ruin, you'll see,' he said darkly. 'Baya can't be trusted.'

'Missing the stables already, are you?' said Hetep.

The day before they were due to set out Hetep's uncle appeared at the compound gates. He looked weary, and his feet and legs were covered in dust.

'Don't tell me,' said Hetep. 'You've only just noticed I was gone.'

'I've been searching the whole Delta for you. What are you doing?'

'I'd have thought the fact that I'm in the middle of a military camp would have made the answer to that obvious.'

Nebenteru looked around, and if he saw anything he approved of his expression did not show it.

'Well, you're to come home – immediately. I can't manage two farmsteads at once.'

'You're the one who stole my land. If you can't tend it, that's your problem. Anyway, even if I wanted to I couldn't leave now. I'm a charioteer, under military discipline.'

'You haven't the wealth! Now stop this foolishness and–'

'No, I don't have the wealth,' said Hetep. 'You've seen to that. But I don't need it any more. I've got patronage now, from one of Egypt's leading men.' A half lie at best, but the less he said about Baya the better. 'So this time you can't stop me. We're leaving for the Libyan border tomorrow.'

'Libya?' Nebenteru's face went from scorn to horror in a heartbeat. 'Thoth preserve us, you'll never come back! If the heat doesn't kill you the savages will.'

'I'm touched by your concern. But I'm still going.'

279

'Listen to me. All this chasing after gold and fame, all this chariot nonsense – what has it got you except toil, injury and grief at seeing your comrades die? And look at you! All scrawny and dark from the sun, when you should be plump and soft skinned, with a good roll of fat on your belly. Don't you care what people think of you?'

'Just go home will you? There's nothing you can do to stop me this time.'

'What if you're killed? You have no heirs and the family line will die. Who will offer sacrifices to your *ka* then? And who will tend to your father and to me once I'm gone?' There was a note of desperation in Nebenteru's voice that stirred a faint pity in Hetep, but he kept his expression hard.

'And even if you don't die,' his uncle went on, 'you could be crippled or maimed. Remember that man – what was his name? – who came back blind after he was struck in the head in King Seti's wars. What is he now? A doorkeeper who hasn't a clean rag to dress in, and has to beg for extra grain. And all the other cripples we've seen, their lives ruined. What if that happens to you?'

Hetep could see the men of the squadron gathering for the midday meal and smelled the bread baking in the ovens.

'I need to go,' he said. 'I'm sorry.'

'Please, think again.' But when Hetep only shook his head Nebenteru bowed his own. 'So be it,' he said with a quiet resignation. 'You are going to death or worse. May your father, and the gods of our household, witness that I tried.'

CHAPTER 31

It took three days for Baya's squadron to cross the Delta and reach the western-most edge of the cultivated land. Beyond lay the desert, a barren, rubble-strewn plain broken by irregular outcroppings of wind-carved rock. Here and there wadis cut the surface like slashes made by a huge knife, and the only vegetation was a few patches of scrub, burned almost to blackness by the sun. And over it all lay a haze of drifting sand, giving the whole landscape a tinge of red – the colour of death.

The road ran in an unbroken line straight towards the western horizon and they moved along it in single file. As they left the farmland behind, with its cooling irrigation ditches and water basins, the heat enveloped them, the air so hot and dry that it hurt the lungs to breathe. After only an hour the men were sagging in their cars – all except Baya, who was leaning forwards, hands gripping his chariot's rail, and staring with a feverish intensity at the far horizon.

Both Hetep and Sebeku had been keeping a careful watch on Baya, but the commander had shown nothing more than a reserved awkwardness in their presence, as if he was ashamed of his former malice – which was suspicious behaviour in itself, but nowhere near as puzzling, or indeed unsettling, as the change in his demeanour they now witnessed.

'It's as if he can't wait to get to grips with the Libyans,' said Hetep, remembering Baya's words about seeking glory. 'Look at his face!'

'I know, and it's getting worse,' said Sebeku. 'The man can't keep still. But as for the Libyans, it's hard to imagine meeting anyone – friend or enemy – out here.'

For ten monotonous days they followed the trail, seeing nothing living but a few insects and lizards. Then, on the morning of the eleventh day, as they were creeping along under a coppery sky, parched and nearly blinded by the light glaring from the pale rocks, there came a waft of cool, moist air and the scent of vegetation. The horses' ears pricked forwards, their nostrils dilated, and without prompting they accelerated into a trot, eager for water. Soon the squadron reached the lip of a crest, and there before them lay the first of the great water-filled depressions that made up the Bahariya oasis.

It looked like a huge green bowl sunk into the stony landscape and was filled with palm groves, reed beds, grain fields and vineyards. Corrals held sheep and cattle, and clusters of mudbrick houses stood on the humps of raised ground. It was as if the men of the squadron had died and were seeing the Field of Reeds, so green and perfect did it look; indeed, many of them dismounted and offered prayers of gratitude, lifting their arms to the sky.

They followed the road down, delighting in the coolness of the air and eager to reach the shade of the trees. They passed a cemetery, which held everything from elaborate tomb chapels to simple stone markers, then a group of mansions and beyond that a temple to Ramesses, its gates flanked by a pair of statues of the pharaoh at which he would receive the oasis folk's worship. And here were the inhabitants themselves, hundreds of them, pausing in their labours to stare at the charioteers, the first new faces they must have seen in months.

The men stopped beneath the palms and drank until they thought they would burst. Baya, his fey restlessness still upon him, would not let them linger and soon they were off again, climbing the road back to the desert.

Ahead of them lay more depressions, stretching all the way to the horizon, with crowns of trees just showing above the plain. They skirted them one by one, still heading west, and by the next afternoon their goal was in sight: a mudbrick fortress built on a raised outcrop right on the western edge of the oasis, its buttressed walls painted with crude images of a nameless pharaoh massacring panicking Libyans.

The squadron rolled in through the gate and halted at the parade ground – a square of packed earth bordered by a workshop, barracks and a small shrine to Amun, all with crumbling brickwork. A few slaves were moving about listlessly and some dogs were digging into a rubbish tip, but otherwise the place looked deserted.

A door crashed open and a score of shabby-looking infantrymen trudged out of the barracks and formed a ragged line, their weapons held ready in a parody of military ceremony. They were lead by a fat man with a wide, crimson face and a nose riddled with broken veins, who was wearing a patched suit of linen armour bearing the insignia of a commander-of-five-hundred. He came stumping over, accompanied by a scribe, and introduced himself with more cheerfulness than the situation warranted as Khamet, the garrison's commander.

'What a fine body of men,' he declared, beaming like the sunrise. 'Now if you'd just give my chief scribe here your names we can see about getting you fed and watered. Can't issue rations to just anybody who wanders in, can we?'

They were assigned sleeping places in the barracks and fed with bread and goats' cheese, washed down with sour-tasting beer. Afterwards Baya insisted on a meeting with Khamet and invited Hetep to accompany him – probably, thought Hetep, as a sign of trust, but with Baya's strange

283

restlessness in evidence he was still wary.

'It seems we truly are needed here,' said Baya once he, Khamet and Hetep were settled. 'You look somewhat short handed.'

'Indeed we are,' admitted Khamet. 'But it wasn't always so.' He was drinking wine, although he made no move to offer any to Hetep or Baya. 'We used to have a much bigger garrison but last year something evil got into the well.' He paused for another gulp of wine.

'And?' said Hetep.

'They died, of course – almost a hundred in all. Their bowels fell out. So we mostly stick to the beer now.'

Baya grimaced. 'I shall tell my troopers to do the same.'

'Good idea,' said Khamet. 'Don't want to lose them as well. We've only got a couple of chariots and even they haven't been working for a while. And if there's one thing that keeps the Libyans quiet its chariots. They haven't got any of their own, of course, being only foreigners, and they're in awe of ours.'

'All the better. Now when can we expect to do battle with these savages?'

'Battle?' Khamet snorted. 'We skirmish now and then with the odd band of raiders but that's it. Most of the tribesmen hereabouts are nomadic herders and all they care about is feeding their animals.'

'Nomads, bandits... what's the difference?' sneered Baya. 'Thieving is a way of life for all unsettled peoples. I hope I do not need to remind you, commander, that we've come here to uphold Ma'at, not collaborate with savages who do not revere Amun.'

Khamet looked bemused. 'Bandits? Hardly. They're mostly family groups – women and kids. A few hunters, maybe, but not many are warriors.'

'Families?' Baya was frowning. 'You are mistaken, surely.'

Hetep was trying not to smile at Baya's obvious disappointment. The man clearly imagined that he would already be slaughtering his way to renown through legions of floundering tribesmen, and was finding the reality of their situation difficult to come to terms with.

Khamet must have realised it too, for he was grinning. 'Yes, families. You've come to the wrong place for glory, my eager young warrior.'

'Then what were we sent here for?' Baya looked at Hetep as if expecting him to supply the answer.

Hetep shrugged. 'Don't ask me. You're the one who seems to want a war out here.'

'You won't be idle if that's what you're worried about,' said Khamet. 'For a start you can help us scare off the bolder raiders. Just accompany the foot patrols, ride around a bit, kick up some dust, that sort of thing. As I said, the tribesmen are in awe of chariots. And of course, it makes an impression on the oasis folk.' He chuckled and gave a sly smile. 'Oh yes, indeed.'

Dawn found Hetep alone in the storehouse, inspecting his chariot's frame. It had been a punishing journey from the Delta and already two of the squadron's machines had all but fallen apart in the arid air, and he was anxious not to disgrace himself by making his the third. He was crouched over, testing the tension of the sinew that strapped the axle to the cab, when he heard the scrape of a foot behind him.

He stood and turned, and saw Baya standing barely a spear thrust away. His mouth went dry and with his heart pounding he stepped back, searching around for a weapon. There: a pile of javelins and some khopeshes, stacked at the corner of the corral. If he made a dash for them he was sure he would reach them first...

Baya followed his gaze and smirked.

'You won't be needing any of those,' he said. 'Not today, anyhow.'

'What do you want?' The hairs on Hetep's arms and scalp slowly settled.

'To talk. In private.' Baya looked about him as if to be sure they were alone. 'We didn't have much of a chance on the journey here – although there was, in truth, little enough for us to say to each other. Still, I hope our time together in the desert has made you realise you can trust me. Remember, I'm not your enemy here.'

'Then who is?'

'The Libyans of course. That commander is a drunkard and a fool – we can both see that. We may need to take matters into our own hands. Can I rely on you, when the time comes?'

'Comes for what?'

'For us to seize command of the garrison. It's obvious Khamet panders to these savages and that they take advantage of it.'

'Obvious, after only one day?'

'You believe it too, and if you say otherwise you're lying. So I ask you again. If we need to take command, do I have your support?'

'I'll do what I think right, according to the requirements of Ma'at,' said Hetep stiffly.

'Of course.' Baya gave him a searching look. 'Remember, we need to win a victory here. Otherwise neither of us will get back to where we belong.'

He left as quietly as he had come while Hetep stared after him, his pulse gradually returning to normal.

Later, as the squadron readied the horses for their first patrol, he told Sebeku what had happened. 'I know Khamet's a bit unconventional, but I'm willing to give him the benefit of the doubt. He has been here a long time, so he must know what he's talking about.'

'And if he doesn't?' said Sebeku. 'We could be dead before we find out for sure.'

'What else can we do? Usurp Khamet's authority? It's a sin you know. Still, I suppose it means that Baya and I are now allies. I mean, if he really does need my help taking over from Khamet he's hardly likely to murder me, is he?'

'Perhaps. Or it could be that he's just putting you off your guard. He can't kill you here – there's too many people about. So he'll wait for a chance to do it in secret, when nobody from the rest of the squadron can see. He hates you; I can see it every time he looks at you.'

'All I see in him is the fanaticism. It's like Pharaoh when the god's strong in him – a face set like wax, with eyes like little bits of fire. It makes me shiver.'

An hour later Baya lead his squadron out, following one of the desert caravan trails. They were barely two miles from the fort and passing an area of low scrubland when they saw their first Libyans: a band of goat herders, naked save for loincloths or phallus sheaths, with long braided hair and beards; a few were armed with spears or javelins and one of them, sporting a gazelle-skin cape that reached to his thighs, was wearing a long dagger. They stood like statues and watched the Egyptians pass, their eyes gleaming in impassive faces as dark as aged leather, and it unnerved Hetep to see them. He remembered what Khamet had said about the Libyans' awe of chariots, but saw precious little evidence of it here.

Baya had the squadron circle around, keeping the Lib-

287

yans in sight. The tribesmen simply stared back, unmoved, until at last they gathered their flock and headed west, vanishing into the desert haze. But to where? wondered Hetep. And what lay beyond this dry, stony land? He found it hard to believe that even Libyans could live in such a place. There had to be more oases, and fertile land, further to the west. Did they have cities, and ports and ships?

He shared his musings with Sebeku, who dismissed them with a grunt. 'They live in holes dug in the sand and eat raw meat. How can men like that build cities?'

In the days that followed more herders were seen, and with them came bands of armed men, who prowled within sight of the oasis road only to fade back into the desert whenever the chariots closed.

'I thought you said it was quiet here,' said Hetep to Khamet, after he and Baya had returned from one particularly long patrol in which they had shadowed a peaceful-looking but heavily armed group of Libyan families all the way to the dunes half a day's march beyond the oasis.

'It is,' said Khamet. 'We haven't been attacked yet, have we? And nothing – not a sickle, not even a single water pot – has gone missing from the farms. And it's all thanks to you.' The commander was drinking again and he raised his wine cup in salute. 'Montu bless the brave charioteers.'

'Where do you get all this wine?' asked Hetep. 'It's not on the ration lists. I've looked.'

'Never mind that,' snapped Baya. He had been growing increasingly testy as, day after day, they had failed to find the Libyan troop concentrations that had made up his earlier fantasies. 'What about the armed tribesmen? What makes you sure they're not massing for an invasion?'

'They're just looking for a way in for their cattle. They want to use the fields to graze the herds.'

'Then we must drive them away, beyond the edge of the desert,' said Baya.

Khamet shook his head. 'Can't do that. The oasis folk need them. After the harvest we let the herders in. The cattle eat the stubble and their dung puts the life back into the fields. You may not have noticed but we're a long way from the Nile. The goddess Hapi can't help us here.'

'Don't tell me you let these savages into the oasis people's fields,' said Baya with disgust.

'It's an arrangement from before the Time of the God. Anyway, some of the oasis folk are Libyan settlers; they've got kin among the tribesmen.'

'Yet they're the ones we're supposed to be keeping out!'

'No, it's the raiding parties and big bands of migrants we have to stop. The herders we encourage. They only stay a few weeks and, like I said, the cattle dung helps with next year's crops.'

The look on Baya's face made Hetep laugh.

'Well, isn't this marvellous,' he said. 'We've come to fight off invaders who've already settled.'

Sebeku found nothing to be amused about when Hetep told him that evening what he had learned from Khamet.

'Clearly the man's been at the wine again. Libyans are like all foreigners – a threat to Ma'at.'

'There's plenty of foreigners in Egypt,' said Hetep. 'Even my mother was one, remember?'

289

'The ones at home are tame and regulated, so Ma'at isn't threatened. But you've seen what they're like here: wild and savage, and a danger to our whole existence.'

'You're beginning to sound like Baya.'

'Not at all. Baya wants to murder them for his own glory. I'm content to leave them alone – as long as they don't bother us.'

CHAPTER 32

The next morning Hetep found Khamet forming up a squad of the garrison's spearmen alongside a train of donkeys.

'You're in command of the fort for the next few days,' he was saying to Baya. 'Just follow the usual routine, understand? No going off on your own.'

'What's happening?' asked Hetep. 'Where are you going?'

'Not far,' replied Khamet. 'Just to the main oasis and back. Won't be long. Right, carry on.'

Baya and Hetep stood watching as Khamet lead his little caravan out of the gate and off down the road.

'What do you think he's up to?' said Hetep.

'I don't know.' Baya's face was set like stone. 'But I'm certain that the man's not fit for command. Abandoning one's post like this is a capital crime.'

One of the garrison's remaining spearmen must have overheard, for he came ambling over.

'Oh, don't you worry sir,' he said. 'The commander'll only be gone a couple of days. He's on a resupply mission.'

'But our granary's still half full,' said Hetep.

'He's not interested in barley – it's the wine he's after. Plus a few other dainties for us loyal troops, of course. The first of the new jars should be ready about now. Some of it's carried east on donkeys – they say it's better than the Delta stuff, begging your pardon, sir – but before it's sent our Khamet, may the gods bless him, goes and charges them a toll.'

'But that's corruption,' said Baya, sounding shocked.

'You'd know all about that,' muttered Hetep.

291

The spearman shrugged. 'Who's to stop him? We're the only soldiers for miles around. And it reminds the oasis folk that we're here; makes them feel safe. They're glad to pay the price.'

'And if they don't?' said Hetep.

'It's never come to that, and never will now you're here. They're scared of you. It's why the commander had you patrolling so often: so you'd make an impression. I wouldn't be surprised if he comes back with double the usual haul.'

'How long has this been going on?'

'Ever since we got here, ten years ago.'

By the afternoon Baya's outrage over Khamet's conduct appeared to have abated, and he summoned Hetep and the other two troop commanders to a conference. To Hetep's disquiet he was once more the shining-eyed man of destiny.

'I've been listening to the infantry scouts Khamet sent out yesterday,' he said. 'And what they say is deeply troubling.'

The other two troop commanders waited in respectful silence for enlightenment. Not so Hetep, who guessed what was coming next.

'You were told not to do anything rash,' he warned. 'Anyway, what's changed? The scouts have been reporting the same thing to Khamet for over a week, and we all know the herders are gathering beyond the oasis roads.'

'The situation has changed for the worse,' said Baya. 'This very morning there was a skirmish with some farmers.'

'Remember what Khamet said: the Libyans are just getting impatient. Their cattle need the forage. Another week or so and we can let them in.'

'This is about more than feeding cattle – I can feel it.

Remember what happened at Sumur when those Habiru scum infiltrated the city. We had thefts, assaults, even full scale rebellion.'

The other two troop commanders – neither of whom had been at Sumur – were drinking in every word and could not agree quickly enough; both declared the Libyans to be the greatest threat to Egypt since the Hyksos invasion. Hetep just stared, astonished by the depth of Baya's self-deception.

'The Libyans should fear us,' Baya went on. 'Instead they flaunt themselves, sometimes within sight of the fortress itself! I tell you, they're planing mischief. And it's our job to stop them.'

'But Khamet told us to stick to the regular patrols,' protested Hetep.

'And what have they achieved except wearing out the chariots and laming the horses? No, if we are to bring these savages to battle we need to go and meet them in their own land.'

Baya took the entire squadron, along with the youngest and fittest of the garrison's infantry. The latter had been made to leave their armour behind and were told to keep up with the chariots, as if they were properly trained runners. Hetep felt sorry for them as they puffed along beside the cars and asked Baya to slow down but the commander would not hear of it.

'The scouts have told us where the enemy's concentrating,' he said. 'We must strike them before they can organise for their next raid.'

They left the road and veered off into the desert. It was the same kind of flat, stony land they had passed on the way from the Delta, except that here the rock outcroppings were higher and the wadis deeper; some of the latter still held dribbles of spring water, around which clumps of vegetation stood out bright green against the dull ochre of the rock. As they advanced one of the outcrops began to rise above the rest until it dominated the skyline. It looked like a massive head, its wind-etched face staring out across the desert, and reminded Hetep of the statues of Ramesses and his predecessors back home – only this was on a vaster scale, as if carved by gods rather than human masons.

They sighted a band of Libyans on the plain near the outcrop's foot. Baya had the chariots redeploy into three columns, one for each troop, and halted them at the crest of a hillock.

'Now do you see?' he said to Hetep, pointing. 'Where are the cattle? And women and children... do you see any? I told you, Khamet's a fool.'

'They're probably a hunting party,' said Hetep. 'Or maybe their families and herds are out of sight. Look at how broken this ground is. You could hide the whole of Re division among these rocks.'

By now the Libyans had spotted them and were running for the shelter of the outcrop.

'If they're as innocent as you claim why do they flee?' said Baya. A gleam came to his eye and he swept out his khopesh. 'Ma'at will be restored,' he cried.

'Wait,' said Hetep. 'We've no proof they're raiders.'

'You should applaud what we are about to do.' Baya turned to the chariot behind him. 'Trumpeter, sound the charge.'

The horn blared, echoless in the open desert, and the chariots surged forwards, the excited young warriors shouting prayers to their personal gods – all except Hetep and his troop.

294

'Well?' said Sebeku. 'Do we follow this maniac or not?'

'I won't kill innocents,' said Hetep. He could almost feel the eyes of his men boring into him and the skin on his back itched.

'Look at them,' said Sebeku. 'The idiot has them moving too fast over the stones. See, one of the chariots has overturned already. He's going to get them all killed. We can at least try to make them slow, if not turn aside.'

As Hetep watched a second chariot foundered. 'Perhaps you're right,' he said, and reluctantly ordered his troop to advance.

The two troops following Baya were closing fast with the Libyans, who were still running across the open plain. Ahead of them more tribesmen appeared at the lip of a gully and formed into a rough line. And these were no simple herders but spearmen and archers; even from here Hetep could see the face paint and oxhide capes that marked them out as warriors.

One of the troop leaders lead his column in a turn, the trailing crews shooting wildly and with little effect, but Baya, still waving his khopesh, lead the other troop straight on, as if determined to run the Libyan warriors over.

'He's getting too close to them,' said Hetep. 'What's he doing?'

Baya's chariots slowed as they reached the rougher ground near the outcrop and went plowing through the Libyan line. They turned, but they were not nearly fast enough and now their enemies were rushing the cars, stabbing at the crews and horses with spears. Hetep called an order to the men in his troop and as they reached the Lybians they turned and raced along parallel to their line, he and the other archers shooting at the tribesmen wherever they massed around Baya's men. Once they were clear Hetep led his men around in a tight loop and they retraced their path, breaking up the clusters of warriors with volleys of arrows and allowing Baya's troop to fight its way free. Then Hetep lead the entire squadron clear.

Baya, seemingly unaware that he had been saved from disaster, was laughing with abandon. He shouted something incoherent, called his surviving charioteers together and lead them back towards the outcrop. By now the Libyans had reached the rocks and were shooting at the Egyptians with bows and javelins; frustrated, Baya wheeled his two troops aside and in moments they had disappeared behind the outcrop.

'He's mad,' said Sebeku.

'Mad or sane we have to follow him,' said Hetep.

Sebeku lashed the reins and they surged forwards, with the rest of Hetep's troop close behind. They rounded the outcrop and saw more Libyans, strung out in the open. Most were women and children, herding a flock of goats and a dozen or so cattle.

Again Baya lead his chariots straight through the Libyans, but with so few armed men facing him there was little danger and the charioteers cut their victims down in heaps. He took out his bow and as the surviving Libyans scattered before him he started shooting, as methodically as if he was on the practice field.

'Stop,' yelled Hetep as he closed. 'They're just herders.'

Baya ignored him and kept shooting.

'This is murder. I said stop!'

As his chariot caught up with Baya's he grabbed a javelin and used it to knock the bow from Baya's hands. Baya stared about him in baffled fury, then snatched the whip from his driver and lashed at Hetep's face and arms. Sebeku got his shield in the way and smacked its edge into

Baya's jaw, and Baya's chariot went wheeling aside.

The dust churned up by the wheels was settling over the land, and through it Hetep saw dismounted charioteers clambering over the outcrop and slaughtering the remaining Libyans there. Meanwhile a few scattered chariots were roaming hither and thither, their crews killing at will, all order gone – a testament to Baya's pitiful skills as a commander.

Without prompting Sebeku halted at the edge of the rocky ground, and he and Hetep dismounted. The former kept his shield ready and they both held khopeshes, but it was a needless precaution, for there was not a single Libyan left alive on the plain.

'Over there,' said Sebeku, pointing towards a pile of corpses. They walked over and saw that it was a group of women; one was huddled over a small bundle from which poked a tiny hand.

'You know what it's like in battle,' said Hetep. 'When Montu is with you and you can't see because of the dust it can be hard to tell who's an enemy warrior and who isn't.'

Sebeku spat. 'Why did you even say that? You don't believe it any more than I.'

'You're right – I don't.' Hetep wiped a hand over his eyes and turned away. 'I'm sorry.'

In the distance he saw parties of Egyptians searching over the plain and collecting hands. Meanwhile Baya had seated himself in front of the growing pile of trophies, his face lit by the setting sun.

'We should go and tell him what he's done,' said Hetep. 'I'm not sure he realises.'

By the time they had returned to the chariot and driven over to Baya the pile of hands was complete.

'How many?' said Baya. His face was flushed with

297

excitement and his breathing came quick.

His driver consulted a sheet of papyrus. 'One hundred and nine,' he said. 'But three were left hands rather than right and should be deducted, else we run the risk of counting a single slain enemy as double. So that makes one hundred and six rebels.'

'Now let us see the booty.'

One of the troop leaders brought up a pair of cows and the few surviving goats. Baya looked delighted.

'I am Baya, favoured one of Set the Destroyer,' muttered Sebeku. 'Like Sekhmet in her fury I laid the foreigners low. I killed their children and took their goats.'

There was a collection of weapons, too. Most were spears, clubs and daggers – the typical possessions of impoverished nomads – but there were also a few axes and khopeshes, and among them a sword: a bronze wedge two cubits long, its blade so highly polished it reflected the sun like a liquid.

'That's curious,' said Hetep quietly. 'It's Sherden. Remember last year when we fought those sea pirates?'

'I wonder what it's doing here,' said Sebeku.

Hetep shrugged. 'Perhaps Libyans got it in trade. The Sherden's ships must call at places all along the coast.'

'Wherever it came from, it does not justify this.' Sebeku indicated the pile of hands and the corpse-littered plain. 'We've slaughtered a group of herders, or at the worst a raiding party bringing back booty from a rival tribe. These people were no threat to us.'

'I know,' said Hetep.

'Then what are we going to do about it?'

CHAPTER 33

They made camp that night, but not before, at Hetep's insistence, they had moved well out of sight of the battlefield and its potentially vengeful dead. At dawn they started back, leading the cattle and goats, their chariots laden with the captured weapons and the bodies of their dead comrades. Of course, the Libyans were left to rot where they had fallen.

The men were silent and avoided each others' eye, as if with the sun's renewal they had finally realised what they had done. Baya chafed at their slowness and sent messengers ahead so that the fort's garrison could prepare a fitting welcome for the returning heroes.

They reached the fort at dusk and found Khamet, returned from his own expedition, waiting for them. The messengers must have reached him for scarcely had the charioteers dismounted than he advanced on them, his jowls quivering, demanding to know what they had been up to.

'The job you should have been doing,' said Baya mildly. 'Culling Libyans.'

'You fool!' shouted Khamet. 'For ten years I've kept the peace with these people, and in one act of stupidity you've undone it all! That place you attacked – that big rock – is one of their sacred sites. And you've defiled it!'

'I neutralised a threat to Ma'at.'

'You murdered herdsmen!'

Baya pulled the Sherden sword from the booty pile and threw it at Khamet's feet.

'Herders?' he said. 'With this?'

'There's always a few warriors. They protect their

299

animals from rival tribes. But there's rarely more than a dozen or so.'

'What you call a dozen I call a war party,' said Baya.

Khamet turned a furious eye on Hetep. 'Did you see any of this?'

'About twenty or so were armed warrior fashion,' said Hetep. 'But the rest...' He was conscious of Sebeku's gaze on him. 'They had no weapons. They were just... people, really.'

'But you attacked them all the same.'

'Not me,' said Hetep. 'It was Baya who ordered the charge.'

'Which you did nothing to stop,' said Khamet, his face hard. 'Well, only the gods can help us now. These people practice blood feuds and the local tribes can muster ten times as many warriors as we have soldiers here. So you'd better get out patrolling again, first thing tomorrow, because now we really do need you.'

Baya shrugged as if Khamet's words were of no consequence and walked off to attend to his chariot. The rest of the squadron dispersed in shame-faced silence, while slaves came to see to the dead.

Hetep was aware that Sebeku was still glaring at him. 'What?' he said.

'It was Baya who ordered it, not me,' he said, mimicking Hetep's voice. 'Khamet's right. You're a disgrace.'

'You think this was my fault?' shouted Hetep. 'I didn't see you trying to stop him. Always ready with the snide remarks, but when do you ever do anything useful?' Even as he spoke he knew it was a foolish and unjust thing to say. He exhaled and rubbed his eyes with one hand. 'I'm sorry. You're right: I should be ashamed. And I am. Just leave me be for a while, will you?'

Later, finding he had no appetite for the evening meal

he went up to the battlements to brood. It was after sunset and the moon had risen, bathing the land in a soft, pale light that masked its harsh redness. Feeling sick in his *ka* he mouthed a prayer to the god Khonsu, trying to invoke the moon's powers of healing, but it did little good.

In the end it was his sense of duty that brought him out of his melancholy. At dawn the squadron would be out patrolling again and they might well find themselves in a pitched battle with Libyan warriors, and he had to make sure his chariot was fit for the task. He descended the steps and crossed to the storehouse; it was dark inside and he lit one of the lamps, and by its light he inspected the chariot's frame, searching for cracked wood or damaged joints. As he ran a hand over the axle he could feel how dry the wood had become – a reminder, as if he needed one, of how arid it was here. Better get some oil rubbed into that, he thought.

He became aware that someone else was in the store-room and was not surprised to see Baya appearing out of the gloom beside him.

'What do you want?' Yesterday's events had confirmed in his mind his physical and moral superiority over Baya, and he was no longer afraid of being caught alone with him.

'I thought we had an agreement. What you said to Khamet can only damage our cause here.'

'You murdered those people. I had to tell Khamet the truth.'

'Murder?' said Baya, with a look of mild puzzlement. 'One murders humans, not animals. What do the lives of savages matter against the maintenance of Ma'at? We're securing the border from attack.'

'As if you care about Ma'at. All you've done is weaken

us here. You heard what Khamet said: the tribes are going to want revenge.'

'That bloated sot! He told me he's writing to the vizier to ask for more troops, as if I can't deal with these vermin myself. Where's my glory now? Where's my victory?'

'Terrible having one's deeds unacknowledged, isn't it?' said Hetep. As he spoke he noticed that Sebeku had slipped into the storeroom and was standing in readiness to spring at Baya. 'But I'll make sure what happened yesterday isn't forgotten.'

'What are you saying?'

'Once we're finished here I'm going to let people in the Delta know what you did – that you lost control of the squadron and massacred a band of goat herders. And this time I have witnesses.'

'So this is how you repay me, is it? I made you what you are, gave you this posting, and now you're trying to ruin me again.' Baya's voice was rising. 'It's my destiny to lead men in battle and gain honours from the hand of Ramesses. Would you deny me that?'

'You're no chariot warrior. You're a disgrace. It wasn't Antef who let the army down at Irqata, it was you. You're not fit to command supply wagons.'

'Not fit, you say?' screeched Baya, his face livid. 'Not fit? Who in the name of all the gods do you think you are? I'm the one who saved the army at Irqata, not you. And what was my reward? Exile, in this hateful backwater. Well, I've shown them now – just as I did at Irqata. Shown them that I'm destined for greatness.' His eyes shone with a sudden mad intensity. 'My tomb will rival a vizier's and my epitaph will fill a wall of rock!'

Abruptly he stopped, staring as if horrified by the re-alisation of what he had said.

'I'm sorry,' said Hetep – and he was, which surprised

302

him. 'But people need to be told.'

'Perhaps you're right,' said Baya in a resigned voice. He turned as if to slink away, then without warning sprang at Hetep, a dagger held high in one hand. Hetep stumbled backwards as the dagger came flashing down, and then Sebeku had one arm locked around Baya's throat, his free hand gripping his arm. Hetep wrenched the dagger from Baya's hand and together they shoved him away.

For a long moment all three stood, breathing hard and glaring at each other.

'Kill him,' said Sebeku. 'Now!'

Hetep looked down at the dagger in his hand. Slowly he let his arm drop.

'No,' he said. 'It has to be done right, so everyone can see. Not here, alone in the dark.'

Baya was smirking now. 'Don't have the stomach for it, eh?'

'I want to make sure everyone at home knows what kind of man you are. And this time it won't be a priest or a mayor who'll judge you. I'll go to the vizier, or Pharaoh himself if I have to. Let's see you try to bribe them.'

'Empty threats,' sneered Baya. 'You'll not live long enough to get back to the Delta.' He shot a glare at Sebeku, turned on his heel and stormed out.

Sebeku watched him go, his eyes filled with hate, then rounded on Hetep.

'What's wrong with you?' he said. 'That's the third time he's tried to kill you. But you just let him walk away as if nothing happened.'

'Didn't you hear? I want him to be tried, properly. Anyway, we still need him. He has a hold over the men of the other two troops and they won't follow me if he's not there. We need all our chariots if we're to stop this invasion Khamet says is coming.'

The squadron split up, each troop patrolling separately so as to cover more ground. For two weeks they searched the gullies and outcrops, but they found no sign of the Libyans; indeed, since the day of the massacre the whole land had become eerily quiet. The stillness unsettled the troopers, and in the evening they prayed at the Montu shrine or huddled in the barracks as they fingered their protective amulets. Meanwhile the oasis folk kept close to their villages, fearfully watching the western horizon. Even Khamet had lost his easy manner, brooding over his wine and snapping at his subordinates.

Two weeks after the massacre Khamet at last had news, and summoned Baya and Hetep to the barracks.

'They're gathering at the sacred rock,' he told them.

'How do you know?' said Hetep.

'I sent some scouts that way this morning. Only one came back.'

'You told us there'd be no more Libyans there,' said Baya, affronted at what he obviously thought was a slight to his authority. 'Why didn't you send us?'

'Because I needed you elsewhere in case I was wrong. And I didn't want a repeat of you earlier performance. We're not slaughtering civilians this time.'

Baya stiffened at the jibe but before he could reply Hetep broke in.

'This isn't the time to argue. Khamet, what do you want us to do?'

'We must break up the gathering before it gets too big. I know these people. They still fear us, and for now they'll content themselves with boasting among themselves. But as more come in they'll get bolder. A hundred, two hundred, and they'll stay there. But any more than that and something in them changes, and before you know it they're a howling, vengeful mob, who won't stop until all the villages are burning.'

'So we need to time our attack to the very day, then,' said Hetep. 'Too soon and we won't be killing enough; too late and they'll attack us, and we'll be overwhelmed.'

Khamet nodded. 'And from what the scout told me, tomorrow should be about right.'

'A hundred or a thousand, it doesn't matter,' said Baya. He spoke casually, but his eyes shone with the now familiar lust for glory. 'We'll annihilate them and watch as a monument is carved with our names on it.'

'Don't think it'll be that easy,' said Khamet. 'These people are tough fighters when they're roused. We'll have to trap them. Once we're near the rock I want the chariots to circle around the Libyan camp and charge them from the rear. They'll panic, of course – as I've said, they fear chariots. I'll have the infantry deployed in their path. Just drive them towards me and, Montu willing, we'll get them all.' He spoke with a lack of relish that drew a sneer of contempt from Baya, but made Hetep feel easier in his mind with what they were about to do.

Chapter 34

Although Khamet lead the force out before sunrise it was long after midday that they sighted the Libyans' sacred rock. He deployed his infantry in ambush at the bottom of a wadi, leaving only a few skirmishers on the lip to keep watch.

'It's up to you now,' he said to Baya. 'Remember, you're to panic them, drive them towards us. Then we'll kill them.'

The squadron moved out in a wide circle, keeping only the tip of the rock in sight. The sun, despite the lateness of the day, was pouring out a torrent of heat and the haze wavered over the baking ground. Dust reddened the air and at the far boundary of the world the earth and sky were mingled together – chaos violating the cosmic order.

'I dreamed of this place last night,' said Sebeku. 'It was not a good dream.'

'It's just memory,' said Hetep. 'We have been here before, you know.'

'No, it's not that. There's too much red in this land, too much of death's colour.'

'Not afraid are you?' said Hetep, forcing a lightness he did not feel. 'Just think of the enemy as foreign rabble.'

'I said that once, didn't I? At Irqata.' Sebeku fingered the scar on his neck.

'How about dangerous foreign rabble? Is that better?'

It was late by the time they reached the point opposite the wadi where Khamet had concealed his infantry. There Baya deployed the squadron in a single line, with himself in the centre and Hetep's troop on the left flank. He gave the order to advance and the squadron rolled forwards, climbing towards a low ridge that lay across their path. Hetep saw figures moving near the peak of the rock – were they signalling, perhaps? Then the squadron crested the ridge and they saw for the first time the Libyan camp, lying at the bottom of the down slope.

'Gods, will you look at that,' said Hetep.

'I told you,' muttered Sebeku.

There must have been scores of tents, mixed with animal corrals and great piles of stores, the total covering more area than one of the villages in the Delta. And where there should have been panic at the Egyptians' arrival there was instead only an eerie stillness, with a few columns of wood smoke rising in the dusty air and not a soul in sight.

The squadron kept going and as they neared the camp a great mass of Libyan warriors appeared out of the haze on the far side: huge, savage-looking men in hide capes, their oily, matted hair pierced with ostrich feathers.

Hetep drew out his bow. 'What exactly happened in this dream of yours?' he asked.

'Best you don't know.'

The Libyans were prancing and screaming insults, as if daring the Egyptians to attack. Baya stood tall in his chariot, his face alight with the same look of exultation it had worn during the massacre two weeks before. He raised his bow and ordered the charge.

The chariots accelerated, shaking and bouncing as they sped across the stony ground. Dust rose up, and over the drumming of hooves and rumble of wheels came the jeers of the Libyans, who were standing firm, as if heedless of the ruin that was hurtling towards them.

With a wild yelling a second mass of Libyans appeared, clambering out from a wadi on the squadron's flank; others seemed to be appearing out of the ground, where they had lain hidden under earth-covered blankets and hides.

'It's a trap,' cried Hetep.

There would be no slaughter of the helpless now and Baya's expression changed to a look of panic. In a shrill voice he yelled a confused string of orders which, purely by good fortune, sent the squadron wheeling towards safety. But not quickly enough: more Libyans were boiling out of another wadi a bare hundred paces away, moving to cut off Hetep's troop.

'Use the bow, you fool!' cried Sebeku. 'Have you forgotten your job?'

As the Libyans closed Hetep started shooting, as fast as he could grab the arrows, while Sebeku wheeled the chariot around, searching for a gap in the thickening ring of their enemies. He saw Baya looking back and for an instant their eyes met, before another band of Libyans appeared out of the dust, racing towards them and blocking their escape. Sebeku yanked at the reins and the chariot came around again, the wood creaking, and from under Hetep's feet there was a loud crack.

'What was that?' shouted Sebeku.

Hetep peered over the side. Sunlight and shadows flashed over the cab as the wheels spun, making it hard to see if there was any damage.

'Just the wood settling,' he said. 'Don't worry.'

The Libyan trap had closed, forming a loose ring of screaming, gesticulating warriors, but aside from Hetep's only two other chariots had been caught. A glance across the battlefield showed the rest of the squadron wheeling about as if forming up to attack.

'If Baya charges he can scatter them and we can break out,' said Hetep. 'Be ready.' He shouted to the other two chariot crews to stay close. Meanwhile the Libyans were hanging back, fearful of the horses and the lethal arrows shot from the Egyptians' composite bows. But more were massing behind, and it would only be moments before their growing numbers swelled their courage and they closed again.

As Sebeku took them around in another turn Hetep heard the squadron's trumpeter sound the retreat and he stared, unbelieving. Baya was watching him and the moment their eyes met he smiled and gave Hetep an ironic salute, before turning to follow the rest of the squadron as it retired.

'He's abandoning us,' shouted Hetep. 'Look at him!'

'Just do your job, will you?'

Sebeku steered for the thinnest part of the ring, the other two chariots close behind. Hetep and the other warriors concentrated their arrow shots, making a gap; Sebeku lashed the reins and the chariot accelerated towards it. A javelin came skimming over Ibis's back and an arrow pierced Sebeku's arm; he cried out but kept his grip on the reigns. A Libyan hurled himself at Vengeance, only to fall and be trampled under his hooves; Hetep grabbed the rail with one hand and Sebeku with the other as the chariot went bouncing over the body, and then they were through.

He turned, hoping to see the others close behind. But the ring had closed, and as he watched a spear thrust crippled one of the horses drawing the second chariot, making it stumble. The driver stared at Hetep in mute appeal before he fell, pierced with javelins. Behind it the third chariot had pitched over; a mass of Libyans was surging around it, and the sunlight gleamed on bronze as they hacked at both men and horses.

Hetep looked away.

'It's just us now,' he said.

They raced on, away from the camp, but also away

309

from Khamet and the supporting infantry, with a horde of Libyans in screaming pursuit. But not even the desert's hardy savages could keep up with an Egyptian chariot and after a while Sebeku slowed the horses.

'What are you doing?' said Hetep in alarm.

'Ibis is tiring,' explained Sebeku. 'The one of the left,' he added, testily. 'If either he or Vengeance stumbles or goes lame we're finished.'

In an hour they had run their pursuers out of sight. But still they kept moving, with the bloated sun setting in an orange haze behind them, and only once it was fully dark did they roll to a stop.

Sebeku jumped down to tend to his horses, speaking softly and calming them after the excitement of the battle. Without prompting Hetep dismounted and knelt down to peer under the car.

'What do you see?' said Sebeku.

'The axle's cracked. We're lucky it didn't snap clean through. How are the horses?'

'Tired but sound. They at least were up to the battle.' Sebeku looked up at the starlit sky, then around at the blackness of the surrounding desert. 'The cold will come down to us soon. And we have no blankets.'

'I don't mind that. It's water we need.'

'Then we'd best find some.'

Sebeku let the horses walk free and to his proud delight Ibis lead them to a wadi that had a spring and few puddles of water at its bottom. They decided to rest there for a while.

'Did you see that vile creature Baya?' said Hetep, once they had eaten the last of their rations.

'I caught only a glimpse; I was too preoccupied watching the horses. But I know that he abandoned us.'

'Abandoned? He was laughing, absolutely waving us on our way to the West.'

'I doubt he intended us to get so far. The Libyans would never have given us our proper rites and Baya would not have returned to do so. We'd have been feeding the vultures for days instead of enjoying our eternity in the Field of Reeds.'

Hetep's fist clenched as it rested on his knee. 'If we get out of this Baya's going to die,' he said.

'Ah, now – that's better. Sense at last.'

'What do you mean?'

'You've been a fool. And I more so for following you here. I've been trying to convince you all along that Baya's an evil man, that he never forgave you for what you did to him.'

'You didn't have to come here.'

'If I hadn't you'd probably now be dead. But as it is...' Sebeku held out a bloodied arm. 'See? Again I am wounded. What if an evil god visits me here? I might die. And all because of you.'

'Would you rather have stayed at home? Remember those stables.'

Sebeku exhaled and closed his eyes. 'You're right. I'm sorry... I'm tired, and in some pain.' After a moment he looked up again. 'Are you're serious about taking revenge?'

Hetep nodded. 'I'll kill him. I swear it.'

'So there'll be no more excuses for the man? And no hesitation when the time comes?'

'None. It's not just about taking revenge for us, you know. Baya's a danger to Ma'at, and so to all Egypt. For that reason alone he has to be stopped, and quickly, too.'

'Ever the idealist, eh?' Sebeku gave a rare smile. 'Now let us see to this chariot car.'

They wetted a leather thong and bound it around the axle, twisting it tight.

'It may get us home,' said Hetep. 'But we'll have to go slowly.'

They rested another hour before moving on. The day's heat had all but gone and as they travelled Hetep could not stop himself from shivering. Deep in melancholy, it seemed to him as if the *akhs* of the men he had killed were pursuing him, their mournful voices carried on the chill nighttime breeze. He felt for his amulet and instead drew out Elissa's gift. He smiled at the memory of her; perhaps this was the time she meant, when he would need protection in a foreign land. Its touch seemed to make the darkness recede.

They steered by the Portal of Heaven, that point near the far horizon about which the Undying Stars wheeled as the sky dome turned. By now the moon had risen, which was a blessing, for without it they might have foundered on the broken ground. Twice they saw figures moving in the distance – Libyan warbands, hurrying to catch up with their main army – and they had to make wide detours to avoid them.

The next day they laid up in a wadi, each taking a turn to watch while the other slept in what little shade the chariot car could provide. They were down to their last skin of water, which they gave to Isis and Vengeance, knowing that their lives depended on the horses' continued good health. That night, tormented by thirst, they set out again. Hetep wanted to steer clear of the Libyan's sacred rock but Sebeku would not hear of it.

'Another night of this will kill us. We'll have to risk taking the straight route.'

In the last hour before dawn they came upon the aftermath of a battle. Libyan corpses lay scattered on the rocky ground; among them were discarded weapons, a dozen dead horses and some broken chariot cars. Many of the dead were half eaten by scavengers and the remaining flesh was bloated and stinking.

'So Khamet beat them after all,' said Hetep.

They stood on a rise and looked around them. Even in the moonlight they could see the chariot tracks carved deeply into the dirt, and it was easy to read the flow of the battle. There, beyond the rise, Khamet's infantry had halted its retreat and formed a battle line, and beyond was where Baya's fleeing chariots had drawn the pursuing Libyans into Khamet's trap – doubtless unwittingly, thought Hetep.

Some of the corpses carried waterskins. He and Sebeku drank a few mouthfuls of the warm, bitter-tasting liquid, and again gave the remainder to Ibis and Vengeance. Then they mounted and set out again, and at the far side of the battlefield they discovered piles of Libyan weapons and severed hands.

'Baya's work,' said Hetep. 'Khamet wouldn't have done this.'

'Indeed. And look at the tracks. They just heaped up the trophies and went home, without sending anyone to look for us.'

'Baya again, making sure we'd die.' Hetep looked up and smiled grimly. 'I think he's in for a bit of a shock when he sees us.'

CHAPTER 35

The sight of Baya cheerfully waving them to their doom had kindled a rare fury inside Hetep, which grew until it burned like rising bile. As the desert rolled by under the chariot wheels he gripped the cab's rail and stared ahead into the moonlight, his thirst, hunger and fatigue all forgotten in his desire for revenge.

Not long after dawn they met an infantry patrol and stopped to get news. The patrol's commander blanched when he saw them and reached for his protective amulet; and no wonder, thought Hetep, with a glance at Sebeku, who looked barely human with his bloodshot eyes, sun-cracked lips and whitened, salt-encrusted skin. The commander told them that Khamet and the rest of the garrison had returned in triumph the day before; indeed, he said, it must have been a victory foretold by Amun, for this very morning men had come from the Delta to reward Baya for his defeat of the Libyan horde.

The thought of Baya once again claiming credit for another man's achievement set Hetep shaking with rage. Sebeku must have felt it too, except that his anger was colder, expressed in the tight set of his head and jaw. Without a word the driver urged the tired horses into a canter, leaving the infantry commander staring after them.

They reached the fort and swept through the gate, trailing dust. In the courtyard stood a pair of yoked chariots and a train of donkeys, the latter still being unloaded by slaves; Hetep spared them no more than a glance. As their chariot came to a stop he drew out his khopesh from its holder and leaped from the car; Sebeku followed, a dagger in one hand and a pair of javelins in the other.

Hetep marched up to one of the slaves.

'Where's Baya?' he demanded.

The slave took one look at his face and fled.

'Baya, you worm,' shouted Hetep from the middle of the parade ground. 'Come out!'

Silence. And then Baya appeared at the stable door. He looked puzzled, but when he saw Hetep his face paled. 'You!' he said in a strangled voice.

'Yes, me,' said Hetep.

Baya's hand moved to his waist to snatch at a dagger that was not there. Realising he was unarmed he took a step back, his hands raised.

'Wait! I can explain.'

'Keep the others away,' said Hetep to Sebeku. He advanced, his khopesh gripped tight, his eyes intent on Baya's face.

With a cry Baya turned and fled into the stable, and Hetep went racing after him. The sudden darkness inside left Hetep almost blind and he stumbled forwards, sweeping the khopesh before him and roaring Baya's name. The reek of dung and horse sweat filled his nostrils, while from all around came the snorting and stamping of the horses, agitated by the noise.

'Where are you, you treacherous offal?' he shouted, but there was no reply from the darkness. From outside he heard shouts and running feet – soldiers from the garrison, he guessed, roused by the commotion. He knew he could rely on Sebeku to keep them from interfering.

He crouched, trying to peer between the horses' legs. There, a shadow deeper than the others, half hidden by the reed screen bordering the last stall. He advanced, silently now, the khopesh raised to strike, and with a shout leaped forwards and slashed down.

There was a yelp and he cut through empty air as Baya hurtled out from the darkness and sprinted for the door. In an instant Hetep was after him and in four running strides had grabbed Baya's tunic and yanked him back. Baya struggled, then froze as Hetep jammed the tip of his khopesh under his chin.

'Stay still, curse you,' he said. He shifted his grip and locked his free arm around Baya's neck.

'Please, don't kill me,' said Baya. 'I'll give you what you want.'

'You can give me what I want by dying,' said Hetep. The khopesh pricked Baya's neck and a trickle of blood ran down the blade.

'For the love of Amun wait,' said Baya, gabbling in fear. 'I can get you reinstated. It's what you really want, isn't it?'

Hetep hesitated. He could see Sebeku blocking the stable doorway and beyond him the silhouettes of several men, including a massive figure with a great bald head.

'Don't come any closer,' shouted Hetep. 'I'll kill him!'

The large man pushed Sebeku aside and stepped in through the door.

'You are many things Hetep, but you are not a murderer.' The voice sounded like Nui's – but how was that possible, this far from Sumur?

'This isn't murder it's justice,' said Hetep. 'Baya left us with the Libyans to die.'

'Whatever he did, this is not the way.' The figure came closer, and now Hetep could see his face.

'Nui,' he said. 'How–'

'Later. First you have to let Baya go.' Nui's voice was more gentle and coaxing that Hetep thought possible. 'If you think he's done wrong then we can arrange a hearing to find out the truth.'

Hetep tightened his arm around Baya's neck. 'No,' he said, while Baya gurgled in terror. 'He'll just bribe the magistrate like he did at Pr-Ramesses. He stole my credit, and now he's tried to take my life.'

'It's not true,' croaked Baya. 'The Libyans cut us off. I swear it!'

'Then what about Amurru? You sent Zuratta to kill me.'

'So far you are guilty only of rashness,' said Nui, taking another step closer. 'If you kill Baya I can't help you. Let him go and we can discuss what to do.'

'You can be reinstated,' said Baya desperately. 'Nui came to tell me I'm rejoining the army. We're going to Kadesh to fight the Hittites. You can join us, I promise. I'll get my father to have you reinstated – I swear it, by Amun himself.'

'Let him go,' said Nui, 'and I'll see that he keeps his promise.'

Hetep's arm quivered as he fought against his indecision. Baya was an affront to all that was decent and a danger to all Egypt – he had to die. And yet he was being promised what he wanted, the chance to distinguish himself in battle under Pharaoh's eye – a promise made in front of Nui, a man he respected and trusted more than any but Sebeku and Teppic. And how could he get away with killing a man in front of so many witnesses? Nui, Sebeku, a half-dozen of the garrison's spearmen, even Khamet – all were watching him, as still as statues, their breath held.

Hetep shoved Baya away from him.

'Just keep him out of my sight,' he snarled.

'Is that it?' cried Sebeku in disgust. 'You're just going to let him go?'

'I can't kill him with these people watching.'

317

'You swore you'd do it!' Sebeku still held his dagger, and with a snarl he turned and thrust it at Baya's heart. Nui grabbed his arm and the stroke went wide. Then he twisted Sebeku's wrist and the dagger fell with a clang on the packed earth floor.

'Now get out,' he said to Baya. 'The rest of you, too.' This was to the staring garrison troops. 'There's nothing more to see.'

Nui took them to the officers' quarters where they could talk without being disturbed. He called for beer; it took Hetep two jugfuls to wash the taste of the desert from his mouth and afterwards he sat, enjoying the pleasant, drowsy feeling of pain and fatigue draining from his limbs. Beside him Sebeku was brooding over his own beer cup and darting occasional looks at Nui, while from outside came the sound of Khamet restoring order to his garrison.

'Better now?' said Nui.

'I suppose I did overreact a bit,' said Hetep, feeling sheepish. Sebeku made a disgusted sound and muttered something into his cup; Hetep ignored him. 'I suppose I was lucky you turned up when you did. But I can't see how. Why aren't you in Sumur?'

'My job there's done. I've been back home this past month, training the division for the campaign. You did fine with Ramesses, by the way – I was right to trust you.'

Coming from Nui the words were praise indeed and Hetep felt a glow. Smiling he turned to Sebeku, only to receive a withering look that sent his *ka* sinking again.

'There's nearly a thousand troops at Sumur now,' Nui went on. 'And we're raising an Amurrite chariot division, too – and all fed from that grain I stockpiled. So you see, there was a plan after all. Oh, and before I forget: the lady Elissa sends her greetings. Her brother doesn't, of course, the ungrateful cur.'

Hetep touched the amulet Elissa had given him. 'She saved us in the desert. Baya left us there to die, you know.'

'So I gather from today's performance. But you were right to let him go. One of the men who came here with me is Stablemaster of the Residence, and is also one of Baya's uncles. You can imagine the fuss he'd have made if you'd killed his nephew.'

'Why's he here?' said Hetep, with the sudden alarming vision of Baya's family pursuing a vendetta against him.

'Don't worry, it's nothing to do with you. Baya was sent out here so he couldn't do anything to embarrass his family while they cleaned up the scandal involving Mehy. The man was thick with a gang of tomb robbers and the taint was strong enough on Baya to make them nervous. Anyway, the robbers were tried and impaled – all in a single day, too, so there wasn't time to beat the names of all their accomplices out of them. And now Baya can't be implicated his family want him back. They sent out the Stablemaster with his shiny new commission, all written and approved by Ramesses. I'm just along to inspect the fort's defences – you've no idea the panic Khamet's letter caused in Pr-Ramesses. The Royal Butler nearly had apoplexy; he thought the Libyans were invading. But it seems Baya's dealt with them, so as the hero of the hour he'll be doubly welcome back in civilisation.'

'It was Khamet who won that battle against the Libyans,' said Hetep quietly. 'All Baya did was massacre some goat herders and provoke the tribesmen. People have to be told.'

'It won't make any difference. Who cares about a bunch of dead foreigners?'

'So he gets away with it again.'

'He should have died in that stable,' said Sebeku, breaking his silence. 'Instead, thanks to your weakness, he'll be back with Re division, and gods help the men he's going to command.'

'No fear of that, at least,' said Nui. 'He's being assigned to Ramesses' messenger squadron. It's an important posting in its way, but they're just scouts and dispatch riders – he won't be giving any orders. He'll get to fight beside Ramesses, though.'

'I'm surprised his family didn't get him command of the whole of Re division. With their influence they could make him vizier if the post was going free.'

'Not now they can't. There's been some changes since you were away. That hearing you convened really stirred things up. Ramesses forced the Royal Butler to have that priest of Thoth dismissed for taking bribes. Of course, everyone knew that Baya's family were responsible, and they lost a whole chunk of influence. In all the maneuvering Teppic's lot managed to grab a bigger share of the priesthoods at Karnak, which means you've got some powerful friends now. Which should keep you safe from the Butler, at least.'

Out of the corner of his eye Hetep saw Sebeku shake his head.

'Then Baya's promise to me, about reinstatement...'

'There were too many witnesses for him to renege on that one, and I've just enough heft myself to see that he keeps his word. But I'm afraid Re division's at full strength, so you'll likely be assigned to the same squadron as Baya. I'll keep an eye on you, though, and tell Antef to do the same.'

'Antef?'

'He's back in command of first squadron. One of the

many concessions Baya's family had to make.'

'I see.' Hetep drank his beer, thinking. 'So I'm going with Baya, then, all the way to Kadesh.'

'Sorry. If there was anything I could do...'

'No, it's fine. In fact, it couldn't be better.'

Sebeku looked up from his beer again. 'Are you really that easily bought? You talk of Ma'at but practice expediency, while Baya's very existence mocks both us and the gods. Well, you're going to Kadesh on your own. I've had enough of you and your hypocrisy.'

'You don't understand. If we're to be in the messenger squadron we'll be close to Baya. It's a long road to Kadesh and it goes through some pretty wild country. And somewhere along it, one dark night, Baya's going to get a knife between his ribs.'

Sebeku's eyes narrowed. 'Is this to be another broken promise? Am I to be disappointed again?'

'The only reason he's still alive is because there were people watching. Next time it'll be just us and him. He'll be dead before we get to Kadesh. I swear it.'

'Then you have a chariot driver again,' said Sebeku.

Nui was frowning. 'This isn't like killing a foreigner on a battlefield, you know. It's premeditated murder of an Egyptian, and by rights I should do everything I can to stop you. However...' For a moment he examined his beer cup, then sighed. 'However, our first duty is to increase Ma'at.' He looked up again. 'Just make sure nobody sees you do it, understand?'

CHAPTER 36

In the three months Hetep had been away Pr-Ramesses had changed almost beyond recognition. On every spare scrap of ground armouries and workshops had sprung up, and craftsmen from all over the empire were churning out weapons, armour and chariots in numbers comprehensible only to the scribes, while the canals were jammed with ships bringing wood, tin and copper by the ton to supply them. And there were troops everywhere: Egyptian charioteers, bowmen and assault infantry; levies newly conscripted from their farms; and Libyan, Nubian and Sherden mercenaries, their foreignness tamed so that now they would work for the restoration of Ma'at rather than its destruction.

Hetep had Sebeku drive them to the compound housing Re division's charioteers. There they found the men of first squadron resting in the shade at the edge of the practice field, covered in sweat and dust, their chariots standing idle. Many of the faces were new to him – recruits, he realised, enlisted to replace the losses incurred at Irqata – but there were plenty he recognised and the greeting they gave him when they saw him warmed his *ka*.

'Welcome back,' said Teppic, coming over. 'We all heard about the victory in Libya. Well done! It must have been exciting.'

'It was dull and hot, and the people little better than savages,' said Sebeku.

'Don't mind him,' said Hetep. 'His old wound's sore again.'

'At least you got to fight. Not like us, stuck here for

weeks with nothing to do but train. We all envy you, you know. But enough of our troubles. We should celebrate your return. I'm sure we can extort some extra beer from the quartermasters for the evening ration. You are staying with us, aren't you?'

'Sorry, no. We've been assigned to Pharaoh's messenger squadron. With Baya.'

'Ah.' At the mention of the name Teppic's face fell, but he soon rallied again. 'Still, at least the pharaoh will see you fight – which is more than the rest of us can hope for. And in such a fine-looking chariot, too.' He took in the chipped frame and patched-up axle, and patted the rail. 'Tried and tested, eh? All the wood settled in nicely, too. And such magnificent horses,' he went on, with more conviction. 'We've been given nothing like these.'

Praise for his horse team took the edge off Sebeku's ill humour.

'Are they not beautiful?' he said proudly. 'This is Ibis and the other is Vengeance-of-Amun. They can run all day, and can outpace anything that lives.'

'Then you've nothing to fear when we get to Kadesh,' said Teppic. 'Come on, I'll show you around. You've missed a lot while you were away.'

Teppic introduced them to the squadron's new members, and described Hetep's deeds at the battle outside Irqata in terms that made Hetep blush and Sebeku roll his eyes. They felt far more at ease when he at last took them to inspect the squadron's chariots. Each of the cars had been modified to carry more weapons: a second set of javelins, a spare khopesh, and more arrows, eighty in all; Hetep remembered the battle outside Irqata and wondered if even that would be enough.

'You'll get this too, of course – all the squadrons are to be equipped the same. And we're being issued with

323

better armour. In fact, you're just in time – it's coming today.'

Over the midday meal the recruits talked eagerly about the coming campaign, of the easy slaughter of hapless foreigners and of the great heaps of plunder they would bring home. They all knew that Seti had once beaten the Hittites at Kadesh and they quoted the inscriptions on the great king's monuments, in which he had described how he had smashed the Hittites and their allies and trampled their armies, leaving their kings lying prostrate in their own blood. But some of the men who had been at Irqata looked sombre and shook their heads, and related their fathers' recollections of the same campaign. No one commented on the difference between the two accounts and a thoughtful silence fell, lasting until the beer jugs had been drained.

'Ramesses has been driving the generals hard,' said one of troopers. 'They say he wants to start the march early.'

'It's so we'll be at Kadesh before the Hittites,' said Teppic. 'May Amun grant that it's true. Then we'll be rested and ready when the they come.'

There was a murmur of agreement and a few prayers of hope, for they all knew that whichever side reached the battlefield first would enjoy a huge advantage. Hetep remembered with a trace of unease what he had told Ramesses of the Hittite spring festival. What if I was wrong? he thought.

A commotion near the gate made him forget his worry and brought them all to their feet. It was the donkey train bringing the new armour, and they ran to meet it. Until now most of them had been wearing nothing thicker than a linen corselet, supplemented by odd bits of Canaanite equipment looted from battlefields in the time of their

324

fathers and grandfathers, and they chattered like excited children as they watched the donkeys being unloaded.

The new suit proved to be a single knee-length hauberk of soft hide covered in scales of thick leather hardened by boiling in wax, and looked much like a leather version of the bronze armour worn by Pharaoh and the chariot commanders, although of course not as pretty in the sunshine. Each came with a matching helmet.

There were more than enough to equip all the squadron's archers. Teppic draped one of the spare sets over a wooden target dummy and he and Hetep shot a quiver full of arrows at it. The scales were so tightly overlapped that few of the arrowheads pierced the hide backing, a result that pleased even the most fatalistic among them, for although none doubted the effectiveness of their protective charms or the good will of their personal gods they all agreed that there was no substitute for a stout set of armour.

Hetep told Sebeku the good news.

'I see there's none for us drivers,' said Sebeku.

'Sorry,' said Hetep, feeling as if it was his fault. 'But don't forget you're the one with the shield.'

'Indeed. And since you're going to be so well protected from now on I need only use it for myself. A welcome easing of my burdens.'

During his final week in Pr-Ramesses Hetep tried to get to know his new comrades in the messenger squadron. It was no easy task, for they were as aloof as only the sons of the nobility could be; worse, Baya had already been with them for many days and it was obvious that he had wasted no time in poisoning their minds against him. To them Baya was the warrior hero who had crushed the

325

Libyan hordes and saved the oasis people, and Hetep, the son of a provincial scribe and jealous of the achievements of the better man, had tried to steal Baya's credit. When Hetep heard this he felt only a wry amusement, and his smile grew predatory when he noticed Baya's discomfort when near him and the pains he took to avoid him, postponing the confrontation they both knew was coming.

A few days before the army was due to march Hetep went home to pay a final visit to his father. At the village he found almost the entire population – adults and children alike – out in the fields harvesting the wheat and barley. With the early raising of the levies each farmer had to do the work of two, and overseers were pacing along the raised field boundaries, encouraging the workers to greater efforts with blows from canes. Hetep's uncle was there, standing on a dyke with a sheet of papyrus in one hand and a pen in the other, making the inventory and watching the labourers with a jealous intensity as if unwilling to lose even a singe ear of grain.

'You're back, then,' he said when he saw Hetep. 'Dare I hope it's to do some honest work?'

He looked haggard as if from lack of sleep; perhaps, thought Hetep, supervising the harvest while short handed was taking its toll.

'Sorry, but I'm part of Ramesses' messenger squadron now. We march to Kadesh in a few days.'

'Kadesh, is it?' Nebenteru grimaced as if in pain. 'So that's the name of the city I see in my dream.'

Hetep had expected anger, or at the very least scorn, and the cryptic response left him at a loss.

'What dream?'

'Every night for the past two weeks it has come. I see a city standing high on a mound and the plain before it covered in bodies. I see you lying beneath its walls, scavengers feeding on your unburied corpse. And now I know the city's name.'

Hetep shivered, as if a shadow had passed across the sun.

'It's a sending from an evil god,' he said. 'It must be.'

'I spent a night in the shrine's incubation chamber, in the very presence of its goddess, and the same dream came again. Don't you understand? It is a sign of what's to come.'

Nebenteru looked old and tired, and very much afraid, and Hetep found himself unexpectedly moved by his uncle's distress.

'Dreams can twist the truth,' he said, trying to assuage his uncle's fears as much as his own. 'I'm sure any diviner will tell you that. There's nothing to worry about – the Hittites will be no match for us. You should see the army that's assembled at Pr-Ramesses. We're taking all four divisions; that's more than twenty thousand men. We can't lose.'

'Who doubts that Ramesses will be victorious? He has Amun to guide and protect him. But victory comes at a price, as you should know by now. How many of your comrades will be lost? How many families are fated to die out because of this?'

'We just have to make sure that it doesn't happen to us. That's why I've come. But I need your help.'

'What are you talking about?'

'All you've done these past few years is belittle my achievements. It's no wonder father's ashamed of me. But if you tell him what you've seen me become – envoy for Nui, and now chariot archer under Pharaoh's personal command – he'll relent, and with his blessing I'll survive the campaign. He won't believe me if I tell him alone. But if we go to the tomb together I'm sure he'll listen.'

327

'Together?' Nebenteru stared, as if unable to comprehend the meaning of the word.

'In Libya I was given a share of the spoils won after the battle, so this time I can pay for a proper *ka* priest. And for sacrifices, too – more than some men of higher rank get. And with father's blessing, when I come back from Kadesh I'll have gold and slaves, everything I need to make this land like it is in the Field of Reeds. Then we'll need never work again. And I'll have the wealth to support a family. I'll take a wife, and I promise we'll fill the house with children.'

Nebenteru studied his face. 'You'll go to Kadesh no matter what I say. I can see that.'

'I need to. But with your help I'll survive and return. Please, come with me to the tomb.'

'Very well,' sighed Nebenteru. 'But not before I've finished the audit on the last of these fields. Will you help me with them?'

'Of course,' said Hetep.

CHAPTER 37

It was the ninth day of the second month of Harvest and the army of Ramesses was forming up to begin its long journey to Kadesh. All night the torches had burned in the assembly areas at Pr-Ramesses while the troops were paraded and counted, their weapons issued and their final loyalty oaths to the pharaoh taken. Now, as the torch flames paled in the dawn's growing light, the army was at last settling into its marching order.

At its head, in his gilded travelling chariot, stood Ramesses, as tall and graceful of form as the god Atum, as resolute and warlike as the god Montu, Lord of Thebes. In the light of his presence waited the vizier and General Huti, the Field Marshal of Chariotry; bodyguards, priests, fanbearers, musicians and royal concubines; and three of the royal princes, the youngest barely twelve years old, there to learn the art of war from their father, the living god. Behind, along a two-mile stretch of road, the troops of Amun, Re, Ptah and Set divisions had assembled: sixteen thousand infantry and two thousand chariots; while at the very rear, in a great mass of noise and disorder, waited the baggage animals, and the slaves, cooks, smiths, brewers, craftsmen, diviners and physicians, without which the army would disintegrate in a matter of days.

From the compound far to the rear Hetep and Sebeku emerged, their chariot going slowly through the tangle of camp followers. Hetep had returned late last night from his trip home and had woken from a deep sleep in which he had seen his father smiling approvingly at him from the Field of Reeds. So warming was the dream to his *ka* that he had lain long in his blanket, while in his mind the smiling Ramesses rewarded him for his glorious deeds in the coming battle with ever more elaborate gifts. Now he and Sebeku were bickering as the latter wove a route through the milling confusion of the baggage train.

'Can't you go any faster?' said Hetep. 'We'll be late for the start.'

'Another word and I'm turning back.'

'But that's desertion!'

They made better progress after reaching the army's main body, skirting the road past the column of troops. As they neared Re division Hetep could hear Nui roaring orders over the noise and he saw Antef hurrying along the line, checking equipment and pushing the slower chariot teams into their positions.

Teppic was there, waving at Hetep and grinning as if they had already won their victory against the Hittites. He pointed to his chariot; its rails had been gilded and the bare wood polished so that it blazed like a lamp where it caught the sun.

'What's all this for?' said Hetep, after telling the grumbling Sebeku to pull over.

'I've been made troop commander,' said Teppic, smiling proudly. 'I had the car done up to mark the occasion.'

'Well done,' said Hetep. 'It looks very... shiny.'

'Not sure if Ipu approves, though,' said Teppic.

They all looked over at Teppic's driver. He was ignoring them, instead inspecting his car's stock of arrows one after another, his eyes darting and intent, and tossing every fourth or fifth aside.

'What's he doing?' asked Hetep.

'Sorting them out according to the colour of the flights.'

Ipu looked up, his gaze sharp. 'Green is the colour of life, and should go at the front,' he said, indicating the forward quivers on the car. 'Red is the colour of death, and makes the arrow bundles look untidy.' He cast another aside.

'There you have it,' said Teppic.

Hetep shrugged. 'We've just been picking out the straightest.' A horn sounded near the front of the column – the signal for the march to begin. 'Better go. Mustn't keep Pharaoh waiting.'

'A moment,' said Teppic, reaching out to put a hand on his arm. 'I've been asking around about Baya. He's made himself popular in this messenger squadron you're both in, which means if there's trouble he's got help. You should come and bivouac with us when we stop at night. There's not a man in first squadron who doesn't hate Baya for what he's done, so you'll have plenty of protection.'

'Thanks for the warning, but I've got no intention of avoiding Baya. It's different now. He's not after me – I'm the one who's hunting him.'

All day the army marched, following the eastern flank of the Delta and pursued by a great cloud of mosquitoes. They went slowly, conserving the strength of both men and horses for the long journey ahead, for it would not do to arrive at Kadesh too exhausted and depleted to fight. The chariots especially needed a great deal of care; each crewman took turns driving while his companion walked beside the car, to ease the strain on the wooden axles.

At sundown they reached the first of the forts that guarded the Way of Horus; so large was the army that most of the troops had to bivouack outside its walls. As the sun set and the watch fires sprang up Hetep noted carefully where Baya had chosen to bed down – after all, he did not want to miss him in the dark. An hour later he and Sebeku were crawling through the camp, daggers held

331

ready as they worked their way silently through the rows of sleeping figures. They reached the spot where Hetep was sure he had last seen Baya, but all they found was a patch of bare earth. A whispered argument followed, with Sebeku accusing Hetep of getting lost, cut short by the sleepy protests of their comrades. Then it dawned on them that Baya was probably stalking them in turn and they crawled away to what they thought was a safe distance before lying down for a night of tense watchfulness. When the morning came Hetep saw that Baya had moved to the other side of the camp; the latter smirked when their eyes met.

The morning's bread and beer rations emptied the fort's storehouses and the army marched an hour after dawn, leaving the lushness of the Delta behind. Bad tempered from lack of sleep Hetep and Sebeku quarreled for most of the morning, but in the end both were forced to agree that the camp, even in the dark, was far too busy for murder, and Baya far too wily to let it happen. Still, each night thereafter Hetep made a point of changing their sleeping positions, and each dawn they saw that Baya had done the same.

On the tenth day of the march the army crossed the border of Egypt and entered southern Canaan, a collection of minor kingdoms and city states which had been vassals of Egypt since soon after the expulsion of the Hyksos. Overawed by the size of the Egyptian force the mayors, princes and petty kings made grovelling obeisance to Ramesses, promising double the agreed supplies of grain, while mercenaries and levy troops flocked to the divisions' battle standards in their hundreds – mostly archers, unarmoured and carrying simple wooden bows, but a few were sufficiently well equipped to join the ranks of the assault troops.

The march slowed as the men wearied. The days were hot with too little water, and the bread and beer, made from grain taken from foreign granaries, had a disagreeable flavour. During the nights the darkness seemed to close in, cold and hostile, with only Ramesses' divinity and the arched body of Nut high overhead to protect them against Canaan's otherworldly dangers, and the native Egyptians grew increasingly unsettled, their sleep disturbed by evil things they could not name. Several times Hetep went crawling through the camp, searching in vain for Baya, and with each failure to kill his enemy his frustration grew, even as his hatred transformed into a slow-burning anger.

In another week they had reached Meggido. Beyond, along the inland road, lay cities only nominally in Egypt's grip and which had not been coerced into storing sufficient grain to supply all four divisions. Now the army would have to live partly off the land, and to do that it needed to spread out. Ramesses, his guard troops and Amun division would take the lead, following the road through the Valley of the Cedar and thence to Kadesh; a half-day's march behind would come Re division, far enough away to not have to camp on land already stripped by Amun's troops, but close enough to support them if there was trouble. Meanwhile Ptah and Set divisions were to take the coastal road, gathering provisions assembled by the cities there and reminding the local rulers of their loyalty oaths, before sending scouts to link up with the newly raised force at Sumur. Then they would swing inland, taking the main trade roads, and on the eleventh day of the third month of Harvest they, the troops from Sumur, and Amun and Re divisions would converge on the plain outside the walls of Kadesh.

The horologists examined the sky and consulted their

papyrus charts – not only for omens, but to ensure that the army's separate bodies would indeed meet simultaneously. The date chosen looked to be a particularly propitious one; better still, with the Hittite's Crocus Festival only now ending, they would arrive at Kadesh with time to spare.

Hetep was with Teppic when the army began to break up into its separate divisions.

'I envy you,' said Teppic. 'You'll be at Kadesh before the rest of us. Just remember to save a few Hittites for us laggards at the back.'

'We're supposed to be getting there before the Hittites, remember?'

'Yes, of course.' Teppic sighed. 'I guess I'm just afraid of missing out on the glory. By the way, how's Baya?'

'Still alive, unfortunately. It's not easy to kill a man in the middle of an army.'

'You might still get your chance. This country's pretty wild.'

'Trees,' said Ipu. He had been standing by his chariot and scanning the densely wooded hills flanking the road. 'You can hide things in trees. And there's still a long way to go.'

Teppic looked bemused. 'That's just about the first thing he's said since we entered Canaan.'

'He's right,' said Hetep. 'I don't like all these hills and trees. A man should be able to see the horizon.'

They entered the Valley of the Cedar, Ramesses and his guard troops in the lead and Amun division following in a tight column. So tall and heavily forested had the hills become that by day the troops walked in a green twilight and they bunched together, afraid of being too far from Ramesses' protective aura. At night, unsettled by the forest's looming presence and the nocturnal sounds unheard in the Nile valley, the men slept close to each other, while nervous sentries prowled the camp's perimeter, challenging shadows and half-seen animals. In such a tightly packed mass Hetep realised he had no chance of getting Baya sufficiently isolated to kill him, and all he could do was swallow his frustration and hope for an opportunity once they reached Kadesh.

On the eighth day of the third month of Harvest the division emerged from the valley and entered the gentler, lightly wooded hills of northern Canaan. It was Hetep's turn to drive the chariot and Sebeku was walking beside him, watching his handling of the team and ever ready with a sharp-tongued rebuke. They were becoming more common now as Hetep grew increasingly tired, both from the march and the nervous strain of having to contain a consuming anger that had no outlet. His mind kept rehearsing the same impossible schemes to isolate Baya from the rest of the army; all he needed was a moment, and it would be done.

Sebeku was talking but Hetep only half heard.

'I said there's something in the trees,' repeated Sebeku, pointing.

'Where?' Hetep glanced around in alarm. Memories of Ipu's warning came to him and he had a sudden vision of a horde of Hittite warriors pouring out of the woods in ambush.

'They've gone now. But I think it could be trouble.'

It seemed other eyes had spotted the movement too, for at an order from General Huti a trio of chariots peeled off from pharaoh's entourage and rolled up the hill flanking the road, heading for the trees.

'It's Baya,' said Sebeku, jumping into the car. 'Here's

335

our chance. I'll get as close as I can; if there's a fight you can put an arrow in his back. Then we're done.'

Hetep looked up the hill and saw Baya's chariot, the last of the three, trailing behind. He handed the reins to Sebeku, who urged Ibis and Vengeance into a canter. As they turned aside from the road a few of their comrades called out, wondering what they were doing, but Hetep ignored them. He drew out his bow from its holder and tried to string it, but found it impossible in the moving car and in the end he thrust it back and grabbed a javelin.

By now the crews from the leading scout chariots had dismounted and were moving cautiously into the trees, while Baya and his driver were hanging back as if afraid to follow.

'Slow down,' said Hetep. 'I can't do anything yet with all these people watching. Wait for the attack.'

They stopped behind Baya, who seemed not to have noticed them. A long, tense silence followed. Then came a cry from somewhere in the woods and Hetep stiffened, his javelin ready. The next moment a pair of figures burst from the undergrowth and came hurtling towards them. They were unarmed and looked terrified; in close pursuit came the dismounted charioteers.

'Can you see any more?' said Hetep. He scanned the tree line but there was no more movement. His anticipation turning to a sick disappointment he lowered the javelin.

'That appears to be it,' said Sebeku. 'We might as well go and see who they are.'

The running figures fell and lay panting with exhaustion and terror. Hetep and Sebeku reached them at the same time as their pursuers.

'Please, don't hurt us,' they said, breathless. 'We're friends.'

'Who are they?' asked Hetep.

'Shasu,' said one of the scout charioteers. 'They must be from one of the northern tribes – see the face tattoos.' He looked down at the cowering figures. 'Well, my friends, you're a long way from home.'

Sebeku looked livid. 'All this fuss just for a pair of vagabonds!' He spat.

'Would you have preferred a Hittite ambush?' said Hetep.

A chariot came rolling up beside them. It was Baya, joining them now he knew it was safe. Hetep still held his javelin; he gripped it hard and raised it ready to throw.

'Now now,' said Baya. 'Not with all these people watching, surely?'

With a snarl Hetep thrust the javelin back into its holder.

'You look disappointed,' said Baya.

'That's because I am. I never expected you to get this close to Kadesh.'

'Likewise.' Baya gave a thin smile. 'But there's time enough – you'll see. Now, I suggest we do our duty and escort these men to Ramesses.'

The pharaoh met them in the road, flanked by Sherden guards. Without prompting the two Shasu prostrated themselves in front of him.

'What are you?' he demanded.

'We were sent here, Majesty, against our will.'

'Sent? By whom?'

'We were taken from our families and forced into service. "Go scout for us," they said. "Find the army of the king of Egypt that we might meet him." And so we came, searching, and found you.'

The pharaoh towered over them. 'Who said?'

337

'The Hittites, Your Majesty.' There was a gasp from Ramesses' attendants and a gabble of talk, quickly silenced by the vizier. 'But we wish to be servants of Your Majesty, not servants of the king of Hatti. Yet when we saw you, looking like Ba'al in his glory, we grew afraid and hid.'

'Are others of your kind here?' As Ramesses spoke he scanned the hillside, as if his gaze could pierce the trees and see what was hidden from lesser men.

'No, Majesty. They are far away with the men of Hatti.'

'How far?'

'They are camped near Aleppo. The king of Hatti fears Your Majesty and his army has become rooted like a stand of trees.'

'That's a hundred miles away,' said one of the chariot commanders. 'By Amun, we really are here first!'

Ramesses held up a hand. 'One moment. Tell me why the wretch of Hatti does not press on.'

'He set out late from his homeland. And now, knowing that Your Majesty will be waiting for him at Kadesh, he hesitates, afraid to move, and tries to swell his army by raising troops from among the Habiru.'

'Then it is just as I foretold,' said the pharaoh. 'Their very gods betray them.'

Hetep remembered uneasily what he had told Ramesses of the Hittite spring festival. Back in Sumur it had been easy to believe Mursili's seemingly unguarded chatter about his land's gods and their needs; now, in this foreign wilderness, so close to the enemy kingdom of Kadesh, he was beginning to have doubts.

'Can we take the word of this one man?' said Huti, and there was a murmur of agreement from some of the others.

'If the vile men of Hatti were here we would have seen them,' said Ramesses. 'But they are cowards and they fear My Majesty. Last year they were afraid to send troops to support the men of Sumur and I took their city, and it became mine. And now they fear to oppose me at Kadesh, and soon that will be mine, too.' He turned, and his face was as shining and resolute as the god Montu's. 'Recall the scouts. From now on we double march.'

'Is that wise, Majesty?' said Huti. 'Without our scouts we are blind. We could–'

'My father speaks the truth,' interrupted the eldest of the princes. 'Why waste time searching the woods and gullies for phantom armies, when within days Amun will place Kadesh in my father's hand? Then let the Hittites face us if they dare!'

'Majesty, please, we must be cautious.'

The pharaoh turned to Huti, his eyes gleaming like bits of polished stone. 'When Tuthmosis, my great forbear, went to punish the rebels at Meggido, his own generals tried to hold him back. "Take the easy road," they said; "be cautious," they advised; for they were afraid. But caution would only have diminished his majesty, and trusting to Amun-Re he chose the bolder course. He set forth at the head of his army and came upon his enemy unawares. Montu and Amun, rewarding his courage, strengthened his arm, and the enemies whom Re hates he slew in their ranks. As it was with Tuthmosis, so it shall be with me.'

There could be no argument after that. Ramesses ordered that messengers be sent back to Re division, telling them that there was nothing now to fear from the Hittites and that they were to press on, and the Shasu were released – unwisely, thought Hetep, but he lacked the courage to say so.

The division formed up again and marched without

339

rest until sunset, when they pitched camp on the crown
of a tall, rounded hill. The hill was bare of trees, giving
a good view of the land as it fell away towards the plain
through which wound the Orontes river. From the east
the dusk was advancing, a great wall of shadow chasing
the departing sun, but the river stood out plain like a
ribbon of dulled silver. And there, on its western bank,
surrounded by patches of greenery, lay the city of Kadesh,
its walls catching the last of the light. When Ramesses
saw it he stretched out his hand and closed his fist upon it,
and when he opened his hand again he looked displeased,
as if he really thought Amun would have so easily given
him his prize.

CHAPTER 38

At dawn on the ninth day of the third month of Harvest Ramesses stepped from his tent looking like Re in his glory, and like Montu all decked in the accoutrements of war. As the camp broke up around him and the drowsy troops assembled into their ranks he turned his face towards the plain of Kadesh, his eyes glittering in the first of the sun's light. His driver Menna brought up his war chariot, and the twin gold disks on its yoke glowed as if they were molten, while his peerless horses, Mut-is-Content and Victory-in-Thebes, stamped and tossed their heads, as if impatient to begin the task of restoring Ma'at by trampling Hittites and Canaanites alike under their bronze-hard hooves. The pharaoh mounted, waited until the last of the dawn prayers had been said, and raised his arm. Horns sounded, and with a rolling of drums the advance began.

In a column the men of Amun division wound their way down the road to the Orontes river. With their goal in sight and the forests now behind them their spirits lifted, and as they marched they sang hymns of victory to Montu and Amun-Re. At the ford the advance slowed, the troops spreading along the bank like spilled oil; the river was broad but sluggish and the infantry waded knee deep, while the chariots slid over the rocky bed, water sloshing over the leather matting on the floors of the cars.

Once they had crossed the march resumed, with Ramesses and his guard chariots taking the lead. The wind lifted the dust from the bone-dry grassland and a blanket of haze hung in the air, fading the land's already muted colours. To the left the plain stretched away to a series of hills, pale with distance; to the right, a mile off and parallel to the route of march, a dull-green line of trees and scrub marked the path of a stream – one of the Orontes' many tributaries. And near the northern end of the trees, high on a mound formed after centuries building and rebuilding, Kadesh rose like a mountain against the featureless sky.

'Where's the garrison?' said Hetep. He was standing tall in his chariot and squinting through the haze at the unmanned ramparts. 'They must have seen us by now.'

Sebeku shrugged. 'Perhaps they ran away. They're only foreigners after all.'

'Are you serious?'

'You heard what the Shasu told us: the Hittites stand trembling in their chariots a week's march away. Perhaps the locals are scared, too.'

'If only it were true,' said Hetep. 'But something's not right – I can feel it.'

The sun climbed, and as the air grew hotter the advance slowed. There was no singing now, instead an unending chorus of coughing from throats irritated by the dust, accompanied by the monotonous tramp of feet and hooves on the grass, while Kadesh rose gradually higher, silent and eerily still.

A mile to the west of the city they saw signs of excavations. Hittites – or so thought Hetep and many of the younger men, until the veterans told them they were seeing the traces of King Seti's camp, made thirty years before during his own campaign in Canaan. Seti had driven off the Asiatic hordes and captured Kadesh; now his son would make use of the very same camp and from there try to emulate, if not surpass, his father's achievements.

The guard troops made for the site's centre where, with the help of the army's diviners, they began the task of setting up Ramesses' campaign tent and the shrine of Amun that was to stand next to it. The work had to be done with care, for a single flaw in one of the rituals or a misplaced protective device would leave the pharaoh vulnerable to attacks from the land's malign gods and demons. Meanwhile to the weary infantrymen of Amun division was allotted the task of laying out the rest of the camp and digging out the perimeter ditch. As the soldiers worked, listless and grumbling in the midday heat, Ramesses sat on his golden throne, flanked by his fanbearers and shaded by a vast linen awning. He looked at ease, his earlier eagerness seemingly forgotten, as if Kadesh was already his and the Hittites no more than a rumour. The princes and many of the younger officers, taking their lead from their pharaoh, rested under their own sun shades, as unworried by the torpor that had descended on the camp as by the silent, brooding walls of Kadesh. Only the veteran troops showed any concern; among them was Huti, who was pacing about the camp, fuming at the troops' indolence.

Sebeku was watching with a wry amusement. 'He's going to do himself a mischief if he keeps going on like that,' he said.

'Somebody has to,' said Hetep, 'or we'll never get the siege started. Still, at least they're getting the horse corrals sorted out.'

Hetep and Sebeku unyoked their chariot and while they waited to be assigned a place Sebeku went to inspect his horses. Hetep spent the time gazing across the plain towards the still-lifeless city; even the sky above it was empty of birds – a strange sight to a man from the Delta, where flocks of marsh fowl sometimes darkened the sun. He shaded his eyes and squinted until he could make out the hill on which they had camped last night. Re division should have reached it by now, he realised. But there was little comfort in knowing that his friends, and another five thousand troops, were still a half-day's march away.

'How are the horses?' he asked.

'Better than I had hoped.' Sebeku ran a hand over Vengeance's forehead. 'Truly they are a team fit for a god. Even now, after a month on the road, they could outrun the wind.'

'Good. Because once you're finished we'll yoke them up again.'

'Are we going somewhere?'

'I don't know.' Hetep hesitated, then made an impatient gesture. 'Just do what I say, will you?'

They had just finished tightening the last bridle strap when they heard raised voices from the pharaoh's tent and saw Huti storming out, his face livid. On his heels came the eldest of the royal princes, almost choking with indignation.

The general stopped and whirled on him.

'Enough!' he shouted. 'When you have as much experience as I, *Highness*, I'll listen to what you have to say. But you, your brothers, and your divine father – may he have life, health, and prosperity – are wrong. And if he wants to stop me he'd better send the Sherden to arrest me.'

The general's eye fell on Hetep and Sebeku. Seeing them standing by their yoked chariot his face brightened.

'Now that's what I like to see: initiative.' He strode over, smiling fiercely. 'If even half the army was like you I'd be a calmer man. I've a task for you.'

'Well done,' muttered Sebeku, with a dark look at Hetep.

'I want you out there,' said the general, pointing to

344

the trees by the stream, south of the city. 'Find out why it's so quiet around here. Don't just stare. Go!'

'Alone?' said Hetep. Then, realising he might be thought afraid, he added, 'I mean, it's a lot of ground to cover for one chariot crew.'

With a snarl of impatience Huti swept his gaze around the corral. A half-dozen chariot teams were still waiting to be unyoked and in a voice that startled both men and horses he ordered their crews out. They were all from Amun division, newly trained for the campaign, and Hetep, on account of his two years' seniority, found himself put in command.

He lead his resentful little troop out onto the plain, Sebeku fuming quietly beside him. A mile out he called a halt and stood up straight in the chariot to search the far horizon all around. But as before he could see nothing moving, and the only sounds were the distant murmur of the river, the buzzing of insects and the hiss of the wind over the grass.

'What is it?' said Sebeku, testily.

Hetep reached for his protective amulet and, just as on that night in Libya, his hand closed instead over the pendant Elissa had given him. Anat, the Lady of Heaven, he thought; he was certain it had been her influence and not his father's that had saved them in the Libyan desert. He wondered if she would be able to do the same for him here and felt a pang of guilt knowing that he still doubted his father's good will. He exhaled and shook his head.

'Nothing,' he muttered. 'We'd better get to the trees.'

They moved off again, heading now for the woods by the stream. As Hetep looked back to make sure the rest of his ad-hoc troop was keeping pace he saw another pair of chariots trailing them at a distance. He shaded his eyes and squinted. It was Baya, without a doubt, accompanied by another crew from the messenger squadron.

'We've go some unwelcome company,' he said. 'Look.'

Sebeku twisted about, and the moment he saw Baya his ill temper vanished and he smiled fiercely. 'He thinks he can kill us where few are watching,' he said.

'He might be right. We're outnumbered two to one.'

'Then we must use our wits. We'll take to the trees and wait in ambush.'

As they accelerated Hetep felt his heart beating faster – not out of fear, but with anticipation. For too long he had been cheated of his chance for vengeance and his hatred had become a festering ache inside him. It was almost a relief to feel it flaring up again, like a fire given new kindling.

At the scrub bordering the strip of woodland they dismounted and Sebeku tethered the horses.

'If anyone harms Vengeance or Ibis I'll strangle him with his own intestines,' he muttered.

'Come on,' said Hetep. 'They'll have seen us. We'd better move quickly.'

He took his bow and a dozen arrows then handed Sebeku his khopesh, and together they plunged into the deeper woodland, the puzzled voices of the Amun charioteers fading behind them. At first the going was easy for the trees were widely spaced, enclosing clearings filled with flowers and dappled sunlight. But further on, where the ground sloped down towards the stream's edge, the trees became thicker, with tangled undergrowth beneath which the shadows looked black.

'Here'll do,' said Hetep, indicating a fallen tree. 'I'll pick him off when he appears. Get over there and hide.' He pointed diagonally across a clearing. 'You can deal with his friends if they make a fuss.'

'You mean murder them?'

'Just subdue them or something. But it won't come to that. Trust me.'

Sebeku pursed his lips but he went all the same, stalking off into the undergrowth. Meanwhile Hetep crouched behind the tree, his bow ready. For the first time he heard bird song, loud over the voices of the other charioteers, who were still calling after him. Then came the snap of a twig somewhere to his left. That's odd, he thought; how could Baya have got over there?

He stared, trying to pierce the shadows beneath the trees. There: someone was creeping up from near the bank of the stream. He fitted an arrow to his bowstring and waited, his heart pounding, but the figure vanished. For a long while he crouched motionless, his ears straining, then he heard more movement from somewhere behind. He twisted around and saw not twenty paces away a squat, bearded man wearing linen armour. This was no Egyptian charioteer, he realised; perhaps it was one of the Canaanite auxiliaries from the camp.

The man saw him and straightened.

'*Mannu atta?*' he demanded. Then, realising who Hetep was, he whipped out a sword and advanced, glaring and belligerent. '*Musraiu!*' he shouted. '*Mus–*'

Hetep shot him in the chest. The man stood rigid, the look of belligerence turning into a ludicrous expression of shock as blood dribbled from his mouth. Then he collapsed in a bubbling heap.

There was no doubt the man had been calling to hidden companions, and sure enough just as Hetep ducked back into cover there came a crashing in the undergrowth and two men burst into the clearing. Both were armoured like the first, only these were carrying bows. Then a third man appeared: huge and muscular, with pale skin and a beardless face, and long, straight hair hanging down his

347

back; a sword hung at his belt and in one hand he held a spear. Gods help us, thought Hetep: the Hittites are here.

Movement beside him made him jump, but it was only Sebeku.

'I heard some noise,' he said, dryly.

Hetep mouthed the words 'Shut up!' and pointed to the Hittite, who was bending over the wounded man. The latter was too badly injured to report what had happened, and after a moment the Hittite straightened and scanned all around him. He signalled to his companions to split up and search the woods on either side, then began pacing across the clearing, straight towards Hetep and Sebeku.

Hetep readied another arrow while Sebeku tensed, his khopesh gripped tightly. Then they heard voices, this time Egyptian. One of Baya's charioteer friends stepped into the clearing, saw the Hittite and went rigid with fear. In one smooth motion the Hittite turned and flung his spear, transfixing the Egyptian through the belly. His victim made no more than a choked cough before he crumpled. A heartbeat later the charioteer's driver came stumbling out from cover, followed by Baya, his eyes wild and searching.

'There he is,' whispered Sebeku. 'Kill him!'

The Hittite roared a challenge and charged the Egyptians while Hetep drew and shot. The arrow struck Baya in his throat and he staggered, clutching at the wound, before pitching over. The Hittite leaped over him and, drawing his sword, ran straight for the driver. The latter raised his shield and flailed desperately with a dagger; the Hittite feinted, ducked, and gutted him with one thrust of his sword. Then he turned, saw Hetep and grinned hatefully.

'It'll be us next unless you do something,' said Sebeku.

348

Quickly Hetep drew and shot, but the arrow only pierced the Hittite's leg. The latter came on, hobbling now, the bloody sword raised high and his face ugly with rage.

'Now you've made him angry!'

Sebeku scrabbled sideways, hidden by the tree, while Hetep backed away and drew his dagger. With a roar the Hittite lunged, just as Sebeku sprang at him from behind and slashed him across the side of the neck with his khopesh, almost severing his head.

'Thank you,' said Hetep, wiping away the blood that had sprayed over his face.

'Hush! There might be more.'

They stood listening, the air around them filled with the smell of crushed flowers and gore, but for the moment all was quiet. Sebeku caught Hetep's eye and together they crept over to where Baya had fallen. It took them a while to find the corpse, for Baya had crawled into a hollow at the base of a tree. There he had died, and there he lay, a pathetic, huddled thing, the flies already exploring the wound in his neck.

'So that's it,' said Hetep. He felt no sense of triumph, only a mild queasiness, and he turned away.

Sebeku stood pondering the corpse. 'So much for the glory of the charioteer's life,' he said. 'One squalid little battle under the trees and that's it: another life extinguished.'

'I can't tell if you're feeling sorry for me or him.'

'I'm just saying. We're not exactly winning renown under Pharaoh's gaze, are we?'

'What should we do about the body?'

'Let the jackals have it. It's what he'd have done to us.' Sebeku looked around. 'Come on, it's time we got back to the others.'

They were halfway across the clearing when there was a shout and a band of Hittites came charging out of the trees. At the same time the remaining Egyptians appeared. There was a short and vicious fight, at the end of which all the Hittites were down at the cost of six Egyptians.

'There's two still alive,' said Sebeku, indicating their fallen enemies. One, dazed but otherwise whole, was sitting up and rubbing his head, while another, rather noisier, was clutching his bleeding leg and rolling from side to side in pain. 'We should take them back to the camp. They might be able to tell us what's going on.'

'Not yet.' This was Baya's chariot driver. With the battle safely over he had emerged from hiding and was now staring accusingly at Hetep. 'Where's Baya?'

'I don't know. I think the Hittites got him.'

'Show me the body.'

'What makes you think I know where it is?'

They stood eyeing each other while the other Egyptians watched in puzzled silence. From across the stream came the crash of booted feet through undergrowth.

'We'd better get back before we're knee deep in Hittites,' said Sebeku.

Still Baya's driver wanted to stay but the other Egyptians, none of whom knew Baya, were unwilling to risk looking for him. Quickly they bound their two captives and dragged them with them out of the woods.

CHAPTER 39

Back at the camp work had stopped on the ramparts, although the ditch was just a shallow scrape in the ground and the shields stuck into the raised earth mound behind it to form the wall were so uneven they resembled a row of broken teeth.

'Pathetic,' said Sebeku. 'It wouldn't keep out a gang of cripples. And as for them...' He indicated the infantry, most of whom were lying in the sun and snoring like hogs, save for a group in the far corner who were drinking beer and quarreling over a game of senet.

'They'll wake up soon enough when they hear about the Hittites,' said Hetep.

The vizier himself came to meet them. Seeing their prisoners he hurried them to the royal enclosure, where Ramesses was still on his throne, as unmoved and unmoving as one of his massive stone likenesses back in Pr-Ramesses. At the vizier's prompting Hetep approached, one arm outstretched as a sign that he was bringing important news.

'Majesty, may you have life, breath and health,' he said, 'the Hittites are here.'

The pharaoh looked at him blankly, as if hearing words in an unknown tongue. 'What did you say?'

'Hittites. We caught some spying in the woods, by the river.'

'That cannot be. You lie!'

'It's the truth, Majesty,' said the vizier. 'See what this man has brought.'

The Sherden dragged the Hittites to the foot of the throne and forced them to kneel. Ramesses frowned as he

351

looked down at them, seeming more puzzled than alarmed.

'What are you?' he demanded. He leaned forwards to inspect them more closely. 'Why are you here?'

The Hittites remained silent, their heads bowed. At a nod from the vizier the Sherden seized them up, dragged them away and beat them with sticks, then flung them back into Pharaoh's presence.

'Speak!' commanded Ramesses. 'What are you?'

One of the Hittites raised his head, but it was only to spit at Ramesses. Enraged, the Sherden beat them until their faces looked like bloody sacks of meat, and again Ramesses asked them what they were. This time one of the Hittites answered.

'Fool,' he rasped; blood and broken teeth drooled from his ruined mouth. 'Our king, Muwatalli, is here and his army darkens the land like locusts.' He pointed. 'There they lie, hidden, north of the city – infantry and chariots, all armed, their numbers like grains of sand. Your soldiers will die and my king will drag you to Hatti in chains.'

Slowly Ramesses shook his head. 'No. It is impossible – it cannot be,' he said, as if the act of denial would keep real his belief that he had arrived at Kadesh before his enemies.

'Majesty, look!' said the vizier, pointing.

Atop the walls of Kadesh banners were breaking out and on the ramparts the garrison appeared – Canaanites and Hittites together. There could be no denying the truth now and Ramesses stared, horrified. Then came a flush of anger, spreading from his neck and up over his face.

'I have been betrayed,' he cried. He turned a livid eye on his courtiers. 'You, who should have advised My Majesty... where was your counsel? "Press on," you said. "Your Majesty has nothing to fear; the vile men of Hatti are far away." Was none of you able to tell me the truth?'

All of them – princes, chariot commanders, even the vizier – looked down in silence, as frightened and shame-faced as chastened children. Hetep tried to slip out of sight, guiltily aware of his part in misleading Ramesses, and his heart nearly stopped when the royal gaze fell accusingly upon him. He opened his mouth, ready to gabble excuses and apologies, but Pharaoh's gaze had already moved on, to settle on the commanders of the Canaanite levy troops. 'And you! Did not one of you know enough of his own land to tell me what passes through them?'

'Majesty, please, there's no time for this,' said Huti. 'We must send messengers to summon the other divisions.'

'I'll go,' said Hetep, anxious to be out from under the pharaoh's gaze. 'My chariot's already yoked.'

Huti nodded quickly before turning to issue his orders to the army's commanders. Hetep, taking the nod as a dismissal, slipped gratefully away.

'Have you gone mad?' said Sebeku, once they were out of earshot. 'That's the second time you've landed us in trouble.'

'You want to wait here to be overrun by an army of Hittites? We'll be safer with Re division – they're our friends. Besides, if we hang about here Ramesses might remember who told him about that Hittite festival.'

Officers were striding about the camp, roaring commands as they tried to bring order to the sudden chaos. The concubines and youngest of the princes were herded out of the west gate, escorted by chariots and Sherden; with them went messengers tasked with seeking out the new division from Sumur and urging it to hurry. The few infantrymen under arms manned the ramparts and stood watching fearfully to the north and east for the first signs of the Hittite attack.

353

At the south gate Hetep joined the vizier and the other charioteers who were to summon the army's scattered formations. Re division was less than four miles away, marching towards them after crossing the ford, and would reach the camp in an hour. But Set and Ptah divisions had taken the road to the west of the Orontes and could be anywhere in the forests and hills beyond the ford, and the vizier was chafing with impatience as his driver fussed with the bridle straps on his horse team.

At last the chariots were ready and they set out, speeding south along the plain. Their route took them close to Re division, and as they closed Hetep could see Nui in the vanguard standing tall in his chariot and first squadron following him in a tight column, their horses stepping smartly. But the infantry block had lost all order as the less-fit foot soldiers had straggled behind their sturdier comrades, and on the flanks the other chariot squadrons were strung out in long lines.

The vizier was in too much of a hurry to stop but he hailed Nui and pointed north.

'Make haste,' he cried, his ancient voice like the call of a vulture. 'To the camp! Your pharaoh stands alone and is in need.'

Then he veered aside, leaving Nui and his officers staring after him.

'Slow down and turn,' said Hetep to Sebeku. 'I want to talk to Nui.'

'That's disobeying orders. There'll be trouble.' But Sebeku did as he was told, peeling off from the escort and bringing them around in a wide curve. As they closed Teppic waved at him from the head of his troop.

'You're going the wrong way for glory,' he shouted. 'Or is Baya after you again?'

'Baya's dead,' said Hetep. 'We've bigger worries now.

354

The Hittites are here.'

Teppic's grin faltered. 'Is this a joke? They're supposed to be days away.'

Nui and his officers came driving over; the infantry commanders, still marching with their troops, were looking on, their faces worried.

'What is it?' asked Nui.

'Hittites,' said Hetep. 'They're waiting of us, north of the city.'

All eyes turned to Kadesh, where the only movement was the waving of the banners atop the walls.

'I can't see anything,' said one of the troop commanders, frowning.

'They're there. We even killed some of their scouts.'

Nui scanned the plain all around, but there was nothing to see except the ever-present haze. He turned.

'Teppic, get your troop out in front of us and form a screen,' he ordered. 'The rest of you get back to your men. Tell them to string their bows and close up those columns. And someone get the infantry moving faster!'

Messengers raced off while Hetep and Sebeku followed Teppic as he lead his troop around the head of the column. The infantry stared dully at them, stupid with fatigue; then came a flurry of orders that sent the whole column into further disorder, with groups of men bunching together and others falling back as they sought out their officers and subunits. Meanwhile Teppic's troop spread out into a skirmish line, guarding the column's front.

From the woods by the stream came the cries of birds, shrill with alarm, and a cloud of them rose up in a tempest of noise. Then a horn blared, and from the cover of the trees burst a long line of Hittite chariots. Each carried three men armoured in bronze, their long hair streaming in the wind. From the crews' throats came a great shout,

355

like the voice of their Storm God when he roars down from the sky.

Hetep gaped, numb with shock. Beside him Teppic was calmly giving orders to his troop.

'Form up and wheel about. Trumpeter, you're with me. And all of you – keep those intervals wide.' He reached over and shook Hetep's shoulder. 'Wake up! It's time we earned all that free food and drink Pharaoh's been giving us.'

'You're going to attack?' said Hetep, horrified. 'You're drunk!'

'No, he's mad,' said Sebeku. 'But what's the alternative? Run away?'

'Trees,' announced Ipu, with a satisfied air. 'Didn't I tell you?'

Teppic's troop accelerated as it came around. The Hittites ignored them, instead converging to form a column aimed straight at Re division's flank. Then a second wave of Hittites came surging out from ambush, and a third after it.

'We have to retreat,' shouted Hetep. 'There's too many of them!'

But Teppic was beyond hearing. He was leaning forwards, eyes intent as his troop bore down on the leading Hittite column.

'Now,' he shouted, and as the trumpeter sounded the order to turn the chariots swept around, the warriors shooting. But they may as well have been gnats for all the effect they had, for most of the arrows were stopped by armour or shields, and only a couple of Hittites fell.

'That showed them,' said Sebeku, as the troop raced north to safety.

A whole squadron of Hittites peeled off in pursuit while the remainder kept going, bearing down on the helpless troops of Re division. The few escorting chariots that were battle ready were overrun and like a huge spearpoint the Hittite column smashed into the ranks of marching infantry, and the screams of pain and terror came loud over the pounding hooves and grinding chariot wheels.

Hetep felt sick as he watched the pursuing Hittite squadron.

'Gods help us, it's like Irqata all over again,' he said. 'Only a hundred times worse.'

'Will you settle yourself?' said Sebeku. 'We'll get away yet.'

Indeed, the Hittites were rapidly falling behind and soon they gave up the chase. As Teppic halted his troop they were met by Nui, who had managed to gather up a squadron's worth of chariots to follow him.

'Get to the camp, both of you,' he ordered. 'Tell Pharaoh what's happening.'

'You think they can't see?' said Hetep.

'Not in all this dust they can't.' Indeed, the Hittite attack had churned up so much of the stuff that it was hard even from close up to see the full extent of the carnage.

'What about you?' asked Hetep.

'I'll try to save what I can. By the way, I may not get a chance to ask you again: how's Baya?'

'We killed him. But it doesn't seem to matter much now.'

'Oh, it matters, all right. After all, we're here to restore Ma'at aren't we?' Nui grinned and clapped him on the shoulder. 'Well done. Now get to the camp.'

His driver lashed the reins and the next moment he was gone, brandishing a spear and roaring a challenge as he lead his chariots straight for the Hittites.

'We can't let him go on his own,' said Hetep.

'Make up your mind,' said Sebeku. 'A moment ago you wanted to run away.'

Teppic must have felt the same as Hetep for he hesitated, reluctant to give the order to retreat. They watched as Nui's ad-hoc squadron charged the Hittites, only to be swallowed up by their third wave; at close range the Hittite crews' spears and javelins killed horses far more efficiently than did arrows and the Egyptians were soon overwhelmed. Meanwhile the enemy's main column had smashed its way through Re division's infantry block, cutting it in two. Officers were screaming orders over the panicked cries of their troops, and now men were running in terror, flinging away their weapons.

Hetep pulled on Teppic's arm.

'Come away, now,' he said. 'There's nothing left for us to protect.'

As Re division disintegrated the bulk of the Hittites kept going west, leaving the way clear for Teppic's troop to reach the camp. They found it in uproar, with leaderless soldiers running this way and that, officers yelling, men scrabbling for weapons, and charioteers struggling to yoke rearing horse teams. The troop dismounted, the men calling for water – Hetep and most of the other crews for themselves, Sebeku for his horses – while General Huti hurried over, demanding to know what was happening.

'Hittites,' said Hetep breathlessly; he had to force himself not to gabble in panic. 'They've destroyed Re division. I think they're coming for us next.'

They all stared across the plain to where, among the fleeing remnants of Re division, they could see the great column of Hittite chariots curving around in an arc. As they watched its course steadied, its vanguard pointing straight at them.

Huti cleared his throat. 'I think you're right,' he said.

'Come with me.'

He lead the way through the camp, Hetep and Teppic beside him. At the centre Ramesses was standing beside his chariot, a pillar of calm amid the confusion, calling out in a ringing voice for the chariot squadrons to assemble, while the Sherden were forming a battle line to protect the royal enclosure. The pharaoh looked indomitable, a bulwark against which Egypt's enemies could only dash themselves in vain, and Hetep felt his panic draining away. Bowing, he approached and made his report.

Let the Hittites come,' said Ramesses with a thin smile. 'With my father Amun at my side they are men without heirs.'

The eldest of the princes was on hand, his eyes shining with worship.

'A thousand warriors cannot withstand you. Even a million will stand stupefied with fear!'

With a noise like the breaking of a storm the Hittite vanguard came smashing through the camp's western perimeter. The Sherden gave an answering shout and charged to meet them; caught in the middle, camp servants and still-arming soldiers were cut down in heaps. Then more Hittite chariots appeared, surging over the broken wall of shields, only to slow as the horses became entangled in the tents and piles of stores. Men fought with spear, axe, khopesh and sword; others with their bare hands. Hetep saw screaming Hittites dragged from their cars by their hair and gutted, while others leaped out to fall on the close-packed Egyptians, stabbing and hacking in a frenzy of bloodshed.

And still the Egyptian chariot force had not finished forming up, with many of the crews still battling to yoke their horses, or calling desperately for arrows and javelins. The noise grew and the Sherden, pressed hard by the flood of Hittites, fell back; in moments it seemed the enemy would reach the east gate, the only safe route of escape. Ramesses called out again, ordering his guard troops to stand firm and his chariot warriors to hurry their preparations, and his voice calmed both men and horses alike. Yet even then they might have been surrounded and destroyed if the god Re, aided perhaps by Set the Destroyer, had not come to the pharaoh's aid, maddening the Hittites with a lust for plunder. As the attackers left off slaughtering the Egyptians to loot the camp the Sherden rallied and pushed forwards, making space for Ramesses' chariots to equip in peace.

At last they were ready and the pharaoh lead them out of the gate in a column. They swept around the north of the camp and came upon the rear of the Hittite force, whose chariots were jammed together in their crews' eagerness for a share of the loot. There were no drums or horns to order the attack, no battle standard but Ramesses himself; a light shone about him, and his chariot blazed as brightly as Khepri, the dawn sun.

Like a flock of raptors they fell upon the Hittites, who were so densely packed there was scarcely need for the archers to aim. Five times they attacked, racing in and out against the helpless column's flank; a few groups of chariots peeled off to counter attack, but their horses were spent after their charge through Re division and most of the crews were killed before they got near. The wheeling chariots threw up great curtains of dust, blotting out the sun, and when at last the surviving Hittites broke and fled they vanished into a lurid orange twilight.

Now the Egyptians were pulling back to rest. The attack had taken its toll on the chariots and scarcely thirty remained intact. The crews sagged with exhaustion, and the dust caking their faces and arms was striped with dark lines of mud where the sweat had run down them. Only Ramesses still stood tall in his chariot, his more-than-human will holding his body up against the crushing fatigue, and his face glowed with the joy of victory.

Hetep, tired already from the earlier skirmishes, felt a pain like fire in his arms and across his back, and could scarcely lift his bow; beside him Sebeku looked grey and hollow eyed, too worn out even for sarcasm. Teppic and Ipu were still alive; they shared the remains of their water, and Hetep grimaced as he swallowed the last of the blood-hot, foul-tasting dregs.

Then they saw, in the clearing haze beyond the broken chariots, the unfought Hittite reserves forming into a line. As the fleeing remnants of their main column rallied around them they began their advance, the tired horses only slowly building up speed. Their numbers barely amounted to a full squadron, but there were enough to overwhelm the remaining Egyptian machines.

Ramesses stared at them, grey with horror. He raised his arms and in an anguished voice called Amun's name, beseeching the god to remember his past loyalty and asking why he had been so cruelly abandoned. Seeming to hear no answer he shrank down in his chariot car, his shaking hands gripping the rail – and in that moment he was just a man like the rest of them, crushed by fear, his godhood extinguished.

Hetep looked between Ramesses and the advancing Hittites. He has to surrender, he thought – either that or we'll all get massacred, for we're spent now. He wondered what life would be like as a slave in a foreign land. He pictured his father, watching him from the West and mocking his earlier conceit, and remembered his uncle's dreams, that now seemed so prescient...

Menna, the royal chariot driver, was shouting some-

361

thing and hauling Ramesses upright. The pharaoh tried
to shake him off; then something the driver said must
have penetrated his despair, for he wiped a hand over
his weeping, dust-reddened eyes and stood tall again. He
looked about him at what remained of his chariotry and
his face set itself into a look of grim fatalism. He raised his
bow and shouted Amun's name; the remaining Egyptians
echoed his cry, and once more took up their weapons.

Ramesses charged and the Egyptian chariot force followed, although the horses could manage to move no faster
than a trot. At two hundred paces the weary routine began again: shoot, reach for another arrow, shoot again,
ignoring the agony in muscle and sinew, and then they
were through the Hittite line. By the time they had finished their turn the Hittites were barely a hundred paces
away, and now they shot into the open backs of the cars.
Then the Hittite line came around, closing up before the
exhausted Egyptian horses could pass through again.

The chariot lines collided; horses, felled by spears and
javelins, dragged their cars over, spilling out the crews.
Hetep saw a Hittite machine careering towards him, its
horses mad with panic; two of its crew were dead but the
third came at him with an axe and he slashed with his
khopesh, while Sebeku kept a second chariot at bay with
shield and spear. Then a third Hittite chariot appeared,
its warrior standing poised with a javelin. And there was
Teppic and Ipu, both on foot, rushing the enemy crewmen
and spearing them down. Teppic turned; his face was
bruised and blooded, but he was grinning with a mad
delight.

'We'll hold them here,' he shouted. 'You'll see. Now
get away.'

'But you'll be trapped,' said Hetep.

'We've no chariot. Go... and tell Ramesses how we

362

fought.' Then he started laying about him with spear and khopesh, his cracked laughter mingling with the screams of the dying and Ipu fighting beside him with a cold precision. Together they opened a gap in the wall of Hittites and before Hetep could protest Sebeku had driven them through.

A few Egyptian chariots were still moving, struggling to free themselves from the periphery of the melee. Ramesses was there, exhorting the men around him to fight on and felling Hittites as if the god Montu himself was guiding his arrows. He accelerated forwards and the remaining Egyptians followed in a straggling column, with Hetep and Sebeku at its tail.

More Hittite chariots appeared, threatening to block their escape. Ramesses swerved and the tireless Mut-is-Contented and Victory-in-Thebes carried him clear; Sebeku tried to follow, but as their chariot turned there came a crack of wood and the car listed, its axle snapped. Hetep grabbed the rail; an instant later the frame collapsed, the wood screeching as it was dragged along the ground. He was flung out sideways and Sebeku came tumbling down beside him while the remains of the car vanished, carried away by the panicking horses.

The pursuing Hittites rumbled past and in their wake came a mob of dismounted charioteers, fresh from killing the Egyptian stragglers. Hetep glanced around wildly; corpses lay everywhere and he snatched up a spear and tossed it to Sebeku, then grabbed a khopesh from its owner's dead hand. Then they stood, shoulder to shoulder, facing the onrushing Hittites.

Sebeku stabbed one and parried another's wild attack, but a third cut through his guard and he fell, a great slash along his ribs. Hetep braced himself to meet the fourth, hooked the man's shield with his khopesh and pulled it

363

down, then stabbed into his unprotected face. Then he straddled Sebeku's prone form, slashing wildly about him, almost blind with fear. No burial, he was thinking – the second death, for me and all the others. His enemies held off, wary of the slicing blade; he wondered why they did not simply shoot him down. Quickly his arm tired and the khopesh drooped in his hand, and like jackals around a wounded bull the Hittites closed in.

'No! This one's mine.'

A warrior shouldered his way through his companions – tall and wrathful, his face a mask of gore thickened by dust, his hair matted with blood. He raised up an axe then brought it down, brushing aside Hetep's feeble parry. At the last moment the axe head turned; the bronze butt struck Hetep's head and he sank down, dazed.

'Lie still if you want to live,' came a fierce whisper, close to his ear.

As if through fog he saw the Hittites running past as they pursued the fleeing Egyptians. Then someone was dragging him away by one arm. He must have lost consciousness, for suddenly he was aware that he was on his feet, propped up between a pair of Hittites.

'You're not much of a battle trophy. But I think, my friend, you are not entirely without value,' said the Hittite.

Hetep opened his eyes. 'Mursili,' he said, at last recognising the voice.

'I told you not to come back to Canaan, that it would mean your ruin. Can you stand?'

'I think so.' Hetep rubbed his head, feeling the lump growing on his scalp. 'My friends, Teppic and Sebeku. Where–?'

'We must leave their gods to decide their fate. We cannot stay here. See?'

Mursili was pointing across the battlefield to a jumble of wreckage and corpses, all that remained of the Hittite reserve squadrons. Hetep stared, unable to comprehend what had happened; it was as if the god Amun himself had destroyed their enemies, for he knew Ramesses' chariot force was finished. Then he saw the Sherden – some formed into a line, the others in small groups, killing the last of the Hittite charioteers – and understood. They must have completed the slaughter of the Hittites plundering the camp in time to come to the pharaoh's aid.

'So we've won,' said Hetep.

'Only for the moment,' said Mursili. 'Now come with me.'

With Hittites all around him Hetep had no choice but to obey and he let himself be lead away from the camp. He found Mursili's presence oddly reassuring and he felt little fear, but much curiosity.

'Who are you, really?' he asked. 'And why are you here?'

'To fight of course. Like you I am a chariot warrior – at least some of the time.'

'A charioteer with no chariot,' said Hetep with a bitter smile, remembering his uncle's words.

Mursili gave him an odd look. 'It was destroyed, like so many others, and the horses killed. My driver too. You met him in Sumur; his name was Tagi. I believe it was one of your arrows which killed him, in that last attack.' The grief in his voice was clear.

'I'm truly sorry,' said Hetep, knowing the words were inadequate yet unable to think of any that would lessen Mursili's pain.

'He's not the only man to have died today.'

More Hittite stragglers joined them, one of whom was driving a chariot. Mursili barked an order, and without

365

demur the other dismounted and handed him the reins.

Mursili indicated the chariot. 'Get in.'

'Where are we going?' asked Hetep.

'You have nothing to fear. I swear it, by all the Thousand Gods.'

Mursili drove, leaving the other Hittites behind and heading for the woods north of Kadesh. In the growing quiet Hetep could hear the cries of vultures and he looked up to see them circling high above, drawn by the abundance of food. From the distance came the eager barking of wild dogs.

The sun was low in the sky as they skirted the northern flank of the city. At the bank of the Orontes they came to a ford where a column of chariots was crossing from the far bank; many were Hittite, with their three man crews and solid cars, but others were of designs Hetep had never seen before, crewed by pale-skinned men in fur-trimmed coats.

'Behold,' said Mursili, 'we have brought troops from all across the empire. Ramesses' valour, while commendable, has only delayed the inevitable.'

Hetep, his *ka* sinking inside him, said nothing as they abandoned the chariot and crossed the ford on foot. On the eastern bank waited yet more chariots and their crews – again the same mixture of Hittites and their outlandish-looking allies. And standing among them was Hattusili, the general who had marched on Sumur the previous year. He spotted Mursili and stormed over, shouting and gesticulating; Mursili answered coldly before pulling Hetep away with him.

'He doesn't like you, does he?' said Hetep.

'No, and he never has. He's my uncle – you may remember I told you something of him the first time we talked in Sumur. He has since become even more insufferable, if such a thing is possible. Now he blames me for failing to destroy your encampment.'

'If it's any consolation I'm glad you didn't.'

'It was not my task to do so – I was told merely to locate your army. The error was his: *he* is the commanding general, not I, and it was he who should have reined the chariotry in instead of letting it advance unchecked. Still, I am the crown prince, so if blame is coming I shall doubtless take my share.'

'Prince? But you said you were a merchant. All that talk in Sumur about the trade colony... You were lying!'

'It was no lie, I swear it, and my uncle's arrival with the provincial army was as much a shock to me as it was to you. He never does tell me anything. In truth he despises me for being the son of my father's most junior wife, for all that I am the heir to the throne.'

'But you lied to me about that festival, didn't you.'

'Not at all. I simply omitted to tell you that when necessary a substitute for the king can be used; indeed, even a suit of his clothes can be sufficient. And I was telling the truth when I said that trade would benefit us more than war. Let us hope that my father is in a mercantile frame of mind once this is finished and he leaves your Ramesses enough of an empire to make it worth trading with.'

'Father?'

'Muwatalli, king of Hatti of course. And you, my fortunate friend, are about to meet him. So mind your manners.'

They left the road and climbed a wooded hill behind the ford. Near the top the trees thinned and they came to a cordon of heavily armed foot soldiers, who glowered at Hetep but moved aside at a command from Mursili.

Beyond the guards, at the crest of the hill, stood a little knot of men. At their centre was a scarred, heavily

367

built warrior with a mane of long hair hanging down from a bald top scalp and furious, bulging eyes. His companions, who looked to Hetep like priests or magicians, were fussing over him, one anointing him with a liquid and another reciting what sounded like a litany, while a third was consulting an animal skin on which had been written rows of strange-looking symbols.

'Behold Muwatalli, servant of the Storm God and the favourite of the god Tarhunna,' said Mursili. 'And a rather quick-tempered father,' he added in an undertone. He bowed low and after a moment grabbed Hetep by the neck and forced him to do the same. 'As I said, manners...'

Muwatalli shoved his attendants aside and stormed over, glaring like a demon. The hilltop gave a good view over the plain and he pointed at the Egyptian camp and raged at Mursili, much as Hattusili had done. This time Mursili's answers were more conciliatory and he indicated Hetep; what he said must have pleased the king for suddenly the latter grinned and slapped his son on the back.

'I told my father you're the Egyptian I met at Sumur. He knows all about you, and is particularly grateful for what you told us about the organisation of your army.'

The king spoke again, while Hetep's face burned with shame.

'He wishes to know the whereabouts of the rest of your army,' said Mursili.

'I don't know what you mean.'

'Oh, come now. I remember your boast in Sumur, even if you do not. Four divisions your army has: Re, Amun, Ptah and Sebeku.'

'Set,' corrected Hetep. 'After the god. Sebeku's the name of my driver. I think he's dead now.'

'Of course: Set. But only two are here, and we have destroyed them. Tell me: where are the others?'

Hetep clamped his mouth shut and shook his head, then flinched as Muwatalli raged at him, spraying his face with bits of spittle.

'As you can see, my father is not a patient man. So please, where are they?'

'I don't know,' said Hetep. 'I swear it. We sent the vizier and a troop of chariots to find them. All I know is they're far away.'

Mursili translated and the king ground his teeth in frustration. Then a blast of horns from beyond the ford made them all look. The Hittite chariots had finished crossing the river and the whole formation was accelerating away, heading for the Egyptian camp, now little more than a dark smudge in the early evening haze. Hetep strained to see, his heart beating fast; there, barely visible, was Ramesses, withdrawing to reform his few remaining chariots and with a cordon of Sherden before him.

'Better for you Ramesses if he had chosen peace instead of war,' said Mursili sadly. 'Now it will soon be over. Yet it is such a waste.' He shook his head then turned to Hetep. 'But at least you, my friend, will survive. Of that I am glad.'

'Don't think Pharaoh's finished just yet. He's a god, remember?'

'And my father, though but a man, is a loyal servant of *our* gods, and it is unthinkable that they should fail him.'

The Hittite chariots vanished into the dusty twilight. The king was staring, his whole body taut; Mursili, unconsciously, was gripping Hetep's arm, while they both strained to hear the first sounds of the coming massacre. And then, faint on the breeze, it came: screams, shouts, and the clashing of weapons against shields and armour. Now the clamour was growing, the shouts becoming cries

369

of panic, and out of the haze came the Hittite chariot squadrons, the formations ragged, many of the cars missing crewmen. Hetep heard Mursili draw a breath, while the king's brow clouded with a sudden, baffled fury.

'What in the Storm God's name...' began Mursili. And then came the answer: a wave of chariots, Canaanites from Sumur accompanied by the remnants of the Egyptian squadrons, pursuing the fleeing Hittites, and Ramesses among them shining like the dawn come early.

The Hittite charioteers plunged into the river – some at the ford, others sliding into the water like crocodiles. And it was there that most of them died, drowning in their heavy armour or pierced by the Egyptians' arrows until their corpses jammed the river like logs. Hetep saw a few mud-smeared figures dragged from the water by men on the near bank; one, wearing gilded armour, was roaring and sputtering while his comrades held him up by the ankles to drain him of water.

The Egyptians and Amurrites stopped at the edge of the river and raised a great shout, giving thanks to the gods Montu and Ba'al. Drums rolled and horns blared, sending out a deafening wall of noise. Then, abruptly, the noise ceased, and the chariots turned and rolled back across the plain.

Muwatalli fell to his knees and howled like a wounded animal, tears running down his cheeks. He raised his arms and shouted at the sky, uttering words both anguished and bitter; Hetep did not need to understand the tongue to know that the king was talking to his gods. Then, his prayers and tears spent, he rose to his feet again. His eyes moved wildly, first to his magicians, who shrank back in terror, then to his bodyguard, who looked away, ashamed; finally they fixed themselves on Hetep. He spoke again, this time in rage, and his hand went to the sword at his

370

belt.

Hetep sprang clear of the king's reach. The body-guard, still stunned by their army's defeat, were slow to act and as Muwatalli came at him again Hetep ducked aside and ran out of the cordon. He heard Mursili calling after him and the sound of pursuit as he raced down the hill, then he plunged into the woodland near the river, arrows clattering against the trees all around him. Men shouted orders, others came after him in noisy pursuit, and he dropped to the ground and crawled through the undergrowth, head twisting this way and that as he tried to keep track of his enemies. The next moment his arm flailed against nothing and he slid headfirst down the muddy river bank. A tree root offered enough of a hand-hold to stop him splashing noisily into the water and he pulled himself sideways, deep under a tangle of shrubs and low-lying branches.

Boots thudded on the dry ground above him and he heard voices, puzzled and angry. He wormed his way deeper into the undergrowth and lay, face pressed against the damp soil, listening fearfully as the Hittites searched for him. Twice they drew near and once a party waded into the river, but their eyes could not pierce the leaves and shadows that hid him. Only after what seemed like hours did the search move away and the voices fade.

He wondered if he should risk trying to swim across the river but the moon was up, illuminating the bodies of the drowned Hittites as surely as it would illuminate him, and he remained hidden despite his discomfort. The evening chill was working deep into his bones and he began to shiver, but he was so exhausted that after a while he closed his eyes and before he knew it he was asleep.

Chapter 40

He awoke to the sound of bird song. It was still dark and the moon had set, although the sky was showing the first traces of dawn. He raised his head and listened, but aside from the birds and a few scurrying animals he could hear nothing over the murmur of the river.

As quietly as he could he slipped into the water and swam for the far bank, crossing easily despite the stiffness of his limbs. It was another matter getting out, for he had to clamber over a pile of Hittite corpses, but at last he managed to drag himself up the far bank and he lay there, shaking with fatigue and cold.

Gradually the sky brightened and through a gap in the trees he could see the Egyptian camp as it stirred into life. Work gangs appeared at the ramparts to repair the damage made by the Hittite attack and others began digging a burial pit to hold the Egyptian dead. As the night receded he saw, beyond the camp, the troops of Ptah division drawn up in battle order. They must have forced marched through the night; beside them, looking battered and bloody, stood the surviving troops from Sumur.

Smoke drifted up from the camp's cooking fires and the sight made him realise how hungry he was; he had eaten nothing since noon the day before and his stomach was beginning to complain. He stood, and as soon as he broke cover he heard a cry of surprise and a gaggle of harsh, foreign-sounding voices. Hittites, he thought, and in a sweat of panic he whirled about, ready to flee, and only then saw the squad of Sherden standing not twenty paces away. They rushed towards him, bellowing challenges and with their swords drawn.

'It's all right,' said Hetep, his hands raised. 'I'm Egyptian. Friend!'

As the Sherden crowded around him their officer peered suspiciously into his face.

'Re,' he decided, seeming to recognise Hetep; the way he spoke made it sound like an insult.

'Er...yes. Re division. At least I was. You may have seen me in... Hey, what are you doing?' cried Hetep as two of the Sherden seized him by the arms.

The officer spat in his face. 'Coward,' he snarled. He barked an order to his troops and they began to frogmarch Hetep towards the camp.

At first Hetep tried to resist but the Sherden were too strong for him and in the end he let them take him – it was either that or suffer the indignity of being dragged along, his heels scraping. He wondered if there was trouble at the camp – were the Sherden in revolt, perhaps? But the place had looked peaceful a few moments ago. Perhaps it's just a misunderstanding, he thought, and we'll clear it up once we get back.

He began to worry in earnest when they turned aside and headed for a hillock on the open plain, on which stood a group of about a hundred men surrounded by a cordon of Sherden. He wondered if they were Hittite prisoners, then came a chill of foreboding when he realised they were all Egyptians.

'What's happening?' he said, and began struggling again. 'I'm one of Pharaoh's charioteers. Do you understand me? He'll have you impaled if you harm me!'

'Re division. Coward,' said the officer. They seemed to be the only words of Egyptian he knew.

They reached the cordon and Hetep was flung inside onto his face. Someone helped him up; he saw it was one of the chariot archers from second squadron.

'What's going on?' he said, dusting himself off.

'Nobody knows. The Sherden dragged us out of the camp at dawn. They were picking men at random, all from Re division.'

Hetep looked around at his fellow captives. Some were infantrymen but the bulk were charioteers – as he would expect, for with their better mobility they would have been more likely to have survived the rout, especially after Nui's act of self-sacrifice. Most just sat or lay on the ground; only a few were armoured, and none carried weapons.

A horn sounded and from the camp came a single chariot. Sunlight blazed on its gold plating and on the bronze armour of its sole occupant: Ramesses, resplendent in his full battle dress. Behind him, on foot, trailed a little band of officials – a priest, the eldest of the princes, the vizier and the senior officers from Amun and Ptah divisions. They formed a line, facing the mound; witnesses, thought Hetep – but to what? Meanwhile Ramesses rolled his chariot to a stop, sending blinding rays of reflected sunlight into the captives' eyes, many of whom fell to their knees and held out their arms, protesting their loyalty.

The pharaoh dismounted and stood, his eyes on the horizon, as if waiting for a sign. Then his gaze shifted, not to the frightened Egyptians but across the river, to where a cluster of men stood on the far bank near the ford. Hetep peered at them and recognised Muwatalli among them, watching the Egyptians.

Ramesses nodded as if satisfied and at last turned to look at the captives. He held an arrow and he weighed it in his hand as he considered them.

'My Majesty elevates his soldiers above all other men,' he said, his tone mild, his voice carrying in the nervous silence. 'They want for nothing; they only have to say

374

"I wish..." and My Majesty provides. Never before has a king done so much for his army. Yet behold! You have done cowardly deeds and are unworthy of the gifts I have given you.'

He signalled to the Sherden, who drew their swords. Some of the men around Hetep backed away; others wept and begged for mercy. The pharaoh ignored them.

'What will they say to you in Egypt when you tell them "I was at Kadesh," when all will know that on that day you failed My Majesty?' Ramesses held out the arrow, his arm straight. 'A day when only my father Amun stood at my side, and you, wretched traitors, turned with faces of fear and ran like mice.'

He brought the arrow down and the killing began. The Sherden did it with swords alone, cutting down the defenceless men of Re division. Some of the victims fought back, but bare hands were useless against bronze blades and armour; others stood, stoically awaiting their fate, perhaps believing that death was indeed a just punishment for failing the Son of Re; still others fell on their faces and redoubled their pleas for clemency. The Sherden killed them all, regardless.

'No officer was with me, no charioteer, no soldier of the army, no shield bearer,' said Ramesses, his voice rising. 'I, alone, went out to face the host of the vile man of Hatti.'

The ring of Sherden closed in; Hetep, jammed near the middle of the crush, looked around desperately, but there was no escape.

'I scattered them like chaff; I made the ground pale with their corpses. And when they fled they looked back to see only I pursuing them. Not you. Not you!'

The last words came out as a scream. Abruptly Ramesses wheeled about, lurched over to his chariot and drew out his khopesh. It was a beautiful weapon, polished and gleaming, and its edge sang as it sliced through the air.

'I left a million of them lying prostrate in their own blood!'

With a howl he flung himself at the men of Re division, slashing right and left with his khopesh. His victims went down like animals at a hunt; not a single one dared to resist or fight back. The awed Sherden held off, leaving the Son of Re alone to avenge himself against those he thought had broken their solders' oath.

All around Hetep the men were crowding closer; nearer and nearer came the pharaoh's blade, the blood flying off in great arcs each time it swung back, the sickening thud of metal hacking into flesh coming each time he swung it forward. More men went down, close enough to Hetep for their blood to spatter his face. Then Ramesses was in front of him, glaring and breathing like a ox. And in that moment Ramesses saw the Amurrite charm hanging from Hetep's neck. His eyes widened and his arm stopped, the khopesh raised to strike.

'Anat, Lady of Heaven – my shield and my sword,' he whispered, and with his free hand he touched the amulet. 'How did this come to be here?'

'It was given to me.' Hetep was shaking and he fought to keep his voice steady. He remembered Elissa's last words to him, spoken on the quay at Sumur what seemed an age ago. 'It's a gift from the goddess. She said–'

'She spoke to you? Impossible!'

Hetep realised the pharaoh's mistake. 'Yes, she spoke. In Sumur.' It was only a small bending of the truth, for he had little doubt that in Sumur at least Elissa was the voice of the goddess. And his words were enough to give Ramesses pause.

'Who are you that she would do such a thing?'

'I am Hetep, who fought beside Your Majesty at Irqata.

376

I killed the city's prince – as I think Your Majesty knows – but another man was rewarded, and Ma'at was weakened. And I fought here, alongside Your Majesty, as did many of my comrades. Your Majesty saw that, too.'

Ramesses was looking at him, at once puzzled and fascinated, as a man might examine a strange insect.

'Majesty, to punish when one should reward is an offence to Ma'at,' said Hetep, his choice of words guided more by desperation than hope. 'The army has been given its lesson in loyalty. Let it now see Your Majesty's justice; let Ma'at be strengthened.'

Slowly, as if prompted by a will other than his own, Ramesses lowered his khopesh. For a long while he stared at Hetep, a muscle in his face twitching as if in response to some inner conflict. Then his expression cleared, and like a man recovering from a blow he passed a hand across his face and shook his head. He turned and walked unsteadily back to his chariot. There he mounted and with a hoarse order gathered up the Sherden and the group of officials, then lead them at a walk back to the camp.

In silence the men of Re division watched Ramesses depart. For a long time they stood, surrounded by the smell of blood and the cries of the wounded, scarcely daring to move. Then, one by one, they gathered their courage and slunk away.

CHAPTER 41

Back at the camp Hetep sat with the surviving members
of Re division's first squadron. They spoke in halting
sentences about the division's rout, recalling the names of
the men who had been killed; it was a long list. Several
had seen both Nui and Antef fall, and although none could
tell Hetep what had happened to Teppic or Ipu there was
little doubt they were dead, for few save Ramesses had
survived that last desperate charge against the reforming
Hittite squadrons.

From there the talk moved to Ramesses himself and his
uncanny shifts of mood – one moment quietly joyful over
his miraculous escape from defeat, the next raging at the
treachery of his army and refusing to admit that any man
but he had fought the Hittites. Of course the god Amun
had been with him, and Ramesses had spent more than
an hour in the god's shrine offering sacrifices. Equally
honoured were his horses Mut-is-Content and Victory-
in-Thebes, whose speed had saved him from the Hittite
counterattack; indeed, many had seen him kneeling before them in the royal stable and filling their grain trough
with his own hands. Some even said that he had been
weeping in gratitude, but most dismissed the claim as an
exaggeration.

They were roused from their musings by drums and
shouted orders, reminders that the battle was still un-
decided and that another day of slaughter was about to
begin. The army – Ptah division, along with the remnants of Amun division and the force from Sumur – began
its advance towards the ford where Muwatalli had earlier
stood. Wearily the men of Re division came to their feet

and joined the ranks; after all, said one, they were still charioteers, and if there was to be a battle it was their duty to fight at the pharaoh's side and perhaps, in doing so, redeem themselves.

On the far side of the river the Hittite army emerged from the trees. There were few chariots but thousands of infantry – both spearmen and archers, the former heavily armoured; Hetep wondered why Muwatalli had not committed them to the battle on the previous day, for they would have overwhelmed the camp, even after the arrival of the reinforcements from Sumur.

The two armies halted and faced each other in silence. In front of the Egyptian line Ramesses was standing in his chariot, his armour gleaming, the blue streamers on his war crown fluttering in the breeze. Around him clustered a little knot of priests and officers, and Hetep could hear General Huti among them, arguing with the elder prince. He moved closer to listen.

'Majesty, please,' the general was saying, this time to Ramesses. 'If we attack now we'll be overwhelmed. We lack sufficient chariots to counter their infantry.'

'Can you really imagine that Amun-Re would let a pack of vile, Ma'at-less Asiatics triumph over the living god?' said the prince. 'Even a million foreigners are no more than chaff; they will drown in their own blood!'

A few of the men voiced their agreement but most stayed silent, looking worried; clearly Huti was not alone in having misgivings. And it was obvious why. The Hittite infantry stood like an immovable wall, their shields grounded and their spearpoints a thicket of bronze points, while the Egyptian troops, exhausted after yesterday's fighting or a night of forced marching, looked as if at any moment the strengthening breeze would sweep them away. Ramesses, beloved of Amun, might indeed win his victory, but if he did he would likely be the only Egyptian left alive to enjoy its fruits.

Hetep had the impression that Ramesses realised it too, for the Lord of the Two Lands was biting his lower lip. Then the mask of god-like imperturbability snapped back into place and he listened without apparent emotion as one of the diviners spoke.

'Majesty, it is true that none can withstand you on the day of your wrath, but are we certain when that day will be? Perhaps it is on a future campaign that Your Majesty is destined to destroy the Hittites.'

'Like a blast of fire I scattered the men of Hatti, and now Kadesh lies at my feet,' said Ramesses. He turned a cold eye on the diviner. 'Are you suggesting I withdraw?'

'Gods, no, Majesty,' cried the diviner. 'Forgive my clumsy choice of words. It's just that Your Majesty has given the army its lesson in loyalty and you have shown us that Amun-Re goes at your side – who but you could have performed such deeds yesterday? And now, to complete your triumph, you can make the Hittite king crawl to you and beg for peace.'

Ramesses gazed thoughtfully at the Hittite army but said nothing.

'Majesty, it would be a fitting end to a glorious campaign,' said Huti. 'And remember: your soldiers are mortal, and can only endure so much. Their loyalty waxes and wanes according to the justice of Your Majesty's demands.'

A veiled threat, which had Ramesses frowning until the diviner broke in quickly.

'May I remind Your Majesty how unclear the omens were at the sunrise augury. Make the Hittite king beg for mercy and you can complete his destruction on another day when your glorious arm is more rested.'

Silence fell, while they waited to hear the decision that would decide their fate. The diviner and General Huti watched Ramesses, their faces strained, as if silently willing him to see reason, while the prince looked at them in disgust.

'You are certain that we can defer matters until another day?' said Ramesses. 'It will not offend my father Amun?'

The diviner assured him that it would not, and for all his composure Ramesses could not stop a flicker of relief from passing across his face.

'Then the fallen man of Hatti has one hour in which to beg for his life. If he does not, I shall descend on his troops like a griffin and smash them into the dirt.'

'We'll have to send an envoy,' said Huti. He looked over at the Hittites, whose chariots were already crossing the ford. 'Although it might be a death sentence for the man we choose.'

Ramesses cast his gaze about him, and everyone tried to shuffle away without appearing to do so. His eye fell on Hetep.

'Ah, yes,' he said, smiling thinly. 'Who better than the man who enjoys the protection of the Lady of Heaven?'

Hetep swallowed. 'Majesty, I am yours to command,' he said.

'Naturally.' The smile tightened. 'Now make haste, and bring the wretch who sits on Hatti's throne to me.'

'Your Majesty,' said Hetep, 'may you have life, breath and health. Amun willing, I'll not fail you.' He felt as if someone else was mouthing the words.

Huti stalked off among the guard troops and came back a short while later leading a chariot. Its driver must have already been given his orders, for he looked like a man facing certain death. At Huti's invitation Hetep mounted the car.

'Now remember, we're not surrendering,' said the general. 'In fact, it's the opposite. Tell their king he has to come here if he wants to live.'

'I'll do what I can.' Hetep had a momentary vision of Muwatalli's violent temper and Hattusili's cold hatred, and shuddered. 'But he may just want to fight.'

'Then we'll do what we can to avenge your death,' said Huti, with a twisted grin that did nothing to settle Hetep's nerves. 'Now go. It all depends on you now.'

CHAPTER 42

By now the Hittite chariots had crossed the ford and were deploying into a line to screen their infantry. The sight made Hetep's stomach turn over with fear; worse was the sense of guilt knowing the part he had played in bringing about yesterday's near disaster. He should never have let Mursili goad him into talking so freely about the organisation of Egypt's armies and he felt the accusing presence of his dead comrades' *akhs* all around him. But perhaps he had been given the opportunity to make amends. He could only hope that it was Mursili who commanded the vanguard, for if it was Hattusili he had little doubt he would be the first to die in this day's fighting.

As Hetep's chariot approached them the Hittite crews took up their bows and javelins. His driver blanched and glanced at him, and he had to clamp his jaws shut so he would not give the order to withdraw. The Hittite commander snapped a command and the weapons vanished, then he drove out ahead and as he came nearer Hetep let out a long sigh. It was Mursili, and he was beaming as he leaped down from his chariot car.

'My good friend,' he said, 'how I rejoice to see you alive! Your flight was so precipitous that I feared you had fallen into the river and drowned.'

Hetep dismounted to meet him.

'Sorry I didn't wait to say goodbye. But it seemed too unhealthy to stay.'

'Nonsense. My father was angry, yes, but he'd not have laid a hand on you. We are not murderers. There are laws against such things. Now to what do I owe the renewed pleasure of your company?'

'I've been sent to demand your surrender,' said Hetep. He shrugged. 'Sorry to be so blunt, but it's the truth.'

'No apology necessary,' said Mursili. 'However, surrender is quite out of the question. In fact, my father was about to send me to ask the very same of your Ramesses: surrender to him, or face the consequences. Which, I am told, will be rather severe.'

Hetep looked back and forth between the two armies. 'But you can't possibly win. We destroyed most of your chariots.'

'Perhaps so,' said Mursili, his face grave. 'But we outnumber you in infantry, and ours are not like the peasant militia you fought at Irqata. We also have the support of the city.'

'We've got more troops coming. Set division – they'll be here soon.'

'But not soon enough to tip the scales. Oh, yes: our scouts have found them even if yours have not. They won't arrive for many hours yet.'

'I see.' Hetep's spirits sank. 'Then we're at an impasse.'

'Indeed.' Suddenly Mursili was grinning again. 'Look at you, standing there all grim and serious, when you should be rejoicing. Yesterday you were just another chariot warrior, while today you are a royal envoy.' When Hetep protested he went on, 'Come now, this is no time for false modesty. That is what you are. Who knows where you'll be tomorrow.'

'Dead, if our armies fight again. Along with most of the rest of us. And I think even Ramesses know it.'

'Does he now?' Mursili searched Hetep's face. 'Let me tell you something – and you are to repeat this to nobody. The Assyrians are causing mischief again. They are a violent and insolent people who menace our eastern

384

border, and we shall need the army intact to deal with them. For that reason, if for no other, my father also has misgivings about another day of battle, which can only maul both sides for little gain. And you are sure that your Ramesses feels the same?'

Hetep knew that to admit the truth would be to betray Ramesses the god, who was as fearless as he was unconquerable. Yet he had seen, briefly, Ramesses the man, who was anxious for the welfare of his army knowing that, if the battle resumed, many hundreds more would surely die. And what if the impossible happened, thought Hetep, and one of those was the pharaoh? What of Ma'at and the security of the world then?

'Yes,' he said at last. 'I'm sure of it. And he's not the only one. Even our Field Marshal of Chariotry is worried.'

'Then perhaps we can come to an arrangement.'

'All it takes is a token of submission and I think we'll all get to march home. You'll keep Kadesh, of course, so in a way you'll have won.'

'And Ramesses?'

'He saved the army. And he's taught the generals a lesson they won't forget.'

'Ah, so that explains this morning's little performance.' Mursili's face wrinkled with distaste. 'We assumed it was purely for our benefit.'

'I think it was for everybody,' said Hetep, grimacing at the memory of his recent ordeal. 'He also showed us that Amun-Re is still with him. It may be enough.'

'Let us hope so. Can you wait a moment while I talk to my father?' When Hetep eyed the Hittite chariots he added, 'There's nothing to fear. You have my word they'll not harm you. You're a royal envoy, remember?'

The moment stretched into an hour, in which Hetep grew increasingly uncomfortable, and not just with the growing heat. He kept his gaze fixed beyond the Hittite chariotry, watching for Mursili, while he could almost feel the eyes of the whole Egyptian army on him, a burning on his back to rival that of the sun.

At last Mursili returned, bringing his father Muwatalli and a cortege of bodyguards. Hetep ignored the king's ferocious glare, instead focussing on Mursili's grinning face.

'It can be done,' said Mursili. 'Now with your permission we shall escort my father to see the mighty Ramesses.'

The pharaoh received the Hittites in the royal enclosure. Hetep, his task completed, was left outside – for which he was thankful, for it spared him from having to endure the stifling protocol of an official audience, even though it left him wondering what was being said. The prospect of another day of fighting – with all the dust, heat and exhaustion; the pain and the fear – made him nauseous, and he could only hope that Muwatalli was keeping his temper in check long enough to give the appearance of suing for peace. It was some reassurance knowing that Mursili was there with him – ostensibly to translate but also, Hetep knew, to soften his father's words.

Tired of standing and waiting he crossed the camp to the perimeter wall. On the plain the detritus of battle stood out clearly in the morning light and he saw parties of slaves and soldiers moving out to begin the task of recovering the Egyptian dead. He knew that somewhere out there Teppic and Sebeku still lay, their bodies perhaps already beginning to rot in the sunshine. The thought was unbearable; no, he said to himself, not them. He returned to the camp and picked out some bundles of spare linen clothing, then went out to search for his friends.

It was easy to read the tale of the battle from the

distribution of the wreckage and bodies. There, a hundred paces from the camp, Ramesses had launched his first counterattack; further on, a dense cluster of corpses marked where the Hittite remnants had broken and fled; and half a mile to the east more corpses marked the place where the Hittites had fought them in close melee after Ramesses' final charge. There, among the shattered chariots and dead horses, the Hittite and Egyptian dead were intermingled, some locked together as if still fighting. And it was there that he found Teppic and Ipu lying side by side. One had been cut down with an axe, the other speared.

He used the linen to wrap their bodies then took out the gold *wadjet* amulet and pushed it under Teppic's wrappings. A couple of nearby infantrymen helped him to drag them to the burial pit and he rolled them in. A lector priest was there intoning spells from the Book of Going Forth by Day; Hetep repeated some of the words and afterwards added a few of his own prayers. As a final touch he picked up one of the offering jugs standing nearby and poured out some beer as a libation.

'To the happy dead,' he whispered. He stayed there for some time, staring into the pit, knowing that his grief was only just beginning. At last he turned away.

Back on the battlefield he retraced the route he and Sebeku had taken as they had tried to escape from the ring of Hittites. Many of the bodies here had been disturbed by scavengers and some were partially eaten; further on, where he and Sebeku had fallen from their chariot, it was worse, and all that remained were disjointed bones clothed in a few scraps of flesh. He searched for a long time while vultures wheeled overhead, their cries mocking, but he found nothing that he could identify as coming from Sebeku's corpse. It was then that he sank down and began to weep, for to die so completely, without leaving even a trace of a body, was the worst thing that could happen to a man.

He was still sitting, his head resting on his knees, when Mursili came to find him. At the sound of the Hittite's greeting he looked up, wiping away his tears.

'Well?' he said. 'Is there peace?'

'I think – I hope – that we shall all be going home soon. But I must say, your Ramesses is a difficult man to reason with. There's to be no formal truce. He could not even utter the word, let alone talk of peace.'

Hetep stood, feeling the ache of tiredness in his limbs. 'So we're still at war, then.'

'I'm afraid so. Which means that it's still our duty to try to kill each other.' Mursili's tone was so serious that Hetep experienced a moment's fear, until with a smile the Hittite went on, 'But I appear to have left all my weapons on my chariot.'

'I don't even have a chariot any more,' said Hetep. He gave a wan smile in return.

'Then we shall have to postpone hostilities until the next time.' Mursili's face became grave. 'There will be a next time, you know, unless Ramesses gives up this foolish claim to northern Canaan.'

'He won't do that.'

'He will, in time.' Mursili looked around at the scattered bones. 'I saw you grieving just then. Some of us have been doing the same. We lost many warriors yesterday; indeed, hardly a family among the nobility has been spared – even two of my own brothers lie dead. And we have lost many of our allies' princes and kings. Some came from the very ends of the empire; it took them a month to march here.'

'A long way to come just to end up like this.' Hetep

gestured at the bodies.

'I could say the same to you Egyptians.' Mursili turned to face him again. 'Was it worth it? For you, I mean.'

Hetep shrugged. 'I got to fight at Ramesses' side. I thought that was what I wanted, but now...' He shook his head. 'I don't want to go through this again. There must be better ways of strengthening Ma'at.'

'I remember once telling you as much,' said Mursili gently. 'And now I'd best be getting back, before my father wonders where I've gone – there's still a great deal to discuss. I shall see you again, before you go. And much later too, I hope. When I am king I shall welcome an envoy such as you.'

'Envoy? Hardly. I'll be lucky if I end up as a scribe again. It was partly my fault Ramesses was so reckless, and I don't think he'll forgive me for it.'

'Not so. He's pleased that you persuaded my father to beg for mercy. As a reward you are to be made Messenger to Canaan – or as much of it as Egypt will be allowed to keep once my father is finished here. I believe Ramesses is to issue the decree today.'

'Please, I'm in no mood for jokes.'

'This is no joke,' said Mursili. 'My father respects courage and he was much impressed by the audacity of your escape. He was able to demand a few conditions from Ramesses, one of which was to have you represent your people here and act as intermediary between us in the coming days. It seems that your pharaoh was moved by some spirit of justice, and agreed. What's that word you keep using? Ma'at, isn't it? So there it is. Order has been restored, justice has been served. Congratulations. I only hope you find it some recompense for your loss.'

It took a moment for Hetep's weary mind to catch up with Mursili's words. 'You're sure of this?'

389

'I saw one of the scribes writing out the commission as I left. So now you'd best be getting back. Your pharaoh might already need you.'

Slowly Hetep made his way back to the camp. Messenger to Canaan, he thought – a lofty-sounding title indeed, and this time there was no Baya to steal it from him. For the first time he thought he could feel the beneficial influence of his father's *akh* and he whispered a quick prayer, promising the old man a double ration of offerings when he reached home.

He tried to imagine what Teppic and Sebeku would have said about his change of fortune, and the little solace Mursili's news had brought was swept away in a new upsurge of grief. It was as if something was stabbing into his gut and he had to stop, bending over and breathing hard, until the pain faded into a dull ache. Again he thought of his new title, and this time felt nothing but a sick emptiness. He wondered how much of the pleasure one derives from receiving awards is due to the admiration of others. He shook his head, irritated by the thought's selfishness; just be thankful you're alive, he told himself.

At the camp's south gate he was met by one of the Re division charioteers.

'I've been looking all over for you,' he said. 'One of the physicians wants you. He says there's a patient at the infirmary making a fuss.'

'Which patient? Who?' asked Hetep, but the man had already gone.

He knew that he should report to Ramesses. Perhaps the pharaoh already had a task for him, and to delay might jeopardise his newly won standing – and he would be fortunate indeed to see another such opportunity for recognition. So it was with some surprise that he found himself walking in the opposite direction, towards the infirmary.

It was similar to the one at Irqata, but if anything even more crowded and noisy, and the smell was intolerable. One of the physicians saw him and came hurrying over; Hetep recognised him from the camp at Irqata.

'Ah, good, it's you,' said the physician. 'Come with me. He's asleep now, but when he wakes just try to keep him quiet, will you? He's upsetting the other patients.'

He lead Hetep to where Sebeku was lying, unconscious and with a bandage around his torso.

'Some of the Canaanite troops found him this morning. He'd crawled halfway to the camp before fainting. They thought he was dead and dragged him to the burial pit, but when they went to toss him in he started kicking and hollering, demanding to know what they'd done with his horses. Some god must be watching out for him – I've rarely seen a man survive so many wounds. But he should do well.'

Hetep squatted down beside Sebeku and placed a hand on his forehead. It was dry and cool, without a sign of fever, and his breathing was strong. In the flood of relief he wanted to wake him and thank him for surviving, for not leaving him alone in this foreign place. And then what? he thought. Tell him that all their friends are dead? Best to let him sleep.

He stayed there for a long while, no longer minding the infirmary's smell and noise, watching Sebeku and musing over his changes of fortune. Messenger to Canaan, he thought, and this time the title made him smile. Of course, it was nowhere near as lofty as the much-coveted Envoy to Foreign Lands, but he knew he would never count another bread ration again. And possibly never fight from a chariot again, but he no longer considered that much of a hardship. Perhaps his uncle and Mursili were right and it was enough to order the world through good administration.

Whatever his duties turned out to be he would need an assistant, preferably an ex-charioteer. And who better than Sebeku? He was sure that in his sour way his friend would be delighted with the post – Hetep remembered what he had told him of his fears before they had set out for Libya. And what did it matter if he could not read? He could learn, and Hetep could think of no other man he would rather have beside him, looking out for him.

He wondered where his new posting would take them. Perhaps Sumur, a place he now remembered fondly. Or even, if there was peace, Hatti. He was curious to see its capital, and to see its people as something other than enemies. He knew that Mursili would make a welcoming host.

But what of the present, and the battle that had cost him so much? He looked beyond the camp at the city of Kadesh, where the Hittite banners still fluttered atop the walls. Ramesses' campaign was a failure, there was no question of that. But what would the royal annals say? How would the pharaoh claim it as a victory? For victory it must be: it was unthinkable that the Lord of the Two Lands could be fought to a stalemate by mere foreigners. Somehow events would be reshaped, and the world along with them, making Ma'at triumph over chaos. And the only account that mattered would be carved onto the pillars and walls of Egypt's temples – or perhaps, in emulation of Ramesses' forefathers, on the mighty temple pylons, alongside images of the Son of Re alone in his chariot and slaughtering his helpless enemies.

Regardless of where they would appear, Hetep knew that the accounts would say little about the men who had followed the Son of Re to Kadesh. But he felt no resentment at the thought: Ramesses was no Baya, stealing the credit owed to better men, but the living embodiment of Egypt, and had it not been for his courage during the Hittite attack the camp would have been overrun and the battle lost. Still, the fallen would have to be remembered; he felt the looming presence of the *akhs* of his dead friends and whispered a promise to keep their names alive for as long as he had breath in his body. But there was only so much he could do, and as the years passed and he and his surviving comrades died they would take with them to the West the truth of what had happened at Kadesh, and all that would endure would be Ramesses' words, set deep into the stone.

Printed in Great Britain
by Amazon

56783136R00229